D1806398

TWICE UPON A THANKSGIVING

A Love Story In Time

Also by Richard Rees

The Illuminati Conspiracy
The Reikel Conspiracy
Somebody Wants to Kill Me
Dear Abigail

Praise for Richard Rees's first two novels:

The Illuminati Conspiracy

"Extremely enjoyable historical yarn, almost induces reader to cheer. Will please many who like their reading with a Scarlet Pimpernelish flavour." *The Guardian*

"This impressive saga set at a blistering pace, teems with excitement and suspense. A fascinating richly detailed historical thriller worthy of Dennis Wheatley at his best." *Daily Mail*

"This is big screen stuff. The formula is right. Plenty of suspense, action, historical detail and a love interest to boot. A good yarn, a good read. The research must have taken many painstaking hours and the author has recreated the atmosphere of those turbulent times to brilliant effect." *Country Quest*

"A stirring love story and a compelling, richly-detailed historical thriller." *TV Oracle Teletext*

"A splendid period adventure novel and a cracking read, fast moving, never fails to hold the reader's interest." *North West Mail*

The Reikel Conspiracy

Richard Rees's research is as meticulous as Frederick Forsyth's, or George Macdonald Fraser's. *Press Association News. London*

A colorful and intriguing tale. *Gregory Peck*

TWICE UPON A THANKSGIVING

A Love Story In Time

RICHARD REES

Copyright © Richard Rees 2015

First printed in this edition 2015

Kindle edition published December 2014

This revised edition 2019

www.richardhrees.com

The right of Richard Rees to be identified as the author of this work has been asserted by him in accordance with the Copyright, Designs and Patents Act, 1988

This book is sold subject to the condition that it shall not, by way of trade or otherwise, be lent, resold, hired out, or otherwise circulated without the author's consent in any form of binding or cover other than in which it is published and without a similar condition being imposed on the subsequent purchaser.

ISBN: 978-1-5148501-7-6

Front jacket cover design: Louise Payne, www.louisepaynearts.com

Book design: Dean Fetzer, www.gunboss.com

To Barbara, for enabling me to love and hope again

*The "Thanksgiving" story idea was suggested to me by
my daughter, Elisabeth, a month before she died,
and I've now written it for her.*

Richard Rees

INTERNAL E-MAILS

From: Amanda Nye

To: Nick Cronin

Subject: **TWICE UPON A THANKSGIVING**

Comments: I'm new here, started this week. My first project is a "faction" story I'd like to pass on to you to read.

Summary: Starting on a Thanksgiving Day in present Plymouth, MA, it's about a young woman's recurring dream experience which takes her back in time to the year 1621, six months after the First Forefathers' arrival in the "New World" on board the "Mayflower".

Is it her subconscious making her face her guilt for entering a marriage for selfish reasons, and in so doing repressing her sexuality?

OR IS IT MORE?

Is it an out-of the body experience, an actual regression in time, in which the events she is being drawn into are for real – and from which she might not return?

From: Nick Cronin

To: Amanda Nye

Subject: Re: TWICE UPON A THANKSGIVING

Welcome to our happy team, Mandy.

Books on lucid dreams have been done before, and are almost as old as Time itself.

Give me a potted publishing history.

From: Amanda Nye

To: Nick Cronin

Subject: Re: TWICE UPON A THANKSGIVING

First ever book on dreams – an interpretation of dream symbols – is known as the Chester Beatty papyrus. The original was written for the Ancient Egyptians, who believed dreams to be messages from the gods (part of the supernatural world) sent as early warning of disaster or good fortune to come. The musical, *Joseph and the Amazing Technicolor Dreamcoat,* was based on such a dream.

The Ancients Greeks also believed dreams carried divine messages. Homer, in his "Iliad", includes a scene in which Agamemnon receives instructions from a messenger of Zeus in a dream. Plato believed they could greatly influence peoples' lives, telling, in his "Phaedo", how Socrates studied music and the arts because he was told to do so in a dream. Aristotle, however, was against this thought. In his "De divinatione per somnun" he states that: "most so-called prophetic dreams are to be classed as mere coincidences, based on no more than a recollection of the day's events."

In his "Oneirocriticon" (Interpretation of Dreams) the Roman philosopher, Artemidorus, c.AD.150, claimed that dreams are unique to the dreamer, the symbols being affected by a person's occupation, social status, health. Its success encouraged Astrampsychus (another philosopher) to produce *his* "Oneirocriticon", which was the forerunner of the type of dream books written, two millenniums later, by English Victorians. The first of them to capitalise on what quickly grew to be a craze for books on the subject was Robert Cross Smith, with his best-selling "The Royal Book of Dreams", written under the pen name of Raphael.

There is also the best-selling Holy Bible, which contains many dreams, among them being Jacob's dream of a ladder from Earth to Heaven; and the dreams of the Egyptian Pharaoh interpreted by Joseph (already mentioned above). Saint Augustine and Saint Jerome both claimed the direction of their lives were affected by their dreams. But taking the opposite standpoint, Martin Luther pronounced (as was his wont) that dreams were the work of The Devil, and could only be diabolical.

Probably the most famous of modern dream philosophers is Sigmund Freud. His theory is that although dreams may be prompted by external stimuli, the root behind most of our dreams is wish-fulfilment, mostly sexual. To Freud, *every* dream holds an important meaning, but its *latent* content – containing the unconscious sexual wish – is allowed to appear only if disguised as manifest content, such as, for example, using symbols: ie: objects that otherwise would have no sexual meaning at all, for instance:

Symbols suggesting penetration: swords, umbrellas etc. – or, as in Damaris Moore's "Twice Upon A Thanksgiving": pointed sticks.

Symbols suggesting orifices: tunnels, caves, boxes, purses etc. – in "Thanksgiving": the overhanging branches of a tree, offering shelter.

This view was disputed by Carl Jung, once a student of Freud's. His belief was that dreams remind us of our wishes, which enables us to realise the things we unconsciously yearn for, and helps us to fulfil our own wishes. Dreams are messages, Jung believed, *from ourselves to ourselves,* and we should therefore pay attention to them for *our own* benefit

Most psychologists now agree with Jung's theory, and also that dream interpretation is something we might so use in our everyday lives.

From: Nick Cronin

To: Amanda Nye

Subject: Re: TWICE UPON A THANKSGIVING

Mandy

You are new here. I should have been more specific and not used the phrase 'as old as Time itself'. I meant <u>recent</u> publishing history, as in how many OBE (out of body experience) stories have been successful – such as Barbara Erskine's "Lady of Hay"?

But being that you're in this vein, give me the latest thinking on OBEs versus Lucid Dreams. Are they similar phenomena? If not, what are their differences?

From: Amanda Nye

To: Nick Cronin

Subject: Re: TWICE UPON A THANKSGIVING

Comparison of Lucid Dreams to OBEs (taken from an internet website):

LUCID DREAM	OBE
Dreamer can consciously program the dream.	OBEer is a passive, objective observer.
Dreamer and his/her physical body are still integrated.	OBEer perceives himself/herself as separated from the physical body, which is inert and thoughtless.
Consciousness is often vivid, with mystical qualities.	Consciousness is more ordinary, like being awake.
Dream is seen as a totally personal (subjective) production of the dreamer's mind.	OBEer does not see it as a subjective personal production, but rather as objective reality.
Dreamer's physical body isn't visible.	A physical body (not necessarily that of the OBEer's) is usually visible.
Few dreams have a lasting positive impact.	OBEs usually have a highly positive, lasting impact.

Comments: Based on above, the phenomena experienced by the author of "Twice Upon A Thanksgiving", would seem to suggest — on all points — more of an out-of-body experience than a lucid dream. Personally, I think they are one and the same thing, the realism being due to the author's — an artist — own imaginative nature.

Except that two aspects of her dream cannot be so easily explained:

The *recurring nature*, night after night, of the same dream.

And her facial *weal marks* one morning, when she awakes.

From: Nick Cronin

To: Amanda Nye

Subject: Re: TWICE UPON A THANKSGIVING

Mandy

I note your personal opinion. But seeing (from your first note) that most of the story is set in/around New Plimoth at the time of the First Forefathers' arrival in the "New World", you may as well finish your daunting research by letting me know the views (if any) on this subject, of the Native Americans who then occupied the land.

ps. also send the ms

From: Amanda Nye

To: Nick Cronin

Subject: Re: TWICE UPON A THANKSGIVING

Native Americans (like the Australian Aborigine) have inhabited their lands for over 40,000 years, during which time they have come to believe that the universe is charged with a power – a voltage *more potent* than the ordinary powers of man – which exists in all things, not only in spirits and deities, but also in the things of nature, trees, rocks, water, animals, and even in "human beings" if they can but reach for it.

The Algonquians – who occupied the land "claimed" by the First Forefathers – called this power *manito*, which is best translated, not as something holy, but as "wonderful", which can be manifested in any/all of the following:

(1) DREAMS. They believed that gods and supernaturals manifested themselves in dreams, which have an importance unimaginable to modern man/woman, sending revelations to the supplicants from the spirits. Interpreted correctly, dreams could influence lives, sometimes conferring gifts on a favoured person: such as the gift of prophecy, ability to cure illness, and heal wounds etc. etc.

(2) VISIONS. Here the visionary's soul goes to a spiritual place where teachings are given. These can be teachings about the:

x

a) Past — to recover wisdom that has been lost; or the

b) Present — to apply that wisdom to today; or the

c) Future — to see into things still to come, "prediction visions", premonitions of events to be either encouraged to happen, or to be avoided.

(3) OUT OF BODY EXPERIENCES. This it was believed, occurs when a human being is asleep. His/her vital part (ie, the soul — which is the core of the self) becomes detached from the body. Although the subject's body is still there (and can be seen by others) his/her vital spark is somewhere else, *maybe inhabiting another person's body*, and thus the subject's *real self* has greater mobility — including even in *time* — whilst he/she is sleeping.

What is being experienced by the author of "Thanksgiving" (ms attached) could be any one of these.

A Lucid Dream? A Vision? An OBE?

Which one is revealed as the story unfolds.

From: Nick Cronin

To: Amanda Nye

Subject: Re: TWICE UPON A THANKSGIVING

Okay, Mandy, you've managed to intrigue me. I'll read it. I'm opening it right now & will get back to you.

TWICE UPON A
THANKSGIVING

DAMARIS MOORE

Copyright – Damaris Moore – 2015

- Prologue -

PLYMOUTH, MA – TODAY

Today is Thanksgiving but I've gone right off them. Not that I've become a killjoy, but last Thanksgiving my ego was badly hit. Robert, my two-faced, two-timing heel of a husband, left me for – *of all things!* – a *floozy* named Stella Slater. I'd not even suspected it, he'd kept her a close secret (an equal shock to me, I thought I could read him like an open book) but her reputation, so I later discovered, was such that any woman – even a plain Jane, and without sounding conceited I'm *no* plain Jane – would have lost her self-esteem.

What's more, he walked out on me before dinner, on which I'd spent some considerable time, and even though I'm not the best of cooks (nothing near, being very honest) if that's not rubbing salt into the wound, then I don't know what is.

Don't misunderstand me, I'm not pining for Robert that I've gone all to pieces – though he was sort of comfortable to have around, rather like an Old English sheepdog, and yes, I do miss that side of him. But now that he's chosen his new bed to lie in (both metaphorically and literally speaking) then if that Slater *woman* (being polite to her here, having established already she's a *floozy)* can manage to stir his libido – if she can find it, that is – she'll not just be welcome to it, she'll also be a magician. She can only have been after him for his money, not for anything else.

But Katy misses him. Katherine, my wonderful, precious seven year old daughter, the second-most immaculate conception in history, because not even when I realised I was pregnant, counted back six weeks and it landed on Robert's birthday, I still couldn't remember it happening. Even though I knew both the likely date and the occasion, it didn't ring any bells in my memory – or any other part of my body, for that matter – but as it rarely lasted more than a few minutes, five tops (though in fairness to Robert, I should mention he had an impotency problem; or rather, a potency problem, he had no trouble at all with impotency) my mind must have wandered on to something else, my current painting probably.

Painting? Yes, that's what I do, I'm an artist, Expressionist (aged thirty-one, for the record) with my work in considerable demand, except I can no longer fulfil it, not now that Robert's no longer here, at home, to help with Katy.

By help with Katy I should have explained that, two months before Robert left, she was in a freeway pile-up in which all four of her grandparents were killed. Miraculously, Katy survived, but the terrible trauma of such a horrific crash left her unable to speak, and since then she's been my all-in-all to me, with very little time to devote to my work. Not that I in *any way* begrudge having to put Katy first. Even though she wasn't planned, in the whole of my life she's the best thing that's ever happened to me. If ever I had to make the choice, I'd willingly give my life to save hers.

Nevertheless, I miss my art. Being married to Robert, it was my one and only passion.

Still, putting all this aside for a moment, Katy, and my lack of output – and often still wondering why Robert, of all men, if he'd had enough of me, would choose a sexual piranha like Stella Slater instead of a rosy-cheeked, American apple pie type (who I could more easily envisage him with) – are not right now the only things on my mind.

Do you believe in regressions?

You know, where you're supposed to travel back in time, to be someone else, in some other age, centuries before you were even born?

Until twelve weeks ago, I didn't either.

But then, it was exactly twelve weeks ago today that Andrew Hartford, my ex and only previous lover (*yes!*, my *only one!* – hard though it is to believe in today's "seven's a norm" society) came back into my life. And it was then that it started.

I don't know if there's a connection? Or whether it's just a coincidence. But I do know that's when it all began.

It…?

The recurring dream I've just mentioned.

Okay, so I said regression. But that was overstating it.

It has to be a dream, or at worse, a nightmare.

It just *has* to.

What else can it be?

And yet, it's so damned vivid, so frighteningly real, I confess I sometimes find myself wondering…

- one -

It came to me again last night. The nightmare.

Yes, on Thanksgiving Eve (a year less a day to when Robert left me) despite literally falling exhausted into bed after a long evening preparing this year's dinner. Despite having gone off the celebration I'd made the effort, not just for Katy's sake, but Alex – my best friend, Alexandra – and John, her latest, were joining us. And Andrew. Yes, the very same Andrew Hartford, my ex-lover (and *still* "ex" I'd like to stress, right from the start) but who has so unexpectedly come back into my life.

I'd given Mrs Bassett the day off to sort out her own family meal, and so, as I crawled under my duvet, I was so bushed, hardly able to keep my eyes open, I was hoping, praying almost, that I'd be allowed to crash out until morning, and my sleep would be undisturbed.

But no such luck. What's more, I was fully aware of the dream. I always am. It's as if I'm not really asleep, but held in some strange subconscious state halfway between slumber and reality.

In it, I'm always running, fleeing for my very life through a dark forest. Chasing me are demons. I can't see them and so don't know how many there are. But I know they're demons. I can hear them behind me, screaming their fiendish howls. And prodding me with pointed sticks, cutting off any escape.

4

The deeper I'm being forced into the forest, the taller become the trees. Silent and sentinelled watchers of my helpless flight from my pursuers, their dark branches towering above me, shutting out the sky, creating a shadowy labyrinthed prison in which the path I'd trodden behind me is lost, and the way before me has no end.

Hampered by a strange heavy homespun skirt down to my ankles, and many underslips underneath – and of all things, old fashioned, black buckled shoes I wouldn't be seen dead in (when I go it will be in stilettos, and black, narrow leg jeans) – the switches of the undergrowth writhe toward me, long snaking tentacles seeking and stretching out for my body as if trying to ensnare me and entangle me in their wooded webs.

But not so the demons. Instead, they seem to be floating through the brush, making no sound other than their hideous cries, not even disturbing the matted sea of dead twigs and cones carpeting the bone-dry earth.

Suddenly, ahead of me, I see a huge beech tree.

It looks familiar, its glossy-leafed branches hanging thickly down to the forest floor, forming a sheltered cave around its massive, smooth-barked trunk. To my panic-stricken mind it seems to offer protection, somewhere where I can hide. Even in my disturbed sleep I know I'm thinking irrationally. How can I possibly lose these blood-curdling fiends with them so close behind me they can touch me, so near I can feel their hot breath on the back of my neck?

Yet, amidst all of my dark, forbidding surroundings, this tree seems to offer hope. A wooded church formed by God over the centuries, a sanctuary from these evil spirits so relentless in their chase. I turn toward it. As if guessing my intention, the front-runners increase their pace, passing me without effort, then running backwards, their faces daubed with paint, still taunting me and shrieking, then closing-in on me until I'm surrounded by them, a running cageling in their tightening circle.

Pulling up my heavy skirt and petticoats to enable me to run faster, I stumble on a protruding root and fall to the ground.

My pursuers give a yell of triumph, followed by a terrible silence. Then they converge in on me, five of them, and encircle me. Pulling me over on to my back, they leer down at me, their devilish faces blotting-out all but the pointed tops of the tall firs, still baiting and poking me with their pointed sticks.

Always, at this point, the nightmare fades away, allowing me to resurface, trembling in my bed, afraid to open my eyes.

But last night there was no such escape.

Lying helpless on the forest floor surrounded by the slanted-eyed hellions, they open up letting in their leader. He walks toward me with the feline stride of a stalking cat and leans over me. I recoil in my sleep. He has Andrew's face.

Andrew! Why is he in my nightmare? And now ripping open my buttoned bodice, then my chemise, his eyes lusting as they rivet on my breasts. The other five devils stay gloating silently down at me, then kneel beside me, tearing at my skirts and petticoats and pulling them up to my waist. Underneath, I'm wearing nothing else to hide my nakedness. I clutch frantically at my torn garments, trying to cover myself, hide my nudity, yet knowing it's no use, fully realising my fate.

Bare-chested, face exultant, Andrew's hands go to the flap of his buckskin breeches to pull it aside. His ring of demons force my legs apart for him.

I scream as loud as I'm able to…

- two -

My scream woke me up. But only partly. Still held in a misty nightmare-land between then and now, I slowly surfaced from the forest floor of branches and cones digging agonisingly into my back, to some faraway, but nearing awareness that what was underneath me was firm and warm, that wrapped around me was some sort of puffy cocoon, and my head was nestling in pillowy softness.

But the hellions were still there. Although my eyes were still tightly closed, I could sense them circled around me, staring hungrily down at my supine body, but more an evil presence than a reality. Yet I was conscious that their eyes had turned a vicious yellow, angry that my climb back to consciousness had placed a barrier around me, taking me out of their reach.

Each time it happens, it is getting increasingly more than just a recurring bad dream. The black forest, the pursuing demons, the choking fear, are becoming more and more real. Even worse, it is getting to be a regular nightly occurrence, making me terrified of bedtime, of closing my eyes to sleep, knowing I will be chased by the same painted devils. What's more, it no longer feels like just a nightmare, that's what's so petrifying. Each time it is getting to be more and more real, until now it's as if I'm actually regressing, regressing back in time to be someone else, in another time, another age, and the terrors I'm facing are actually taking place, that the unspeakable horrors looming over me should I fail to wake up, will one night transpire before my recall back to the present time, and the terrible fate awaiting me back there will truly happen.

But now, my fear has been taken to a new and inexplicable dimension. Last night, with Andrew appearing in the dream, eyes full of lust and all lascivious to ravish me, I was taken past all previous bounds.

I forced myself fully awake. My body was moist with terror, my limbs were aching and heavy with running, and across my face I could feel the whiplash stinging of the thin boughs which sought to impede my flight. One arm and hand was shielding my breasts, my other hand was covering my pubes, desperately trying to hide my nakedness from the demons' leering gaze.

Full of dread as to what was actual, or what was imaginary: the hellish chase, or the lulling comfort, I slowly allowed my eyes to open, but holding my body stiff, terrified of finding the yellow-eyed hellions still surrounding me.

Instead, the wan light of early dawn creeping in through the small panes of the large bow window with its cushioned curved seat, was enough to reveal the dim but welcoming security of my bedroom. Seeing the familiar outlines of my antique New England furniture, the pine door to the bathroom, the spread of my king-sized bed with its centuries-old brass headboard, I let out a sigh of relief. Then the all too vivid flashes of my nightmare came flooding back into my mind and my fear returned.

Unable to control myself from shivering, I drew my knees up into the pit of my stomach, curled myself into a tight foetal ball and nestled deeper into the mattress, pulling the duvet around me, like a warm comforting shawl.

Why was the same dream assaulting me? Over and over again?

And why had Andrew suddenly entered it?

Why him waiting to violate me while the demons held me down? And why the Puritan clothing, nothing else under the many slips, leaving me naked and exposed?

What did…what *does* it all mean?

I know that women in Elizabethan times didn't wear pantalettes (if that's what they called them then) under their dresses – okay, so it was the hoi polloi women that didn't, and maybe ladies of refinement did (though not *all* of them from what I've read). But in *my* dream, did their absence have some sort of Freudian meaning for me? Some hallucinatory, psychosexual longing bottled up inside me and striving to…?

Hearing Katy's feet on the landing carpet, I quickly raised my face back on to the pillow. The door slowly opened and my daughter's pretty, oval face, with its sleep-tousled dark hair peered around it. Seeing me awake, the rest of her followed, wearing her "Pocahontas" nightdress, and clutching brown, patchy-fur "Big Ted" – bought by Robert the day she was born – under her arm.

Rubbing her eyes, she crossed the room and sign-languaged to me, 'You were shouting again.'

'It was only that same, silly old dream, sweetheart,' I reassured her.

Pulling down my nightdress – why do the damn things ride up so high? – I raised the duvet. Katy climbed in and snuggled her warm back into my front. Cuddling my daughter in the crook of my body, drawing comfort and security from her, and from the familiar sweet, sleep smell at the back of her neck, I whispered, 'But it's getting less and less, and will soon stop altogether.'

Reassured, Katy nestled tighter against me. I buried my face into her hair and kissed it. Its fragrant shampoo smell helped reassure me, reminding me of the normality of our daily lives, and recollecting the fun we'd had during Katy's bath-time last evening, splashing each other until my shirt-top was soaked through.

'Now close your eyes and get back to sleep,' I gently admonished her, stroking her head, 'or you'll be too tired to help me with Thanksgiving.'

Sighing with contentment, Katy screwed her eyes shut, squeezing "Big Ted" to her chest. Soon, her regular breathing told me she'd drifted off. But there were at least a couple of hours before I needed to think of getting up to finish off yesterday's late preparations, and I was too fearful of falling back into slumber-land, no matter how lightly, in case the dream returned.

Needing something else to occupy my mind, and realising it was only when Andrew had reappeared on the scene, that this recurring nightmare had started, I thought back to when I first met him, hoping that something, somewhere, would provide some clue as to what was happening to me?

- three -

I first saw him in a modern art gallery in Greenwich Village. I was nineteen, going on twenty, a student at New York Art College and still chaste. Yes, at nineteen, hard though it is to be believed, and living alone in a small apartment in the swinging Big Apple, of all the places to try to stay that way. But I had my reasons, I always do. That's the calculating part of me – a strong part of me, I should add.

I noticed him as soon as I entered the gallery. In his late twenties, at a guess, maybe early thirties, he was very "Pierce Brosnanish", as in his "Thomas Crown Affair" heyday. Dark tousled hair, the appealing, quizzical look as he studied a fine Cubist painting, and immaculately dressed in a dark blue suit and open neck, dark blue shirt. The sort of man, handsome, wealthy-looking, I'd fought-off all my previous boy friends for, keeping my virtue (in the archaic sense, that is) for the first night of my honeymoon in a luxury suite of a six-star Barbados hotel. Once upon a time, in my pre-Robert days, there was the hope, a dream of romance in me.

I was also impressed with his obvious appreciation of the painting he was viewing. Bold strokes, strong colours, it was far and away the best in the gallery. Pretending to be fully concentrating on other works, I slowly sidled toward him, deep in contemplation, and deliberately bumped into him.

I looked up, all startled and apologetic. 'I'm sorry,' I said. 'Please excuse me.'

He turned and studied me. I'm five six, with long slim legs, which, when I'm wearing my tight-fitting black jeans with high-heeled tan boots, as I was that day, look as if they go on forever, and didn't have to raise my eyes too high to meet his. They were dark brown, brooding, almost black. He gave me a crooked smile that made my heart lurch.

I'm not big-busted, but I'm not flat either, and I mentally congratulated myself for also deciding to wear one of my tight sweaters. Polo-necked and tucked into my belted jeans, it was pulled even tighter. With its tan colour complimenting my boots, my open, light brown duffel coat, and my shoulder length tawny hair slightly but deliberately ruffled, I knew I looked good.

'Hello, there,' he drawled. His voice was rich and deep, in keeping with the rest of him. 'I didn't know Diane Lane had an identical younger sister.'

This was obviously a day for film-star comparisons and I rewarded him with one of my friendliest smiles. Open, with just the right touch of averting my gaze to show I was embarrassed, yet shyly flattered. I kept it for only the briefest of moments, before raising my lashes (thick and curling) to let him know I was also bold enough to return and hold his appraising gaze. I didn't say anything, just let my eyes do the talking for me.

It was he who looked away first, glancing at my art portfolio.

'Artist?'

'Student.'

He indicated at the painting. 'What do you think?'

'Magnificent. Bold, with a fantastic mix of colours. He's just had his first big exhibition. The gallery must have bought it in.'

'Destined to be famous one day then?' he questioned.

'Without a doubt.'

'So it could be worth double, maybe even treble in a few years?'

I felt momentarily disappointed that he was obviously regarding it more as an investment than a work of art. If there was one thing I was passionate about it was art. When I first read that Vincent (van Gogh, that is) had sold only one painting during his lifetime, and that was just to pay for a meal, I used to wish I could reach him, wherever he was now, and tell him that today he was recognised as one of the greatest, and was being sold for tens of millions. I'd have liked him to have known.

But back to Andrew Hartford. I quickly shrugged my disappointment away. He had too many other, very obvious, redeeming qualities – and also, if I was right, hidden ones as well – to let this come between us.

'Triple; quadruple,' I answered. 'Probably more.'

'Great.' Now he was really interested in the painting. He moved closer to it and studied it at greater length. 'The only question now is – will it go with the colour scheme of my new apartment?'

I felt another drop of spirit, but again I swiftly dismissed it. It wasn't everyday a girl bumped into Pierce Brosnan's youthful double, nice shoulders, flat stomach, a deep sexy voice, and *very obviously well-off.*

He turned to face me and gave me a smile, still crooked but suddenly sort of unsure. I felt my knees go weak.

'I hope you won't think me forward,' he said, sounding kind of nervous of me biting him, 'but I've a favour to ask. Oh, I'm sorry, I should first introduce myself. I'm Andrew. Andrew Hartford. I'm a writer, and college lecturer, in Native American Studies. My new apartment's just a stone's throw from here. I'm moving in over the weekend and I'd like to have everything in place for next Monday's house warming party. In return for an invitation, would you oblige me by giving me ten minutes of your time – to tell me whether you think this painting will blend in with the décor?'

I hesitated. An invitation to dinner at some top restaurant and I'd have grabbed his arm and led the way. But to go with him alone to his place, that was something quite different. He might be dishy, but he was a complete stranger. Deciding who to lose my maidenhead to was one thing, having it taken away from me by forcible rape was quite another.

Andrew noticed my indecision.

'Hey, I understand your reluctance,' he said, his voice all concerned. 'For all you know, I could be New York's "Jack the Ripper" or "Boston Strangler". If it will make you feel any better there's a hall attendant. You can leave your portfolio at the desk and tell him if you're not down in ten minutes he's to call the nearest Precinct.' He paused, giving me a moment to think, then produced another of his crooked grins. I felt myself wavering, right down to my curled toes. He must have seen my expression changing, because he repeated it. 'Well, how about it? Willing to take a risk?'

I still dithered, wanting to say, "yes", he was so appealing. His eyes went all sort of unsure again as he waited, begging almost. That swung it. 'Sure. Why not?'

We made for the door. He held it open for me – instead of going through first, as so many males do, letting it slam back on you. I liked that. There are far too few gentlemen around these days and besides, I love being made a fuss of, it makes me feel good. Exiting on to the sidewalk and mingling with the passing crowds, he crooked his arm invitingly. As I took it, he said: 'Now that you know my name, you haven't yet given me yours?'

'Damaris,' I replied. 'Damaris Hopkins.' Actually, at that time, being young and single, it was still Wyman, but I'd already decided (with much calculated thought) on using Hopkins in my future career. Being able to trace my bloodline back to one of the First Families, the signature should add to the value of my paintings.

'Damaris. An unusual name.'

'It's said to be Greek but it's origin is Celtic, after their goddess, Damara. My American first forefather was Welsh. I was named after his daughter, my great-great-etcetera-etcetera grandmother.'

'Forefather?' Andrew said, openly amused by my use of the term. 'You make him sound like one of the Mayflower bunch?'

'He was. Stephen Hopkins, one of the original hundred-and-two,' I replied, with the usual element of pride I always get when mentioning it, and enjoying seeing the smile go from his face, to be replaced by an abashed look. But he quickly recovered and turned the tables on me by pausing and giving me an exaggerated Elizabethan bow, with full hand action, right there in the middle of the crowded street.

'My! I'm impressed,' he said, oblivious of the passing stares and theatrically raising his eyebrows. 'To find myself in such eminent company. I'm deeply honoured, my lady.'

'Don't be absurd,' I returned, sorry now that I'd boasted.

Snatching his arm, I lengthened my stride, forcing him to do the same. 'Shouldn't we hurry, before someone else buys the painting while you're deciding?'

'I'd put a deposit on it before you came in,' he said. 'We've got until closing time

- four -

The apartment was very modern, in its design, furnishings, other paintings, and scattered sculptures. Not my style, but very swish nevertheless, and everything obviously expensive. Patently, Andrew had paid interior design consultants to advise him. But I loved the stone fireplace with its deep recess and log-effect brazier. The wall above it had been left empty, presumably for him to make his own contribution in his choice of the main painting.

The door to the main bedroom was open. The bed was king-sized. I felt my heart sink as I realised he must be married. *Trust my rotten luck,* I thought. It should have occurred to me, someone as achingly handsome and eligible as this. Until then it hadn't entered my head.

'It's fantastic, I love it,' I forced myself to enthuse. 'What does your wife–?'

'There's no Mrs. A Hartford,' he cut across me with yet another of his crooked smiles, 'present or ex.'

Taking my portfolio from me – I hadn't bothered to leave it with the attendant – he placed it against one of the sofas. 'What will you have to drink?'

I hesitated again, just as I had on being invited here to advise on the painting. Was this the start of a planned seduction? If so, was I going to submit? Describing him as appealing was putting it mildly, and something told me he'd be more than a good lover. No youthful fumblings. No college student rough stuff. But it wasn't in my plan. I'd long ago made up my mind to keep myself virgo intacta until the nuptial bed, keeping my intended dangling (figuratively speaking…) no matter how wealthy – with hints it would be more than worth it, beyond anything he'd imagined – until the gold ring was on the third finger of my left hand, and I had a claim to half his assets if things went subsequently wrong.

See? I said I was calculating.

'Coffee? Tea?' Andrew listed the two options. 'The kitchen was connected up today. I'm dying to try out my culinary skills.'

I relaxed.

'Or maybe some orange-juice? I'm particularly skilled with cold drinks.'

With the threat of him making a pass removed I decided to show him I was sophisticated. 'I'd like a white wine if you have any in, a medium dry?'

'Any one in particular?'

'I'll let you choose.'

My reply wasn't only deliberate to make him feel expert, it was also to let me off the hook. Other than knowing there were various types of grapes – Merlot, Cabernet Sauvignon, say – I knew little about wines. At the same time I made a mental note to redress my lack of knowledge, just in case (cross fingers) our chance meeting developed into something more potentially permanent. Always wise to be prepared.

'The best I can offer is a Chablis. I've not yet had a chance to stock up. And I'll join you. A toast to my good fortune in finding an art connoisseur when I most needed one.' Turning to the cabinet, he asked over his shoulder. 'Speaking of which, will it go with the room?'

I answered honestly. 'Perfectly.'

He faced me, holding two wineglasses half-filled, and handed me mine. 'Miss Hopkins, thank you for your help. In return for which – and I won't take no for an answer – as well as the invite to Monday's house-warming, I'm now taking you to the best Italian *ristorante* in Chelsea which – by the sheerest coincidence – is just around the corner from here.

He clinked his glass against mine. 'Here's to your health, Damaris. I love your name, by the way. Drink up, then give me a moment to phone the gallery and we'll go.'

I panicked. 'But I'm not dressed for–'

'Damaris,' he said, looking deep into my eyes. 'You look perfect.'

The following Monday evening, I paused outside his apartment and looked down at myself. I'd splashed out and bought a simple black dress, elegant, tight fitting, accentuating my figure, a three-string pearl choker with a central pearl pendant, and matching black, open strapped, stiletto heels which made my spray-tanned legs look even longer. Opening my black evening purse, I checked my hair and make-up in the mirror and, quietly satisfied, rang the doorbell.

I was a little puzzled by the lack of noise from inside. I'd deliberately arrived half an hour late, to make an impression. By now the party should have been in full swing.

I was even more puzzled when Andrew opened the door, wearing expensive looking dark-blue jeans and crew-necked, navy-blue, Armani sweater (the name was cross stitched across the chest, in the same shade blue). Past him, I could see into the sitting room, lit by four large table lamps. Flames from the log-effect fire were dancing high in the wide stone recess. It all looked cosy and inviting. But it was empty of people.

He took my arm to draw me in but once again I hesitated. I still wasn't sure of him. 'Am I early, or have I got the date wrong?'

He was good, I'll give him that. Taking gentle hold of my arms, he looked deep into my eyes. 'This *is* the party. I wanted your company to myself. But I was afraid you'd refuse if I said there'd be only the two of us. I truly hope you'll forgive the deception...?' He paused. 'Especially as you look so stunning.'

I was of half a mind to run, but then he gave me that sexy smile of his and quizzical raised eyebrows.

'Am I forgiven?'

'You're forgiven,' I replied and walked into the room

Into the spider's web.

The rest (as they say) is history. Private history, which I've never shared with anyone, not even Alex, despite her telling me – right from when we first met in Art College and immediately cottoned to each other – *everything* about her own busy love life, and that was enough to curl an Eskimo's hair on the coldest day of an Arctic year.

Andrew was the perfect host. Placing me on one of two long white sofas facing each other, and sitting himself opposite, with a low coffee table between us, he was a wonderful conversationalist, with a whole range of subjects and humorous anecdotes to keep me laughing, classical music turned down low in the background, and subtly filling up my wine glass before it got empty, so I wasn't aware of how much I was drinking.

All this, and the seductive atmosphere of the room (the Cubist painting looked fantastic in its allotted place over the stone fireplace, which made me feel rather smug with myself) that by the time it was eleven and he offered to drive me back to my tiny apartment on the other side of Greenwich, I was all upset inside, completely demoralised that he'd not tried to make a pass at me – not *one*. Didn't he find me attractive? In fact, my partially inebriated, hurt feelings went deeper than pique. Over the evening as he sat talking, his lack of interest in me as a (though I say it myself) sexy, mature woman (I'd also slowly edged my skirt up to thigh high) became such an insult, it made it an increasing challenge for me to tempt him into my arms, to kiss me, to caress me, and – as the wine went more to my head, and all thoughts of waiting until Barbados evaporated – to slowly, *very, very, slowly* undress me, and make love to me in that king-sized bed of his I knew was only feet away, on the other side of his closed bedroom door.

So, when he stood to help me to my feet, I fell against him (looking back, rather like a sucker prey willingly – no, more than willingly – *anxiously* entering a Venus fly-trap) then pressed my body against his and challenged him with my eyes.

When he pulled back the duvet and laid me down on the bed, now wearing only my black lace bra and miniscule matching briefs, bought to make *myself* feel good, not with any forethought of enticing Andrew (truth, I'd *honestly* thought it was a party I was coming to) I whispered, as if imparting a confidence.

'It's my first time.'

'I'll be gentle,' he promised.

And he was...very, at first...but as the tempo slowly increased, I was suddenly sober and just couldn't get enough of him. And then deep down in my...well, loins, using a poetic, rather than any of the more generally used and somewhat descriptive words...there was the most wonderful tingling sensation, which increased, and *increased*, and became so exquisitely unbearable that I simply had to scream...and bite...and scratch...until, just as I thought I could take no more, all that thrill-filled part of me seemed to implode, an ecstasy which shot up my spine and took-off the top of my head – or so it felt.

I fell back on my pillow. So this was what I'd been missing. But no more. I was awake at three, and again at six, just to prove it.

Every Tuesday and Thursday evenings after that, I could hardly wait for his apartment door to close, before backing him across the drawing-room to his bedroom, unbuttoning his shirt on the way and falling on top of him across the bed. We'd make love until gloriously satiated then get dressed and go out to one of the many restaurants nearby, then back to Andrews' apartment to start all over again, finally falling asleep in the small hours of the morning, wrapped in each other's arms.

Unfortunately, this was only twice a week – though I suppose it did give us a chance to recharge our batteries in between. But on Mondays and Wednesdays, Andrew had evening lectures, and on Fridays had to drive to New Haven to help his mother care for his terminally ill father. It was a filial duty he never missed. Nor did I ever ask him to. I respected him for it. *Not many sons* – I thought – *had the love for their parents that Andrew had.*

Meanwhile, Alex guessed something was going on, and kept probing:

'Dris, you're getting to look more and more like a contented cat with a ready supply of cream. There's only one thing that could make you look like this. Sex, fantastic sex, and plenty of it. Own up, Dris. Tell Alex. Who is he?'

But I never once let on. Alex may have been my friend, but she was also gorgeous and man-mad, experienced with naturally (take my word for it) Marilyn Monroeish blonde hair. And though I trusted Andrew (implicitly) I wasn't taking the risk of introducing him to her. As for the other girls in college, whenever I overheard any of them boasting about their current boyfriends' "assets" and staying powers, or bemoaning the lack of them, I'd smile to myself, knowing they regarded me as a stuck-up, someone who preferred her own company – apart from Alex – and think smugly how little they knew.

As our first year together approached, Andrew and I were by now so much in love, we were talking marriage once my studies were over, a commitment for life when no storm of fate could possibly keep us apart. And as for our sex life…well, from now on I'll draw a veil over it, if that's okay, and keep all the intimate detail to myself – especially as to how adept I was getting – except to say that after each time I'd think it just couldn't get any better. But it did.

Then came the Friday I'd been waiting for, when the results of the 'Finals' were published and Andrew and I could go public. I'd gained a first, with honours (as had Alex). Knowing how pleased Andrew would be, and not wanting to wait until Monday when he returned from his mother's, I took a cab to his apartment. His father had worsened at the start of the summer and Andrew had spent the vacation, and the following Christmas break with them, until his father finally passed away, just before the current semester started. At long last we could start planning our future together, I thought, and over the weekend, he could tell his mother about me, she should be getting over the worst of her grief by now.

The traffic was bad. By the time the cab dropped me off, I was so impatient I rushed up the stairs, not even able to wait for the elevator to come down.

I was about to press the bell (Andrew hadn't given me a key, 'security reasons,' he'd explained) when I saw the door wasn't properly closed and let myself in. Hearing movement in the bedroom, and realising he was packing for Saturday's journey, I tip-toed across the carpet to surprise him, and saw some silver framed photographs I'd never seen before.

I glanced at the nearest, on a side table. Posed in front of a large, colonial-style house, it showed Andrew standing, arms linked with a slim, elegant, dark haired woman, wearing a French-navy dress (obviously expensive) and exquisite jewellery, a simple gold necklace with matching earrings, brooch, and a delicate gold wristwatch. Standing in front of them was a good-looking boy of about six and a pretty little girl of about three, with Andrew resting his right hand on the girl's shoulder and the woman holding the boy's with her left. On her third finger was a gold wedding ring.

It was a intimate photograph. A family picture. I went into instant shock as I realised what it meant, and spun around to run out of the apartment, but then I heard a female voice murmur from the bedroom. I don't usually swear — not the vulgar expletives, that is; to me they're evidence of a limited vocabulary (that's only my personal opinion, of course, I'd never sit as judge and jury on the rights of others to so express themselves) confining myself to "blast" and "damn", and the occasional "frig" — but this was different.

You prick! I thought. *You absolute, fucking, prick! And I fell for it! Well, so help me, Andrew sodding Hartford, you're not getting away with it! No way, you rotten sh-*

Stifling the word, I pulled myself together and entered the room as if I owned the place. 'Sorry, darling,' I exclaimed, 'but I left my—' then paused in pretended surprise.

Wearing an evening-suit and looking as handsome and immaculate as ever, Andrew was zipping up the black evening dress of the woman in the photo. His face drained white. The woman stepped back as if I was an intruder about to attack her, her eyes opened wide with fright. Partly recovering, she stammered: 'Who…who are you? How did you get in?'

I managed to look all upset. 'Oh, I'm so sorry, Mrs Hartford,' I stammered, 'I didn't know you were in town,' then deliberately hurried my reply to her question. 'I used my key, the one Andy gave me.' I'd never once called him "Andy" – I detested abbreviated names, especially with a "y" tagged on – but it added a nice touch of familiarity.

I turned to face Andrew, all apologetic and anxious to leave. 'Sorry again, lover. I was in such a hurry this morning I left my thongs behind, and just dropped by to pick them up. I thought you'd already left for New Haven, what with your mother still being so distressed after losing your father.' (Thongs? No way, I tried them once, never again, it felt just as if I was being split in two. But they added a more provocative, in more ways than one, undertone.)

'Losing his father?' his wife repeated, staring at me all goggle-eyed, as if not believing my presence in the room. 'Andrew's father's alive and...'

Her voice tailed off as she realised the significance of the words I'd dropped and rounded on Andrew, who was still standing there numb with shock.

'Thongs! Lover!' she exclaimed. 'Andrew, what's going on here? Who is this – *this girl?*'

I answered for him as if I thought he shared everything with her, on an open marriage sort of basis. 'Oh, I genuinely apologise, Mrs Hartford, truly, but I assumed you knew? I'm Andy's squeeze – Tuesdays and Thursdays at least, though I suspect there's a Monday's and Wednesday's, as well. But I surely don't want to cause any trouble between you, so I guess I'd best leave you to sort it out in private. Let me know if it's still on for next Tuesday, Andy?'

With that I exited the bedroom and managed to stroll unhurriedly across the living room. Well before I reached the apartment door, I heard Andrew's wife's voice explode in anger, with Andrew pleading to be given a chance to explain. How the hell he hoped to manage this, caught with the goods and all that, I didn't know, but if anyone could, he'd be top of my list. But as for me, as soon as I closed the door behind me, I dropped all pretence, and as I hurled back down the stairs, I was flooded with tears.

I still can't recollect how I made it back to my apartment. I can dimly recall asking the hall attendant to call a cab. But I do remember that sometime during the small hours of the night, my tears changed from heartbreak over love lost, and turned instead into anger at myself for being so easy for a practised seducer like Andrew to pick up and lay…and for never suspecting him, not *once*, over the twelve months.

Boy, did I feel dirty…and used.

I got out of bed and showered. And scrubbed myself all over. Three times. The water as hot as I could bear it, without it blistering layers of my skin off.

It worked…but then I was left cursing my stupidity, and my naivety.

And determined I would never let it happen to me again. *Ever.*

Never again would any man get to make a fool of me, I vowed, and that was for sure. Next time, I'd be in control. Meanwhile, the thing that mattered most now was my career. After this, I was going to make it to the top if it killed me, but I couldn't make it alone, not without money, especially during the early years of building a name for myself. I could, of course, go back home to live with my parents, but as much as

I loved them that wasn't for me. After three years of being on my own in New York, I couldn't again be answerable for my comings and goings.

And so, with early dawn lighting up New York's sky-scrapered skyline, I got out of bed, put on my robe, and sat in a chair near the window to consider all my available options.

By six-thirty, I'd decided. By seven I was packed and in a cab on my way to Grand Central Station, where I posted Alex a quickly scribbled note, saying just enough. By eight I was on the train back to Plymouth.

Three months later I married Robert – "Tub" Moore, from my high school days before I left for Art College. The one who used to follow me around like a faithful sheepdog, his worshipping eyes showing complete loyalty, willing to ignore my flirting with other boys (provided they were good looking, of rich parents, that is, and only flirting, *nothing more* – to prove to myself I possessed that certain something to attract the right sort of husband in the future, tall, dark and handsome, and preferably *wealthy,* at a stage higher on the scale than rich – except I was now back to being willing to settle for just rich, and also forget about the tall, dark and handsome) hoping that one day I would come around.

Well, that day had come. "Tub" was now a qualified architect. His parents *were* rich (though not quite rolling in it, but still, near enough). They and my parents also happened to be the best of friends, and our union was greeted with enthusiastic approval all around, no expense spared by mine for the wedding (I chose the most gorgeous dress, purest white, from head to toe) or for the reception, with hundreds of guests, and hundreds of wedding presents. Alex was one of the bridesmaids. Even then – unhappy about the explanation in my note – she did her best to pump me for the truth, the whole truth and nothing but the truth, about my sudden departure from New York – she just knew there'd been someone – but I kept it all to myself. A secret shared can quickly get to be gossip and is therefore best kept secret, even from one's own best friend.

Our wedding present from Robert's parents was a beautiful old New England house, a converted farmhouse with outbuildings, standing in its own grounds, just a few miles south of Plymouth.

And from mine a fortnight's honeymoon in the luxury bridal suite of a six star Barbados hotel.

With no worries about Robert guessing at my extra-curriculum activities in my last year in college.

He wouldn't know what a virgin felt like.

- five -

I brought my mind back to my room, with Katy still fast asleep beside me.

No, unless I'd missed it, nothing about my "New York thing" seemed to explain why Andrew had suddenly intruded into my nightmare.

And besides, *why* was it happening to me? And not just once, but nightly? Was I being given some sort of psychic warning of some terrible event awaiting me unless I avoided it? I don't understand them, but I've read about such things. People being given premonitions in dreams. Being told that the flight they are about to take is going to crash. They refuse to board. And hours later, it does.

So what was I being warned against? Not to go for a walk in the woods?

For some reason, I got a mental picture of me as Gretel, holding hands with Robert as Hansel, as we walk through the forest picking flowers. We meet a withered old witch named Stella, with hooked nose and zits, who locks Robert inside a cage in her ginger-bread house, with a red light over her front door. Then zooms me by broom to a Disney-style castle in the clouds – with just one room, a bedroom carpeted with purple shag pile, dominated by a huge, phallic shaped Cubist painting – owned by a smoothie-type giant called Andrew, who tries to tempt me into his massive bed with a thick slice of American apple pie, laced with a powdered aphrodisiac.

Considering the massive difference in our sizes, I don't know what he's hoping is going to happen between us, but it causes me to smile, restores my humor, and makes me dismiss the picture.

If this dream thing continues, maybe I'll go and see a shrink.

Raising my pillows, I turned my gaze through the bow window (I sleep with my curtains open) and lay there, watching the dawn rise, silhouetting the dark outline of Plymouth Bay. The blurry red curve of the rising sun grew slowly bigger over the horizon, reflecting across the waters. As it became clearer outside, revealing familiar landmarks, window light after window light switched on across the seaport town as the early risers awoke to get breakfast out of the way, before starting the final cooking of their carefully thought out dinners in celebration of this special day.

Special day – for most of them, maybe. Dads. Moms. Kids. Grandparents. And in many of the homes, close uncles, aunts, and chosen friends, plus their kids. All merrymaking together, with inevitable squabbles breaking out. But nevertheless, together, as families.

But not for Katy and me. Not with Robert's and my parents dead, and Robert somewhere – Heaven only knew where – boring the pants off Stella Sla-

No, he'd never ever think of removing them that way, either.

Besides, she'd probably left him long ago, grabbing all the money he took with him – $200,000 – having liquidated a couple of his investments earlier that week and transferring the proceeds into his ordinary account, then drawing that amount out in cash the day before he left.

So rather than Katy and me being alone this Thanksgiving, I'd invited Alex (who moved here from New York a couple of years ago, and now has her own art-gallery) as I do every Thanksgiving – and last year she'd been a great support when we thought Robert had gone missing – and also John, her latest conquest, an aspiring poet, five years younger than her, very good-looking and nice with it, whom she seems to be genuinely fond of. More than any of her previous lovers. So much so she's let him move in with her, something she swore after the failure of her only attempt at marriage, she'd never do with any man again. So maybe something will come of this one. I hope so. She's a fantastic friend. I'd like to see her with someone permanent, someone caring like John, who so obviously adores her, to settle her down.

I've also invited Andrew. He's moved here to Plymouth, too, and…well…despite the way he beguiled me (in the "tricked me" meaning rather than "charmed") in New York, I couldn't leave him on his own, not on Thanksgiving.

He arrived at my door three months ago, recently divorced and cleaned-out by his wife, looking all pathetic – and unaware, so he said, until I told him, that I was a successful artist, or that Robert had left me – explaining he'd come to look me up and apologise for New York, before moving to Florida – where his now widowed mother had retired to – to care for her, and to write books on Native American history full-time.

But instead of spending just the one day, he went and checked into a motel, mooched around the area for a week, and fell for the place. Next thing – I don't know how – he'd got himself an evening classes lectureship at Plymouth college, leaving him free to write during the day. And so, instead of Florida, he now lives in a sea-front house (leased) leading on to the beach, and his lecture course, "The History of Early America from the First Arrival", is so damn popular his classes are over-crowded, with a fair number of those attending being women smitten by his suave charm.

Not that he's interested in any of them (or so he claims). After the divorce and the way Cecilia took him for every cent, he's seemingly off women for life. Except for me, that is.

Within only days of me walking out on him in New York, he realised he'd lost the only true love of his life (there were tears in his eyes as he told me, which he had to keep wiping away, but very discreetly for me not to notice) but by the time he'd nerved himself to do something about it, it was too late, because by then I'd married Robert.

He confided all this to me when he called on me late one evening, *long* after Katy's bedtime, and having first strengthened himself with Southern Comfort – it took him all of half a bottle, so he (very reluctantly) confessed. I was in my robe, as I usually am that time of night, relaxing by the fire, and didn't want to let him in, but he was so insistent he had something he needed to tell me, I hesitatingly gave in.

He started off (stammering it almost) by admitting that when he first met me in the gallery, he'd simply been attracted to me. But, being married, he hadn't meant to fall in love with me, that just happened out of the blue when he took me to that Italian *ristorante*, the first day we met. Nor had his plan been to get me into bed, perish the thought. ('Please, Damaris, don't *ever* think that of me.') But on that Monday evening in his apartment – although he'd tried hard to hide his feelings by engaging in conversation – when *I* stumbled against him and he read what was in *my* eyes, well, yes, he'd been weak, unable to resist, I was so attractive, so damned sexy, he defied any man in the same situation to have been able to refuse me.

After that, he'd tried many times to 'come clean about Cecilia', but he'd simply been unable to, in case I walked out on him, he was so frightened of losing me. The inevitable result was that he'd 'screwed it all up', but still didn't realise how much he *really* loved me, until, as he said, it was too late. But, 'please, please Damaris', would I forgive him…and could we be friends again? Only friends, he wasn't expecting any more. Just as long as he could be near me, that's all he asked, especially now that Robert was no longer around and an emergency could arise in which I might need to turn to him for help. And also be an 'honorary uncle' to Katy.

I didn't believe a damned word of it, but neither do I believe in holding grudges either, and so I said: Yes, of course I forgave him. Lots of water had flown under the bridge since New York. We were both older, more mature, there was no reason why we couldn't be friends – but only *friends* (I stressed) nothing more. He not only accepted the conditions, he's also kept to them, except for the other evening, that is, when he…(but no, I'd prefer to forget that particular lapse, if that's okay, because I was just as much to blame).

Anyway, since then, if Alex is free to look after Katy, we've occasionally gone out together, but only to public places, concerts, cinema, the odd meal out – central tables in hotel dining-rooms, I'm insistent on that, not secluded tables in *trattorias* reeking of Italian atmosphere, with red candles in Chianti bottles streaked in red wax, and a guitarist strumming Napoli love music, like his around-the-corner, get-you-in-the-mood, Greenwich stamping place.

And so, he was joining us for Thanksgiving. But not with Katy's blessing. She didn't like him much. She may just be a child, but Katy has a natural ability for weighing people up. She studies them not saying a word, then makes up her mind. And once she has, nothing can persuade her to change it–

Without warning, the memory of my nightmare flashed into my mind, jolting me out of my brooding.

Slowly, knowing what to expect, yet unable to prevent myself, I turned my gaze to the side-window. Far off in the distance across the rolling countryside, I could see the massive beech tree of my dream – left standing there on its own, as the forest-line had been pushed further and further back over the centuries.

Its hanging branches, heavy with leaves, reflected the beautiful orange-brown shades of this year's abnormally late Fall. Studying it, I wondered whether it was the constant sight of it that was prompting my dream?…my nightmare?…my whatever? Anything – other than it being a time-journey, or a regression. And I don't give a hoot that Captain James T Kirk, Spock, Doc, Scotty, Uhura and the crew of the USS Star Ship "Enterprise", were constantly going in and out of time warps in their never-ending, split infinitive quest, to boldly go where no man has ever been before.

I know a little about them, *Star Trek* was Robert's favourite TV programme, and if I had nothing better to do, I'd sometimes sit and – while reading a magazine – watch it with him. But although time travel may be gospel for Trekkies, it's not for me.

Nor did I intend wasting time considering it. Just to imagine it being some sort of weird journey back in time. Oh, no! Even thinking about it and all its implications could send one crazy. Like: If as a result of involving myself in past events, Stephen Hopkins, my *Mayflower* ancestor, had been prevented from going to bed with my great, etcetera-etcetera grandmother, Elizabeth, the night my own direct forbear was conceived, would I still have been born? But I must have been born, I'm here now, aren't I? See? To even dabble, let alone wrestle with such thoughts, could drive you more than just normal crazy, it could send you completely loco, to end up in a padded cell wearing a straightjacket, and the key thrown away for ever.

Admittedly, I've read plenty of articles in which people, sane, sensible people, swear they've personally had these experiences. But if they did, then why didn't they try again and go back in time to strangle men like Hitler, or Stalin, or Attila the Hun at birth, and save all those millions of lives? The answer, of course, is that they couldn't. How *can* one go back and change history. It's impossible. It just doesn't make any sense, despite what eggheads like Einstein claim – if that's what he did claim, that is? I confess I'm not too sure. Physics was never my best subject.

So, mine just had to be a dream, or at worst, a nightmare. Anything more would be simply mind-boggling. The first step on the slippery slope to that padded cell in the asylum – banged up, certified as being bananas; and not just one banana but a whole great big bunch of them.

Digging my nails into my forehead, I forced all such thoughts away. Don't even go there, I told myself. Such superstitious nonsense may have gone down well in the Dark Ages when imaginations ran rife, and people believed in magicians, and hobgoblins, and all manners of malignant spirits, with cloaked Witch-finders riding from hamlet to hamlet, convincing the susceptible that women living amongst them, their neighbours, best friends even, had the evil-eye. Then "trying" them by immersing them in ponds in ducking-stools and finding them "innocent" if they drowned, but "guilty" if they survived, and burning such "proven" alive at the stake. A real no-win situation. Like the happenings that took place in Salem, not too far from here, and only three hundred years ago. But in today's world, such things just didn't occur, and that included regressions. They were nothing more than heightened dreams. Realistic, maybe. But dreams, nonetheless.

Okay, so it still didn't answer what was happening to me, or why. The same nightmarish events, night after night. I hadn't an inkling. But until the reason for them was revealed, it would have to remain that way. With me dreading falling asleep.

To give my mind something else to occupy it, I switched on the TV from the bedside controls…

- six -

Keeping the volume low not to disturb Katy, I flicked through the early morning channels.

At this early hour the choice of programmes was poor, but I finally settled on Channel 15's "Twelve Months Ago Today" – a documentary reminding viewers of various incidents, humorous and serious, which had happened throughout the States of New England on last year's Thanksgiving Day.

I forced myself to concentrate, to try to eliminate every vestige of the nightmare – and all the stupid questions – right out of my thoughts. On the screen was a film clip from a cell phone recording. Judging from glimpses of paint-flaked sides and rusting bolts, it had been taken from the deck of some tramp ship, and showed the keeled hull of an overturned boat being carried high on a wide grey ocean by rollers, then dropped into troughs by its swell.

Dubbed over the pictures, the commentator's voice narrated:

"Discovered in mid-Pacific by a Panamanian freighter, *Mariola*, this swamped hull was thought to be tragic proof of the loss of round-the-world yachtsman, Sean Wolfe, who left Boston in the August of last year, to single-handedly circumnavigate the globe. Two months later, after rounding South America and heading into the

Pacific, all contact with his yacht, *Samoset Three*, was lost during a violent storm. Despite an air-sea search lasting a week, no trace of the yacht was found. The hunt was called-off and Sean Wolfe presumed lost."

The shot changed to the yacht being winched on board the ship, water pouring out of her, then the clip focused on her name, *Samoset III Boston*, faintly readable on her stern.

The voice continued.

"With the discovery of the yacht, the worst was assumed and Sean Wolfe's death confirmed by inquest." On screen appeared a couple of shots – one facial, one whole – of a seemingly tallish man (good-looking, in his early thirties – how sad) with fair coloured hair.

"And that, it was presumed, was the end of the story. But then, last Thanksgiving, right out of the blue, Wolfe – said to be a solitary man who preferred his own company – arrived back at his lonely Massachusetts estate, having been luckily rescued from a remote Pacific island by a passing merchant ship on her way to Seattle, and then flown home."

The voice paused, long and melodramatic.

"Only for tragedy to strike again, when, within only hours of being welcomed back by his sole relative – his uncle – Wolfe suffered a fatal heart attack, caused, it was assumed, by the privations of his long months with little food and water."

The picture again changed to show a private burial place, surrounded by a white fence in a peaceful glade ringed by trees with hanging branches. The camera shot closed-up on one of the rough granite headstones, with just "SEAN WOLFE. Aged 33." engraved on it.

"And now he lies at rest, surrounded by his ancestors, among them being the famous Samoset of history, the Abenaki Sagamore who was the first Native American to approach the First Forefathers when, in 1620, the Mayflower dropped anchor in Plymouth Bay. The following year, 1621, with only fifty-one – exactly half their number – having survived the first winter, they held their first harvest festival on American soil, which over the centuries has become the national celebration we now call Thanksgiving. This is Howard Burrows signing off, wishing all my viewers your own happy Thanksgiving Day."

I glanced at my bedside clock – it was time to get up – and switched off the set. But thinking back to the documentary, I vaguely recollected catching the end of the coverage of the yacht's departure, and the subsequent search for it when it was declared missing. I'd been unaware of the owner's connection to Samoset, which might have increased my interest – after all, my own great-great-etcetera grandfather and grandmother, Stephen and Elizabeth Hopkins, were among the fifty one survivors of that first terrible winter, and must have met the young chief – extremely well-stacked, by all accounts, six foot two and built like Tarzan – giving the women, Puritan wives included (and great-etcetera grandmother Elizabeth, too, I shouldn't wonder from all I'd read about him) the most impure thoughts.

But why the dead yachtsman had named his boat *Samoset III*, and not *II*, when, to my knowledge, there'd been only one Samoset famous in our history, was a mild puzzle. As for what happened to him next, his return and his tragic end, this was news to me, such matters having been driven from my mind by the shock of *my* last year's Thanksgiving, when Robert was seen driving out of town with Stella Slater, a stranger to me at the time until the police told me *all* about her (and a *virgo vestalis,* it seemed, she was anything but) which only added to the puzzle of what, other than his money, could have first attracted her to him?.

And Robert being drawn to Stella, that's what was so strange. Acting so out of character. He'd been so disinterested in s-e-x that if I'd ever told him one evening I had the hots, he'd have thought I was having a fever and got me a powder; and a chance remark about longing for an orgasmic thrill would have had him responding that the fun fair was closed that late at night, but if I still wanted one the next evening, he'd take me there for one–

Beside me, I heard Katy gasp. She was staring up at the side of my face, her eyes open wide with concern.

'What's the matter?' I asked.

'Marks on your face,' she sign-languaged.

Throwing-off the duvet, I crossed to my dressing table and peered in the mirror. Across my cheek were two angry red weals. My heart skipped a beat as I remembered being struck in the face during last night's nightmare flight through the undergrowth. I felt a band tighten across my chest, restricting my breathing, as panic once again took hold.

I sat there motionless, unable to move, staring at myself in the glass, then saw that Katy was sitting bolt upright, looking anxious at me.

'Are you all right, Mommy?' she hand signed.

'Of course, darling,' I turned and somehow forced a smile. 'It happened yesterday while I was gardening, but is only now showing. It's nothing to worry about.'

Still trembling inside, I got back on the bed, stretched for my pillow and crept with faked threat on my beautiful daughter. 'Now, are you going to stay there all day, or are you going to get up and help me with Thanksgiving?'

Grinning with delight, Katy gestured, 'Stay here,' and picked up her pillow.

I let her launch the first attack, pretending to wilt under the onslaught.

- seven -

I didn't find this out until later, but at the same time that Katy and I were pillow fighting, an internal flight from San Francisco was docking at Boston's Logan Airport. On board was a man, a stranger to me then, which is why, at this point, I don't want to give his name.

Even before the plane came to a halt, passengers were scrambling to their feet, grabbing flight-bags from overhead lockers, and pushing and shoving toward the exit-doors like there was no second to spare, as if Thanksgiving would be over and all the turkeys and pumpkin pies eaten up, unless they could reach their waiting transport and destinations in the shortest possible time.

The man – six one, lean, early thirties, deeply tanned by being weather-beaten, collar length hair made blonde by the sun – stayed seated until he was the last to exit. Wearing a faded, blue denim jacket, narrow jeans over boots, he sauntered down the aisle.

Two stewardesses, one dark haired, the other fair, immaculate in their uniforms and both pretty, were standing by the exit door (waiting for him, so he later claimed, but that was probably his wishful thinking – but there again, maybe not). As he approached them, they gave him "come-on" smiles (more wishful thinking?) but he ignored their invitations, merely responded in a deep, New England drawl: 'Thank you, ladies, for a most enjoyable flight,' and exited into the corridor.

By holding back he'd timed it right. Every luggage carousel was thickly surrounded by passengers also arrived from other incoming flights. With nothing to collect he threaded through them and mingled with those already making for the "Arrivals" hall. Staying away from the crowded barriers and voluble greetings of waiting relatives and friends, he made straight for the exit doors and out on to the front sidewalk area.

Almost before he had time to look around, a black Mercedes with dark windows drew up alongside him. A rear door opened. He entered. The door closed. The Merc pulled away from the kerb, smoothly changed automatic gears and headed for downtown Boston.

'Everything okay?' asked a flat voice alongside him, that of a stocky, Italian looking man, in his middle fifties, wearing a dark suit and dark sunglasses.

'Uh-huh,' the man confirmed. 'Thanks for wiring the money, Carlo.

Carlo Vicenze gave a thin smile. 'No problem. But next time, gimme some warning first. I almost died of shock on the spot.' He paused. 'I'm already re-negotiating a new deal. Once they've faxed me their bid, we can take it from there. But we'll talk more in my office.'

The younger man stared brooding through the car window, then looked in, 'Give me a couple of days first, Carlo? I'd best get back and find out what's been going on while I've been away. Then try putting it right – if it's not too late. Until I do, I accept my share of the blame. With his track record, I should have known better than to leave him in charge.'

Vicenze thought about it a moment then nodded. 'Sure. Makes good sense. It will also give me more time to try upping the ante.'

He instructed the driver. 'Drop me off outside the building then take Route Three South, exit at Six, and follow the South Carver signs.'

- eight -

I let Katy win the pillow fight then took a quick shower, towelled and talced, hid the weals on my cheek with a concealer stick and make-up, pulled on black, narrow leg designer jeans (as is my day style) and a black polo neck sweater, and went downstairs to make breakfast.

Katy wanted her usual cereal, but I wasn't feeling hungry. Toasting myself a piece of brown grain bread, I turned to gaze out of the kitchen window, seeing, but not taking in, the lawns carpeted with multi-hued leaves fallen off the landscaped young trees and shrubs, surrounded by centuries-old oaks, beeches, and elms, and beyond them, open fields.

Instead, with last evening's preparations spread across every kitchen surface, bringing twelve months ago flooding back, I was picturing Robert in his habitual brown and green tweed suit and floppy hat, slowing down his dark blue Lexus SUV to casually wave to Katy and me as he drove past, puffing his briar pipe as usual so as not to cause suspicion, then his wheels crunching along the winding gravelled drive and through the wide gateway into the narrow country road, out of sight.

And out of our lives.

He'd come down that morning looking edgy, pausing only to say he'd no time to eat and would be "gone maybe a couple of hours". Such a statement, in contradiction to his habit of always acting to routine – previous Thanksgivings, after eating a hearty breakfast (cereal, two eggs sunny side up, bacon, buttered toast and marmalade, large black coffee) he pottered about the grounds, then came in and settled by the sitting room fire with a book (on architecture, what else?) until his parents and mine arrived – I could hardly believe my ears. In answer to my questioning, he would only say "it's to be a surprise", and hurried out through the door before I could reply.

"Surprise" wasn't a word in Robert's vocabulary. He was so goddamn stolid, so frigging predictable, he never did anything – except maybe go to the john – without discussing it with me first. But as it turned out, "surprise" was the operative word. Afterwards, all the tell-tale signs he'd had something on his mind, had, on reflection, been there for me to see, months before. His new habit of disappearing for long walks through the surrounding countryside, and returning to brood – or in retrospect, to plan – in front of the log-fire, chewing at his pipe rather than smoking it, before retiring earlier than normal and be fast asleep – or pretending to be – by the time I'd pop my head around his bedroom door to say 'goodnight'.

I admit I should have noticed, but I'd been so worried about Katy lying in intensive care in hospital; and then having to come to terms with her losing her speech; and also finding time to help Alex with her PR work and brochure design for my forthcoming exhibition, that I just hadn't.

It doesn't say much for me, I suppose, because he could have been ill, but as he'd never looked particularly healthy – a little too bulky, not much colour – I'd not taken much notice. Not surprising, not to anyone who knew me, especially during my teen years. I'd always been…well, "a selfish bitch" (as the other girls in my grade used to call me) which is why throughout High School, I'd kept my own company, except for sometimes talking to, or occasionally a little light flirting – crudely known as "p-teasing" – making sure I still had it – with (as previously mentioned) the best-looking rich boys (as previously mentioned). Aloofish.

The same in art-college, apart for Alex. We hit it off from the moment we first met, something to do with the attraction of "opposites", I suppose. But as an only child, pampered by my parents – especially my Dad (and later, worshipped by Robert, but more as an icon than female flesh and blood, with a body allowed to be touched) my every wish had always been granted. Again in retrospect, even my affair, my "New York thing"with Andrew, had in all honesty, been as much for the erotic pleasure of it, as for what I'd convinced myself was love.

In fact, the only one I've ever loved unconditionally is Katy, and that was only from when I first held her in my arms. Before that extraordinary moment, I hadn't even wanted a baby – the "it" growing inside me was going be an interference in my life, an unwanted restriction on my work. But then, when they gave her to me to hold, and I looked down at her as she snuggled against me, so beautiful and so trusting, and realised the miracle of her, that it was *me* who'd given birth to her, that without me she would never have existed, that was the first moment in my life I ever experienced the kind of love which takes your breath away. The one you'd be willing to die for, if something ever happened to force you to make that choice.

That's exactly how I felt, sitting and sleeping by her bedside in the hospital after the car accident, her life hanging by a thread. If, by giving my life for hers, it would have ensured she would live, I wouldn't have thought twice about it. And as for when she'd finally been allowed home, work had taken second place. I didn't even attend the exhibition, nor did I feel particularly excited when Alex phoned to say that every painting had been sold within hours, and raving for me to produce more of the same ('but only when Katy's well enough', she'd added, in all fairness) for my next showing.

Maybe I'd assumed it was worry over Katy, and grief over the loss of his parents, that was on Robert's mind during that time – the reason for his solitary walks, his pensive moods, and retiring early to bed. But we'd grown so far apart I'd not really taken much notice, nor in truth had I much cared.

And all that time he'd been planning his new life with Stella Slater.

Possibly…probably…it was *my* indifference that drove him to seek another woman's company in the first place. But of all the ones to pick, why someone with *her* reputation? Hearing that Billy Graham had once run off with Mae West, could not have surprised me more.

Nevertheless, I tried to find him. After reporting his disappearance to the police (who straightaway lost interest on finding out *who* he'd gone off with and closed the file) I then hired a private investigator, but only because there were things – financial matters, mostly – to sort out. As far as I was concerned, if Robert preferred someone like *Stella Slater* to me, then *I* certainly didn't want him back. However, as I've said, Katy missed him. What with losing her grandparents, her voice, and then her Daddy, all in a matter of months, that was one hell of a lot for a six year old to take – she cried for weeks, right through Christmas and into the New Year – and so my searching for him was as much for her as for myself. But when he didn't even try getting in touch with her (too busy creating a new life, I thought, at first; and then I started wondering if he'd had some kind of mental breakdown, because that would explain everything: Stella; walking out on his work; his home; and especially Katy, who he'd worshipped). Then Katy slowly came to accept it, and now rarely mentions him.

But despite having his vehicle license, bank and credit card numbers, the investigator failed to find any trace of the pair – not even Stella's mother had known about Robert (at least, not by name, or so she claimed) only that her daughter had been planning to run away with "some married man whose wife couldn't hold her man". And so, after six months of paying the PI's fees and expenses for no return, I discharged him and handed it all over to Paul Chapman (Robert's attorney) to sort out, and tried to get on with my life.

At least, I'm fortunate in not having any money worries. But as for Paul, maybe that wasn't such a good idea. Living a quarter of a mile away, he's taken to calling here on his way home from his office, not only to report on the continuing lack of progress, but also to 'check I'm okay' (quote) – except his idea of checking doesn't coincide with mine. Like the other evening, when he arrived later than usual, knowing that Katy would be in bed–

Katy's fed-up sigh turned my attention away from the window. She was toying with her cereal, left elbow resting on the table, her face propped in her hand.

Dropping the spoon in the bowl, she signed: 'Why does Andrew have to come to dinner?'

Not again, I thought, *we've been through all this before.*

'Because he's an old friend from New York. And he's on his own.'

'I don't like him. I'd rather have just Aunty Alex and Uncle John.'

'I know you would, sweetheart, but it's only for dinner. Besides, Andrew's trying so hard to be friends with you. Bringing you presents, and playing games with you and Harry.'

Harry (Harrison) was our bearded collie. With a string of names as long as your arm, not even Europe's noblest family could have such a pedigree. Bought by Robert as a pup to keep him company on long business journeys, and as a family pet, Harry was as irresistible as he was ungovernable.

'Harry doesn't like him either. And Andrew only brings me presents because of you.'

'Now you know that's not true, darling,' I argued, yet knowing full well it was. Lately, he'd started holding my hand on our evenings out, and trying to kiss me good night on the lips after driving me home instead of on my cheek, except I kept turning my face aside. As for last week when he arrived unexpectedly, knowing (just like Paul) that it was after Katy's bedtime...

No, to repeat, I really don't want to think about that night.

But children were so damned discerning – and Katy especially so, even more since she lost her speech. As if her other senses had increased in compensation.

'There's nothing between Andrew and me.' I protested. 'We're just old friends from way back, that's all.'

'Well, I still don't like him,' Katy sign-languaged back.

'That's because you don't try.'

'No, it's not. It's because I don't like him.'

'Well, I'm sorry, Katy, he's coming and that's that.'

Katy began to add something more. But you can't argue with children's logic, so I turned away and glanced about the kitchen, checking last evening's preparations.

Not being much in the mood for celebration, I'd kept to the basics: roast stuffed turkey, giblet gravy and cranberry sauce, mashed sweet potatoes, peas, onions in cream, and curled celery, followed by pecan pie – but as for extras like pumpkin pie and so on, I hadn't been up to making the effort.

In the corner of my eye, I could see Katy still poised, waiting to continue the argument. To change the conversation, I joked, 'If Benjamin Franklin had had his way we wouldn't just be *eating* turkey today, we'd be saluting it. He wanted it to be America's symbol instead of the bald eagle. That's why someone made up the rhyme about us having two national birds: "May one give us peace in all our States, and the other a piece for all our plates".'

Katy shrugged as if to say "who cares?". She was spending the morning with her best friend, Jo – Paul and Suzanne Chapman's only daughter – at Suzanne's express invitation (which is almost tantamount to a royal summons) probably to keep Jo out of her mother's immaculately coiffured hair while she preened herself even more to welcome her specially invited guests (an equally royal invitation) to her Thanksgiving dinner, a real highfaluting annual event if ever there was one – from what I've heard, I'd always avoided her majesty's bidding. So, before Katy could get back to Andrew, I said: 'Finish your breakfast, Katy, or we'll be late for Jo's,' and turned back to the window.

I stared out again over the garden. What had I been thinking about?

Oh, yes, Robert…

If I was partly to blame (or maybe more than *partly*, as will have been gathered from what I've so far said about myself) well it wasn't *all* my fault. Okay, so he'd never had much stamina, often out of puff and all that; I was always on at him to exercise, and to go for a check-up. Still, exercise or not, he'd been so undersexed, so indifferent, he'd have made top eunuch – *without* the operation – in the most exotic of harems, but he'd refused to talk about it, far more interested in his work, Katy, his home comforts, in that order, with intimacy very much an also-ran. To be honest, that was my real reason for suggesting separate rooms when I found I was pregnant, saying I felt so restless I needed my own bed to stretch out in, so as not to keep him awake and lose sleep because of me. He'd made no protest, anxious to please as always, even agreeing 'if that's what the doctor advises, we must do whatever's best for you and the baby.'

After Katy's birth, my pretext was that caring for her during the day meant I'd sometimes have to paint into the early hours, and what with the 2am feed as well, and not wanting to disturb him getting in and out of bed, maybe it would be best if our sleeping arrangements continued a while longer? Robert had again thought it "a sensible idea", so much so he'd not once raised the subject of my returning to the nuptial bed, during the seven years it had continued.

Andrew Hartford, on the other hand, was *over* sexed. A hundred and ten percent over. Sure, he'd managed to keep it under control during his first months of settling in Plymouth. But that, as it transpired, was only to try to lull me into a sense of security (false).

Then, last week, he'd pounced.

Oh, hang it, if I'm going to keep remembering it, I clearly need to exorcise the memory of it, so it might as well be now…

He arrived unexpectedly, and late, as I've already mentioned, expecting Katy to be in bed fast asleep. But I'd given her an extension for a mom-daughter cuddle as she'd been feeling sad that day, missing "Daddy".

Anyway, she eventually became heavy-lidded. Having persuaded her to give Andrew a dutiful peck on the cheek, I took her upstairs and settled her in with a story. A *long* story, I think she was determined (enough to revive herself) to keep me from going back down to Andrew. But finally, though reluctantly, she allowed me to leave.

Returning to the sitting room, Andrew and I settled down to chat. The lights were low, the flames of the log fire were casting flickering shadows across the oak-beamed ceiling, and I had classical music (Vivaldi, with Joshua Bell) playing in the background. Despite fighting it, the ambience of the room was evoking memories of the first evening he invited me to his Greenwich apartment, and the first time we made love (using a polite euphemism for what happened next, back then).

To make it worse, I was getting used to having him around me again, and that evening the old familiarity suddenly returned, the memories rose-tinted, creating a cosy warmth between us, amounting almost to intimacy and banishing the reality that he'd all along been two-timing me. Also, after years of not being held, I was feeling the need of a man's strong arms around me making me feel snug, secure (and yes, alright I admit it, with a certain, but unmistakeable tingly sensation suddenly invading my nether region) especially after all I'd gone through the last twelve months – losing my parents, and in-laws, Katy's accident, then finding she'd lost her power of speech, and Robert leaving.

Looking back, maybe it *was* my fault. He'd obviously timed his call, hoping I was ready for him to try his luck, nevertheless, I must have conveyed my mood to him, because he suddenly crossed from his chair and sat beside me on the sofa. At first, he just casually laid his arm along the top of the settee, barely touching my shoulders. I remained sitting stiff for a few moments, listening to the music and fighting the dictate of my body, telling myself that if things got out of hand and it went too far, it wouldn't be right, not with Katy asleep upstairs, above us…

But when he dropped his arm lower, I stopped resisting, sank against him and rested my face on his chest. From then on, the only excuse I have is that he'd been subtle. Making no sudden move in response, he gently caressed the nape of my neck, and then the top of my spine. I know I should have stopped him, but "damn it to hell!", I kept thinking (preparing a defence for myself for after) the last time was eons ago, and that was with Robert and over in minutes, which also included raising his interest and hardening his resolve.

And so, rather on the lines of Hoagy Carmichael's *My Resistance Is Low*, I turned my face and buried it into the nape of Andrew's neck. Still stroking me, his hands moved slowly and all too familiarly down to my breasts. Cupping them over my thin sweater, he gently thumbed my nipples, and suddenly (moving from Hoagy Carmichael to Billy Daniels) with me being already more than half way there, *"that same old magic has me in its spell"* feeling took hold. Being honest, it was exquisite. Within seconds he'd taken me to the point where there was no going back. Putting my arm around his neck and giving him my mouth to kiss, I conveyed to him how I was feeling and slid on to my back on the sofa, inviting him to go all the way.

With his lips responding to mine, I made only a token protest when his hand went under my skirt (which, by coincidence, I happened to be wearing that day, instead of my habitual black jeans). Crooking his thumb over the top of my underwear (small) he slowly slid them off, assisted by some helpful wriggling on my part. Pushing his slip-ons off at the heels with his toes he wrestled to unzip and remove his trousers. Then, just as they reached his ankles…

Katy banged her drum from the top of the stairs.

'What the hell's that?' Andrew swore, sitting up with a start.

I sprang to my feet. 'It's our signal. Katy wants me for something.'

'Damn! Of all the blasted moments to pick.'

Feeling all guilty and full of shame, I was already making for the door, smoothing my skirt straight. 'Coming, darling,' I called out.

Andrew's voice followed me: 'Hurry back. We've got some unfinished business.'

Running upstairs, I didn't respond.

Katy was back in bed, curled under the duvet, with only her face in sight, her eyes searching mine just in case she was in trouble, yet knowing full well she wouldn't be.

'What's the matter, sweetheart?' I asked, sitting down beside her and stroking her hair. 'Why aren't you asleep?'

She looked up. Katy has such appealing eyes, especially when she's tucked up in bed, wearing her nightie and looking vulnerable. They always melt me.

'I can't,' she signalled, pulling her hands from under the duvet. 'When I close my eyes, I keep thinking of Daddy...and Grandma and Grandpa...and Granny and Granddad. Will you stay with me, Mommy?'

'Of course, darling,' I replied, hugging her. She clung to me, arms tight around my neck. We stayed locked together for some time before I sat up and tucked her in once more. 'Now doesn't that feel comfortable and safe. Snuggle in and close your eyes tight. I won't go, but this time try getting to sleep.'

Holding her hand, I looked down at her, amused at the fierce determination on her face, all screwed up, attempting to force slumber to descend on her.

She looked so innocent and trusting, I felt suddenly ashamed for not being a fit mother. You really are a selfish Monica, I said to myself, "making it" downstairs on the sofa, and Katy lying so innocently in bed right above you.

The flush of guilt made me aware of being naked under my skirt…

(Hey!, wait a goddamn moment, maybe *this* was why I imagined myself naked under my clothes in last night's dream? My subconscious remembering back to that evening…? It could well be, better a rational explanation than a psychoanalysis one…?)

Still, putting that thought aside and returning to Katy, kissing her on her forehead, I said: 'I'll be back in a moment.'

She nodded, eyes suddenly heavy-lidded.

By the time I returned from my room wearing new underwear, she was out to this world, fast asleep. I kissed her again and crept out, leaving the door half open for the landing light to filter through into her room, for her to feel safe if she woke up.

Returning downstairs, Andrew was lying on the couch, waiting, in what he obviously thought was a provocative pose. Still minus his trousers, and wearing only his black silk, designer boxers (shirt, socks removed) his ardency was so very evident – having maintained it for so long, he'd obviously lost none of his libidinous drive (or taken one of those erectile enhancing pills they persist in trying to sell you by spam email, irrespective of whether or not your first name is female, hoping, I suppose, that your husband might need them) – he looked so ridiculous, I burst out laughing.

'Hold it a moment longer while I get my camera,' I spluttered. 'I could make a fortune, selling snaps at next week's lecture. At the same time, would you like a coffee?'

Looking all hurt and offended, he sat up. Struggling into his clothes, he tucked his shirt in, and with his ardency only slowly deflating, making him look even more absurd, and not wanting that part of his anatomy caught in his zipper, causing a nasty accident, he *carefully pulled it up,* fastened his belt, and put on his socks and shoes.

I paused in the doorway, on my way to the kitchen. 'Or maybe you'd prefer a cold Coke to cool you down?'

'Sure, I don't think,' Andrew replied, in an even worse huff. Glancing at his watch, he grated, 'I'd not realised the time, I'd best be getting back.'

Moments later he'd left, without giving me a kiss on even my cheek.

He'd phoned only once since then, to confirm the time for Thanksgiving dinner, and hadn't mentioned the episode, although it had been there unspoken between us – especially for Andrew, who'd obviously taken it as a rejection of his charms, one in particular – and still wasn't seeing the funny side of it.

Men! Why were they so damned touchy if you made a joke about anything to do with their sexuality? Their attraction, their performance. No matter how playfully it's intended, any adverse comment, particularly (according to Alex who says she's often used the ruse to break off with someone she's gone off) about the later, and they take offence like hurt little boys. I was dreading the first few minutes of seeing Andrew again, realising how tinder-fused the atmosphere would be. Hopefully, Alex's and John's presence would help to cloud the episode from his mind.

But thinking of men – men in general, that is – did they divide into only two categories? The Andrew Hartfords? Or the Roberts? Weren't there any in-betweens? Men who were dependable yet sexy; reliable though with a sense of humour; and more than anything (from what I'd personally experienced of other women's husbands – not just Andrew, but Paul Chapman too, he also sprang into my mind) men capable of staying faithful to their wives, and not always on the make for something in the extra-marital department.

If there were any, I'd never met one. Not free and unattached, that is. The rare ones I'd met, the ones with that certain, extra something, were inevitably happily committed, and so few in number, they should be designated a protected species.

In which case, rather than risk another Andrew, or another Robert, I'd prefer to stay single, and keep expending my passion on my art, thanks very much.

Looking back into the room, Katy was still playing with her food. Glancing at the clock and seeing it was almost nine, I grabbed my sheepskin coat (light tan, three-quarter length, lined in white wool, with cuffs turned back, it's a favourite, even though it's years old).

'Okay, Katy Moore, leave it, we're late. You know what Jo's mom is like about being on time. Put your coat and boots on, and don't take long.'

Katy slid off her chair, ran into the hall and up the stairs to her room.

I shouted after her: 'Katy. I'm going for the Jeep – lock up behind you, and bring the key.' Choosing my heeled, tan leather boots to go with the sheepskin, and pulling them up over my black jeans, I made for the door.

As my feet grounded the gravel drive leading to the U-shaped outhouses and ex-stable block behind the main house, my eyes were once more drawn to the beech tree dominating the skyline. It was exactly as in my nightmare, hanging branches forming a wooded shelter around its thick trunk.

Putting my hands into my pockets and pulling my collar up, I entered the arched tunnel leading to the rear courtyard, unable to prevent myself shivering, despite the coat's warmth.

Deep inside myself, I knew there had to be some reason for the nightly repetitiveness of whatever was happening to me.

The question was: What?

And why me?

- nine -

Meanwhile, getting back to The Man from San Francisco, the black Mercedes was now approaching Quincy. For a brief moment, he was tempted – despite all he'd come through recently – to ask the driver to take the more winding Atlantic 3A route instead. During his time away he'd missed its wild scenery, its rocky, wave-lashed coves, scattered lighthouses and historic sea-ports – Hingham, Cohasset, Scituate, Duxbury, with their eighteenth- and nineteenth-century clapboarded houses, and fishing-vessels and yachts riding at anchor in their harbours.

But the mysterious pull inside him made him keep to the faster and more direct Route 3. Not even taking-in the familiar countryside, the landscape sped by. The many farms became repetitive blurs, green fields and grazing cows going unnoticed, as did the sloping valleys and rolling hills, the meandering rivers and streams, and the narrow country roads winding alongside them, following their course, sometimes crossing shallow fords or flowing under historic 18th century covered wooden bridges, and others arched and made of stone.

His mind focused on journey's end, distant hamlets sped by, white steepled churches on emerald greens, ringed by wooden houses, surrounded by forests of red- and sugar-maples, beech, hickory and oak aflame with the greens, reds, brown and gold of a delayed autumnal Fall. As for the rolling hills beyond them, back-dropped in the hazy distance by mountain ranges with their wild and rugged forests of spruce, balsam fir, hemlock, conifers and tall white pines, he hardly noticed their passing beauty.

Drawn by a compelling, but inexplicable inner force, his overwhelming urgency was to reach his destination. He'd told Carlo he was anxious to get back to discover what had been going on in his absence. That much was true.

But it was not the reason for his exigency.

That came from the singular dream he'd been having recently. Especially the last one, when he'd fallen asleep on the flight from San Francisco to Logan, and which had left him with the strange certainty that to get back today could well affect the rest of his life.

And could also mean the difference between life and death.

But *his* life? Or that of the young woman's strangely dressed in Puritan clothing, fleeing through the dark forest, desperately trying to escape her pursuers?

He didn't know. The dream had ended too soon.

All he knew was that he was her only hope.

Provided he got to her in time.

Today's time…

Or past time…

It didn't matter.

As long as it was in time.

- ten -

'Damn,' I muttered, seeing Suzanne exiting her large, double front doors as I drove up the Chapman's curving drive. 'Damn and blast.'

If there was anyone I wasn't in the mood for right now it was Suzanne *haut-et-puissant* Chapman. But it looked as if I was going to be stuck with her. I prayed Paul would remain hidden. Not only should his eye be showing purple by now, but I didn't know whether seeing it would make me want to laugh, or give him another one for a matching pair.

Jo was already standing inside the columned porch. Taking hold of her daughter's hand (and adopting the pose of a dutiful mother) Suzanne waited for us to reach them.

'You go,' Katy hand-signed, hearing me swear and realising why. 'I'll say you were in a hurry.'

'It's okay, darling,' I ruffled my daughter's hair. 'Just have a fun morning with Jo.'

I stopped my Jeep (a Patriot – ideal for the forest tracks I subjected it to with my work) at the foot of the steps leading up to the big, ivy-walled, stone house. The Chapmans and myself were neighbours only in as far as their land joined with mine, but our driveways were a quarter of a mile apart. Jo was "Jo" to everyone else but Suzanne, who either gave her her full name, Josephine; or in the company of high society: Josephine-Louise. Shades of Gallic imperial grandeur, I always thought, by a woman so proud of her long past,

65

French-noble blood, she believed – genuinely believed – that it set her a class above the rest of us.

I gave Katy a hug. 'Enjoy yourself. I'll back for you at two.'

Katy hugged me back, jumped out of the Jeep, and ran up the stone steps, signalling: 'Good morning, Mrs Chapman,' as she approached Suzanne, who replied automatically: 'Good morning, Katherine. Sweet child.'

Giving me a final wave, Katy linked hands with Jo and they disappeared into the house. Brought up by a caring nanny, with most of her time spent in the domestic quarters with the "servants", Jo was as down to earth as her mother was always up in the sky.

Even at this time of the morning, with dinner preparations obviously in the hands of the cook (sorry – *chef de cuisine*) and staff, Suzanne was wearing an almost diaphanous lilac dress with matching high heels, and her hair immaculately styled, ready to meet her guests of approved relatives and appointed friends.

As she daintily negotiated the steps, I looked up at the house with its green gabled roofs and dormer third-storey windows. It was one of Robert's finest commissions (his particular talent was designing and overseeing the restoration of old New England properties for which he'd been in demand from New York State to Vermont and Maine). He'd spent endless hours drawing (and redrawing) various plans, and umpteen sketches, for its external and internal modernisation to meet Suzanne's demands, mostly histrionic, but that was typical Suzanne – in becoming a pampered wife she'd missed her true vocation as a spoiled prima donna (but there again, perhaps not, because in effect, that's what she was). Despite all this, Robert had still managed to keep its unique old New-England charm. The final result was a beautiful house in which he'd been justifiably proud – although I doubted Suzanne appreciated the effort he put into it.

I pressed the button to lower the passenger-side window. Suzanne inclined herself elegantly from the waist (conscious, as always, of her every movement, as if film-cameras were permanently on her) and peered in.

'Damaris, thank you for letting Katherine keep Josephine company while we entertain. Are you sure you won't change your mind and join us? Josephine would love for Katherine to stay to dinner with her in her room. To tempt you, this year we're breaking with tradition and having a French *haute cuisine* menu. Puree of game soup. Hors d'oeuvres of olives farcies, canapes of caviare. Lobster in shells garnished with oyster crab. Small timbales, Bretonne. Filet of venison with artichokes, and so on and so on. You'd really love it.'

No I wouldn't, I thought, *I'd hate it*. Not the food but the company, and all the false airs, graces and conversations. 'Sounds delicious, Suzanne,' I lied (and the food sounded too rich for my taste, too) my nerve ends instantly jangling as I saw Paul descending the steps to join us, 'but as I explained, Katy and I decided on a quiet celebration. Alex and John are joining us. And Andrew. Andrew Hartford. Thanks all the same. Maybe next year?'

As Paul approached the Jeep, *I don't know how he has the gall*, I thought, not after the other evening, when he'd called "to check I was okay," except that this time he decided to give me a physical by pinning my arms back and groping under my sweater. As I didn't consider this to be part of an attorney's brief in his concern for his client, I'd struggled free and…well, turned down his appraisal.

His eye was a beaut. And I was right about the colour. A deep shade of mottled purple. I still couldn't understand how he had the nerve to join us, but maybe Suzanne would have wondered 'why?' if he hadn't? Or perhaps he just wanted the excitement of outfacing me, hoping to make me feel embarrassed by the fact he now knew what I felt like – above the waist, anyway.

As he reached her side, Suzanne moved to make room for him. As cool as a cucumber, he placed his arm around her waist. Sunbed-tanned, wearing knife-creased dark blue slacks, dark blue polo-club blazer with a gold-weave badge, gleaming white shirt, dark blue cravat finely dotted with white-spots, the eye looked incongruous with the rest of his immaculate appearance. 'Hello, Damaris', he said, looking into the Jeep, but his abashed smile at least showed he was conscious of how he'd acquired it.

'Just look at Paul's eye, Damaris,' Suzanne yakked, giving me Paul's version for it. 'The silly buffer hit it on something the other night, garaging his Ferrari after getting home late from his office. And our guests will be arriving soon. How *should* I punish him?'

'Looks like he's been punished enough, Suzanne,' I replied, turning to the sartorial vision. 'Home late again, Paul? You really shouldn't be giving your clients such attention. Not with a beautiful wife like Suzanne to rush back to.'

Suzanne, who accepted compliments as her due, simpered – and Suzanne simpering is a nauseating sight. She took proprietary hold of her husband's arm. 'I keep telling him the same thing, Damaris. He should learn to delegate more to his junior attorneys.' She turned to Paul. 'I'm trying again to persuade Damaris to change her mind and join us, but she still refuses.'

Paul gave me his gleaming, white-toothed smile; it looked forced. 'How disappointing, Damaris,' he smarmed. 'And now you're on your own, maybe an opportunity lost. A couple of my client-friends from Boston are joining us. Both recently divorced, extremely wealthy and very eligible. Either could have been the catch of the year.'

'Except that hooking fish was never my sport, Paul,' I gave him an overly sweet smile in return. 'You never know what's going to be on the other end of the line. They may look like minnows, but then – as I recently experienced – they can unexpectedly metamorphose into octopuses with eight tentacles to fight off. No, Katy and I are happy as we are, thanks very much.'

Detecting a hint of hidden repartee between the two of us, Suzanne looked sharply at her husband. 'You've no need to worry about Damaris, Paul,' her voice hardened, 'she doesn't need *your* help to sort out her social life. She's got that handsome Andrew Hartford coming for dinner. I don't think either Daniel or Michael could compare.'

Paul pulled back, flushing at his wife's rebuke. Returning to me, Suzanne commented. 'I heard a whisper that you and Andrew are old friends, Damaris?' She paused, then added.

'Someone said that you and he...' she gave me a saccharine smile, clearly returning the compliment for whatever my exchange with Paul was all about '...*knew* each other *well*, during your college days in New York?'

Hearing the emphasis, and knowing Suzanne's penchant for gossip – and elaborating on whatever she heard – this wasn't something I had any intention of discussing. 'Yes we did, Suzanne,' I put my hand on the gearshift and smiled back, answering her question all open and innocent. 'He was one of my tutors,' I said, unable to stop myself from adding, 'The best. I invited him to join us knowing he'd be on his own otherwise, especially as he knows Alex and John.'

Suzanne arched her eyebrows. 'Then it must one of those odd coincidences, him choosing Plymouth, of all places, to live?'

'It must have been,' I answered, letting the Jeep roll away. 'I'll be back for Katy about two.' Raising the window, I pulled away, spinning the wheels and creating a spray of gravel behind me.

In my rear mirror, I could see Suzanne standing there in the drive, glaring after me. Paul took her hand. She flung it away and stormed up the steps. Paul hurried after her. It looked like he was going to have some difficult questions to fend off. More difficult, I suspected, than any he had to face as a practising attorney.

If so, then maybe I'd gone too far. Paul wasn't a man to cross.

He'd want his own back.

- eleven -

Exiting the drive, I turned for home. There, in the near distance, silhouetted on its hill, was that damn beech tree again. It seemed determined to haunt me. Again I wondered whether it was the daily sight of it that was causing my nightmares–

My heart missed a beat as the picture of Andrew standing over me flashed into my mind, pulling aside the flap of his buckskin–

Buckskin breeches! Of course. The realisation hit, making me gasp with relief. How stupid of me. My dream wasn't about demons after all. It was a war-party! An "Indian" war-party. That's all it was. Nothing more sinister, nothing more foreboding than that.

What's more, Andrew's lectures – one in particular – must have been the cause.

I'd attended them from the start, persuading Alex and John to join me. They'd both enjoyed them. One thing about Andrew, he was gifted with an almost mesmeric ability to transport his listeners' imaginations back over the centuries, and make them feel they were actually witnessing the events he was describing.

But there was one that had stood out. The Pequot Mystic Village massacre of 1637, some 17 years after the First Forefathers arrival in the New World. He felt strongly about it. And from a night back in New York, when we'd exchanged secrets in bed, I knew why. Tracing his paternal line all the way back to that time, he'd found he had Pequot blood in his veins.

Because of this, he had presented that lecture with extra passion, his sympathies clearly evident as he described the terrible carnage in almost photographic detail.

'Of all the North Eastern woodlands tribes,' he'd begun, 'it was the Pequot who gave the early settlers the most trouble. But their resistance to the White Man's penetration of the New England forests in search of new farming land, could not prevent them the loss of their traditional hunting grounds.'

Raiding along the Connecticut Valley, killing and scalping all before them, the Pequots increasing activity had determined the colonists to form an expeditionary force, volunteers and militia, to stamp them out.

Aided by Uncas – who had broken away from his father-in-law, Sassacus, chief of the Pequots, to form his own tribe, the Mohegans – and sixty of Uncas' braves, the small force crept up on a Pequot palisaded village on the Mystic River and surrounded it. It was evening. Hearing the sound of revelry coming from the enclosure as the Pequots celebrated the success of another raid, the force decided to delay its attack until dawn, and opened it with Uncas' Mohegans shooting fire arrows at the wigwams as all inside slept. The blaze quickly spread, turning the village into a hellish inferno. Waiting in the forest, muskets lined, the settlers shot down every Pequot who tried to escape, including the women, old and young, and every baby and child; while inside the palisade, some six hundred or more burned to death.

Brilliantly presented, in Andrew's unique style, and made more evocative to our ears by the reaction of so-called Puritan Christians amongst the striking party – like New Plimoth's Governor, William Bradford, who described the terrible slaughter as "a fearful sight to see them all frying in the fire", yet calling it "a sweet sacrifice", and giving God the praise for it – it just had to be Andrew's lectures that were causing the dream.

What's more, it explained why it had only started when he came back on the scene. It all fitted. Especially when I thought back to my coming home all upset from the Mystic one, and later that night, dreaming about it, tossing and turning in my bed, imagining the Pequot women, babies and children, blazing as torches, while the settlers just stood and watched, glorying in their "victory".

The following night, the nightmare of me being chased by demons through the forest had started. And had continued ever since.

I'd not made the connection before, never having seen their painted faces. In previous dreams they'd been without shape or form, only shadowy apparitions chasing me, screaming their fiendish yells, and prodding me with pointed sticks—

A blaring horn cut short my brooding. Looking up, I saw I'd wandered lanes. A car was coming toward me. I pulled at my wheel, narrowly missing a head-on collision. The driver glared at me, tapped his temple with one finger, telling me I was "nuts", stuck it up for me to see it in my rear mirror, and continued around a corner, still angrily honk-honking.

I took a deep breath. That was close. Too close. The damn nightmare seemed determined to get me – one way, or another. But having solved it, maybe it would stop? If not, then I could at least cope with it now.

With a long morning ahead of me without Katy, I made for home.

- twelve -

I drove through the arched tunnel and across the paved quadrangle to the old stable wing housing my studio, and backed the Jeep to the door. The block opposite, connected to the main house, held an indoor swimming pool and small gym (where I used to work out and still occasionally do, but Robert rarely did). Completing the U-shape were the garages, garden and tool sheds, stone walls covered with honeysuckle, climbing roses and other clinging plants, as was the house itself.

When Robert and I discovered the rambling, centuries-old property two months before we married, it had been empty for over five years and fallen into neglect. But Robert had seen its potential and asked his parents for a loan. Instead, they gave it us as their wedding present. Returning from Barbados, we lived in a town apartment for a year, with Robert spending all his free time designing the conversion and working alongside the builders on the alterations. The result, from the outside, was more than just a beautiful house, it was idyllic, and as for inside it was, despite its size, a home, cosy and inviting, that everyone who saw it fell in love with at first sight.

Just looking at it now, every alteration, every improvement, was a reminder that Robert's work had been his passion. Katy had been his love. And I'd been his comfortable companion, a few degrees higher on the scale than Harrison, which was all he had seemed to want out of me – and which, whenever I brooded about it, made his running off with Stella Slater all the stranger.

With my warm blood, it was no wonder I'd felt so libidinally frustrated (or in plainer words, sex-starved). Maybe I should have taken a lover instead of cold showers. It wasn't as if I'd not had offers. I had. Plenty. From men (most of them rather dishy) who'd seemed to guess my pent-up frustration. But although I'd oftentimes been tempted, a couple of times very tempted, and though I have my faults, infidelity and sneaking into motel rooms just isn't my style. (It really isn't. When I first met Andrew, if I'd known he was married our "New York thing" would never have started. And that's the truth. Especially with it dashing my plan for my "first time" to be in a king-sized bed in a six star Barbados honeymoon suite, with a handsome rich – wealthy – husband, preferably young, well and truly hooked.)

Maybe this was why I'd thrown myself into my painting. A catharsis – I might even say a cathexis (apart from Katy) – to release my pent up emotions by concentrating my mind on my work, trying to keep the other side of me (the one I keep bottled up, but which recently has strangely started to re-surface) from wanting to be held…to laugh…to feel joy…

To be loved.

Oh yes, above all else, to be–

But banishing all maudlin thoughts aside, I'm not complaining, because over the last six years, the result of it has been that my reputation has continued to grow, with my output unable to satisfy the demand, especially the last fifteen months when – because of looking after Katy – I've managed to complete only four paintings.

I entered the building. The door opened into a snug, with a soot-stained stone fireplace and comfy old chairs, where Robert and I had often taken our coffee breaks and lunchtime snacks, microwaved in the kitchen beyond. To the left was Robert's study. Harrison hurtled out to greet me, standing on his hind legs, body twisting, tail wagging, and massive paws on my shoulders to reach and nuzzle my face, before dashing outside to find Katy.

'Harrison!' I called after him. 'Katy's not here.'

The crazy dog took no notice, but hurtled into the tunnel, skidded on his front paws into the wall, shook himself, and hurled himself at the rear door to the house, clawing at the panes as he stretched up, pressed his nose against one and peered in, hoping to see Katy.

Through the open door into Robert's study it was easy to guess his nature (or at least, the one he displayed at home). It was as on the day he left. The uncluttered green-leather topped desk edged in gold, the orderly shelves for his text books, and document boxes for his plans, taped on the outside with the names of each client. Pinned to green-baize display boards mounted on the walls, were "before" and "after" photos of his favourite projects. Everything in its place, as tidy as his life – or as uncomplicated as I'd thought it to be, until last Thanksgiving when, after he failed to return and I reported him missing, the police had discovered different. If only I had taken more notice of his changed mood and confronted him, maybe we could have worked something out…?

I turned away. What was the point of going over it again? Even if tomorrow he phoned out of the blue asking to come back, I wouldn't have him anyway. Not after he'd been with *Stella Slater*. Not for one million, two million, three million ad infinitum dollars.

Entering my studio, I switched on the light, leaving the blinds drawn across the patio window and large skylight. It was like entering another world to Robert's. Since deciding to keep Katy home from school for a year, I'd added a second door directly into the house through the end gable wall, which should have prompted me into trying to keep the room tidy. But it was a total mess, a disaster area, even for a painter. Charcoal sketches, drawing pads, loose canvasses, brushes, paints, rags, lengths of metal and wood for framing, spread all over the floor. Finished paintings, already framed, stacked against the walls. And pine shelves with scores of books on art, stacked any old how.

Nevertheless, any art historian of perception entering the room and seeing the sketches pinned to the walls, would be able to trace my development and changes of style over the years. As a student in New York, I'd been greatly influenced by American Indian art, especially the findings of archaeological digs revealing their decorative style from before the arrival of the "White Man": the bilateral designs of the North Eastern woodlands tribes, their geometric patterns – triangles, diamonds, squares, circle motifs, crosses representing the four corners of the universe, solar symbols, mixed with swirling interlocking spirals – and their strong use of colour: red, white, black, blue, green, sepia, yellow.

A feeling of incredible power and energy had emanated from them to me, not only in terms of cultural and aesthetic quality, but in spiritual expression as well, as exemplified in the words of Native American artists like Linda Poolaw of the Kiowa-Delaware: "You have to stay around and focus and listen, and the answer will come to you." And Rina Swentzell of the Tewa-Santa Clara Pueblo: "Art should be more than a deliberate act. It should come from a deeper source somewhere within you, a part of the act of living."

Further into my studies, I read that American Indian art was similar in spirit to that of Paul Klee, an early 20th-century German painter who used colour to express his feelings. Experimenting in his style, I began using strong light and vivid colours to give harmony to my subjects and crystallise my own feelings, and after completing my studies and returning to Plymouth, the physical frustration of my early years of marriage to Robert caused me to release my passions into my work. This was the period when I felt I truly became a painter, and this was confirmed by the ever growing interest in my exhibitions, and the glowing reviews of the critics.

But my best work was still to come. Through Paul Klee, I discovered his friend Franz Marc, also a German, and his thoughts on painting coincided exactly with my own. The way he conveyed his mysticism and veneration for nature through animal paintings, which utilised all the Expressionist devices of distortion and colour symbolism, spoke to the very depths of my soul. His use of colours for symbolic reasons – blue for hope, green for peace, varying shades of red for passion, anger, danger – and the way he used tones to stir the sensuous in the viewer, joining the underlying affinity between modern art and my own first love of primitive tribal art, had completed the full circle for me. Through it, I finally achieved my search for my own method of expression – a form of extensive expressionism, in which was manifested a heightened relationship between my inner self, the artist, and the external world.

Around me, in the seascapes, the countryside, the forests and woodlands of New England, was all I needed to express Rina Swentzell's "inner source within, part of the act of living."

My new method was my own. Travelling around, I would see my subject. Deer in the woods, horses grazing, whales surfacing and blowing. Then using my eyes like the close-up lens of a camera, I developed the ability to focus on my subject, taking in its form and line, and eliminating all insignificant particulars encircling it which might disturb or hinder. Etching them into my mind, I found my subconscious able to retain the subject itself, and the main elements surrounding it. Making only snatched charcoal sketches I'd then return to my studio and straightaway draw the intended outline on canvas, almost as if using my very soul as the photographic negative from which to develop the finished painting.

But then came last Thanksgiving. Almost without realising it, and despite my reduced output my style again evolved. From 'extensive expressionism' to 'intensive expressionism' by which my paintings now convey – for want of a better way of describing it – the innermost feelings of my repressed self, revealing my own inward experience of life, uncovering the reality lying hidden under the surface I display outside the sanctuary walls of my studio.

Such were the four paintings – my finished output for the last fifteen months – placed upright between protective sheets alongside the door and destined for Alexandra's gallery. Realising I wasn't in the mood for outlining, let alone painting, and not wanting, for many reasons – needing a change of scenery; feeling somewhat low, despite the relief of having now realised what had prompted my dream – to spend the morning in the house on my own, I decided to take them there now, for Alex to hang tomorrow. I had a key to her gallery and could let myself in.

Taking two in each hand, lifting them by their cords, I carried them out to the Jeep, opened the rear door and put them inside. Already in the back was a fifth painting, finished only last week. Not understanding the dreamlike state in which I'd painted it – nor the style, which was completely opposite to anything I'd ever painted before – I'd hidden it out of the way in the utility and covered it with a large sheet.

Still puzzled by it, I slammed the rear door shut.

Harrison was straying about, sulking at not finding Katy. Calling him into the back seat, I gave him a tranquillising pill. I hated doing it, especially as he'd not long woken up and been let out, but for safety's sake I didn't want any of his sudden leaping about when I was driving, and all the more so after my recent near-accident. Better safe than sorry.

Starting the engine, I drove through the stone archway, down the drive, and made for Route 3, toward Plymouth.

Across country on the South Carver road, The Man from SF was nearing his destination.

'Turn left into that forest road up ahead,' he said to the driver.

As the Merc entered the trees, a horseman was trotting his steed along the track, in the same direction as them.

'Slow to a crawl.'

The Man from SF lowered his tinted window as the car drew level with the horseman. Seeing him, the rider's face paled. He pulled up his horse. Elderly, thin-mustached, wearing a tweed jacket, jodhpurs, yellow waistcoat, check shirt, yellow tie, he was a typical product of old New England society.

'Follow me to the house,' said the Man from SF, "You've got some explaining to do.'

Before the horseman could reply, the window closed and the car continued.

'When you get back to Boston,' the Man from SF instructed the driver, 'tell Mr Vicence I'll call him later today as soon as I've put things right.'

- thirteen -

As I headed for Plymouth, the trees thinned. Coming up around the corner was one of my favourite spots, a scenic pull-in overlooking the town. I saw it was empty and glanced at my watch. It was still only five minutes to ten. I turned in, switched off the engine, and sat back to look at the scene stretched below me.

Route 3 was unnaturally quiet, but Plymouth was coming alive with cars and traffic on the streets. Beyond its smaller bay was the wide expanse of Cape Cod Bay, opening up to the vast, grey Atlantic. On the distant horizon were two black dots, large ocean-going ships spaced miles apart. Nearer, a number of smaller, coastal ships were riding at anchor, while in the harbour, fishing vessels clustered at their moorings, surrounded by private yachts and boats lying idle, sails unfurled, engines silent.

Prominent among them was *Mayflower II*, a modern-day replica, exact to the last detail, of the sixteenth-century vessel which had brought the First Forefathers – mine among them – to this very place. Looking at it and remembering how proud my father was of our family history, brought both my parents into my mind.

If Katy, a child, was still grieving for them, why wasn't I able to? Even at the time of the accident, I hadn't given in to sorrow. Why? They'd been a wonderful mother and father to me and had deserved more than the few tears I'd shed. Maybe the girls in school had been right about me? Perhaps selfism was my predominant nature. It was certainly true of me as a child. With no brothers or sisters to share my parents' affection, I could twist them around my little finger, precociously playing on their affections, especially my father's, to get what I wanted – and mostly succeeding – except when my mother saw through me and put her maternal foot down.

Even in my teens, when they wanted me to study art nearer home, I refused, determined to go to New York, yet expecting them to pay my fees and my expenses as my right. As for Robert, marrying him for security, just to further my career, knowing I would never love him, nothing could have been more selfish.

But maybe I was being too harsh with myself – not being able to grieve, I mean? The shock of my Mom and my Dad being killed in that way, Robert's parents, too – I'd been genuinely fond of them – all four at the same time, had been too much to take in. Thinking back to my stunned state at being told by some stranger at the other end of a phone line, I'd been so numbed by the horror of it I'd been unable to cry. And at the same time, told that Katy had been airlifted to the nearest hospital in a critical condition, my immediate reaction was that my place was at her bedside.

Katy was still in a coma on the day of the joint burials, with Robert and myself standing silent at the gravesides, still uncomprehending all that had happened, torn between the loss of our loved ones, and almost out of our minds with worry over Katy hovering near death in intensive care. Then, when she regained consciousness, came the blow that she'd lost her voice. Maybe this, on top of the deaths of his parents, had proven too much for Robert and he'd cracked as a result? It would explain a lot.

But my own lack of tears didn't mean I hadn't felt pain. I had. I still do. Deep pain. But it's all locked inside me, in my heart, my mind, and oftentimes an agonising ache in the pit of my stomach. Hell, I only wish I *could* cry...and scream...and yell...and try to release it all. But hardly a day goes by without me thinking of them, Mom, Dad, seeing their photos smiling at me from their silver frames, and their eyes following me around the living room.

Even now, looking down at *Mayflower II*, it was evoking memories of my father in my mind's eye. How I loved him. What a gentle, handsome, man he was. And so proud of his heritage. I can still remember him, as clearly as if it was only yesterday, telling me the story of how our family first came to America to live.

I was only six when he told me, relating it as one does to a child.

Simply.

We were sitting together on the sofa on a winter's evening. It was snowing heavily outside. Hanging up on a wall in an ornate gold frame, we had an old portrait, oils finely cracked, of a good-looking man, much like my father, in his thirties, wearing an Elizabethan doublet of many colours, with a rounded hat of blue velvet, the style of clothes (I realised, when I was older) that a gentleman in those times would have worn.

'Who's that man?' I asked my father.

'He's your great-great-great-grandfather, many times removed,' my Dad replied, putting his arm around me. Sensing one of his tales coming up, I snuggled up against him, loving the smell of pipe-tobacco clinging to his jumper.

'His name was Stephen Hopkins. You were named after his daughter, your great-great etcetera-etcetera grandmother Damaris. Although it's said to be Greek, it's a Celtic name. Your ancestor, hanging up there, was of Welsh blood, even though he lived in England.'

'Why isn't he smiling?' I questioned. 'I have to smile when I'm having my picture taken.'

'Because they didn't in those days, sweetheart. When their portraits were being painted, they had to stay still and look all serious.'

'Why is he painted, then? He'd have to stay still a long time. Why didn't they photograph him?

My father laughed. 'Because they didn't have cameras then, angel. They hadn't been invented. They didn't have airplanes, or cars, or big ships either. In fact, do you remember when I took you last year to see that old-looking sailing ship with tall masts in the harbour. That's a replica of the Mayflower, that your great-great etcetera grandfather came here in.'

'But that was made of wood. Where did it sail from?'

'It first started from London, England.'

'Phew, that's an awfully long way away. They showed it to us once on a globe in school. I wouldn't like to sail all that way in a wooden ship. It might sink.'

'I don't think I would either, sweetheart. As for the Mayflower, it nearly did sink — a couple of times.'

'Did great-great etcet…etcet…grandfather sail it all by himself?'

'Etcetera, angel. But no,' his eyes twinkled at my childish thought, 'it had a captain and a crew. And forty-six other men on board to help if needed – as well as fifty-five women and children – all living together in one space below deck, with the women and children not emerging much because the weather was so rough.'

'They must have been packed tight then, all in one room. How long did it take them?'

'Yes, they certainly were cramped, just like sardines in a tin. As for how long the voyage took, it was sixty-six days before they sighted land and dropped anchor. That's nine weeks and three days. Almost two and a half months.'

'Phew!' I exclaimed again. 'That was a long time. Did they have toilets? I didn't see one on that ship in the harbour.'

I can hear my father chuckling. 'No, darling. They didn't have any. Or baths. Or showers.'

'Ugh; they must have been very dirty…and smelly, then. Where did they do their–'

'Damaris,' he cut me short, 'you do have a habit of asking the most unseemly questions. In buckets. They called them slop-buckets.'

'Together! In the same room! Did the women see the men's weenies?'

My Dad tried to look stern, but I could see him trying to stop his mouth from curling. 'I sometimes shudder to think what you hear in school, Damaris. But to answer your question: No, I shouldn't think so, they'd have had curtains to hide them, probably made of sacking. More to the point, where did you get that word from?'

'What word? Weenies?'

'That's the one.'

'From Johnny Batty. He's always showing us his. It's a funny looking thing, like the spout of my toy teapot. But then it sometimes sticks up like a pencil. Why does it do that?'

'I'll defer that answer, sweetheart, until you're old enough to understand.'

'I'm nearly seven.'

'Yes, you're growing up fast. Too fast, more's the pity. As for Johnny Batty, I think I'll have a word with your teacher about him.'

'Okay…Daddy, did slop-buckets have flushes – like we do?'

'No, sweetheart, they didn't. Things were a little primitive in those days by our standards.'

'How did they empty them, then?'

'Damaris, can we change the subject? They waited until they were almost full, then they took them up on deck and emptied them overboard.'

'Ugh! The room must have smelt. I'd have been sick.'

'I expect I would have too, darling. Except if we'd lived then, we'd have had to learn to rough it, just like they did. But back then it was their way of life. They didn't know any other. It certainly wasn't hygienic, and by the time they reached the New World – as they called it – they were nearly all of them ill, and glad to drop anchor and smell clean fresh air again.'

'Then why did they come here then? Why didn't they stay in England?'

'Well, in your great-great grandfather Stephen's case, for business. To trade for furs and things. And because he was an adventurer, as they were called, and wanted to start a new life for himself and your great-great etcetera grandmother, Elizabeth. As for the Puritans, they came to escape persecution in England.'

'What's purs...purs-ic-ussion?'

'It's the nasty things people do to other people, when the stronger ones think differently about things to the way the weaker lot do.'

'What sort of things?'

'Well, with the Puritans, it was because they didn't think of God in the same way the Church of England did, who told the people of England what they had to believe in in those days. As a result, the Puritans were kicked out of their jobs, which meant they didn't have any money to buy food for their families, or pay rent for their houses. Consequently, they and their children were turned out on to the streets and forced to sleep in alleyways, or under hedges. And if they protested about it, they were thrown into prison.'

'That was cruel.'

'Yes it was, but again that's how it was at those days – and sadly still is today in many parts of the world. But anyway, after a while the Puritans had had enough of it, so they got together and decided to start a new life for themselves over here, in America, where there was plenty of land to build new houses, and their own churches, and farms to grow food. But there weren't enough of them to pay for the Mayflower to take them, so they asked businessmen like your great-great granddad, Stephen to join them and share the cost.'

'Then he wasn't…what did you call them?'

'A Puritan.'

'Yes, a Pure-it-un.'

'No, he wasn't. Of the one hundred-and-two who sailed on the Mayflower, only forty-one were Puritans: seventeen men, ten women and fourteen children. The other sixty-one: thirty men, eleven women and twenty children, were not. So to differentiate between them, the Puritans called them "Strangers". And themselves, "Saints".'

'Why did they do that?'

'Because, again, the Strangers didn't think of God in the same way the Puritans did.'

'That's silly. If they were all going to the toilet in the same bucket, they couldn't be strangers.'

This time, my father openly laughed. 'No, Damaris, that's very true. Sadly, they didn't think like that then. I shouldn't be surprised if they had separate buckets, painted "Saints only", and "Strangers for the use of". However they did agree on one thing.'

'What was that?'

'Well, before sailing they'd been told stories by earlier adventurers who'd explored these shores and wanted to appear as heroes back home in England – men like Captain John Smith, the one I once told you was rescued by Princess Pocahontas.'

'Oh, yes, I remember. What sort of stories?'

'That the natives who already lived here were unfriendly, and so savage that they would try to kill the Forefathers as soon as they stepped ashore.'

'Did they?'

'No, as it happens they didn't. In fact, they were very friendly, at least, at first. It was only later that things changed and that was mostly the fault of the White Man. But in the beginning, the Native Americans taught the settlers how to grow new crops, because the ones they'd brought with them from England didn't like the soil or the weather over here.'

'That was kind of them.'

'Yes, it was, sweetheart. Except the settlers had not only believed the stories, but had also paid a professional soldier, Myles Standish, to sail with them, to lead them in case they were attacked. As it happened they didn't need him, because after first sighting land, it took them another month to decide on the best place to settle. By then it was well into December, and their biggest enemy now was the weather. It was so bad, with biting winds and icy rain, then fierce blizzards and blinding snowstorms, that instead of building houses, as they first planned, all they were able to put up were temporary shelters. The only log building they managed to almost finish was a Common Meeting House, making it strong enough to also use as a fort, in case the stories were true and the natives *were* unfriendly. They started on a stockade as well, but again it was only partly built, with most of it facing the forest, because if the Indians – as they called them – *did* attack, that's where they would come from.'

'Did they?'

'No, the Indians left them well alone. So much so, the settlers didn't even see any, only heard them whooping at them from the forest, and that – so the Indians later claimed – was only for fun. Which was just as well, because the settlers were falling like bowling pins with pneumonia, and scurvy, and also hunger, owing to them not having brought enough warm clothing with them from England, to be able to go out hunting for meat. As a result, they were forced to exist on the few stores they'd shipped over in the Mayflower. By February, things were so bad that the Meeting House had been turned into a hospital, leaving only six men and one woman still on their feet.

'The seven tried their best to keep the others alive, making soup, keeping the fires going by chopping wood, washing the bed-clothes and bathing their patients. But when Spring arrived, only half of them had survived, with the dead being buried in unmarked graves in the middle of the night, and the soil raked back over them so the natives wouldn't know how few were left to defend the settlement.'

'Did any of the children die?'

'Sadly, yes, many did, one of them your great-great-etcetera grandmother's and grandfather's baby boy born on board the Mayflower, who they'd named Oceanus. But it was the women who suffered the most. Of the eighteen who sailed only eight were still alive, and Catherine Carver, the wife of John Carver, the first Governor of New Plimoth – spelt P-l-i-m-o-t-h, as Plymouth was then called – was sinking fast. As for Carver himself, he was so heartbroken, knowing he was going to lose her, he didn't want to go on living. Of course, being Governor, he had to keep going, but months later he caught sunstroke when tending the fields and died. It's said that he didn't fight it much, that all he wanted was to join her…'

All he wanted was to join her.

Still sitting in my Jeep in the scenic pull-in looking down on Plymouth, I remembered that even at the age of six, those words had moved me.

Moved then – and still moved by it, even now – by the thought of a man so much in love with a woman he'd not wanted to go on living without her…

Not wanting to dwell on this thought, I swiftly dismissed it, but still hearing my father's voice telling me how, in the March of that year, 1621, the settlers had met their first Native American, when Samoset, a young Abenaki Chief, had boldly walked into the settlement to initiate the first peace talks between the "Whiteskins" and the "Redskins".

Samoset was something special, tall, dark and handsome, as they say, and wearing only a loin cloth (plus a leather belt for his tomahawk and knife, and a cross-shoulder sheath for his arrows) with a fantastic physique – which, it is said, was much admired and appreciated from as close they dared, so as not to let on to their husbands, by the surviving wives.

Even the Puritan women (who, with their strict moral beliefs, should, of course, have averted their gaze) had been unable to resist looking. But though they were later made to pay for their transgression (their pastor, William Brewster – a real dutiful guardian of their morals from all accounts – consigned them to the Meeting House for twenty four hours to seek God's forgiveness in prayer) I'd be willing to bet they considered their punishment well worth it. What's more, it just goes to prove that even when wearing heavy buckled shoes and a close-fitting bonnet, a bodice buttoned up to the neck, and a homespun skirt down to the ankles, underneath them a woman is still a woman for it all.

As for love, getting back for a moment to John Carver, what about him not wanting to go on living without his Catherine? Now, that was love. Real love. More than that – a rare love. Not given to many. At any time during my "thing" with Andrew Hartford – a day, an hour, a minute, a moment even – had he *ever* made me feel that way.

In all truth, I had to answer: No. Never.

Okay, so forget Andrew. Did I think I could ever feel that way about *any* man?

Again, in all honesty, I doubted it. In fact, I was sure of it. Positive. So far, I'd not met one, not one, who could come anywhere near to inspiring such a depth of devotion in me. Even more, was there a man these days, remotely capable of loving a woman to the same extent that John Carver loved his Catherine? Of not wanting to live without her? Or maybe being willing to even die to save her?

Well, speaking from *my* knowledge of men – highly unlikely.

From my experience there were only two things they were interested in.

Sex (Andrew).

Their creature comforts (Robert).

Or both (Paul Chapman).

But of the ones I knew (except my Dad, that is) it was always themselves they put first.

So maybe that's why I am the way I am. Or appear to be. Coming over all selfish. Yet, that's the surface me. Deep inside, I've got so much love to give, it just wants to burst out. Except I'd be frightened of giving it, because I know it would never be returned to the same extent.

I was let down once. And once is enough.

As far as the world outside is concerned — and other than what I reveal in my paintings, and to Katy of course, and sometimes, though not too often, to Alex — I now keep the real me hidden.

I don't want to be hurt again. Ever.

Still gazing down at *Mayflower II*, I felt suddenly faint, as if my mind was drifting away, my spirit parting company from my body.

Panicking, I tried to fight it. Tried to scream but no sound came.

Next thing, it was as if I was floating in space.

And then I *heard* myself scream.

But only as a hollow echo, getting fainter and fainter like it was plummeting down into the depths of some bottomless pit.

Even more frightening was that, far below me, I could see my own body slumped in the driving seat of the Jeep with my eyes closed; and Harrison still flat out in the back.

A fog was creeping over Plymouth and all surrounding it.

The bay. The fields. The forest.

Becoming denser and denser, it slowly obliterated everything from my view.

Then, just as slowly.

It lifted.

- fourteen -

NEW PLIMOTH, NEW ENGLAND, 1621

Feeling as if I was floating bodiless, I was looking down on a half-finished logged palisade, ranging between eight to eleven feet in height, with four breaches for gates: one on a small hill facing open ground to the south; a second and third at both ends of a wall running along the banks of a brook where it entered the sea; and a fourth open breach facing north-west at the surrounding forest. Inside the fort were six crude huts (one-roomed, no more) and four turf roofed dugouts, with smoke holes in place of chimneys.

Five women, and ten or more children of varying ages, were moving about within the stockade, some wearing severe Puritan clothing, others Elizabethan.

Anchored offshore, sails furled, was a wooden ship exactly like *Mayflower II*, but with her decks busy and looking all weather-beaten.

Plying between it and the estuary were two longboats, ferrying stores. Wearing a similar mix of Puritan and Elizabethan clothing, some twelve or so men were rowing the boats, while others were carrying more stores through the brook gate into the settlement.

Oh, frig! I thought as I identified the scene. I'd no sooner solved one dream than another was beginning. Frig…frag…*oh, fuck!*

I pulled my ethereal self together.

Maybe this was just a normal, everyday, nothing-extraordinary-about-it reverie, seeing how one minute I was enjoying the view of modern Plymouth…and the next, without any warning, I was looking down on New Plimoth, almost four centuries back in time. In which case – based on my previous experiences – I'd no choice other than to go along with it. How long would it last, anyway? Ten minutes tops, the length of a nap.

The mild weather, patches of unmelted snow, the position of the sun shining through white wisps of cloud, and the chorus singing of birds from the forest – and also knowing it would be April 5 in the year 1621, before Mayflower set sail on her return voyage back to England – let me guess it was early Spring of that same year.

Curiously, unlike my dream of the girl running for her life through the forest, in this one I felt no fear. Though it was just as *spooky*, yet it also felt pleasant, my conscious spirit and I floating together in space, hovering over the settlement, witnessing all that was going on, an observer looking down on a tapestried scene, but with no body to feel pain – almost like being at a cinema watching the continuation of my father's story.

Despite all their trials – the freezing winter, months of sickness, and losing half their number – the survivors had completed the Common House. Twenty foot square, it stood on a hill facing the forest, alongside the north-west gate. Erected next to it was the beginnings of a watchtower, with a logged platform the same height as the palisade.

Two men were standing on the platform, seemingly discussing the placements of four cannons. One was a stocky man with red hair and beard, wearing a polished breast-plate and a rapier at his side. He just had to be Myles Standish; *Captain* Standish as he insisted on being called – Captain *Shrimp*, as the settlers were said to have called him behind his back. Looking at him, they probably had. He looked a fussy, self-important little man.

The other man was taller, dark-haired and good-looking. He was wearing three-quarter length breeches and black longboots, and a plain white hessian shirt (no ruffles) under a sleeveless brown leather jerkin (sort of an Elizabethan gilet). Immediately recognising him from the oil portrait (now hanging up in my sitting room) I was looking down, hard though it was to believe, at my great-great etcetera-etcetera Granddad, Stephen Hopkins.

How peculiar, I thought, *to be looking down at my own ancestor.* I was very tempted to shout, "Hi, great Grandpa!" down to him, but then remembered I was dreaming (or whatever). Besides, going along with all the time-travelling gobbledegook, hearing a bodiless greeting coming down out of the sky, especially one shouting "Hi, great Grandpa", might have given (or, depending on which timescale I was in, might *give* in the present tense) the poor man a heart attack, and with his daughter Damaris, my namesake and forbear not yet born, or more importantly, not yet conceived, how would that affect my own future? Okay, I knew it was all absurd. Still it had to be considered.

Because if I was right about the year, about it being Spring of 1621, it would be another five years and more before my own great etcetera grandmother was born. Stephen's first wife, Constance Dudley, had died in 1615, leaving three children: Elizabeth Damaris, she'd now be 16. Constance, she'd be 10. And Giles, 9. Then three years later, 1618, Stephen had married his second wife, Elizabeth Fisher (my line) 15 years younger than him. Their first child, Oceanus (the baby who was born on the *Mayflower* while it was still off Cape Cod) caught pneumonia, poor mite, and died during that first terrible winter. But Elizabeth was still due to have five more children, my own ancestor among them, and there was no way I wanted to interfere with Stephen's and her history. And certainly not mine.

So, best forget the greeting.

But space time – what a load of codswallop. How could anyone possibly believe in all that stuff? Still, dream...or whatever, with no painted, tomahawk wielding war-party to chase me this time round, then like I've said, I might as well enjoy it while it lasted.

The open ground to the south, between the settlement and the forest looked as though it had once been tilled before the First Forefathers' arrival – which it had, by the Patuxet tribe who'd lived on this same spot from time immemorial, until they were wiped out by a "white man's plague" picked up from visiting English ships trading for furs.

Working the soil, preparing it for planting, were two youths – Puritans, judging by their plain black clothes – and a young girl about sixteen years of age...

I looked closer at her. There was something strangely familiar about her. Apart from her dark bobbed hair she was–

The very image of me when I was the same age!

99

Although I knew she wasn't for real, the shock of it still made me want to gasp (except I couldn't of course, being bodiless) but the uncanny resemblance to me when I was sixteen – height, face, and from what I could make out of it in her loose working clothes, even her figure – told me I was looking at a young Elizabeth Damaris, Stephen Hopkins' eldest daughter.

Still feeling shaken (this I seemed able to sense, like the pleasant feeling I experienced moments ago when I decided to enjoy the dream, but had now suddenly evaporated) I tried to rationalise what was happening to me. Stephen Hopkins' image I could explain – after all, I'd grown up with his portrait hanging on the wall – but I'd no idea what Elisabeth Damaris looked like. Then, with relief (and that's *really* understating it) I realised my conception of her was probably a sort of mirror flashback to what I looked like (other than the hair, that is) when I was only sixteen.

That calmed me down.

But then I gave the clothes she was wearing a more scrutinizing look, her long homespun skirt, the black buckled shoes, and realised that this was the young woman of my recurring dream. The girl running for her life through the forest, trying to escape the war-party – with me seeming to be inhabiting her body.

If I'd had skin it would have crawled.

And then I remembered something even more disturbing from our family history. That sometime after arriving in the New World, Elizabeth Damaris had gone missing. That she had one day wandered away from the safety of the fort into the forest, and was never seen again – her fate a total mystery.

Oh, God! Was I wrong in my thinking that this, too, was only a dream? With a dream, no matter how deep, no matter how frightening, I would rise out of it. But what if this was something more…more inexplicable?

Oh, please, please, don't let this be for real.

Please, my mind rebelled at the thought, not for real.

Not a…not a regression.

Please let me wake up now. Back safe and sound in my Jeep in the scenic pull-up.

Pleeease!

But my plea went unanswered.

Talking to Elizabeth Damaris was a fair-haired woman, older by some ten years, and pretty. Playing around them were two children, a girl of about ten, and a boy a year or so younger.

At that same moment, my subconscious, my spirit, my essence, my whatever, zoomed down from on high and entered my lookalike's body.

Terrified by this sudden development, I was now seeing all around me, not from up in the clouds, but through Elizabeth Damaris's eyes. It just had to be a delirium, *it just had to be*, I tried over and again to reassure myself, nevertheless it was the weirdest of feelings. Weirder even than the recurring nightmare. What's more, it seemed to me that my lookalike shivered as I passed inside her, a quiver that went through her body.

To add to it all, the other woman must also have noticed it, because in a concerned voice she said, 'Damaris, thou art trembling child?'

Damaris! My double was known by her second name, not her first – maybe always had been, or perhaps only since my great etcetera-etcetera Granddad married Elizabeth Fisher, so she'd not be confused with her stepmother? But whatever the reason this only intensified my feeling of weirdness at what was happening to me. It was as though the woman was talking to me, Damaris Moore.

'Art thou sure thou are sufficiently recovered, child, to be working the soil? It is barely a week since thou rose from thy sick bed. And today, the sun is at its warmest since we reached these inhospitable shores. Comfortless though it be, should thou not return home and lie down for the remainder of the day?'

Elizabethan English! It was getting to be more and more peculiar by the second. Apart from never having heard old English spoken before, their chit-chatting was going to take some getting used to. What's more, it prompted another frightening thought. If I could not only hear and see, but also experience *inner* emotions – like first enjoying the dream, but now the feeling of dread which had replaced it – what about *outer* sensations, like touch, tenderness, soreness…

Pain?

Oh God, I hoped not. Please, not pain. Not the forest experience. Not rape.

But then, realising that this was not at all the same dream, I somehow managed to force the thought aside.

Damaris laughed. It sounded sort of bubbly, that of a happy natured girl. 'No, Mother, it was but a fleeting light-headedness which passed as swiftly as it came.'

By calling the woman 'Mother', Damaris confirmed she was Elizabeth Fisher, her young stepmother, my own great-etcetera grandmother. I'd guessed as much from her resemblance to my own Gran. Also, she seemed all nice and gentle in her movements, and had the same kind expression in her eyes my Gran had. Which meant the girl and boy had to be Constance and Giles, Damaris's sister and brother by Stephen's first wife, Constance Dudley.

Meanwhile, Damaris had turned to view all the activity going on between the *Mayflower* and the fort. 'It seems Captain Jones is anxious to have our stores ashore,' she commented. 'As soon as his hold is empty he will be setting sail on his return voyage back to England.'

My great-etcetera Gran gave a heartfelt sigh. 'Yes, and how I wish we were returning with him, Damaris.'

'Some days, so do I Mother,' Damaris responded, but her opening phrase appeared to qualify her wish. Surrounded by the vastness of her new land, the dense forest, the distant snow-capped mountains, she surely must have had a longing for London, with its hectic activity and colourful life. And no doubt she'd left friends behind, girls of similar age and mind, and parties and theatres to attend (apart maybe from *The Globe*, she somehow didn't look the Shakespearean type). Even more, with young women in those days often married by the time they were fifteen, and dashing young men with swashbuckling swords at their sides, riding up on horseback to pay court to them, she was going to find a pioneer's life very different, what with its hardships and loneliness. So why the hesitation?

Her voice suddenly took on a more buoyant tone. 'Yet, now that Spring has arrived, there is something about this land that seems to call to me. Its beauty, its openness. I've a feeling I am going to be happy here. Especially when more settlers from the old world arrive to join us, and we start becoming a community. The whole thing is so...so exciting, carving out a new life for ourselves. Don't *you* feel it, Mother?'

Hearing her, I was alerted that my spirit (or whatever) was inhabiting the body of a very determined young person, not at all the 'Yes, Mother, no, Mother,' dutiful type of daughter that history tells us was the norm in those days. And confirmed by her using less of the Elizabethan parlance, too, like "you" instead of "thou", hinting that she was her own person, independent minded, and likely to want her own way in things, not someone to be trapped inside, well, for not too long, and certainly not long enough (the dreadful thought struck me) *for this to be also the day she decided to go for a walk alone in the woods.*

Pleeease, I again begged to whoever, whatever was controlling me, *get me out of here.*

But again, no answer. And so I returned to being a passive observer, listener.

'Indeed, I don't, Damaris. I feel nothing of the sort,' my great-etcetera Gran replied with unexpected fervour (she'd fooled me with her gentle demeanour). 'And I'm surprised to hear thou say thou dost. But there again, thee and thy father are so much alike. I think it would have been much wiser of him to have sailed alone, rather than bring us with him;

especially after his failure last year in Virginia. Instead, he should have sent for us to join him, only after knowing whether or not this new venture of his has succeeded.'

My great-great etcetera Gran paused, awaiting Damaris's reply. When it was obvious none was forthcoming, she continued. 'Talk to him, Damaris; he listens to thee. With half the Mayflower's crew victims of the epidemic, and the survivors not yet fully recovered, it will be at least two weeks before she will ready to sail. There is still time enough to change thy father's mind. After this long and harrowing winter, and the loss of little Oceanus, I would give anything to return home to civilisation and England's milder climes.'

Baby Oceanus, bless him, buried in an unmarked grave somewhere outside the fort with the other fifty who'd died.

'It would serve no purpose, Elizabeth,' Damaris replied, taking the liberty of using my great-great Gran's first name. 'After Virginia, Father was determined to bring us with him this time, instead of leaving us behind, if only to show us at first hand his ability to prosper. The vast stores he has brought with him – iron pots, axes, knives and suchlike – to exchange for Indian furs, bear witness to his intention on that score.'

Though she was only sixteen, this lookalike of mine also sounded as if she had an old head on her shoulders. She certainly seemed to know her father well – better, by the sound of it, than my great-great etcetera Gran did, despite being his wife of three years.

Elizabeth rounded on her. I saw the sudden flash in her eyes. *Good for her*, I thought. It was good to know that my side, the Fisher side, also had spunk.

'Such cynicism does not behove thee, Damaris.' There was a bite to my great Gran's voice. 'I blame thy father. Having thee tutored was, in my opinion, a mistake. Knowledge of history and the classics is all very well in a man, but it has given thee an independence of mind which does not sit well on a young maiden. Nor does it give thee the right to speak of thy father in a manner which even I, his own wife, would never dare.'

'Perhaps it comes from my Welsh blood, *Mother*,' Damaris reverted to her previous mode of address (but with unnecessary emphasis, I thought). 'A cynicism, as you call it, born from empathy with my own kinsman, Prince Madoc, who discovered this land five centuries past, but never received the credit. Except when Queen Bess conveniently and recently recalled it, in order to try to register a prior claim to it than that of Spain's.'

'Prince Madoc? A kinsman? That is but thy father's imagination, child.'

'Maybe Mother, yet maybe not. But when Father used to sit me on his knee and tell me the stories Madoc brought back with him to recount to his own children, and their children after them, he swore to me they were true. And if Father believes them, then so do I. As for returning to London, a strong part of me already has a peculiar attraction for this place, an affinity with its forests and its beauty. And a desire to meet its people, who I suspect have been much maligned over the centuries by other voyagers not as generous towards them as was our ancestor.'

Elizabeth came back at her. 'Thy father should never have led thee to believe his tales, child. They are but myths. As for thy sudden liking for this land, for myself I would have preferred to remain in London, where our life was so comfortable. A large house which we owned, menservants, maids. Now it feels as though we are starting from nothing. This is no place for any future children of mine to grow up. Nor Constance and Giles. And certainly not for a young wife such as myself – nor thee, Damaris – with the constant threat of attack and other dire manner of evils constantly hanging over us.'

Glancing at the nearby forest, Elizabeth shivered.

'How its darkness frightens me. How many cruel eyes are staring at us at this moment, even as we talk. Savages!' she burst-out, giving sudden vent to her pent up fears. 'Keeping us awake at nights with their fiendish howling. In league with Satan and all his demons.'

'Mother!' Damaris protested. 'Having never met them, how can you say such -?'

'T'is true, Damaris,' great Gran insisted. 'Why only yesterday, I heard Brother Brewster tell a gathering of his people that every Red Indian – man, woman, and child – all live under the rule of a village elder called a sagamore, who answers to a so-called tribal sachem, and that each of them is under the direct command of The Devil incarnate himself. What's more, Brother Brewster says, with every painted savage we kill, we will release their souls from bondage, for which there will be great rejoicing in heaven.'

'Oh, Elizabeth!' Damaris was openly horrified by the Puritan pastor's scandalous views. 'Surely you do not give credence to such blasphemy? If the natives here are anywhere near as savage as braggarts like Captain John Smith claimed, why did they not kill us when we first landed off the Mayflower and had not even begun to erect our defences? Instead, they let us build our settlement on their land, without once showing themselves. Surely that must tell you something of their true nature?'

Although she'd not yet reached full womanhood, Damaris Hopkins (just as I'd already suspected) was clearly a self-opinionated, argumentative young minx. From which it could be assumed that she was headstrong as well. So, with me now beginning to wonder whether I might – just might – be experiencing something *more* than a dream, it was time to start thinking what would happen to me if my spirit really *was* inside her? If so, I didn't want her doing anything stupid to prevent me returning back to my own time.

Only playing safe, nothing more.

Following up on this, I wondered whether I could tune into her thoughts, and perhaps influence her when she came to making decisions…especially big ones. Like stopping her from going any nearer the damn forest. The tree line was looming too close as it was. Maybe this was why I'd again been sent back in time (if I had, that is?). Only this time (pardon the pun, if it is one) to stop her entering the frigging forest, so there'd be no nightmare flight through any forbidding woods, no shrieking, whooping war-party chasing us, no Andrew lookalike intent on rape (unless, as I've already broached, that came from some Freudian complex within me?).

And if this meant changing the course of history and keeping Damaris Hopkins in the record books instead of going missing, then, in this particular instance, I was all for it.

Anyway, while I was wondering, my great-great etcetera Gran was still distraught.

'Then why their fearful howling, Damaris?' she demanded. 'Especially at night? Why, its *very sound* is sufficient to conjure up visions of demons and all manners of other such fiendish creatures, come from Hell to torment us.'

Naturally, Damaris had an answer. She was going to take some controlling, this mirror image of mine, even if I did manage to enter her mind.

'I suspect, Elizabeth, that it is merely their way of trying to frighten us, to persuade us to return back to our own land, without causing bloodshed either to themselves, or to us.'

Great-great Gran thought to reply, but realised she was wasting her breath and turned away, venting her frustration instead on Constance and Giles, who'd wandered off from her side, and were getting too close to the forest's edge.

'Come Giles, come Constance,' she ordered, her tone sharp. 'Let us return to the safety of the fort. Thee also, Damaris,' she called over her shoulder as she made for the palisade. Giles and Constance dutifully scampered after her, linking hands and gleefully playing some sort of ring-a-ring o' roses around her, without falling down.

Do as she's frigging well telling you, Damaris!, I tried to telepath her. *Go after them!*

Feeling her hesitate, I thought for a moment I'd succeeded. But then she brushed *my* choice of action aside. She really was a strong-willed young madam.

I tried again, screaming it at her.

Go after them! Go after them!

I needn't have bothered.

'Not yet awhile, Elizabeth,' Damaris replied. 'This glorious air is already working wonders on me, helping me to recover my strength. I will follow in an hour or so.'

Great-great Gran spun around. She looked really cross with her. She wasn't the only one. I was feeling exactly the same with her myself.

'There are times, Damaris, when thou testeth the very patience of a saint. Then at least return to thy fellow workers. The earth thou are tilling is too far from them.' Determined to have her last maternal word, my great-great etcetera Gran added, 'And do not, any of thee, cease thy vigilance. They say these savages can move so quietly thou are not even aware of their presence until they are upon thee, and by then it is too late.'

She should have known better and saved her breath. 'Do not fear so, mother,' Damaris responded, 'I will take *especial* care, with my eyes never off the forest, just in case one of them should magically materialise out of thin air.'

A touch of unnecessary sarcasm, I thought, being on my great-etcetera Gran's side, and although there was now a good gap between them (or rather, the three of us) I clearly heard my ancestor's exasperated sigh. 'As usual, Damaris, thou insisteth on having the last word.'

Grabbing Giles' and Constance's hands and putting an end to their ring-a-ring o' roses gambolling, she marched them away, yet still made the final exchange hers as her voice came floating back. 'One of us at least has the sense to be aware of the dangers.'

Damaris gave a laugh, but other than that didn't answer. Instead, the defiant young minx dropped to the floor and lay back. Placing her hands under her head as a pillow, she looked up at the thin bands of white cloud scudding across the blue sky. With the sun's warmth on her face, she closed her eyes.

I now had only her ears to warn me of danger. Tuning in to this one remaining sense, I was immediately struck by the fact that something was wrong, but couldn't hear a thing so intense was–

The silence.

Straightaway, I knew what it was.

'The birds!' I screamed again. *'The frigging birds aren't singing!'*

This time Damaris seemed to hear me, sitting up straight and opening her eyes.

But she was too late.

From behind, a bronzed hand clamped over her mouth to prevent her screaming.

And a knife to her throat forced her to her feet.

Into the dark forest.

At that same moment (so I later discovered) Stephen Hopkins happened to glance up from the watchtower platform where he and Captain Standish were now stacking cannon balls.

Seeing Damaris being forced into the forest at knife point, by an almost naked savage, unobserved by her two companions – who, like true dedicated Puritans, were engrossed in their digging – my great-etcetera Granddad went loco. (Describing his feelings afterwards, he used Elizabethan terminology like "beset" and "demented", but in today's vernacular, "loco" is as good a word as any to define his reaction.)

'My daughter!' he yelled, pointing. 'A filthy Redskin's got her.'

Standish looked up to see Damaris and her captor disappear into the forest.

'Fire a cannon!' great-great Granddad screamed at him. 'Fire a cannon!'

Shrimp, the military expert (recently widowed with no children of his own) stayed quite calm. 'T'would achieve nought, Hopkins,' he observed, 'except perhaps bring down a tree. Moreover, the cannons are not yet primed. The only hope – and that is but a slender one – is to gather an armed party and give chase.'

He paused to think, driving Stephen to almost hit him.

'And with only twenty-one men left alive,' Standish ruminated, 'let alone fit, that would mean calling everyone off the shallop and the longboat–'

Great-great Granddad grabbed him by his ruff. 'Then rogering-well call them! This is no poxing exercise thou bloated buffoon. My daughter is been dragged off into the forest to the Devil only knows what horrors! Who in damnation cares about stores when she–'

Standish pulled himself free and gathered his linen frills back into place. 'Then away with thee Hopkins,' he ordered. 'Muster the men. I will gather the arms from inside the Common House.'

The last words were spoken to thin air. Stephen was already down the ladder and tearing through the fort, bawling of what had befallen Damaris and yelling for help. Elizabeth ran toward him, eyes wild, arms outstretched with fear, but he sprinted past her for the shore, calling to the men on both boats to 'turn back and row like Hell.

- fifteen -

Meantime, though I was terrified (and believe me, that comes *nowhere near* describing how I felt) I'd mentally accepted, in a spirit-like sort of way, that I was in, if not a regression, then in some weird experience I couldn't explain, and even worse could do nothing about, except to hopefully wake up out of it. Maybe (I tried hard, *very hard*, to convince myself) there was something in between a third and fourth dimension? A kind of three point five on the postulated spacial scale? If so, it could very well answer everything, and not just for me but also for others who claim to have had similar mysterious occurrences.

Whatever, despite wishing I wasn't in it, it seemed as if I was stuck with it, and so...

We were now deep into the forest, with Damaris being constantly poked in her back with the point of an arrow by some half naked man whose face she couldn't see. From the corner of her eyes (or *our* eyes – whichever? however? whatever?) she was aware only that he was tall, black haired, bare-chested, wearing buckskin trousers and moccasins laced with leather thongs, but nothing more.

Forced to make her way between towering trees ever deeper into the forest, her long skirt was making her stumble through the undergrowth. There was no path to discern, but her captor was in no doubt of his direction; every time he wanted Damaris to turn he'd dig one of her shoulders – the left to go right and the right to go left, thrusting her into it, as it were, and viciously, too.

Although I didn't physically feel anything (which answered my fear as to whether or not I would experience pain) judging by the way her shoulders jerked every time he poked her, it must have been really hurting Damaris.

But at last I'd been able to tune into her mind and so knew what she was thinking.

Despite her earlier cocksureness, she was, just like me, scared out of her wits. Even the Atlantic storms hadn't made her heart thud like this, or her insides tremble so.

She was in no doubt that she'd been captured by a "Redskin" – her word not mine – but what if Elizabeth was right about the unimaginable things these vicious savages would do to any young white woman who fell into their hands? Every man in the tribe "having his way with her" – whatever Elizabeth meant by that – until she died from loss of blood.

Damaris had a rough idea what her stepmother meant, but not a proper idea. Having a younger brother she'd guessed what bits fitted into what, but she was puzzled as to how something so small and limp as Giles's could enter something so tight as her own body.

(Her ignorance surprised me; I would have thought that most Elizabethan maidens, with marriage at fifteen not at all unusual, would at least have been given a hint – if only a subtle one – by their mothers as to what to expect on their wedding night. Or been whispered it by their now knowing friends who had got themselves hitched, or the more daring, no-longer-a-maiden ones who'd taken the plunge and tried it for themselves.)

Nevertheless, Damaris wasn't the only one petrified out of her very mind by the thought. Especially the dying from the loss of blood bit. With my spirit seemingly trapped inside her body, I again prayed that this was all a dream, a nightmare, or at least a hallucination – and please, please, *pleeease*, not be happening for real.

Because all around us seemed so normal. Here, deep in the woods, birds were singing. Squirrels were scampering up trees. A deer chewing at leaves turned startled to look at us, then darted off into the deeper safety of the forest. Bees hovered over wild flowers, sucking up nectar. Butterflies were flitting about with no seeming pattern…butterflies, for goodness sake; could anything be so normal? It just had to be a dream I was in.

Up ahead, I heard the faint sound of a river. It grew louder and louder, and ever nearer, the thunder of water crashing against rocks.

Parting thicket branches, Damaris emerged on to a well-trodden path extending in both directions along the bank of the river. Swollen by rain and melting snow from the hills, the resultant torrent was crashing against rock faces and boulders, hurling plumes of spray high into the air.

Damaris's captor dug her in the right shoulder, forcing her to the left. It must have been particularly hard and just one too many, because she swung around, snatched the arrow out of the brave's hand, and snapped it across her thigh.

As they faced each other, I saw real hate in the Indian's black eyes.

Even more disturbing, he had a real cruel look about him. Narrow of face with a hooked nose (like the vengeful *Magua* in the Daniel Day Lewis version of *Last of the Mohicans*) he resembled a bird of prey. He was also at least six foot tall. I felt Damaris's surprise at this, it was, after all, some four inches taller than she was used to in the average Englishman of that time, and also that his skin was olive-brown. From the terms "Indians" and "Redskins" given to them by the first English adventurers to meet them, I guess she expected it to be a definite crimson hue.

As for his body it was lithe and powerful looking. He looked as if he could pick Damaris up like a feather and send her flying. And from the way his eyes narrowed as he looked at her, just slits of loathing, if any guy spelt trouble, this one did.

Damaris, I think you maybe let your temper get the better of you. But it's too late to regret it, so I suggest you get the hell out of here. Give him a hefty kick in the crotch with those heavy looking shoes of yours, and while he's doubled up gasping for breath, whack him on the head with that rock by your feet, then start running as if the hounds of Hell are after you.

I don't know if she heard me or whether she worked it out for herself, but I felt her nerve herself to give it a try. But before she could move, "Magua" slapped her hard across her face. Hurled backwards, Damaris fell to the ground. And then he was on top of her, one hand over her mouth to stop her screaming, the other clawing under her skirt and petticoats and up her naked legs.

Damaris's right arm was trapped between her body and his, but her left was free. She scratched his face with her nails. Making no cry of pain, "Magua" removed his hand from

117

under her skirts and wiped his cheeks. Seeing blood, he slapped her again, knocking her head back, then returned to pulling-up her skirts.

Thinking she was groggy, he relaxed his hand covering her mouth. Damaris bit it hard, then went for his eyes, poking her fingers into them.

This time, "Magua" gave way to rage. Pulling his tomahawk from his belt, he raised it above her head. Damaris closed her eyes and stiffened, awaiting the final blow…

There was a thud. The sound of something embedding into flesh.

Damaris peered, hesitantly, through slit lids. "Magua" was still on top of her, eyes open, except they were staring at her unseeing, the eyes of a dead man.

From his back protruded a feathered arrow.

Hitting and kicking out with arms and legs, Damaris pushed him off. His body slid to the ground beside her. Rolling away from it, she got to her feet and stood there, uncertain, looking wildly about her, searching the surrounding dark forest for the source of the arrow.

Oh, Hell, no. Please, no. Don't let this be the start of my nightmare, where that blood curdling war-party chases her. And not just Damaris but me! Me as well, trapped inside her! Whooping and prodding her with their pointed arrows. Playing cat-and-mouse with her. Until she falls. And then they…

From the corner of her eyes, Damaris saw a dim shadow flitting through the dark trees toward her.

Rooted to the spot, her spine suddenly gone stone cold, she waited.

- sixteen -

Out of the trees emerged the handsomest man I've ever seen. And if that's how he struck me (living in an age of film and television heart-throbs and its obsession, especially the media's, with "the beautiful people") Damaris must have thought he was from another species she'd never been told about.

Just from the way her eyes opened wide at the sight of him, I knew she was staring at him in awe. Having heard my great-great etcetera Grandma Elizabeth say that Damaris had been tutored in the classics, I assumed she'd seen inked drawings of Greek gods in books. But as they were of mythical deity, she had no doubt thought that earthly men of similar appearance could not possibly exist. If so, she now knew different – as far as this particular specimen was concerned, at least.

Damaris herself was tall – well, for those days. At a guess, the same height as me, five six – which would have made her about the same eye-level as a man of average height in Elizabethan times. But this Greek-god double was at least six inches taller, six foot, six one, maybe more. He looked to be in his late twenties, eyes dark and deep-set, hair black, short at the front, shoulder-length at the back, with two white feathers denoting (at a guess) that he was some sort of a chief. And as for his physique, there was nothing (or almost nothing) to guess at, he may as well have been in the altogether, wearing only two buckskin loin cloths, one at the front, the other at the back, supported by a leather belt in which was a tomahawk and a long knife. His shoulders were broad, with a muscular chest tapering to a six-pack stomach, and sinew hips leading to well-formed thighs and calves and bare feet.

His walk, as he approached, was like that of a stalking cat.

Damaris gave a sharp intake of breath and I felt her heart quicken. What's more, it most definitely wasn't from fear. If ever a girl was instantly smitten, this was she.

Looking down at "Magua" and seeing the scratch marks across his face, he said (of all things in English, which seemed to confirm I was dreaming – but *some dream,* despite it): 'You fought well.' His voice, though a tad guttural, was deep, gorgeously so, in keeping with the rest of him. 'Massasoit should not have chosen Hawkface to keep watch on your village. Ever since his squaw was taken and violated by white hunters two summers ago and left to die, he had much hate in his heart.'

Lifting Hawkface, as I now knew his name to be (dreamwise that is) over his shoulder as though he was of no weight, 'Follow me,' "Adonis" said, and strode off, following the trodden path. Damaris tucked in after him, her eyes devouring his muscular back.

Some ten minutes later the path emerged into a clearing – at a point where the river ran slower, in a meandering curve. In the centre of the open space was a dome-shaped wigwam about ten foot square, and a longhouse some twenty feet wide and twice that in length, both with walls and roofs made of long pieces of bark built over saplings put into the ground, and bent and tied together by withes. They looked like temporary erections, the longhouse as a night shelter for the thirty or so braves dotted around the clearing, the wigwam presumably for their leader. Two of the braves were waist deep in the river catching fish with nets, more were skinning deer, while the rest were sharpening weapons, or sitting in groups, talking.

What amazed me (and I sensed Damaris thinking the same) was that they all appeared to be roughly the same height as Hawkface, around six foot, with athletic physiques (but not to be compared with "Adonis", who was something extra special) with not an ounce of fat on any of them. If this was just a hunting party, their number was likely nowhere near the strength of all the braves in their tribe. If so, how easy it would have been for them to have overwhelmed the *Mayflower* settlers, and either killed them or taken them prisoner, the instant they set foot on their lands, long before they'd even begun to build their fort.

A silence fell on the clearing as Damaris and her saviour stepped into the open. Every brave stopped whatever he was doing and converged on them.

From the wigwam emerged a man who, by his bearing, was clearly their Chief. Again, about six feet tall, wearing buckskin trousers and moccasins, with five white feathers stuck like a fan into his long black hair, his fine physique made it difficult to judge his age. At a guess, in his late thirties. Stern of face, he was followed by another tall Indian, a few years younger, with three feathers in his hair, who resembled the Chief enough to be his brother.

Damaris's rescuer lowered Hawkface to the ground and addressed the Chief in his own language. Meanwhile, the braves formed a half-circle around us, at first muttering amongst themselves, then falling silent to listen.

The two spoke at some length, the Chief's face giving nothing away. At the conclusion he looked at Damaris, black eyes slowly sweeping her from head to toe, but saying nothing.

Damaris didn't even blink but stared straight back. Only sixteen, she may not have been the most prudent of females (a downcast expression would have been much wiser) but she certainly had guts. Whatever, it seemed to work. I'm sure I saw a flicker of amusement crease his stern face at her temerity.

But the powwow was over. Folding his arms, the Chief stood there, still looking suitably grave as Damaris's rescuer translated to her:

'The Great Sachem, Massasoit, mighty Chief of the Wampanoag, welcomes you.'

Massasoit! This was indeed some dream! Me! – meeting the Native American signatory to the first ever peace treaty between the "Red Man" and "White Man". Something to boast about – had this been for real – to Suzanne *le nez en l'air* Chapman. Still, famous Chieftain though he was, the introduction was somewhat grandiloquent (even if it *was* me making it up). All the same, it was sheer music hearing the "welcomes you" bit.

'Chief Massasoit asks your forgiveness for what Hawkface did to you,' Damaris's rescuer continued. 'In punishment, his spirit will be banished to spend many moons in the place of fasting, before being allowed to enter our happy hunting ground.

'But now that you are here, the Great Chief Massasoit has a mission to ask of you. That under my protection back through the forest, you will return to your people and tell them he wishes to sit with your elders in Council, and discuss peace between his people and yours.'

Damaris didn't need to be asked twice. Not just about being returned to the settlement. Nor her mission to set up a peace treaty.

But the trip back through the forest with this Indian Adonis, who looked like a Greek god, most definitely got her instant "yea" vote.

- seventeen -

They – we – whichever – were sitting against a small boulder on a projecting bluff, looking down from on high on the torrential river far below, forced to curve its way around a steep, thickly-wooded scarp. Stretched before us, in every direction, was an unbroken green and brown-speckled carpet of the tops of dense trees: oaks, chestnuts, pines, spruces, climbing slopes and dropping into hidden hollows as far as the eye could see.

We must have walked over a mile, her rescuer leading the way, when Damaris suddenly claimed she was feeling weary and sat down on a smooth ledge of stone.

Except I wasn't fooled, her eyes were my eyes and I knew only too well what she was up to, *and* where she was looking. Taking sly glances at his muscular body and iron-hard legs, especially his loin cloth, the shameless young madam was going almost cross-eyed trying to work out the shape underneath.

She'd not seen a man so unclothed before, at least not in the flesh. Drawings of naked Greek heroes in her history lessons would have been in outline, with no definition, and for a sixteen year old girl full of curiosity about such things, as any normal, healthy girl would be, even, as was obvious, in Elizabethan times – or maybe *especially* in Elizabethan times from what I've read about them, and the things they got up to in the Virgin Queen's Court – they just made her all the more inquisitive to see…well, "it" (her word, not mine) for real. Understandable when you think about it, considering that back in those olden days when she was living in London, men of fashion went about wearing protruding cod-pieces which must have made the mystery for Damaris and her friends all the more intriguing. Even more so as some men – especially those with especial cause to do so – had had, so I'd read, their cod pieces made somewhat larger than needed, as a vain boast by their owners that under them, they were more endowed than they in fact were. Had I chosen to, I could have helped her – buckskin clings – but with Damaris being only sixteen, it wasn't for me to lead her astray.

Giving up with an inward sigh of defeat, she looked up at his handsome profile instead.

'What is your name?' she asked. 'And how is it you speak English?'

Her rescuer remained silent for a moment, still gazing over the forest, then he turned his dark eyes to look at her. 'I am Samoset, of the Morratigon...'

So, this was Samoset. I should have guessed it the first moment I saw him, especially as I knew from history that Samoset had some knowledge of English, which is why he was the one chosen by Massasoit to first approach the Pilgrim Fathers. No wonder he'd given their women such impure thoughts. Having been with him for an hour or more now, and able to appreciate him, I sided with the Puritan wives. Wedded to men with rounded girths, whose minds were forever on a heavenly plane, I reckon they were entitled to any wicked thought that came their way. And when it was someone this hunky, to make hay while the sun shone.

'...my village lies some five days to the north.' His deep voice was as sexy as his physique. 'From there our tribal lands continue two more days east, from the mouth of the Kennebec River to the lands of the Penobscot, who, like the Morratigon, are of the Abenaki family. Together with the Wampanoag – and other surrounding tribes, who you will not find to be as friendly – we all share a language known as Algonquian. My English comes from your fishermen and fur traders who have visited our shores for fifteen years or more. And from Tisquantum, also known as Squanto, one of Chief Massasoit's advisers, and the last of the Patuxet who once lived on the land you chose to build your village. They were wiped out four years ago by a white man's plague, as were half the Wampanoag.'

Samoset paused, then continued.

'Before then, Squanto was taken captive by an English captain, along with braves from other villages, and sold as a slave in Spain. He escaped and reached your London and there met one of your kindlier merchants, who took him for many years into his home and taught him to speak your language, then paid for his voyage back across The Great Water to rejoin his tribe, only for him to find the Patuxet were no more, only skulls and bones picked clean by scavenging animals and birds, and their lands gone to waste. Chief Massassoit gave him home. Squanto has served him ever since, and each time I visit the Wampanoag he teaches me more of your language.'

'He has taught you well,' said Damaris, glancing again at his loincloth.

'Your language, perhaps, but not your ways or your beliefs. For me they are a mystery, and will always remain so.'

The muffled sound of the river rising up from the depths below, the sigh of the breeze stirring the tree-tops, the singing of the birds, the rustling of small animals, maybe even deer, searching unseen for food nearby…plus very much the presence of Samoset…was so affecting Damaris I could sense she'd have been willing to stay here forever, New Plimoth and her family forgotten, and England a million miles away. (If I'd been her, so to speak, with no Katy to get back home to, I think I could maybe have been persuaded to feel the same. I'd never met *any* man like this before, not even back in my own time – or should I say forward in time, this dimension scale thing was *so* confusing.)

'Such as?' Damaris asked, trying to prolong her time in his company.

'Mostly your need to conquer,' Samoset replied. 'To rule over us. Having been told by Squanto of the White Man's intention to send more and more settlers to our shores, this is the main reason why Chief Massasoit, and his brother Quadequina, wish to be the first to agree a treaty between your people and theirs. With half their braves also lost to the plague, the Wampanoag are being raided by surrounding tribes, all anxious to hunt over their lands. Knowing that White Men's weapons spit out death, Massassoit wishes to treaty with you to protect his own people from such attacks. Furthermore, he believes you are honour bound to agree to it. Had he so ordered it, he could have had you all killed when you first stepped ashore from your tall ship. Instead, he let you live on his lands. By so doing, he chose the path of peace between his people and yours, and other White Men who, as he knows, will follow in even greater numbers.'

'Then why the terrifying howling, keeping us awake at night?'

'Even Indians,' Samoset said the words with irony, 'are able to apply thought to their deeds. It was to make you anxious to talk of peace. But in our talks be warned that you and we hold many opposite views. Unlike the White Man, it is our belief that land cannot be owned. For us, Mother Earth is but held in trust for our children who follow after us. If you demand more than this, we will willingly sacrifice our blood to protect our way of life.'

Damaris was now so captivated by Samoset, she genuinely wanted to know more. 'Your beliefs are so different to all I've been taught. Tell me more about them?' She also had another question she was just aching to ask but hesitated over, then found the courage: 'And how is it that you keep your...' she cast her eyes down, then dared to raise them, '...your physiques so strong and so supple?'

Samoset's eyes, so black, so very deep, searched hers.

'To this,' he said, with an unexpected smile; I felt her heart race, 'by outrunning the deer, which can take half a day. As to our beliefs...'

He looked over the untamed forest, '...it would take a lifetime to tell and we must be on our way. But this I will say...' his outstretched hand swept a circle over all they could see. 'This, our land, was given to us by the Creator at the beginning of time. Here we were made, the people of the first light. Not only did He make us, but every other creature – the moose, the otter, the beaver, the deer – partly to give harmony to all things, and to sustain us, with the right to kill. But only to preserve our own lives. Never, like the White Man, for profit. This is why our prayer to the Great Father, Kietitan, is to thank Him for what and who we are, and our position in the whole of Creation. I will say the prayer to help you understand.'

Walking to the rim of the bluff, he raised his arms to the sky and cried out aloud:

'Great Father Kietitan. Thus it was in the beginning, that for every tribe you created you also gave a homeland, providing grain, fruit and game, such as we need to eat, and with all that we need for clothing. For the Earth You gave us, O Mighty Kietitan, is our Mother, it cares for us, it is part of our body. The mountains and hills are our backbone. The gullies and creeks are our heart veins. For all this, Father Kietitan, we, your children, thank you.'

Damaris was so moved – so much so, I could sense it – that she stayed silent as Samoset remained standing on the edge of the ridge, arms still raised high in reverent thanks.

Savages! I could almost feel her anger as she thought of the dour Puritans back in New Plimoth, and of Brother Brewster's bigoted views. Savages! Never! More defenders of their lands, their ways, their customs and beliefs, in the only way they knew how. But savages? Never! Never! Never!

Turning away from the scarp, Samoset gave Damaris his hand and pulled her to her feet.

'And now we must continue on our way, or your people will be sending an armed party in search of you. One shot fired in anger could start a war between us, before your elders and ours have sat together in Council, and begun to even talk of peace.'

- eighteen -

Back in New Plimoth, Captain Standish was stacking muskets, pistols, pikes, cutlasses and swords against the front wall of the Common House. Governor Carver was still too weak in bed to take part in the search, and Brother Brewster, in his godly concern for Damaris, had chosen to remain inside the palisade to pray for her. But the four men from the shallop, and the two from the fields (who, in Shrimp's expressed opinion, should have been keeping a closer eye on "that headstrong Hopkins wench") had just run in panting to join the twelve already gathered in the muddy square. That made eighteen, plus himself. There was little hope (he thought to himself, but deliberately didn't express it) of finding the wilful gaby alive, but it was, nevertheless, a timely opportunity for him to exercise his motley troops. And from what he'd seen of them so far, they were sorely in need of it.

Squaring his shoulders, Standish strutted forward to review them.

'Mustered', he'd ordered great-etcetera granddad Stephen, by which he'd meant lined-up smartly, awaiting his command. Instead, they'd gathered into two opposing groups, with the "Strangers" loudly arguing the "Saints" contingent's opinion that there was "little purpose in going after that Hopkins biddy, she'll never be seen alive again". Stephen was having to be physically restrained by his menservants, Edward Doty and Edward Leister — neither of who were men to shirk a fight — from striking the young "Saint" who'd made the comment.

The truth, thought Shrimp, who had a soldier's contempt for those he regarded as cowards, was that every jack one of Brewster's lot would give anything not to be the ones chosen to enter the forest and face the damned savages in open combat. Well, it wasn't up to them, the decision was his. But if half his troops' hearts weren't in it, it augured even less well for the chances of finding the malapert maid — or rather, her body, she'd be raped many times over and long dead by now.

Watched by the six grim and silent women left alive after the winter — who were consoling my great-etcetera gran Elizabeth as she sobbed into her apron — and by the remaining twenty four boys, girls, and toddlers, Standish decided his tactics and halted in front of his militia.

'Form two lines,' he commanded.

The quarrelling simmered down to surly muttering, with much bumping and shoving, until they formed two ragged lines. Nine "Sinners" in the front, nine "Saints" in the rear, just as Shrimp had anticipated. Inwardly sighing at each man's lack of military discipline, there was little to choose between them, none were yet recovered to full health, but the "Strangers" at least had strength of purpose, and included the only three sharpshooters: Hopkins, Doty and Leister. This decided it for him.

'Rear line, man the cannons and guard the stockade,' he ordered. 'Take only matchlocks; the rescue party will need all four flintlocks and pistols. Rear line! Fall out!'

Faces barely containing their relief, the nine "Saints" ran to the Common House, grabbed muskets and pikes and scurried away, fanning out to the north, south, and west walls of the stockade, leaving Town Brook wall unmanned.

Standish faced the line of "Sinners". 'Chosen men! Flintlocks for myself, Hopkins, Doty and Leister. The rest: matchlocks. Every man to arm himself with pistol and either a sword, cutlass, or pike And a dagger for close combat. Chosen men! Collect your arms!'

He paced about as they gathered their weaponry. 'Snap to it! Snap to it! No time to lose! Form two lines, one of five, one of four. Apace! We don't have all day! Chosen men! Arms at the ready! Right turn. In double time, make for the Forest Gate. March!'

With Standish trotting alongside, the party moved off. Detaching herself from the other women, Elizabeth ran to Stephen's side. 'Find her, Stephen, find her,' she pleaded with him, 'Merciful God, find her alive and unharmed.'

Shifting his gaze sideways as he double-marched, cleft chin firmly resolved, Stephen tried to reassure her. 'I will wife, I will,' he vowed, despite having little optimism, feeling sick to his stomach at what Damaris must be suffering at this very moment. 'Even though my own life be forfeit.'

The latter circumstance wasn't quite what Elizabeth wanted to hear. Wringing her hands she fell back and watched them lope through Fort Gate, and head for the dark forest.

- nineteen -

As we (Samoset, Damaris and I) emerged from the forest, we saw ten armed men trotting out of the fort and heading toward us across the open ground. Standish was recognizable by his helmet and breast plate. Damaris shouted to them and waved.

Captain Shrimp's voice carried to us: 'Chosen men! Halt!'

But then the stupid man ordered them to: 'Prime weapons! Load!'

And then, of all things: *'Front row kneel! Chosen men, take aim!'*

I could hardly believe it as every man (except great-great granddad Stephen) obeyed his commands, the front row kneeling, the rear remaining standing, and directed their firearms at Samoset. With horror, I realised that the next order was: *Fire!*

Damaris acted, leaping in front of Samoset to shield him, arms outstretched and yelling: 'No! No! Don't shoot! Don't shoot!'

That was her reaction. Me? My horror turned to panic.

What the hell are you doing? I screamed at her, forgetting I was only in a dream, or whatever. *Have you gone frigging nuts? This is no time to play the frigging heroine. Not with me inside you and all those frigging muskets pointed right at us! Get back! Get back! I don't want to frigging die here in New frigging Plimoth, four hundred frigging years before I was even born!*

Next thing, I heard Standish bawl. 'Stand aside, you gaby! Stand aside!'

134

Listen to him, Damaris! Do as you're frigging told! Stand aside! Dive to the ground! Anything! But just get out of the frigging way! Any second now, the frigging idiot's going to yell: Fire!

But then, bless, bless, bless his cotton-picking heart, great-great granddad Stephen broke ranks. Leaping in front of the pointed firearms, he yelled: 'Lower your muskets! Don't fire!'

At the same time, Damaris shouted, 'Samoset comes in peace! In peace, do you hear! To discuss a peace treaty! Put down your arms!'

'I'm in command!' Standish bellowed. 'I give the orders. Take aim, I say–'

But instead, and thanks be to the gods (Whiteskin or Redskin, no matter which) the other eight obeyed great granddad and lowered their arms.

Shrimp turned on them, beside himself with rage. 'Chosen men! Resume firing positions.' But they took no notice of him. Instead, the front rank stood up and they all turned to each other and started talking animatedly amongst themselves. As for great-etcetera granddad Stephen, he was already running to us, arms open wide and crying out: 'Damaris! Damaris!'

As Damaris ran to meet him, I could see the tears running unashamedly down my great-great etc. granddad's face.

At both my ancestors' insistence, anxious to show their gratitude for Damaris's safe return, especially great etcetera gran Elizabeth who, after measuring Samoset up and down…and down and up…was insistent about it, Samoset was to sleep the night under their roof.

Supper was over, Giles and Constance were lying under blankets in a dark corner of the one-roomed hut, and

Stephen, Elizabeth, Samoset and Damaris – the latter as a concession for her part in bringing-in the peacemaker – were talking around an open fire, the smoke drifting up through a hole in the roof above.

'When your Council meets Chief Massasoit,' Samoset was explaining, 'do not forget that when you arrived on his shores but four full moons ago, he had only an idea – learned from Squanto – as to who you are. Until we know you better, we call you *Awaunageesuck* – The Strangers – because you are the ones who are alien to our shores, not us. When Columbus claimed to have found us, it was he who was lost not us, thinking he had reached the shores of Japan by sailing west, but we have always been here and did not need finding.

'We ask you to understand this. This is our land. We have lived here since it was created for us at the beginning of Time. We know you call us savages, but we are an ancient people, a proud people, with separate tribal cultures, and a way of living that once gave rise to large cities. One such, long before your London was ever thought of, was Cahokia, in the land of the Mississippi. A city with a hundred pyramids, and sixty thousand people living within its walls, stretching as far as eye could see. Cahokia's chief lived atop the highest pyramid and from there he and his descendants governed "The Law", as given by Kietitan, The Mighty Creator, to the First Man to live on Mother Earth.

Impressing every word, Samoset looked straight at great-great granddad Stephen.

'Know this, too. The name we call ourselves is *Anishinaabeg*. The Human Beings. Not savages. Massasoit is the proud Chief of a proud nation. If you wish for peace, you should treat him as such.'

Realising the import of Samoset's words, Stephen gravely nodded.

'Nevertheless,' the young Morratigon chief continued, 'peace is as vital to Massasoit and the Wampanoag as it is to you. Having chosen Patuxet as your home, you are surrounded by tribes who will seek to destroy you. And with many braves lost to a white man's plague, Massasoit is as much under threat from them as you are.

'He also knows,' Samoset stressed, 'that more Awaunageesuck will come after you, and the way to protect his people is to smoke the pipe of peace with your people. I will show you your situation for you to understand the danger you yourselves are in.

Scraping a map of the coastline of New England on the dirt floor with an arrowhead, he indicated the positions of the various tribes by their totem-signs, and giving their names:

'You will see,' he explained, 'that apart from the Great Water that brought you here, you are surrounded. To the north of you are the Massachusett and the Pennacook. To the west the Nipmuc. To the south, the Pequot and the Narragansett. To the east, on the land you call Cape Cod, the Nauset. Each of these tribes is against you. Other than Massasoit's Wampanoag, on whose land you have chosen to dwell, the only ones not against you are the Abenaki, my tribe, to the north – but who are becoming more and more under the influence of French traders, who are your rivals – and to the south, the Mohegan, a new tribe led by Uncas, the son by marriage of Sassacus, chief of the Pequot. But both the Abenaki and the Mohegan are too far away to be of help. Your only hope – with the greatest threat coming from the Pequot – is an alliance with the Wampanoag. *This*,' Samoset emphasised, fixing his dark eyes long and hard into Stephen's, 'you must make your people understand. Peace with Massasoit is their only chance of survival.'

Throughout his summary, Samoset sat on his haunches, left foot under his right ankle, his thighs open. Damaris was lying on the floor opposite, her chin in her hand (a position she'd chosen deliberately, I was getting to know her only too well) seeming to be interested in Samoset's analysis, but really to allow her another chance to glance up his thighs in the hope of seeing more than she'd seen in the forest. (Unfortunately for her, his loin cloth was draped straight down and she was going to have to stay disappointed.)

But neither was great gran Elizabeth, immune. Whenever she thought no one was looking toward her, she was also taking sly glances at Samoset's body. (And why not? Though great granddad Stephen was still a handsome man, the more I saw of Samoset – dreamwise again, that is, and not in the same way that Damaris was going cross-eyed trying to see more of him – the more he was confirmed as something special, a real hunk, and handsome with it.)

Further proof of this (had I needed it) were the three Puritan women – widow White and two maidservants, Desiré and Dorothy – who, at this moment, were spending the night in the Common House doing their penance for taking – as ruled on by Brother Brewster – a more than healthy interest in the young Morratigon Chief. Except, I'd wager they were comparing notes and not spending much time, if any, in contemplation of their sins. And that if Brother Brewster was true to himself, his own wife, Mary, should be with them. I saw her peeking while pretending to be averting her eyes.

But Damaris was going to have to stay frustrated. Elizabeth, too. The discussions were over. Samoset was saying (to the clear disappointment of them both – fortunately for great grandma, noticed only by me and not by great grandpa) that he would prefer to sleep on the floor of a rough shelter Stephen had thrown up behind the one-room abode, in which to keep his trading goods.

As soon as he'd gone, Damaris said goodnight to her parents and crept under her blankets in her dark corner. From the way she kept propping her eyes open, I guessed she was trying to stay awake until both her father and step-mother were asleep, and then (if my guess was right, and I just knew it was) she was intending to creep out of the house to Samoset, and hoping things would take their natural course between them, and she would finally find the answer to the mystery now dominating her, of exactly what happened between a man and a woman when they lay down together in seclusion.

(If that was her plan – and I don't think there was any doubt about it – then if other young Elizabethan maidens were anything like Damaris, the history books regarding them need to be rewritten. She was wanton, way before her time…yet maybe not, as I've already said, when I think of the things they got up to back then, not just in in the court of Good Queen Bess, but also in that of her father's, Henry VIII, including dalliances with two of his future wives, Anne Boleyn and Catherine Parr, when they were only 16 and 15. And with Anne's 17-year old sister, Mary, if I remember my history aright. As for Bessie Blount, another of Henry's amours, she was just 14 when he first started to get to know her – "know" as in the biblical sense of the word that is. So on reflection and despite her admittedly naughty mind, Damaris was maybe an innocent by comparison. Although Brother Brewster, if he'd been privy to her thoughts, would, I'm sure, have felt morally called on to speak highly censorious to her, and maybe even tried to get her to join widow White and Desiré and Dorothy in the Common House, despite her not being one of his flock.)

Anyway, sadly – or fortuitously, whatever one's point of view – Damaris's plan was not to be. Fighting the exhaustion of her long day, her eyelids grew heavier and heavier. She tried to resist but failed. Within minutes, she was fast asleep.

And when she woke up at early dawn before the rest of her family and crept out to Samoset, he was gone.

Staring into the empty hut, and seeing the flattened ground where he had lain, burning tears welled up in her eyes.

At the same time, I felt my spirit depart her body, leaving her there, kneeling on the floor, tracing, with her fingers, the shape of Samoset's body in the earth...

- twenty -

PLYMOUTH, MA, TODAY

Tapping on glass brought me back to consciousness, thinking, as I was surfacing, that my great-great, etcetera grandparents' hut didn't have windows, only clear paper immersed and stretched in oil, to allow light to faintly seep into their temporary home.

The knocking continued and with it a woman's anxious voice. 'Are you okay? You okay in there, honey? Wake up! Wake up!'

I forced my eyes open to find myself back in the driving seat of my Jeep – in the scenic pull-in overlooking modern-day Plymouth, its streets, buildings, traffic, harbour, ships, all restored. Straightening up and trying to recover my senses, I turned to the window and saw a woman's face peering anxiously in at me. Blue-rinsed hair, on the tubby side, and wearing multi-coloured rimmed glasses, she was, at a guess, in her early sixties.

I lowered my window.

'You okay, honey?' the woman repeated, her voice concerned. 'Burt and I,' she gestured toward a tall, rake-thin, gray-haired man sitting against the hood of his car, sweeping the bay through binoculars, 'we were worried about you. You were so still we thought you'd fainted. We couldn't leave until we knew you were all right.'

'I'm grand,' I assured her. 'Truly. Just over-tired. I pulled in to briefly close my eyes and must have dozed off. But thanks for your concern,' I said, raising the window and cutting off her response. Taken aback, she returned to her rake-thin husband. Judging from the cold looks I was getting, she was letting him know how badly she was treated, after all her good intent. Getting into their car, they drove off, not giving me a second glance.

Left alone in the overlook, I leant back in my seat and took long breaths, until I felt my heart rate return to some degree of normality.

Another dream…?

Hallucination…?

Or something else…?

What's more, whatever this new occurrence was, it seemed I hadn't solved the mystery of the recurring one, after all. Andrew and his lectures might have something to do with it, but it plainly didn't fully explain it. As for this last happening, it hadn't even come to me in my sleep. The way I'd suddenly drifted, unable to resist, from being wide awake in my Jeep into a completely different, yet equally realistic experience of Damaris, was even weirder.

Which brought the whole mystery back to square one.

Something I couldn't explain.

Whatever, I was able to remember everything that had taken place, just as clearly as if it was all recorded on film. But whether Damaris and Samoset ever met again, I really didn't know; history didn't say. Nor did our family's.

Slowly controlling my trembling, I forced myself to think.

I knew that Samoset, for some reason, wasn't at the peace meeting between the settlers and Massasoit. Squanto was the translator. The upshot was a seven-clause treaty, the most important being that both sides guaranteed to come to each other's aid in the event of attack from any of the surrounding tribes.

Seven months later, Massasoit and ninety-nine of his braves (one of the fussy Puritans must have taken the trouble to head-count them) joined the settlers in the first ever harvest celebrations on American soil, bringing five slain deer with them as their gift. Once again, Samoset wasn't among the revellers – although Damaris was. The Forefathers had provided food and ale from store, wild turkeys shot by a four-man hunting party (probably the three sharpshooters, my great etcetera granddad Stephen and his manservants Doty and Leister – plus of course, Captain Standish) and wine made from local grapes.

All in all the festivities lasted three days, with one devoted (as was to be expected, having met him) to Shrimp showing-off, drilling his militia up and down in front of Massasoit – and to playing various sports, including one similar to today's lacrosse, except the pitch was a mile long and a quarter of a mile wide (bet the Wampanoag won, by a huge score).

However, there *was one* thing in Abenaki history, that suggested Damaris and Samoset did maybe meet again. And if so, that it made a lasting impression on Samoset.

Back in his tribal homeland on a peninsula the Abenaki called Pemaquid – in what is now the state of Maine – the name for one of the rivers there was Madamascontee, which meant 'alewives plenty' ('alewives' as in fish, not "beery spouses"). Sometime during Samoset's lifetime it was changed to: Damariscotta.

Damaris-cotta. It was just too much of a coincidence.

Furthermore, there were blanks in both Damaris's and Samoset's lives.

Damaris was only sixteen when Samoset saved her from Hawkface. The year was 1621, and according to the records she didn't go missing until 1627. During those six years, from sixteen to twenty-three, she never married – very unusual for a young woman to stay single for so long in those early settler days. As for her disappearance, if (as my recurring dream had it) she was ever caught by a marauding war-party, and then taken captive…or killed, nothing was known. Not only were the records blank about it, but nor was any such story handed down in our family stories.

Her fate was still a mystery to this day.

A little more was known about Samoset.

In 1627, the same year that Damaris went missing, he was recorded as having sold 1,200 acres of his tribal land to some Englishman whose name escapes me. For one who believed land couldn't be owned – but was to be held in trust for his children, and their children after them – it was a puzzling thing for him to do. From then, it was another twenty five years, 1653, before there was further record of him, when he sold *another* 1,000 acres. He died only days later and must have known he was dying when he sold. It was all very strange.

Staring through the window, but not focusing on anything, I thought: *I'd give anything to know the answers.* Anything, that is, apart from a repetition of what I'd just experienced. Or my recurring nightmare. Both felt real enough to give me the heebie-jeebies. All I wanted from now on were normal dreams...pleasant dreams...ones with happy endings.

Please, God, or Kietitan, or whoever was sending them, if it's not too much trouble.

I reached to start the ignition, but changed my mind. Getting out of the Jeep, I opened the rear door, took-out my four recent paintings, propped them against the rear bumper, and removed the sheet from the one I'd kept hidden.

I stared at it. The scene was of a sylvan glade, with a small waterfall descending gently into a still pool surrounded by full-leafed branches hanging down to almost touch its surface. The style was pre-Raphaelite, Romantic, no similarity to anything I'd ever painted before. I looked at it, now even more fearful of the dreamlike state in which I'd painted the scene, my brush seemingly guided by some unknown hand.

On the right of the composition was a rocky outcrop. Leaning against it, wearing only a loincloth, and looking as though he was waiting for someone to emerge from the pool, was a man of beautiful physical proportions, looking like a Greek god.

There was no doubt.

It was Samoset.

Face, physique, everything, even to his long black hair.

Had the Samoset of my last vision been influenced by this strange painting?

Or was there more to it all?

Something beyond the world of the subconscious?

With maybe more to come?

Hell, despite Samoset being a hunk, I hoped not.

- twenty-one -

The Man from SF slowly awoke. Moving his hand, he felt the studs and smooth leather surface of the chesterfield. Opening his eyes, he took in the redwood shelves full of books, the mahogany desk topped in burgundy-red leather, the large oil painting of "The First Thanksgiving" – similar in style to the famous picture with the same title by Jennie Brownscombe – the polished wooden floorboards, the large Persian carpet–

'Well?' a familiar voice intruded. 'How often does that happen?'

The elderly rider was looking at him from the depths of a winged armchair, studded and padded in burgundy-red hide, like the chesterfield.

The younger man sat up. 'How often does what happen?' he asked, giving himself time to recover.

'Falling asleep like that. You've been out over ten minutes. Mumbling away in English and Algonquian.'

'Algonquian? You don't know any Algonquian.'

'I've picked up a few words over the years. Enough to recognise the language. But you're ignoring my question. How often does it happen?

'It doesn't. I was just flaked after the flight and couldn't keep my eyes open.'

'If you say so.'

'I do say so.' Crossing the room, the younger man poured himself a brandy, neat, then needing more time to clear his head, he reached for his red, leather-bound note pad on his desk and opened it. The last entry, in his own writing, was a phone number with a Plymouth code. He didn't recognise it, but it would give him extra seconds to get back to normal.

'What's this number?'

'I've no idea. It's all just as you left it. I haven't touched a thing.'

Searching his mind, he had no recollection of jotting it down. But buying himself more time to recover, he dialled it. A machine answered. Listening to the voice, he remembered why he'd noted it, left a brief message and, feeling more himself, faced back into the room.

'Where were we...? Oh, yes, the insurance company. It's my guess they'll be only too willing to settle out of court. They'd be stupid not to. Their money back, plus interest. That should be enough to persuade them not to prosecute.'

He paused. 'The police will be a different matter. There's going to be some questions asked. They're not going to accept you made a mistake. Why the hell did you do it?'

'I told you, they refused to pay up.'

'No excuse. The idea was so dumb, so goddamn witless from start to finish, I can't think what possessed you. What if someone had come checking?'

'No one did. Nor would anyone been likely to – especially now, not after twelve months. If it wasn't for you turning up,' the older man sounded regretful of the fact, 'I still say I would have got away with it.'

'And all I can say is you were damned lucky no one examined the body.'

'They took my word for it. My name still means something around here.'

'Not for much longer. You realise you can't escape trial, and all that'll entail. Reporters yelling at you outside the courthouse. Flashing cameras. The one thing in your favour is your dodgy heart and your age. But leave it to me, I'll get you the best firm of attorneys in Boston, I'll ask Carlo to recommend one. Probably his own: Paul Chapman. A couple of postponements because of your health. Appeals. You'll be a hundred-and-ten before they get to pass sentence, and even you'll never make it to then.' The younger man paused. 'But let me think about it some more. I'll see you later, as arranged. We'll talk further then.'

Looking relieved at getting away so lightly, the elderly man left the room.

The Man from San Francisco returned to the chesterfield and lay down.

What the hell was happening to him?

It was all becoming more and more crazy.

This last experience had been so damned realistic it was as if he'd actually regressed.

Whereas before, it had been nothing more than a dream of a girl who lived way back in time – but whose name he now knew to be Damaris – running through the forest, fleeing for her life from her pursuers.

Then she falls; they tear her clothes off; their snake-eyed leader stalks toward her…

And she starts screaming.

While he stays hidden in the glossy leafed branches of a large beech tree, watching.

Yet her only hope.

- twenty-two -

Although I was still all jittery inside, I'd recovered enough to be able to drive, and fast, as I usually do – unless Katy is with me – giving myself something else to concentrate on.

Exit 5 flashed past. I glanced toward Plymouth, approaching on my right.

I just loved the place. "America's Home Town" as it was called, and home to me. Okay, so maybe it was sometimes criticised for its apparent indecision over whether it should be a modern tourist resort or scenic historic village. And at first sight, the town – with its mix of centuries old houses and buildings, its narrow cobblestone streets, clapboard mansions, its twisting main street and antique shops, contrasting with its present-day motels, souvenir shops and sights-seeing buses – might appear to reflect this conflict. But it was this very singular mix I loved. Modernity and antiquity blended together in its own unique style.

Despite what I'd just come through – dream, hallucination, whatever – my gaze was drawn toward Burial Hill – the once Fort Hill, where New Plimoth's logged palisade had ended and on which the Common House had once stood. And the watchtower, from where my great- great, etcetera-etcetera granddad Stephen looked up to see Damaris being dragged into the forest by Hawkface – some four hundred years back in time, yet in dreamtime only twenty minutes ago.

But it was all too much a reminder that these strange dreams I was having had not gone away, and I turned my attention back to my driving.

Exit 6 was rushing up at me. I shot into it, feathering my brakes as I looked to make sure I was clear to drive straight out, put my foot back on the throttle, and into Samoset Street.

Alexandra's gallery was one of nine outlets on a select precinct. Newly built of rustic red brick with slate roofs, tinted glass windows, they formed a three-by-three-by-three U-shape around a car park, bordered by trees and shrubs. Composing the nearest block as I neared it, was a Ladies Fashion-house, a shop selling New England and European antiques, and the inevitable Law Office. Facing the road, across the car park, was a Men's Clothing outlet, a bibliopole of antiquarian leather-bound books, and Interior Design Consultants. Completing the U-design were specialists in modern Italian, French and Spanish furniture; a restaurant, and finally, 'Bristow Art Gallery'.

Entering the car park, I was surprised to see Alex's car – white Porsche, tinted windows – outside the gallery. With no Thanksgiving dinner to prepare, I'd expected her to be tucked up in bed with John. She must have decided to use the break hanging up the paintings for the exhibition, yet it was still a surprise. Knowing Alex, compared to spending a whole morning luxuriating under the sheets making love, I would have placed waking up early to work in a definite no-win situation.

Still uptight, I left my braking to the last second and screeched to a halt alongside her car facing the gallery's double-fronted, dark glass doors. Switching off the engine, and seeing Harrison still out to this world – I must have given him too big a dose – I patted him, feeling guilty, 'Sorry, Harry,' and got out of the Jeep.

'Hi!'

I looked up. Alex was exiting the gallery looking somewhat flustered, and – unusually for her – her blond hair all awry. She waved as she skipped down the stone steps from the roofed arcade and crossed over to me, smiling as always, except that today it looked a little forced.

A New Yorker, Alex was my one genuine friend; someone I knew I could always rely on. After graduating the same year as me, she'd applied her considerable talent to painting "real life" scenes of The Big Apple, contrasting the grimness of its back streets with the wealth of its colourful high life. But her gregarious nature had found that existence too solitary. 'The loneliness of the long-distance artist', she'd called it, turning successfully to PR and forming her own company, marrying one of her employees (handsome – naturally) in the process, only to find she'd exchanged one form of solitude for another.

'Once the honeymoon was over and the first flush of passion died down, all he thought of was golf and sailing,' she told me, after arriving at my door four years ago, with packed suitcases, her car full of personal items and asking for a bed. 'Okay, so he was good in the sack, good but not fantastic, but what the hell! There's more to life than waiting for a man to come home in a foul mood if he's had a bad game, or the weather's too rough to take the boat out, but ready for instant coitus non-interrupt-us if he's had a great time.'

She sold her firm for top dollar, paid off her "leech" husband, then settled in Plymouth and started the gallery. Before meeting John, she'd drive about in her Porsche, blonde hair blowing free, wearing designer tops with one too many buttons open, and always seeming to have at least three men friends happy to wine and dine her, while she kept her sylphlike body strictly to herself – her new policy with men from now on (or so she claimed) keeping them at bay until Mr Right came along.

I thought he had in John (four years younger than her) especially when she unexpectedly asked him to move in to live with her in her recently built split-level house (by coincidence, near Andrew) close to the beach. That's why it was such a surprise to see her here on this day of all days. Maybe she and John had had a spat?

'Hi, Dris,' she greeted me with her usual hug. 'You in a hurry or something? If so, why the Jeep and not the sports?'

I thought about telling her of my recent dream, then decided against. She'd just laugh it off and accuse me of having drunk too much wine. Besides, it would take too long to tell.

I raised the rear door. 'The why is because I've brought you my paintings. And no, I'm not in a hurry, no more than normal.'

'No more than usual! Come on, Dris, you could've fooled me. I thought you were going to drive right up the steps and into the gallery. Just as well your brakes are working.' She glanced into the Jeep. 'It's a wonder Harry didn't finish up on the hood. Is he asleep, or stuffed?'

I detected a hint of tension in her tone, her good humour a little forced.

'Knock-out pill, I wasn't up to fighting him, especially today. Dear Suzanne requested Katy's company to keep Jo out of her way, but she's in one of her ooh-la-lahing moods, and I don't want to leave Katy there too long. Then I've still got to finish cooking dinner – not that I'm not looking forward to having you and John over – but what with it being a year ago today that Robert...Well, I guess I'm a little uptight, and an exuberant Harry could have tipped the balance.'

'My, I can hear,' Alex arched her eyebrows. 'What's brought all this on?'

'I don't know. Robert maybe? Or Andrew? I'm not–'

'Then let's see if changing the subject can help?' Alex cut across me, which wasn't like her, she was usually my listening ear. 'What's the hurry to bring them in today? With you insisting on still doing the entertaining – despite my saying I'd do it this year – I'd have bet my last dollar on you being bent over a hot stove, all domesticated and up to your neck in turkey stuffing, not come visiting.'

'I did most of it yesterday. But being on my own, with Katy at Jo's, I couldn't settle and decided to drop them off. Come to that, what are you doing here? Don't you ever take a day off? You should be–'

'John got up early,' Alex cut across me again. She really did seem edgy. 'He had some lines running through his head and wanted to get them down on paper. So, like you, rather than hang about, I thought I may as well come in

155

and start on the exhibition. Those them?' she asked abruptly, peering into the back of the Jeep.

'Yes. How perceptive of you.'

'I'm sorry, Dris,' Alex apologised. 'Let's get them inside, then you can follow me back to mine for a coffee and a proper chat.'

I handed her the first two paintings.

She looked at them, and whistled: 'Wow, Dris, they're *fantastic*. Better than even before, and that's saying something. Let's see the others?'

I showed her the other two.

'Sensational! Just sensational! What's made you alter your style?'

'Experimenting.' I still didn't feel up to baring my soul.

'Then keep experimenting. It's getting time for me to change my wheels.'

Both carrying a painting in each hand, we climbed the steps and entered the gallery. The door into the office was shut, the lateral blinds on the window to the showroom drawn. This was unusual, Alex never closed them, she hated the feeling of being locked in, or entering a dark room. What's more, I saw her glance, almost furtively, at them, like she was double-checking. She really was in an odd mood today. But whatever was causing it, I'd wait for her to explain.

Alex displayed mostly abstracts, but today, taking pride of place in the centre of a wall was a large oil painting, similar in style to Jennie Brownscombe's "The First Thanksgiving" showing the Forefathers celebrating around food-laden tables in the open air with Massasoit and his braves, back-dropped by the wide open sweep of Cape Cod Bay. Seeing it after what I'd just experienced gave me a momentary shiver.

I shook the feeling away. 'Who painted it? I asked, indicating the painting and propping both mine with hers against the reception desk and crossing over to study it closer.

'A young Duxbury artist. She called with it on spec. It's not my normal taste, but when I saw it, I just couldn't refuse.'

'It's a bit close to Brownscombe's. Did she ask permission?'

'She didn't really need it, her's is different enough not to be accused of plagiarism. Still, she queried it and showed me the reply. All above board or I wouldn't have taken it in.'

I ran my eyes over the brush strokes, it was wonderfully painted. I read the scrawled signature. 'Avis Wall, she should go far. I tried to buy one like it not long before Katy's accident. I was browsing, searching for scenes to paint and turned into this dirt road. It didn't say private, but driving along it I met the land owner out riding, a nice old guy, and after explaining why I was there and apologising, he took me up to his house to see it…'

Going up to the painting, I looked closer at Damaris, Elizabeth, Stephen and Massasoit, and all the other faces I knew – in my dreams, that is. The only one missing was Samoset, who'd not attended the shindig.

'But nothing would persuade him to sell. Said it had been started by an ancestor, and belonged in the family. As well as the Pilgrims and the Wampanoag, it had the old man's descendants right up to the last one who died. In fact, it was all rather weird. According to the old guy most of his family's faces had been included – though only in outline, but *before* they were even born – and over the passing centuries had been filled in to show who they were by other family members. There was only one outline left. He said something about having to wait for The Great Spirit to tell them who it would be, but…' I laughed, somewhat edgily, thinking back to both dreams, '…I guess he was pulling my leg. Still, I liked it, and kept plaguing Robert about it afterwards, hoping he'd tried to get the old guy to change his mind–'

I turned and found I was on my own. Through the gallery window, I saw Alex lifting the fifth painting out of the Jeep.

'No!' I yelled and fled outside. But I was too late. Alex was gazing at it, not even turning her face as I approached. 'Who's the artist?' she queried.

'Me, I'm afraid,' I replied, trying to grab the canvas from her. 'It's not finished.'

'Afraid! Dris, it's great!' she said holding on to it. 'I love it! I can't wait to see it finished. But you've never painted anything remotely like this before. What prompted it? Repressed sexual urges? Reading too much Freud?' She indicated at Samoset. 'Talk about Superman! You wouldn't like to give me the phone number of whoever posed for it?"

'No-one posed for it, Alex' I replied, taking the painting from her and putting it back in the Jeep and re-sheeting it. 'Just my imagination.'

Alex whistled. 'Wow, and again, Wow! Some imagination! But what a pity. If he'd have existed, he might well have been my Mr Right. I sure could've had a lot of fun finding out.'

'I thought you'd found your Mr Right in John?'

Her face clouded. 'I thought so, too. But we're having problems. Or at least, I am. When he moved in I forgot you also have to put-up with their habits and foibles.' She shrugged. 'Guess I've lived too long on my own and I'm finding it hard adjusting.'

So I was right. Alex's mood was to do with her and John. I waited for her to elaborate, but instead she changed the subject.

'Speaking of Mr Right, the other one suddenly phoned out of the blue.'

Okay, if she preferred not to talk about it, that was all right by me. 'And which of the many would that be?'

'The one I told you about, remember? Mr Hunk, the guy who went all gaga over your paintings. You must remember. I had only two left and he bought them both, but then got upset when I told him I'd run out of your catalogues. He gave me his number in case I came across a spare one, except I went and lost it. I still say Mrs Webb must have thrown it out when she was tidying. Anyway, after all this long time, he's left a message on my machine saying he's calling-in sometime this week. Sad, but all my hinting I was available couldn't have left much of an impression on him. Only sounded anxious to get hold of your profile. No mention of holding me.'

'My heart weeps for you, Alex. You'll just have to make do with John,' I said, giving her a second opportunity to open up. 'Perhaps you should try making more of an effort. I wish I had. Robert may not have been the world's greatest lover but I miss him in other ways...' I paused. 'Alex, like you're always there for me, I'm always here for you. You hinted earlier you wanted to talk about something…?'

Alex went suddenly serious. 'Actually, Dris, it's two things…'

She hesitated, as if unsure how to start, then clutched my arm, stumbling over her words. 'First, you're right, Dris, I should make more of an effort with John. I realised it myself after getting here this morning. Hey! I thought: What *am* I doing in today? It's a holiday, chance for a long lie-in for goodness sake. But if John's already making excuses to get up before the crack of dawn to write poetry, this relationship's not just heading for trouble, it's in it – and deep. So, listen to your heart, Alex, don't go losing him. Today's Thanksgiving, the day for counting your blessings. What better chance for us to sort things out…?'

Again Alex faltered, nervously biting her lip as she searched for her words. It was all so out of character, she was usually well able to express herself.

'So, would you mind if we don't come around tonight, Dris? I know you'll have gone to a lot of trouble but I thought I'd treat John and myself out to dinner, just the two us – candle light, best wine, soft music and then maybe an early night. I'm really sorry to let you down at such short notice, but–'

'Alex, it's fine,' I interrupted, but for some reason still sensed that there was more to her agitation than she was admitting.

What's more, once Katy was tucked up in bed, it meant me being alone with Andrew again. And after last week's episode on the sofa, I'd been banking on Alex and John being there. It looked as if Katy would be getting an extension tonight. Not that she'd mind, she'd welcome it, even more so if Andrew took the huff again and left early.

'Alex,' I said, squeezing her hand, 'don't give it another thought. Katy and I will be fine. We'll just have to eat turkey every meal for the next few days, that's all, but what the heck, it will save me cooking, even if it does get to taste more and more like a dead dodo the longer it lasts.'

'Thanks, Dris.' Alex returned my squeeze, her relief so apparent it seemed out of all proportion to sorting herself out with John. Still puzzled, I asked: 'And the other thing?'

Her grip tightened. She really was acting strange today.

'Dris, on second thoughts it's not that important. It'll keep until after Thanksgiving. And instead of coffee, we'll share my bottle of Gaja 2007. We'll have more time to–'

'Alex,' I cut across her, 'If it's bad enough to break open *that* bottle, I'd rather you tell me now.'

Seeing the look on my face, Alex swallowed. 'Stella Slater's back.'

I felt my heart miss a beat. Then, in a voice which even to my own ears sounded cold and detached, I asked: 'Is Robert with her?'

'Sorry, Dris. All I know is that she was seen in some grocery store–'

Leaping into the Jeep, I slammed the door shut and switched on the engine.

'Dris!' Alex shouted through the closed window. 'Don't cheapen yourself!'

I engaged gear, reversed with a squeal of tyres, spun the wheels, and sped past her across the car park for the exit.

To confront Robert.

But not for myself anymore.

For Katy.

- twenty-three -

Shooting out into Samoset Street without checking either way first, I put my foot down on the accelerator and sped off, but then saw Andrew's silver coupè with its PEQ-OUT plates parked alongside a sidewalk. Slamming on my brakes, I stared at it.

What was Andrew doing here, parked near the gallery? Recollecting Alex's mussed-up hair, her edginess at my unexpected arrival, the drawn blinds on her windows, I realised her real reason for being at the gallery today, why she'd been acting so peculiarly.

Having to tell me about Stella Slater may have contributed to it, but it had sweet F-A to do with John. That part of her explanation was nothing but a lie, except that John's amatory performances must be consistently below her orgasmic par if she was already two-timing him. And of all men, with zipper-always-ready-for-unzipping Andrew! No wonder she'd not wanted to face him across the dinner table, not after what they'd been doing only hours before. But *Alex*? The one person I thought I could trust. Not that I cared if Andrew was having it off with half of Plymouth – but Alex didn't know that. And in my book that was as good a betrayal as one can commit to a best friend.

Finding my cell-phone flat, I'd forgotten to charge it, I dialled her number on my car-phone.

Drumming my fingers on the steering wheel I waited for her answer-machine to switch on. As she was clearly "occupied" with Andrew, she wouldn't be picking-up the phone. But after I'd left my message, our friendship – and business relationship – would be over for good.

'Bristow Art Gallery.'

It was Alex answering. This was so unexpected I automatically said: 'Alex?'

There was a pause before she replied in a shaky voice, 'Hi, Dris. Forget something?'

I recovered. 'Yes, to speak to Andrew.'

A longer pause. 'Andrew? I'm sorry, Dris, but what makes you think—'

'Alex, I know he's there. Put him on. No, don't. Just tell him I hope he's not too late to book in somewhere for Thanksgiving. Maybe he can join you and John? That should make an interesting threesome. As for you and me, Alex—'

'Dris! Don't hang up!' Alex's desperate tone stopped me slamming the phone down. 'It's not what you think. At least not with me. I'm speaking from reception. Andrew's still hiding in my office. *Please* believe me, Dris, but for some reason, he's been pestering me for days now. Joining me on my runs along the beach, making suggestive hints. I keep telling him to get lost, but it's like water off a duck's back. I should have told you straightaway, except I didn't know how to, or whether I should. He must have seen me leave this morning for the gallery and got here not long after, saying he happened to be driving past and saw my car parked outside...'

Alex paused, then rushed on. 'I was just telling him to eff off when we saw you drive in. Andrew dived into the office, leaving me not knowing what to do, especially with having to tell you about Stella Slater. So I decided to stay quiet. It was wrong and I'm sorry, Dris. The guy's a lech, and always will be, even when he gets to using a Zimmer frame. Take my advice, get rid of the slimeball. With your looks you can do way better. Please believe me, Dris, I'd never risk spoiling our friendship. You and I, we go back too far...' Alex's voice tailed off, begging me to respond.

I knew straightaway she was telling the truth.

God, did I feel a heel for leaping to the wrong conclusion.

I *could* excuse myself by pleading I was all uptight about hearing that Stella – and maybe Robert, too – were back in town, but whatever Alex's faults, I really should have known her well enough to realise that disloyalty wasn't one of them.

No, it was typical Andrew. But along with feeling self-reproach, I felt relief. It not only answered any last vestige of conflict about him, it also confirmed to me that New York had been nothing more than a teenage infatuation, born out of a young woman's natural sexual curiosity. But as for it ever being love – not in a million years. And as for comparing him to Pierce Brosnan's "Thomas Crown", I preferred Steve McQueen's anyway – always did.

'Dris!' Alex's voice pleaded out of the phone.

'It's alright, Alex,' I said. 'Forgive me? I've been having one of those bad hair days. And then when you told me about Stella–'

'That's okay, Dris. And thanks. But I would have thought the same.'

165

'No you wouldn't; but I'll tell you about my day some other time. Listen, why don't you lock the office door, then disconnect all the phone extensions at reception and just walk out of there, leaving him trapped inside the gallery? Give him a Thanksgiving he'll never forget. He won't trouble you again, not after that. As for this evening, I'll expect you about six.'

'Dris,' Alex hesitated. 'Would you mind very much if I still say no? Sure, my reason for crying-off was that I didn't want to face Andrew. But the part about John and myself is true or I wouldn't be here today. For all my joking about Mr Right, John's the one for me. I don't want to lose him. So, thinking about it, dinner, just the two us alone, John and me, the right atmosphere, and a lot of serious talking, might help us sort things out? If it's okay with you, that is? I'm sorry if it will cause you any–'

'Alex,' I cut across her, 'now you have us both apologising, and in your case there's no need. It's a great idea. So, have a wonderful evening, both of you. And, Alex, make it work. You and John are so right for each other. A little give and take. On both sides, Alex. That's what I should have done. Except more giving and less taking on my side, than on Robert's. Call you tomorrow.'

'Okay Dris.' Alex's relief was evident, even over the phone line. 'I'll look forward. As for Andrew, I'll do exactly that. Lock the creep in. It'll serve the louse right. And take care of yourself when you get to the Slater woman's. If Robert's there with her, don't do anything stupid. Don't forget you've got Mr Hunk breathing fire to meet you. When he calls again, I promise to sing your virtues to the high heavens. And Dris,

166

don't go shedding any tears for Snake-eyes. Just be grateful you found him out for what he is. Ciao.'

'Bye, Alex. Once again, I'm sorry. You're a one-in-a-million friend.'

Replacing the car-phone, I thought about her description of Andrew.

Snake-eyes! Trust Alex to have noticed it. Why hadn't I?

But now she'd said it, I could see Andrew's dark brown eyes narrowing to serpentine slits as he assessed the effect of his seductive charm.

Calculating the moment to strike.

Stella Slater lived in a treeless street of clapboard houses, all looking the same, with wooden steps up to front decks, patchy lawns, concrete driveways, no garages, divided by six-foot high wire-net fences.

Number 12 was halfway down. I parked outside it. Harrison opened one eye, looked at me, yawned and went back to sleep.

Leaving a window slightly open, I locked the Jeep and hurried up the steps to the front door. Heart pounding, I pressed the bell and heard it chime, but there was no movement inside. I pressed it again. Then a third time.

The door hurled open. 'Okay, okay, sweetie!' Short, bottle-blonde hair, Stella Slater confronted me. 'What's your damned hurry?'

This was the first time I'd seen her. All I knew about her was from the police. Her reputation with men. That, according to her mother, Stella was having an affair with some married man her mother knew nothing about, except

167

she'd overheard Stella talking to him on the phone, planning to run away on Thanksgiving when everyone and everything came to a halt. And finally, that on that same morning, three people who knew Stella had seen her and Robert drive out of town (they positively identified Robert from photos) both sitting cosy together, and Stella touching up her lipstick in the vanity mirror on the sunshield.

'I'd like to speak to Robert,' I said, hearing my voice tremble.

She pretended to look all puzzled. 'Robert? And who in the hell's Robert?'

'My husband.'

Stella affected to look even more mystified. 'Honey, now why the holy hell should I have your husband? Am I supposed to be holding him for ransom or something?'

I saw curtains moving and shadowy shapes peering around them in some of the nearby houses as her curious neighbours watched us confronting. I felt my anger evaporating and embarrassment taking over. But still not out of my mood, I lowered my voice to a cold, though strained undertone. 'Miss Slater.' (I felt so damned false using 'Slater', when what I wanted to call her was: 'Sluter'.) 'If Robert's not with you, you'll at least know where he is for me to contact him. And please don't try to deny it,' I added, seeing her still wearing her blank look. 'You and he were seen driving out of town together, a year ago today.'

Stella's face puckered as she still pretended to be remembering back, then it suddenly cleared. 'Is that who you're talking about, sweetie? In that case, someone told you wrong. We weren't driving out of town, we were driving through it. If the guy was your husband, all he was doing was giving me a lift to the bus depot, nothing more. But you'd best come in, honey,' she grabbed my elbow, glancing at all the twitching drapes. 'Or I'll have to start charging for seats.'

After a year thinking Robert had run away with this woman – even though it was contrary to what I'd thought was his nature – the shock of being told different momentarily robbed me of speech. My face must have paled because Stella tightened her grip on my arm as if she thought I was about faint.

'Okay, sweetie,' she said. 'I've got you,' and pulled me into the house, sundry emotions and questions all milling around inside me, sat me on a sofa, and before I could gather my thoughts there was a glass in my hand. 'You look like you could do with a stiffener, honey,' she said, 'Sip it slow, I made it neat.'

I drank it. Brandy. It hit my stomach, burning it, but clearing my head.

'Feel better, sweetie?' Stella asked with genuine concern.

My first glance of her had been cursory. I now studied her properly.

In her mid-thirties, at a guess, and still with an hour-glass figure, accentuated by a tight sweater, a one-size-too-small mini skirt and the longest of needle-point stiletto heels, she screamed 'sex' with a capital 'S'. If only someone had shown me a full photo of her a year ago, I would have known that despite her obvious (well, seemingly obvious) good heart, Stella Slater just wasn't Robert's type and immediately realised there *had* to be some other explanation for his disappearance.

169

'Yes, thanks. You're saying that's all Robert did – give you a lift?'

'Sure, honey, that's all. That's my trouble. Always has been. Anyone sees me with a guy and straightaway the rumours start. I was on my way to Boston to meet my man-friend, who was married but not getting on with his wife, you know the kinda thing. We were running away together to start a new life. He decided Thanksgiving would be the best day, his wife was waitressing at some restaurant, and wouldn't be home 'til gone midnight. Anyway, my cabbie didn't show up, and what with it being a holiday, I couldn't find another. So there I was, hoofing it along the road to the bus-depot, struggling with my cases, when this utility pulls up, dark blue, expensive-looking, and your...Robert, you said his name is...?'

I nodded.

'A real nice guy, sweetie, and classy with it. Anyways, he lowers his window and offers me a lift. I could tell he was a gentleman, what with his tweed suit, pipe and all, so I thought: 'why not?'. He drove me right to the depot – even carried my trunks inside – then drove off. And that's the last I saw of him, I swear to you, honey.'

Stella arched her eyebrows: 'That I should be so lucky as to be running off with a proper gent like yours. Mine's now doing ten for holding up a gas station. It's why I'm back home with my mother. Boy, do I know how to pick them!'

My whole being – heart, mind, body – was still surging with all kinds of reactions. As for my conscience forever believing that Robert had...Talk about guilt. But one question was uppermost:

'Did Robert make any mention of where he was going?'

'Not exactly. Just that he was on his way somewhere to try to buy some painting his wife liked.' Stella looked at me and gave a long sigh. 'You sure are lucky, sweetie! While I was running-off with a no-gooder, you were getting dinner ready, all nice and cosy at home, not even suspecting your old man was getting you a surprise Thanksgiving gift. I tell you, honey, next time I'll make damn sure I–'

She halted in mid-sentence. 'You saying he never got back?'

I shook my head, my mind churning.

A painting! There was only one I'd kept pressurising Robert about.

'Gee, I'm real sorry. You should've stopped me prattling on. Once I get started, I don't know when to stop.'

'That's okay,' I said, puzzling out aloud. 'I think I know where Robert was going, except I can't understand why he first drove into town?'

'Oh, I can tell you that, honey. He happened to mention he was having to call at his bank manager's house, to pick up some cash to pay for the painting. He thought seeing it bundles rather than a check, might persuade the owner to sell. Said he'd been delayed on business the day before and couldn't get to the bank in time. So he phoned the boss man – a pal of his he said – faxed him his confirmation, and the guy took the money home with him for your Robert to collect. Trusting sort, your old man.'

This dotted the i's and crossed the t's to what the police had found out. But at last, at long last, I knew where Robert was headed. I got to my feet. I had a short drive ahead of me, and this time I was going to go it alone. No more police or circumstantial evidence. But wherever the trail eventually led to, the obvious place to start was the source. The old house, some two miles into the forest, off the South Carver road.

'Thank you, Miss Slater.'

'Please call me Stella.'

'Thanks, Stella. Sorry for the misunderstanding but the police…'

'You don't have to tell me about *them*, honey,' Stella sympathised. 'If there's ever anything I can do, just pick up the phone. Anytime, day or night, makes no difference.'

That reminded me. 'If I could make a quick call? My cell-phone's flat. Just to tell my neighbour I may be a little late picking up my daughter.'

'Sure, honey,' Stella pointed to the wall-mounted instrument. 'Help yourself.'

- twenty-four -

I was speeding along the South Carver road, only passingly aware of the riot of colours dominating this year's late Fall. Almost the end of November and everywhere around me was still a sea of foliaged trees with their variegated patterns of yellows, browns, greens, reds, oranges and gold.

Instead, my mind was still in a state of shell shock at Stella's bolt out of the blue.

Twelve months ago, I'd at first refused to believe that Robert — steady, dependable, level headed Robert, middle-aged before his time — had acted so out of character and run off with another woman. And not a companionable other woman, someone more suited to his nature, but one of Stella Slater's man-eating reputation. But then I also found out he'd liquidated some of his investments and drawn $200,000 of it out in cash, and been seen with Stella in his car, seemingly driving out of town. Not just *with* her but both acting all comfy together, like they knew each other really well. So, with no other explanation, I'd had no choice but to accept the evidence, circumstantial though it all was.

Now, it seemed I'd been right all along in my belief. Which left me not just back at the beginning, but also with a full year lost into the bargain.

Whatever the cause of Robert's disappearance — even if it *was* tragic — I'd rather know than wonder all my life. If it wasn't too late to unravel the mystery, that is. Realistically, even if there *had* been some clues lying about at the time, it was as good as certain they'd be long gone by now.

But if anything, the mystery had deepened.

Starting with Robert spending $200,000 on a painting as a Thanksgiving gift — *no way*, not unless he'd had it valued first and been told it would one day be worth ten times that as an investment. As for it being a *surprise*, surprise was something Robert just didn't do. Other Thanksgivings there'd been nothing, not even something sensible — art brushes, say. Not that Robert wasn't generous, it's just that he wouldn't have thought about it.

The car-phone rang. I picked it up: 'Damaris Moore.'

'Damaris? I tried your cell-phone but it seems to be switched off.'

There was no mistaking Andrew's voice.

Damn! I should have realised he'd have *his* cellphone with him. Resisting the urge to slam down my receiver, I replied in an icy-cold voice: 'And always will be to you, Andrew. Whatever you want to say, I don't want to hear it.'

'Damaris, please listen.'

'Andrew, I'm driving and in no mood for listening.'

'Don't hang up! I can only guess what cock-and-bull story Alex told you, but just give me a moment to explain—'

'Andrew—'

'Dris!'

That annoyed me. Only Alex called me Dris. I felt my hackles rise.

'One minute; that's all I ask. You owe me that.'

'I owe you sweet eff-a, Andrew. From now on, stay out of my—'

'Dris!' his voice intruded out of the earpiece. It had a menacing edge to it I'd never heard before. What with Alex mentioning his eyes, I realised I'd not known the real Andrew until now. Or I'd been blind to him.

'Don't think you can be rid of me that easily.' It was said in a tone so sinister it frightened me.

'I'm putting my phone down.'

'Dris!' he menaced. *There's no way you're getting away from me! So don't try to—'*

I cut the call, pulled in to the side of the road, and punched the check numbers on my receiver to confirm where he'd phoned from. I was right, it was his cellphone. If Alex had locked him in, he'd be out of the gallery in no time, if he wasn't already.

There's no way you're getting away from me!

The threat in his voice had been real. Was he just trying to scare me? Or had he meant it?

For some reason I had a sudden flash from this morning's dream, the recurring one, of the war-party's slant-eyed leader stalking toward me, intent on raping me, while the other painted braves held me pinned down on the ground—

The flash ended as suddenly as it came. But was my imagined, yet uncanny resemblance between "Snake-eyes" and Andrew, some sort of subliminal warning, a sudden realisation from my subconscious to myself, of how *vindictive* a person Andrew could be? What if he was waiting for me when I got home. What if he tried to—?

I checked myself. Subliminal warnings! These weird dreams I was having must really be getting to me. Any sign of him

175

when I got back, I could always stay in my car, lock the door and call the police.

In the meantime, I still had to find out about Robert, and that was far more important.

I switched off my phone in case Andrew tried to ring me again.

Thanksgiving, I thought. *Thanks for what?*

Forgetting the weird dreams, I'd just made two enemies in less than two hours.

First, Paul Chapman.

And now Andrew.

If it was right that things came in threes, who would be the third?

Up ahead, I could see the dirt road snaking through the trees and into the forest, with a long drive ahead of me before I would reach the old house, standing all on its own on a high bluff, with not another house for miles.

Should I change my mind about going on alone? The owner had seemed genuine, refined and well mannered. But outward appearances could be deceiving.

What if he wasn't all he seemed?

What if *he* was the third?

What if Robert had shown him the two hundred thousand and the old guy had seized the opportunity to steal it all? Blasted Robert with a shotgun, then disposed of his body and car somewhere on the vast estate?

Okay, it was far-fetched, but one never knew these days. What about the crazy and tragic events that kept happening – almost daily it often seemed – right across the country, beamed live into our homes and deemed newsworthy for us to watch, sitting comfortably in our cosy armchairs looking at the horrors unfold on our screens, shaken by it all, but mostly hoping it would never happen to us.

With the house so isolated, was it wise for me, a woman alone, to drive up to the house without protection? No matter how subtle my questions, if the old guy had a screw loose, he could panic and kill me as well.

Still pondering, I glanced at the forest.

Wisps of mist were curling out from between the trees. Wreathing toward me like long ghostly fingers, they encircled the Jeep and slowly engulfed it, fogging-up the windows and knitting thicker and thicker, until everything, countryside, forest track and the South Carver road, was blotted from view.

For the second time that morning, my eyelids became heavy.

I fought it, but to no avail.

Again, I felt my spirit seeming to leave my body, and rising high above the mist...

- twenty-five -

NEW PLIMOTH, NEW ENGLAND, 1627

Once more it was as if I was floating bodiless, looking down on a sea of fog. Then, just as before it slowly lifted, and a new scene was spread before me.

The South Carver road was gone and every patch of farmland, leaving only forest as far as my eyes could see.

Soaring swift and free, my reluctant spirit was carried high above the trees. Passing over New Plimoth, there were many more houses inside the stockade than in the Spring of 1621, all now built substantially of logs, lining two streets laid out crosswise. A group of women were chatting, with children playing around their feet. Others were in their back gardens washing clothes in rainwater barrels or tending their allotments. And two new sailing ships were riding at anchor off the estuary, and from them four boats were being rowed ashore, two ferrying people, the other two stores.

The once open ground outside the palisade was sectioned into small parcels. A handful of men were tilling their various plots. There was a look of peace, permanence, and of growing prosperity about the settlement. Though my last dream was only two hours ago, time in New Plimoth had progressed a number of years.

Interesting though it was, my disembodied spirit was rebelling, crying out to be released from this new hallucination?… trance?…whatever?…and be returned to my own time.

Instead I was drawn against my will into the dark forest. Gliding between the trees, I saw Damaris idly strolling, her apron held out in front of her as she paused to gather wild berries.

Behind her, stalking her from tree to tree, were the six war-painted braves, intent on taking her, but prolonging the moment of capture.

Oh no, please no. Not my recurring dream.

And in the middle of the day this time, not in my sleep.

Where they Nipmuc…? Massachusett…?

Or God forbid, Pequot?

Whichever, leading them would be Snake-eyes, Andrew's lookalike.

The third of my enemies, not the old man up in the house, after all.

As I realised this, my plea was answered. I felt it. Some unseen source was giving me the choice. To return to my own time and banish this nightmare from my life for ever, never to experience it again…

Or enter Damaris and warn her of the danger, but then remain within her body.

The first offered me safety.

The second…?

I already knew what the second offered. And maybe more?

What if it was 1627 – my spirit went cold at the thought – the year Damaris went missing?

Taken prisoner, perhaps?

Or maybe killed?

Except…

Crazy though it seemed, what if the nightmares had been sent to me as pre-omens of what would befall Damaris if I *didn't* warn her? What if after weeks and weeks of experiencing them I was now being given the chance to save her? And if I did put Damaris first, before myself…something I *never* do except for Katy…she would somehow escape, despite the seemingly impossible odds?

Okay, I knew I was talking another dimension here.

Mind boggling, history changing stuff.

But what if?

Yes, the mysterious source seemed to stress…

Damaris *will* live.

But *only* if you warn her.

With it came the prompting that in my dream, it was *my* decision, *my* urging, to make for the beech tree. To seek, however illogical it might be, the security of its spreading branches which somehow seemed to offer hope – a wooded sanctuary made by God, from which help would come.

I knew it was preposterous. How on earth could an inanimate tree protect Damaris from a marauding war-party?

But what if this was the purpose of my nightly dream, all along?

And if so, what if I ignored it?

Again, the old time travel conflict and all its many questions, the sheer hocus-pocus of it all, dominated my struggle.

If this was more than just the recurring dream – if this really *was* for real – what would be *my* fate if I was wrong? If what took place here almost four hundred years back in time still happened, with Damaris still being taken amidst all these tall trees…and raped and killed?

Would my spirit – my soul – my very essence – be forever trapped within her dead body, bound here for all eternity in this untamed forest, never to be returned to my own time?

Never to be reunited with my own body?

Never to return to Katy?

In which case, to hell with it.

Yet, despite all that, could I do nothing? Just leave Damaris here to her destiny?

But maybe this needn't be her destiny, the strange source argued.

Maybe her destiny is in your hands.

I realised it was all too absurd – sci-fi baloney with no basis. Even so, as I watched the war-party creep nearer and nearer to Damaris, what a damnable choice I was being given.

In an agony of indecision, my spirit remained suspended over the scene.

The Man from San Francisco was sitting at his desk, dialling Carlo Vicenze's number, when he suddenly felt faint.

Replacing the phone, he tried to rise to reach the chesterfield, but there was no strength in his legs.

Slumping across the desk, he pillowed his head in his arms, and felt his spirit depart his body and soar up into the ether.

As I entered Damaris's body she gave a shiver, just like before, but nothing more. She'd not realised my presence then, so why should she now? But having found out how to tune into her mind but two hours ago – or was it four hundred years ago? – this time it was instant, no problem.

On a day like this it was good just being alive, she was musing to herself as she strolled between the tall trees of her beloved forest, loving the smell of pine, listening to the songs of the birds, catching glimpses of timid animals scurrying for cover, and hearing the rustling of leaves by creatures scrabbling the undergrowth, searching for food.

It was also good getting away from her father and Elizabeth, especially today, when, following their now regular custom with every ship bringing new settlers from England, they would prepare her to meet each and all of the eligible men on board. And by eligible they meant not only the young and hale ones, they meant unmarried full stop – up to and including even middle-aged. Bachelors, widowers, fat, thin, tall, short, hirsute, bald, made no difference. With her younger sister, Constance, wedded for over a year now, they were *despairing* of Damaris doing the same, and this had been their routine for six years now *(six years, oh hell!, then it was the year 1627!)* praising each man's every conceivable virtue to her, but ignoring whatever their faults. To her father and Elizabeth, all maternally minded, with four-year old Caleb and two-year old Deborah, and pregnant again (with *my* own great etcetera-etcetera "Gran", I swiftly worked it out – how weird) Damaris should by now, at twenty-two, be not only wed, but should also have given them their first grandchild.

But the *only one* who existed for her, was still Samoset.

Six years on (totally oblivious of the war-party creeping up on her) she was still carrying a torch for him, preferring to walk the woods alone, rather than be married to some man she didn't love, not just still thinking of Samoset, but still fantasising about him. The same being laid-down-on-the-grass imaginings as before, his lips meeting hers, and his hands moving over her body.

The wanton minx clearly hadn't changed any since we were last conjoined.

Nor did she have the slightest thought of danger being alone in the forest, because the peace treaty that Massasoit had agreed, back in the April of 1621, with the ailing Governor Carver, and then ratified a month later with his successor, Governor Bradford, had been faithfully kept by both sides, without any real incident.

There'd been an anxious period five years ago, in 1622, when the Powhatans had risen up against the English colony down in Virginia, and gone on a rampage, killing hundreds of settlers. News of this had caused the equally hostile Pequot to put on their warpaint. But, threatened on one boundary by the Wampanoag's treaty with New Plimoth, and on their other by Uncas, who was now known as "The First of the Mohegans", their raiding parties hadn't ventured into Massasoit's territory, killing only "White Men" who'd ventured on to their tribal lands, and burning their farms. But things had now quietened down and after six months of New Plimoth being on its guard, life was back to normal.

As for Damaris, she was quite content – or as content as she could be without Samoset by her side – wandering the forest, preferring to be thinking of him, the only man who had ever stirred her emotions so, heart, mind, soul and body.

So much so *(talk about unrequited love, she had it really bad)* she was still ruing not having fought off her tiredness that night he'd stayed with them, and remaining awake to give herself to him. She'd looked for him the next day when Massassoit and a handful of his chosen braves had entered the palisade to open peace talks with the settlers who had survived the first winter, but Samoset wasn't among them. The negotiations were translated by Squanto, who'd then remained in New Plimoth to help in ways such as how to plant Indian corn.

The right time, according to Squanto, was "when the leaves of the white oak are as large as a mouse's ear". The "how" was by fertilising the crops with rotting herring. There'd been much whispering amongst the remaining Saints about the evils of listening to the words of "a savage in league with Satan" (it seemed that Brother Brewster was still busy, keeping up the good work) but the Strangers had prevailed, and just as well, because the eight acres of English crops had failed, and had it not been for the twenty acres of Indian corn they would not have survived the following harsh winter of 1621-22.

But from Squanto, Damaris had learned that Samoset was married – ever since the age of twenty. An arranged marriage to an Indian princess, daughter of the Sachem of the Eastern Abenaki, and they had a son – now about twelve years old – Samoset's heir as Sagamore of the Morattigons, and also heir, through his mother, to one day be Sachem.

Despite this, her feelings for Samoset hadn't diminished. Married or not, how she wished she'd gone to him that night for her to have an even greater bond to dwell on, rather than just yearnings – the memory of their bodies joining together as one, however that was achieved. (Then despite her desire for grandkids, it seemed Elizabeth *still* hadn't told her. You'd have thought she would, only ten years between them, but maybe she was too embarrassed of her stepdaughter knowing *exactly* what her Dad and she got up to under the sheets at bedtime.)

And so, for six years her love for Samoset had remained her passion. There would never be anyone else for her (of that she was determined, totally so, her whole being). Nor would she ever agree to marrying to some short, bald, corpulent old...

Through her eyes, I saw the beech tree, except she was heading away from it, not for it.

I had to get through to her. Before it was too late.

Look behind you! Look behind you! But keep walking! For God's sake, don't freeze!

Damaris glanced over her shoulder and saw a war-painted brave drop behind a bush out of sight. I felt her panic, her spine, her whole body cold with fear, her mind churning.

War-paint! Had Massasoit broken his treaty? Or (thinking just like me – or maybe it *was* me, voicing *my* fear) was the brave from another tribe? Massachusett...? Nipmuc...? Or even worse...

Pequot!

Having heard all the bloodcurdling accounts of the Pequot, the thought of him being one of them made her legs go weak, but from somewhere she found the strength to keep walking, pretending to not have a care in the world for the brave not to know she'd seen him, giving herself time to think.

Was he alone? But even if he was, he'd be too strong for her — unless she was fortunate enough to grab a broken branch, and strike him a lucky blow.

But if there was more than one, her fate was sealed. Especially as the settlement was too far away for anyone to hear her screams for help.

She hurried her pace. Suddenly they were behind her. And now she knew their number. Six. Faces paint streaked, carrying bows, quivers over their shoulders, and tomahawks and knives in their belts.

Despite knowing it was of no use, that her heavy skirt would hamper her, Damaris ran. The braves padded behind her, keeping pace, playing cat-and-mouse with her, prodding her with arrows and whooping to increase her terror. Raising her skirt and ignoring the thin switches lashing her face, she ran faster, a natural instinct to escape, yet knowing it made no sense. It would be better to turn and face them, and beg them to kill her quickly and not ravish her first.

Except she knew they would. And so she kept running.

They closed in around her, still whooping and prodding her even harder with their arrows.

Look left! Look left!

Damaris looked to her left.

The beech tree! Make for it!

She saw the huge tree, its thickly leaved branches hanging down almost to the floor, and ran toward it, oblivious of the switches lashing her face, eyes fixed only on her goal, tripped over a protruding root and fell to the floor. Her pursuers gave a shriek of triumph and closed around her in a tight circle, then parted for their leader to approach. His paint-streaked face loomed over Damaris, eyes slanted and hooded.

Andrew! Snake-eyes! Despite being prepared for it, my spirit flinched.

So did Damaris, recoiling and twisting away from him. Snake-eyes grabbed her buttoned bodice and tore it open. With a lascivious leer, his eyes riveted on her breasts. The braves dropped to their knees beside her, pulling up her skirt and shifts around her waist, exposing her nakedness, and forcing her legs apart.

Frantically, Damaris clutched at her torn garments, trying to cover herself.

Standing, face exultant astride her, Snake-eyes' hands went to the flap of his buckskin breeches to pull it aside.

Damaris twisted and kicked, releasing her grip on her clothes and scratching at the other braves' faces, determined they'd not take her without a fight, and screaming like a loon. A white hunter could be in the woods nearby and hear her. Or one of her attackers might get angry (like Hawk-face six years before, she flash-backed) and mercifully end her torment with a blow of his tomahawk.

Death was preferable to…

Travelling through the swirling mists of time, he heard her scream.

The next moment he was crouching on a thick branch of the beech tree, peering through the foliage.

She was fighting them like a wild cat, scratching and clawing at their eyes.

Taking an arrow from his quiver, he notched it in his bowstring, took aim, and fired.

A kneeling brave screamed, his eyes opened wide with shock, then he buckled forward, his eyes blank, across Damaris's legs, a long feathered arrow between his shoulder-blades.

Snake-eyes dived behind a tree.

The other four war-painted braves hunched and spun around, their eyes searching the undergrowth. In the silence, there was a thud. One of them clutched at an arrow protruding from his chest and fell glassy-eyed on the ground. Then came another thud, a second fell, an arrow piercing his heart.

Lying flat on the forest floor, Snake-eyes began slithering back, moving from tree to tree.

One of the remaining braves got up and ran. A fourth arrow took him in the neck and went through it. Clutching his throat in a vain attempt to stop his blood from spouting, he staggered and fell. His legs twitched in paroxysmal agony and went still. The last brave sprinted for the protection of a thick oak. A fifth arrow took him in his back, hurling him against it. He slid down its trunk, his nails clawing at the bark.

Snake-eyes leapt up and zig-zagged through the brush, staying low. Another arrow shot through the air, narrowly missing him, and embedded in a tree trunk.

Then Snake-eyes was gone. And silence descended over the forest.

Pulling her feet free from under the dead brave, Damaris grabbed her torn clothes around her. I sensed her fear (reliving her Hawkface trauma again) as she waited for her rescuer to appear. Despite having saved her life, she knew it didn't mean that this one was friendly. He could be from another marauding tribe, a hostile who wanted her for himself.

The leaves of the beech tree rustled. A man's lithe body dropped catlike to the ground. Wearing only a loincloth, a tomahawk and knife in his hide belt, a quiver over his shoulder and clutching his long-bow, there was no mistaking him.

Samoset! Samoset! Again! Oh, thank God!

Picking herself off the floor, and letting go of her bodice, not caring that she was naked to the waist, Damaris ran to him. Wrapping her arms around his waist she clung to him, her bare breasts pressed against him and sobbing with uncontained relief.

Samoset held her, letting her release her fear. Damaris stopped trembling. Tenderly, he brushed her cheek, wiping blood from the thin cuts made by the switches as she fled from her pursuers.

'We must go,' he said. 'The Pequot—'

'Pequot!' Damaris's voice quivered, her fear returning. 'Oh, thank God for Him sending you to rescue me.'

Samoset pulled her bodice around her, tying it together with the torn strips. 'Come. The one who escaped will—'

'Andrew Snake-eyes!' Damaris exclaimed, using without realising it, the name I gave her, and shivering with revulsion as she remembered back.

'If that is how he is called, then he was well named. His eyes are those of a pine serpent. But he will be back with other Pequot, seeking vengeance for those I have killed.'

189

'Why are they on the warpath?' Damaris's voice still trembled.

'Why are Pequot ever on the warpath?' Samoset replied. Crossing to the five bodies, he pulled out his bloodied arrows and returned them to his quiver. 'Because that is how Sassacus prefers it. After his recent victories against your militias, the Pequot believe he has magical powers, and Sassacus encourages the belief. Since he became Sachem, he has doubled their tribal lands and now rules over thirty or more villages, each large enough to have its own Sagamore. In your language Sassacus means 'fierce man'. It describes him well.'

Pulling the sixth arrow from the tree trunk, Samoset pointed deeper into the forest.

'We must go,' he repeated.

'But New Plimoth is that way,' Damaris indicated back the way she'd come.

'So are the Pequot. If we are to lose them, we must first circle around them.'

Samoset turned and headed deeper into the dark forest.

Without hesitation, Damaris ran after him.

- twenty-six -

Samoset's long stride soon opened a gap between him and Damaris.

Half walking, half running, impeded by her homespun skirt, she succeeded in catching him up, but already she was panting. 'Shouldn't we stay on barren ground to hide our path?' she gasped, looking back at the straight furrow they were leaving behind them across the forest floor, that even a child could follow.

'The marks of your bare feet on dry ground,' Samoset said over his shoulder, 'will be as clear to the Pequot as the prints of your shoes on wet earth. When we reach the river I will lay a false trail. Until then, speed is more urgent.'

He strode on with Damaris struggling to keep up, penetrating deeper and deeper into the forest. All around was dark and silent, broken by shafts of sunlight slanting in between the tall trees, casting bright patches across the ground. Startled birds took sudden flight, their flapping wings breaking the stillness.

Weighed down by her skirt, Damaris was finding it harder and harder to keep up. I could sense her legs becoming heavier, every intake of air burning her lungs. Finally, reaching the top of a rise, she was forced to stop to take in gulps of air.

Samoset pointed to a narrow meandering gap in the trees below. 'The river,' he said to encourage her. 'Two arrow flights away.'

'I've no strength left.'

Samoset lifted her over his shoulder as easily as if she was a child, then headed down the slope. Looking at his rippling back from upside down, I could sense Damaris enjoying the strength of him. (I also knew what else she was thinking, even in this perilous situation. She really had a wicked mind, this lookalike ancestor of mine, more 21st century than 17th.)

Reaching the river, he lowered her to the ground. Here in the open, out of the darkness of the forest, the afternoon sun shone down, warming Damaris and giving her new strength to carry on.

Though it was the height of summer the river was full. 'We will go upriver, deeper into the forest,' Samoset pointed, 'to find one of Massasoit's villages, but make the Pequot think we are making for your settlement by making faint prints of your shoes at the water's edge, pointing downriver–'

'But,' Damaris questioned, 'will the Pequot be taken in by–'

'I will also leave signs upriver, but easier to find. They will think these to be a false trail and follow the shoe marks downriver instead.'

(*Double deception*, I thought to myself, intrigued by Samoset's cunning and hoping to hell it worked – with Snake-eyes chasing us, hell-bent, as I knew he would be, on revenge.)

'What kind of signs?' Damaris asked.

'Stones moved under the water. I will also snag threads from your skirt to a tree and hide it in the undergrowth for the Pequot to find. You will find it easier to run without its weight. With Kietitan's help, this will make them think the snags and the stones are to deceive them we have gone upriver. I will also throw one of your shoes far, where it won't be found, but sink the other downriver. They will find it and search east, taking them further and further away from us.'

'But my soles aren't hard enough to run with bare feet.'

Samoset pointed upriver, at the rocky sides stretching flat and wide along both banks. 'Across the smooth stone-face they will be. Where it ends, I will take to the river and carry you for your feet to stay dry, letting you run when we again meet rock.'

'But *your*s will then be wet. If your ploy fails to deceive them they will be able to follow your prints.'

'I will stay in the river and make none.'

Damaris removed her skirt and her shoes.

Keeping to the flat rock floor, warm from the sun under her feet, we rounded the first bend in the river, when we heard a piercing yell from downriver.

Samoset beckoned Damaris to silence. Moments passed, then he whispered. 'They have found your shoe prints.'

Damaris strained her ears but could hear nothing.

(Nor could I. Samoset must have had the senses of a bat.)

There was a another piercing yell.

'And now the threads and the stones.'

Damaris clung to his muscled arm, drawing strength from its steely hardness.

From around the bend came a third piercing yell.

'And where I hid your skirt. We will soon know which way they will choose.'

It seemed an age before he spoke again.

'The main party are going downriver. But three are searching this way. One in the water. And one on each bank.'

I could hear the fear in Damaris's voice as she asked: 'What do we do now?'

'Take to the forest.' Samoset pointed to the sloping rock-face above. 'Kietitan is with us. Here the crag stretches inland beyond the river's edge. Come, before they reach the bend.'

He paused as a fourth yell came from further away. 'The ones searching downstream have found your shoe under the water and calling the three braves to return.'

Cupping a hand to his ear, he listened, then said, 'They are still coming this way.'

Taking her hand, he helped her up the spine and along it, until it ended a short distance from the tree line. Lifting her into his arms, and moving slowly so as not to disturb the twittering birds, he carried her across the open ground, stepping from patch to patch of hard earth not to flatten the grass (having seen films like "Dances with Wolves", I realised what he was doing). Reaching the forest, he lowered her to the floor and pulled her down behind some thick shrubwood.

Peering between the leaves, Damaris saw a war-painted Pequot appear around the bend on our side of the river, flickering eyes slowly searching the flat bedrock.

Wearing buckskin trousers and clutching a tomahawk, a knife in his belt, bow and quiver over his shoulder, she trembled as she recognised him.

'Andrew Snake-eyes!' she whispered.

Samoset clamped his hand over her mouth to silence her.

194

A second brave appeared, wading knee-high in the middle of the river. Then a third on the opposite bank. Both as lithe and as muscular as Snake-eyes.

Searching in a straight line, they reached the spine of rock.

Snake-eyes paused, examined the crag and called to the other two Pequot to wait.

Samoset gripped Damaris's arm, warning her not to move.

Climbing the rock, Snake-eyes crouched down and closely inspected the surface. Then lifted his gaze to the tree line, narrowing his eyes as he looked long and hard at the forest, searching and listening for something not right – birds not singing, a shaking bush.

Damaris shuddered. Samoset tightened his hold on her arm.

The Pequot on the opposite bank gave a sharp bark, and he and the other brave continued upriver. Snake-eyes hesitated, still suspicious, gave a last searching glance (it was as if he was looking right at us and I sensed Damaris's heart miss a beat) then he leapt off the rim of the spine, landing catlike on the bedrock below. All three continued in a line upriver and passed out of sight around the next bend.

Trembling like a leaf, Damaris clung to Samoset. He held her for a moment, then stood up. 'We must go. And pray to Kietitan that Snake-eyes will not return and find our trail.'

Once again they entered the dark forest, and I sensed the panic leaving Damaris as the hope they would escape replaced it.

But as for me, I knew Snake-eyes wouldn't give up.

Dream…regression…whatever, I could hear Andrew's voice on his cellphone, and the venomous threat in his tone:

195

There's no way you're getting away from me.

And I knew that Snake-eyes would be equally remorseless.

Vindictive.

Cruel.

No, he wouldn't give up.

He would return.

Find our trail.

And follow.

- twenty-seven -

It was nearing dusk as we crested a high ridge. Stretched below us was a wooded valley, encompassed by a thickly-timbered circle of hills with two gaps – one in the far distance for a river to enter, and the other – for it to flow out – at the foot of the ridge, just below where we stood. A gap twisting its way between the foliage of the trees showed the river's course.

'It looks just like the Garden of Eden,' said Damaris, her voice betraying her exhaustion, and praying that they were going to rest here, if only for tonight. 'It's as though we are the first to discover it. As if no-one has ever set foot in it before.'

Samoset started down the slope. Following zigzag from tree to tree, Damaris slipped, scraping the soles of her feet. She cried out with pain. Samoset lifted her up, one arm around her lower shoulders, the other under her thighs. Damaris rested her face against his chest.

Reaching the valley floor, Samoset made for the sound of the river. Minutes later, we emerged from the trees into a beautiful glade. Formed by a gentle bend in the river, at its furthest corner was a small waterfall, below it was a large pool ringed by trees, their branches trailing green and copper-coloured leaves on to its surface.

I immediately recognised it.

The gentle falls…the sylvan bend in the river's course…the pool's still waters…the heavy-leafed hanging branches.

It was the scene in which I'd painted Samoset leaning against a large rock, and so exact, it was frightening to see it. All it needed was the outcrop, and I'd really start thinking I was in more than just a dream.

I must have conveyed my shock to Damaris. 'I have the strangest feeling I've been here before,' she whispered. 'And yet I know I haven't.'

'I have the same feeling,' Samoset said, still carrying her. 'Though I have never been in this part of the forest. I also felt it when we first met. As if I knew you. It remained with me the rest of the day. But in the morning when I awoke, it had gone.'

'Which is as it was with me,' Damaris replied.

I sensed her becoming fearful, thinking of Brother Brewster's stentorian expressed opinions to all and sundry, regarding spirit invasions of the body.

'Is it possible that when we are together, we become possessed?' Her voice was tremulous, evincing her dread.

She wasn't alone. Feeling dread, I mean. With Damaris, I knew it was me inside her who recognised the glade. But if Samoset had never seen this valley until today, how come he also thought it looked familiar? And that when they first met, all of six years ago (back in 1621, that is, just keeping a check here on our timescale) he'd felt a similar affinity with Damaris on that occasion, too?

Something really weird was going on.

Please, someone, please wake me up. And return me to my own time.

'Possessed?' Samoset repeated her question.

'By evil spirits?'

Samoset smiled. I wished I could have, but I was too distraught by it all. I waited for his answer, in the hope it might help calm me.

'If we are,' he replied, 'it is by good spirits not evil. Six years ago you were saved from Hawkface. Today a Pequot war party. Now we have been led to this valley of paradise where I have seen food enough to sustain us until it is safe for me to return you to your people.'

'But the Puritans say there are no such things as good spirits. Only bad.'

'Then they speak against their own beliefs. The White Man's religion preaches of a Holy Spirit who is all powerful and all good. And home in Pemaquid, I have heard your seamen pray to guardian angels for protection on their voyage back across the Great Water.'

Though I preferred the idea of good spirits to bad, his answer did little to soothe me, but as I'd already been in this dream, hallucination, regression, whatever, for longer than usual, and my pleas for it to be over weren't being answered, it looked as if there was more yet to come and that reply would have to do for now.

"Your feet are cut and bleeding,' said Samoset, still carrying Damaris, 'and have gathered much dirt.' Crossing to the pool, he lowered her to sit on a rocky mound–

A rocky mound!

The outcrop I'd painted!

Hell, the feeling of resignation hadn't lasted long.

A blink of Damaris's eye, no more.

Oh, God, Kietitan, whatever your name is, please let me wake up still sitting in my Jeep by the side of the South Carver road, for me to get the hell back home to Katy.

Please!

But my plea went unanswered.

From all of his six foot one, Samoset looked down at Damaris.

'I will need one of your underskirts.'

'But that will leave me with only two.'

'The night will be warm,' he promised.

It took Damaris but a split second to cast her constraint aside. As I settled once more into a mood of acceptance (it seemed I had no choice, anyway, whatever it was that I was in, it was pretty clear I was imprisoned in it) I sensed my forebear thinking that here in this hidden valley she was not constrained by Puritan rule. Here, she was as free as a bird to do exactly as she pleased. What's more – and "a pox on Brother Brewster and his dogmatic doctrines" – she'd take off her top one, it was thicker and heavier than the two underneath. They would cling to her body more, for Samoset to notice her.

She'd no sooner decided than she was wriggling out of it. Handing it to Samoset, she sat there, bold as brass, as he tore the underskirt into strips, never taking her eyes off him as he wet them in the pool, then returned to crouch in front of her, gently washing and drying her feet.

All the time she kept glancing at his body, thinking how wonderful it would feel to be that free of clothing, so unrestricted, and yet not feel wicked and full of sin, or be told she was heading for "eternal damnation and the unquenchable fires of everlasting Hell" (Brother's regular Sunday sermon punch-line, seemingly. If only he'd lived in my day and shortened his name from William to "Billy" Brewster, the Puritan bible-basher could have been an instant hit with his own religious slot on Sunday morning TV – and a grand mansion, an ethereal-looking family, each with happy faces all glossed, and a white stretch limo into the bargain to go with it, to drive them to his packed services).

Anyway, it was just as well for Damaris he wasn't there to watch. Even though she was unnumbered as one of his sheep (being of the Sinners faction, not the Saints) he'd still have had something to say about her reactions to Samoset's ministrations, and that was for sure.

His touch was so gentle, almost like a caress, it was giving her the most wonderful butterfly feelings in the pit of her stomach, and the strangest fluttering sensation in – of all places – her loins. She wasn't sure why or what it was all about, but she guessed (and guessed right) that they were being caused by impure thoughts at the sight of Samoset's almost naked body.

As soon as she realised this (and in all fairness to her) she tore her gaze away, reminding herself that Samoset was married, with a son only ten years younger than her, and what she was feeling, what she was thinking, what she was longing to happen, just couldn't be right.

Placing a square of petticoat under her feet, Samoset gently wiped the cuts on her face, then stood up and turned toward the forest.

Damaris reached out for him, fearful at the thought of Snake-eyes and the other Pequot finding her alone. 'Please don't leave me.'

Samoset smiled at her. 'I go to search for healing leaves.'

'But what if Andrew Snake-eyes…?'

Samoset put his hand to his ear for her to listen.

The only sounds to be heard were birds singing. A number took to the air in natural but not startled flight. An inquisitive fawn stepped out of the forest, gazed at us with big brown eyes, then slowly turned away and ambled back into the trees.

'We are alone,' Samoset assured her, and was soon back with a handful of green leaves.

Crushing them between his palms to release their juices, he applied some to her cut feet and bound them with strips of her underskirt. Then, gently smoothing the rest of the juice on her facial scratches, he looked up at the cloudless dark-blue evening sky, dotted with stars, and the light of a full moon rising through the branches of the trees.

'We will rest here two days for your feet to heal. Tonight you must sleep in the open but tomorrow I will make you a wigwam. I carry flints to make fire,' Samoset indicated to a hide pouch tied to his belt, 'but we cannot risk it. Thanks be to Kietitan the grass is dry and there will be no rain. But first, I will find you something to eat.'

Again, he disappeared into the forest, leaving Damaris with conflicting emotions. One was the nagging dread of Snake-eyes finding their trail. But other was that she was on cloud nine being alone with Samoset, already dreaming of sharing his promised wigwam with him, and then…(but no – the very thought of it had made her discard all her earlier vows, and I think it best to let her keep her amoral thoughts to herself). As for me, however, I was wishing the very opposite, still praying to wake up in my Jeep and hightail it back home to Katy, to hold her in my arms and never let her go.

Samoset returned with arms full. 'Roots, tubers, berries,' he explained, placing them on a rock ledge. 'With no fire, this is all we can eat until we find a Wampanoag village.'

Damaris must have been ravenous, because she ate everything Samoset put before her, and gulped down the water he brought her in a hollowed piece of wood which he fashioned with his tomahawk and knife. Draining it, her thoughts once again raced away with her as she placed it on the floor and nerved herself to make the first move.

Samoset stood up. 'I will keep watch while you sleep,' he said. 'Nothing will harm you.'

Damaris watched him walk away through eyes blurred with tears.

Lying down on the hard, grassy floor, she followed the moon as it rose above the trees.

The songbirds were long silent, deer and other daytime animals were hushed. But all around she could hear nocturnal creatures moving about, snuffling for food. In the silvery lunar light she could see them coming out of the trees, and crossing the glade to the pool's edge to drink. Around her, owls were hooting their eerie call, and other preying birds of the night their own peculiar cries.

Drying her eyes, she looked at Samoset's dark outline sitting with his back against a boulder, his profile just distinguishable, impassive as he watched the night-black forest.

'Why are you so far from home? Are you visiting Massasoit?'

'No. I was sent to save you.'

She sat up. 'But how did you know I was in peril?' she asked in astonishment.

'The Great Spirit came to me three days ago in a dream and told me you were in danger.'

(Dream! Now we were all having them. A dream within a dream.)

'Three days ago?' Damaris's voice betrayed even greater surprise. 'But I wasn't even in peril then. And it takes at least five days to get from Pemaquid to Plimoth.'

'Only three days to run.'

'You ran? All that way?'

'For much of it.'

Damaris was robbed of speech. I wasn't surprised. It was a little unusual, to say the least, running three days non-stop, just on the strength of a dream.

(Damaris, I don't know whether I should tell you this, but I think you've maybe got your wish. Okay, I know he's married – and yes, that creates a *big* problem – but he wouldn't run all that way, for all of three days without stopping, unless he's got a thing about you. Surely? But as to what you do about it, that's up to you. I'm not interfering any more – or taking a moral stand – especially in things that have already happened way back in time. I did my bit with the beech tree and now just want to get back to my own time.)

Samoset turned to face her. 'You once saved my life when you stood in front of me and prevented the rescue party from firing. I was bound by honour to save you.'

(Sorry, Damaris. But having come to know Samoset as well as you – historically speaking that is, though in dream time only hours – I should have thought of *noblesse oblige.*)

Her shoulders drooped. She'd been thinking along the same lines as me.

'Your wife? Is she...' her voice caught '...beautiful?'

'Her spirit was taken twelve full moons ago. Her body died from the plague that White Men call smallpox, brought by one your tall-ships which visited my village trading for furs. Half my people also died.'

In the darkness it was impossible for us to see Samoset's expression. But I felt Damaris's heart give a sudden lurch. She hesitated over her next question, which she was almost too afraid to ask.

'Your son?'

'He was safe in the forest, undergoing the rite to prove his manhood.'

'Rite?' Damaris asked, though her mind was already occupied with a wild thought: How would her father and Elizabeth take to her marrying Samoset and going to live with him in his wigwam village in Pemaquid? And being a stepmother to Brave Wolf? All things being equal, the ten years age difference was no more than that between her and Elizabeth.

But Samoset was replying to her question:

'When an Abenaki youth is ready to pass from childhood to manhood, then at the time the leaves of autumn start to fall, he is blindfolded and taken deep into the forest, to where he has never been before. He is given only bow and arrow, knife and tomahawk, with which to hunt for food, and has to live in the forest through the winter, allowed to return to his village only when it is Spring again. Little Wolf survived the trial, and having proved his manhood is now called Brave Wolf. With my brother, Yendaneca, to advise and guide him, he is Chief of the Morrattigon until I return.'

Samoset sounded proud of his son. But Damaris was still thinking what must surely have been an impossible dream in those early settler days of 1627 – if she could but make Samoset fall in love with her, what would Brave Wolf say to having a White Woman as his stepmother, especially as his real mother was a Princess of Abenaki royal blood? Would he accept her?

Her gaze moved to Samoset's face and shoulder-length black hair, then down his lean body reflecting bronze in the moonlight.

She wanted him. Boy, how she wanted him. Wanted him like crazy. I could feel her whole being longing for him, aching to be held in his arms and surrender to him, to let him take her and for her to respond with the strange, overwhelming passion that was coursing through her body. But even though she still didn't know exactly how *"it"* happened, her instinct told her that now was not the right time.

'Goodnight, and thank you for saving me,' she said. Lying down again, she half turned on to her side, stretching out on the grass, one hand under her head as a pillow, her two thin underskirts clinging to her hips and thighs.

'May Kietitan protect you,' Samoset responded.

As for me, being from the present day, I knew more than my precocious ancestor did. From where he was sitting in the shadows, Samoset could make out Damaris's shape in the moonlight, the contours of her body revealed by her two remaining thin under-slips. His tone was quite definitely husky with desire, betraying similar feelings to her own.

Just for a flash (and with the obstacle of him being married now removed) I almost changed my mind not to interfere again, and let her know her instinct was very wrong. Samoset was obviously crazy about her…and hers just for the taking.

But then I decided against.

And let events take their fated and historic course.

- twenty-eight -

Birds singing roused Damaris from her sleep. Underneath her was hard, her body felt stiff and sore. Half awake, she moved her hand and felt grass. Suddenly, she remembered and sat up, eyes now wide open to say "good morning" to Samoset. But he was nowhere to be seen.

Panic struck her. Her eyes swept the glade. There was no sign of him. Then, on the ledge above her she saw fresh fruit. Her fear subsided as she realised he must be nearby.

Searching for him, she saw branches move in a dense thicket across the glade. Realising it was Samoset, she got to her feet. The cuts under her soles no longer smarted. She started walking toward him, but neither was there any discomfort and she changed to running, her young limbs suddenly absent of ache, enjoying the pleasure of being without the weight of her skirt, and only two petticoats to encumber her. Her legs, her body, felt so light, so free, it was as if she was floating inches above the ground. So much so it seemed to her, that just like Samoset she could outrun even the deer. What's more (the young minx thought, slowing back to a walk) she wouldn't tell him in case he decided to move on today – another warm night together in this hidden valley and she might yet succeed in tempting him.

Reaching the thicket, she remembered the cuts to her face. She touched them. All soreness had gone, her skin felt smooth. She made her way between the brushwood to where Samoset was kneeling, his back to her.

'Good morning,' she greeted him.

Samoset looked up, smiled back (her heart raced) and continued with his work. He'd cut down a number of leafed saplings, leaving a cleared circle, and pulled the tops of the perimetry ones together to meet in the centre and bound them with withes. He was now threading the lopped leafy branches between the standing timbers, thickening the sides and domed roof, but leaving a low arched space between two saplings to form an entrance.

It was the wigwam he promised her. Damaris peered inside. Rounded, thickly leafed, it looked inviting, intimate, shutting out the world outside. Adam and Eve must have built something similar, she thought, to share while they were still naked and unashamed, before the serpent intruded their paradise.

Samoset stood up, the bower finished. 'Tonight, you will feel safer here than in the open.'

'And you?'

'I will keep watch.'

Damaris's heart sank. This wasn't what she'd been hoping for. Alone together and Samoset now a free man, she'd envisioned them sharing the bower. Once within its rounded walls, by their very closeness their bodies must surely touch in the darkness. When that happened, the rest would follow, and they would make love, and become as one flesh, thus bonding them irrevocably for life, and for all eternity.

Yet in her hurt, I sensed more than just her hopes of their physical union being dashed, the ache in her heart spread to her very soul. But inexperienced as she was, she might not recognise it as the feeling of being hopelessly in love, whose whole world had just collapsed around her (the way I'd once felt when I walked in on Andrew, still thinking then I was in love with him and my young dreams had also collapsed). She didn't have the mind of a modern woman to get over it, she was vulnerable. The pain she was feeling was intense, my heart went out to her, wishing there was something I could do, something I could convey to her, to help alleviate it.

Fighting back the hot tears filling her eyes, she spun away to return to the river, to be alone with her thoughts. Behind her, she heard Samoset starting to chant, but keeping his voice low. She looked back and saw him kneeling back on his heels, arms upraised to the sky, uttering a song of praise to his God. There was no melody to it, just the same note repeated over and over again, with minor inflexions of tone. But there was no doubting its reverence. Despite the way she was feeling she was mesmerised by this side of him, wanting once more to know more about him and his ways. With this, her determination to win him rose within her again, thinking that the more she knew him, the closer she might get to him, and so reach his affections this way.

The chant ended. Lowering his arms and placing his palms on the ground, Samoset now prayed in English to include her: 'We thank you, Mother Earth, for the food you provide for us, as day follows day. I ask the saplings' forgiveness for cutting them down for shelter, as a place to rest our bodies. We thank you, Mother Earth, from who we were made, for caring for us and giving us life.'

Kissing the ground, he rose to his feet and moved to her side. As they crossed the glade, she asked him: 'Is it part of your religion to apologise for harming even trees?'

'We are taught this from when we are children,' Samoset replied. 'Mother Earth gave us life, and provides food and clothing such as we need to live. It is not only man who deserves respect, but each living thing, who all have their place in creation. And not only respect, but our gratitude when we are forced to use them for our own existence. This is why we ask the saplings' forgiveness for cutting them down, and of every animal we kill for food, and their skin for clothing, and to cover our wigwams. Even the muskrat for taking some of his winter store of roots for sustenance – but never the whole, because the muskrat worked hard in gathering them, and also has a right to survive.'

'Do you apply this thinking to all things?'

'To us, everything exists to serve something else. Everything gives of itself. Everything receives to itself. The Sun gives its light and heat so that the Earth may have life. The Earth gives of itself to the plants, and the trees, and the vegetation, all of which give of themselves to the birds and the animals and all creatures that walk, or crawl, or swim, or fly. They in their turn give of themselves to us, the Human Beings. And when, in our appointed time we die, we give of ourselves back to the Earth, to the dust from which we were formed. Thus does the cycle of nature go on, and the Sacred Circle is complete.'

'Sacred Circle?' Damaris questioned.

'White Man's thinking is square,' Samoset replied. 'His mind is trapped in sharp corners, he cannot see beyond their confines. Take your fur hunters. They kill the beaver, remove its skin for profit, but throw the meat away as if the beaver has no other importance.

'But we think of ourselves as living within circles, with no corners to contain us. From the Great Hoop of the Universe, to the Earth circling the Sun, the Moon circling the Earth, and season following season – to the blood of life circling within our bodies. Thus, we kill the beaver only when we need his fur for clothing in winter, or line the inside of our tepees for warmth. But then we also eat the meat, before returning the beaver's bones to his native stream, for his spirit to live among familiar surroundings. So it is that in this way, by killing only for necessity, not for profit, we affirm the beaver's right to exist until it becomes time for him to serve the Human Beings within the daily circle of life, as it was decreed by the Creator from the very beginning of time.'

How different to us, I sensed Damaris thinking. We just take, without giving anything back, and assume we have a divine right to do so. Theirs was a completely different way of life…

Her mind returned to pondering how could she break his defence barrier? Thinking again whether *she*, a White Woman, by sacrificing *her* way of life, could fit into his Abenaki way of life? Accepted by his people? And even more paramount, by Brave Wolf, his son? And my heart felt for her all over again, she was clearly (if not fully realising it herself) in love with this tribal chief. And in a moment of weakness I felt for myself, too. I'd known only two men, Andrew, and Robert, and been so hurt by the first I'd consigned myself to a life without love with the second. What was it about *me* – that I couldn't find someone to love with the same depth of feeling that Damaris had for Samoset?

She decided to be bold; to throw accepted convention to the wind.

'Many years ago,' she said, 'I saw a Powhatan Princess named Pocahontas, being driven through the streets of London in a coach escorted by mounted soldiers for an audience with our Queen Elizabeth, with people everywhere cheering. Yet, her husband was an English commoner, named John Rolfe. If it was the other way around, and a white woman married, say, an Abenaki Chief, do you think it would take her long to learn their beliefs? And once she had, would his people, and his children – if he had any – accept her as one of them?'

That's the way, I told her, recollecting the husky tone in Samoset's voice last night. Tell him how you feel. Don't wait for him to tell you. Either the guy's naturally shy, or he's just unsure whether a White Woman could fall for a so-called Red Man.

Go for it.

Samoset's eyes searched hers. 'It would depend on the white woman,' he answered. 'Yes, if she could adapt to our ways. But if she could not, she would pine for her previous way of life, and two lives, more if they had children of their own, would be destroyed.'

Damaris returned his gaze. 'But if their love was strong enough,' she insisted, following either my prompting, or it came from her own obduracy, 'and enduring enough, then surely nothing would defeat it?'.

213

'Provided there was tolerance and understanding on both sides,' Samoset replied, adding with just the hint of a smile: 'And with a little help from the gods.'

(To me, that seemed – using modern parlance – to be a cop-out answer. But not being too experienced myself, first falling, blinker-visioned, for a sexual predator, then marrying on the rebound his very opposite, maybe I wasn't as worldly-wise as I thought, and had read Samoset all wrong?)

They reached the river. 'And now, a swim,' he said, changing the conversation.

But whether deliberately or not, I couldn't decide. Nor could Damaris, her heart sinking again. And not just hers, but mine as well, feeling for her from the very bottom of it.

Lying on the grass bank, Damaris waited for Samoset to surface.

She had counted up to ninety and he was still under the water. The pool was deep, but she could make out his shape moving slowly along the bottom. Suddenly he shot upwards, breaking the surface with such an explosive surge, his body rose out to his waist, then he sank back to his shoulders, remaining afloat as if standing in the water just by moving his legs. Raising an arm he brandished a large silver fish in his hand, live and struggling to get free. Expressing his pleasure with another rare smile, he said, 'It will still be here later,' and tossed it back into the pool, where it curved and dived straight down into its dark depths.

Bringing his legs to the surface in one smooth movement – like the dolphins Damaris had seen when crossing the Atlantic – he bent his face half under the water and sped to the bank, cupped hands stretching in front of him, feet churning the surface behind. Reaching the bank, he flipped over on to his back and rested on his elbows, his lower half still in the water and the rest of his muscled torso, from rippled stomach up, gleaming wet and bronze in the sunshine, with drops falling from his black hair.

(Talk about Tarzan in the flesh! Forget the falling-in-love-with-him-at-first-sight side of things, it was no wonder Damaris had lustful feelings for him, too.)

Still tied to his belt, the front of his loincloth floated to the surface.

'Teach me to swim,' Damaris said, standing up and removing her top underskirt. Letting it fall to the grass, she stepped out of it. 'It's to dry myself with afterwards,' she explained. (Which was no doubt true except – if my suspicion was right – it wasn't her real reason for removing it. Now left wearing only her thinnest underskirt, and nothing underneath, she was up to something and it wasn't difficult to guess what.)

She entered the pool. With the sun shining hot out of a cloudless blue sky, it was much colder than she'd expected. It was even colder as she waded towards where Samoset was already waiting in water up to his waist.

Waist-high for Samoset was rib-high for Damaris, but moving her hands on the surface for balance she reached him, and fell against his wet chest. He put his arms around her to hold her steady. The sensation was more wonderful than she'd imagined. There was some-thing so…(sensual, I prompted her, as she searched for words to describe the feeling)…so physically pleasurable about the smoothness that water gave to their touching flesh, she instinctively held him tight for him to feel her firm breasts pressed against him.

But again to her disappointment, he pulled away. Although he was a hunk to look at, and a veritable terror with a bow and arrow (a real-life Abenaki "Robin Hood") he was clearly unsure of himself with women. His wife was probably the only one he'd ever been with (and I don't mean just stepping out together, holding hands in the moonlight on a warm Indian Summer's night).

Once more feeling rejected, Damaris pretended to persevere until she was able to swim a few strokes, then made the excuse of being cold to get out of the water.

And suddenly, exactly as she'd hoped it would happen, it happened.

Giving Samoset her hand to help her to the river's bank, he just stood gazing at her.

Aware – as she knew it would when she removed her top one – that her thin bodice and slip were clinging wet and transparent to her body, showing her breasts, and also her triangle of dark hair at her groin (which Elizabeth had seemingly avoided explaining, other than it was "a part of growing into womanhood", but it was enough for Damaris to have guessed, and guessed right, that it might help tempt Samoset). Seeing how he was looking at her, she made no move to cover herself with her hands.

Emboldened, she had no feeling of shyness, and as for what to do next, she didn't even think about it. Lowering the underskirt, and letting it fall to the ground, she stepped out of it and placed her arms around Samoset's neck, and pressed her naked body against his.

Heart thudding, Damaris waited for him to respond. Feeling something move against her lower stomach, she looked down and at last she knew how it happened between a man and a woman. Almost hurting from a sudden feeling of urgency burning in her loins, she raised her face to his and whispered. 'Do your people kiss?'

Samoset's face came down on hers. Their lips slowly met and softly searched each other's fullness, then he gently lowered her on to the grass.

'I have never lain with a man before,' she said, her voice still a whisper.

'I will be gentle,' he promised.

And he was.

The caressing of his fingers was so feathery, that by the time he finally entered her, she was near to frenzy. She had to dig her teeth into his shoulders to stop herself from screaming. Suddenly she arched her body upwards – then cried out, and collapsed on to warm earth.

Samoset moved to lie beside her and held her tight, kissing her hair.

Damaris turned her face and looked into his.

'That was beautiful,' she whispered, then peeped down at his loincloth.

'Doesn't it happen to you as well?' she hesitated, suddenly shy.

He smiled at her, his face full of tenderness. 'I wanted to pleasure you.'

'But doesn't it happen to a man?' she persisted

'When I let it.'

'So you prevented it deliberately?'

'Yes.'

'Then it will happen tonight in our bower,' Damaris said, becoming all bold again.

And it did.

Not the first time. Because Samoset once more stayed in control of himself and made sure he "pleasured" her again.

But Damaris had worked it out in her head the second time. Making him lie on his back while she knelt across him, then lowering herself on to him (which just went to show that it was all instinctive, even for a young Elizabethan maiden like Damaris, and nothing to do with which century we're born in, not even our so-called "liberated woman" age) and they both came together, then fell back in each other's arms.

'Well,' Damaris asked, after recovering, and still bold. 'Did I pleasure you?'

'Very much so,' Samoset answered, not moving.

'Good,' Damaris said, snuggling up to him. Placing her head on his shoulder, she curled her arm across his chest and her leg over his thighs. The light of the moon shone in through gaps in the leaves, illuminating the bower, making it feel warm and restful, and letting her see Samoset's face.

'According to Morattigon law,' she asked, watching his reaction, 'does it mean we are now married?'

'Again, very much so,' Samoset replied with a smile.

'Good,' Damaris repeated, holding him even tighter. 'That means we can sleep the night together and wake up in each other's arms. 'R'wy'n dy garu di,' she said, looking up at him. 'That's Welsh for "I love you".'

'Welsh?'

'Yes. I'm Welsh, a Celt, not English. Just like the Abenaki, the Wampanoag, the Nipmuc, the Massachusett, are different tribes of the Algonquian race, so too the Welsh, the Scots and the Irish, are all parts of the Celtic race. With one thing in common. We are all vassals of the English, who are a separate people made up of many races. It's a story of conquest that goes back over a thousand years. It may already be too late for the Wampanoag, but I will tell it to you in the hope it will help others of your tribes from losing their lands.'

'Then tell me,' said Samoset, looking down at her.

'In the morning,' said Damaris. It was a husband-and-wife phrase and, liking the sound of it, she smiled, almost purring. Sighing with contentment, she closed her eyes.

As for me, I had mixed emotions.

Feeling pleased for Damaris that she had found, and now won, what seemed to be her true love. And also, if from here she went to live with Samoset in Pemaquid, the mystery of her disappearance had been solved.

But uppermost in my thoughts was: How long was I going to stay inside her body? How long had I already been here? If it *was* a dream, it was by far the longest I'd had. Starting from yesterday in Damaris's time, and with night closing in again, it was almost *two days*. Yet if it was still today in *my* 21st century time, I would presumably wake out it – and the sooner the better, leaving Damaris and Samoset to get on with their own lives – but more essentially, letting me return to mine, even though I might be late getting back to Katy.

However, if it was *more* than a dream – I dreaded to think of it being a regression, but it needed to be faced – had my spirit been inside Damaris's body for the same length of time as all that happened to her, 400 years ago, to unfold?

Two days!

If so, then what was happening to Katy back in today's time?

Would I *ever* get back to her?

Or was I stuck inside Damaris's body for the rest of *her* life?

However long, or however short, that might be.

Or *had been*, seventeenth century-wise…

The full story of her disappearance hadn't yet been revealed. Stuck out here in the dark forest, with Snake-Eyes and his two war-painted Pequot braves maybe still pursuing her and Samoset, and the nearest of Massasoit's villages perhaps still a day's trek away, what if there was more still to come?

Leading from this, another dread thought struck me.

That of my comatose body sitting in my Jeep on the South Carver road.

For maybe the best part of two whole days now.

Or had someone found it?

If so, what if I couldn't be revived?

Oh, Katy. Katy.

- twenty-nine -

Damaris was awoken by a hand over her mouth.

I sensed her heart race. She opened her eyes. It was Samoset.

Placing a finger to her lips, he whispered: 'Pequot.'

'Snake-eyes?' she whispered back, knowing the answer. As with Adam and Eve, the serpent had intruded their Garden of Eden. Staying silent, Samoset picked up his longbow and arrows and left the bower. Quickly putting on her underskirt, Damaris crawled outside.

Dawn was lighting the sky. Making no sound, Samoset was moving like a stalking cat between the saplings. He paused, listened, and glided on his stomach across the ground to the thicket's edge, notched an arrow in his bow and peered out.

Watching him through Damaris's eyes, my own heart (as it were) was also racing. I'd been right. Just like Andrew, Snake-eyes hadn't given up. Except, returning to my fears of last night, Snake-eyes was more lethal, and although I knew, historically, that Samoset must survive to another day, nothing more was known of Damaris. If today, in her time, was the tragic end of her in real time (and how sad it would be, I'd so much come to like her) it had already happened some four hundred years ago, and there was *nothing* I could do to change it.

But with me trapped inside her, what would happen to me?

As I was panicking, Samoset took aim…and fired. From the river came a strangled cry, then silence.

Damaris inched to his side. The body of a Pequot brave was floating, face down, in the pool, the surrounding water stained red with his blood.

'Andrew Snake-eyes?' she whispered, begging him to confirm it.

'No,' he whispered back. 'He and the other Pequot are hiding in the forest. I will draw them out.' And before she could stop him, he stood to his feet and strode out into the open, and stood there, daring them to come to him.

Snake-eyes and the third Pequot burst out of the trees, tomahawks raised and howling defiance. But Snake-eyes was holding back, letting the other rush on. He stopped running, notched an arrow in his bow and fired.

As if seeing it in some sort of slow motion, Damaris watched the arrow's flight through the air. It entered Samoset's stomach and passed through him, its point emerging from his back. Clutching at it, he fell to his knees on the ground.

For what, in time, was a split second, but seemed endless, Damaris looked at her lover, blood coming from his wound, torn between wanting to rush out and hold him, or try to make her escape.

Stay hidden!, I screamed at her, my instinct for my own self-preservation dictating to me and to hell with not interfering with history. *Crawl away! Follow the river upstream, try to reach a Wampanoag village. Do you hear me? Slim though it is, it's your — our — only hope.*

But I should have known better. My plea fell on deaf ears.

Regardless of the leading Pequot, now no more than a hundred yards away, Damaris ran out of the thicket and knelt beside Samoset. She held him to her, ignoring his blood issuing over her.

You stupid mad fool! I don't know how, but Samoset is going to survive this. You should have put yourself first. Forgotten about loving the guy. By being so frigging selfless you've gone and sealed your own fate. And maybe mine, too.

'Back!' Samoset gasped, pushing Damaris aside.

Face creased in pain, he pulled two arrows from his quiver. Dropping one on the ground, he strung the other, took swift aim, and fired. Tomahawk raised for the kill, the Pequot kept running, the arrow in his heart, then fell almost at Samoset's feet.

Snake-eyes gave a shriek of anger and threw himself flat to the ground. Slithering like a serpent through the grass, he snaked towards Samoset.

Samoset notched his remaining shaft, aimed and released it. It whistled past Snake-eyes, missing him by only inches. With a rasp of breath, Samoset fell slowly to the floor, pushing the arrow even further through his stomach. Twitching in death agonies, he flopped over on to his back, snapping the protruding shaft. Arms outstretched, he lay there unmoving, eyes wide open, staring lifeless into space.

Dead! Samoset's dead! What the frigging hell's going on here! This can't be right! It can't be! Samoset lived on! Wake up! Wake up! What about Damaris! What about ME!

Damaris remained frozen in fear, kneeling beside Samoset's body.

Oh, God forbid! Was *this* the answer to Damaris Hopkins' disappearance? Taken by Snake-Eyes? Violated, then to die here? Or be forced to go with him to his Pequot village and a life of slavery? Never more to be heard of?

With me, ME, still trapped inside her body?
Four hundred years back in time.
And Katy! What about Katy?

With an exultant yell, Snake-eyes got to his feet. Gripping his tomahawk, he advanced warily across the glade. His serpentine eyes, as he neared us, were filled with triumph.

Damaris was terrified. Reading her thoughts, she was filled with dread knowing she'd be subjected to the most unimaginable defilement before she died. Grabbing Samoset's knife from his belt, she raised it to plunge it into her heart. Snake-eyes leapt to stop her.

Samoset came alive.

Snatching the knife from Damaris's hand, he slashed up with it at Snake-eyes' stomach. The tomahawk dropped from Snake-eyes' grasp. He clutched at the gaping wound and tried to staunch the gushing blood. His eyes glazed over and he fell dead on the red-stained earth.

Damaris clutched Samoset's head to her breast. 'Don't die! Please don't die!'

Samoset tried to smile, then his face grimaced as a spasm of pain shot through his body. He clutched the feathered end of the arrow still in his stomach, 'Do not cry,' he whispered: 'Time ordained by Kietitan for spirit to depart body.' He winced as another spasm hit him.

Digging his heels into the ground, he tried to push himself back toward the pool, but his strength was gone.

'Help reach river,' he begged Damaris, his voice getting fainter. 'Great Spirit good. Give me honour. Make grave for warrior's resting place, next to where I fall in last battle.'

Damaris put her hands under his armpits and raised his upper body. They inched their way over the grass. Reaching a hollow alongside the pool, Samoset rolled into it and lay there, gazing up at the trees and the sky beyond. Damaris knelt at the edge of the hollow tears streaming down her face.

Samoset looked up at her. 'No sorrow,' he said, his voice so weak she had to strain to hear him. 'There is no death for spirit, only a passing on. Father is Creator. Earth is Mother. Body made from her clay. Return to her bosom. Cover with rocks...'

His voice faded. It seemed he had gone. Then he somehow managed to whisper: 'Find two thistledown...Blow over resting place...Love not die. Live forever.'

His eyes clouded over. He fought it off for one final effort. His eyes searched hers. 'Say prayer for spirit...Ri gari di...That right?'

Damaris nodded, too choked to say 'yes'.

Samoset smiled up at her. Then he closed his eyes.

And died.

He wasn't supposed to. It didn't fit in with history.

Nevertheless, here in this sylvan glade, their "Garden of Eden", Samoset died.

Leaving Damaris alive, kneeling there.

Breaking her heart.

Then she forced herself to her feet, to honour her last promise to him.

It took her almost the whole day to carry rocks from the river and cover his body well.

Standing by his graveside, tears again flowing down her face, she recited parts of what sounded like a Biblical psalm, one she thought best expressed his belief, interspersed with phrases from his own prayer to Kietitan.

'O Lord – Kietitan – how excellent is Thy name in all the Earth, who hast set Thy glory above the heavens. When I consider the heavens and the stars that Thou hast ordained; what is Man that Thou art mindful of Him? For Thou hast put all things in his care. The animals that walk in the forest, the fowl of the air, the fish in the waters, such as we need to eat and provide our clothing. The Earth you gave to us is our Mother. She cares for us. She is part of our body. The mountains and the hills are our backbone. The gullies and creeks are our heart veins. By whatever name You are known, how excellent it is in all the Earth.'

Raising her face to the sky, she opened her arms wide.

'How deep is your mercy, O Great Spirit. I commit Samoset's soul into Mother Earth's safe keeping. Amen.'

Eyes brimming with tears, she turned to leave the valley.

It was then I thought I heard a cry coming from Samoset's resting-place.

It was a man's voice crying out in desperation:

Don't leave me here! Don't leave me! The thistledown! Don't forget the thistledown!

I didn't know whether I was imagining it. In all honesty, I was too concerned about my own plight to care. This dream had been one hell of a dream and I was still locked inside it, wanting to be free, back to being myself, Damaris Moore, once again. But some strange force, either from inside myself, or from outside, was compelling me not to ignore it, and I conveyed the plea to my forebear:

The thistledown! I reminded her. *Don't forget the thistledown!*

Without questioning the impulse, Damaris turned back and began searching. And wonder of wonders (this is how it works in dreams, orchids can bloom in winter) although it was not the season for them, she miraculously found two inside the bower, two stems growing from the very earth where she and Samoset had lain together – as if created from their combined seed and specially nurtured by God, their round, white, fluffy downs intertwined

Returning to Samoset's grave and raising both downs to her lips, Damaris kissed them and blew. Like a gentle snowfall the white fluffs filled the air, and from nowhere came a soft wind that carried them upwards and upwards into the sky, until they were out of sight.

How strange! I thought. I'd played the puffball game many times as a child, counting the number of puffs it took to waft all the pieces away as being the hour of the day. Except the seeds had always drifted to the ground. Never before had I seen them float up into the air and disappear.

Kneeling, Damaris kissed one of the rocks she'd placed over Samoset's body.

'Keep him to Thy bosom,' she whispered, 'Goodbye on Earth, my love. Until we meet again, in the spirit-world.'

I suddenly remembered a Native American saying I'd once read and liked so much I'd memorised the words. I gave them to Damaris and she repeated them out loud.

I buried him in that valley of winding waters.
I love that land more than all the rest of the world.
A woman who cannot love her lover's grave
is worse than an animal.

And then she walked away.

Reaching the top of the rise she gave one last look at her valley of paradise and, barefoot, wearing only a bodice and underskirt, headed down the other side.

All alone now, she once again entered the dark forest.

It was then that for me everything went suddenly black.

- thirty -

PLYMOUTH, MA, TODAY

I came to slowly, as if ascending from a black bottomless pit.

From a far distance I could hear my own voice echoing the words: *I buried him in that valley of winding waters...valley of winding waters. A woman who cannot love her lover's grave is worse than an animal...*

The dark curtain of my closed eyelids became gradually lighter, from ebony to purple, then to dark red, a hazy crimson, finally a yellowy orange, telling me I'd reached the surface and was into the daylight. I forced my eyes open, fearful of what I might see.

I was back in my driver's seat by the side of the South Carver road. Around me, the strange mist was lifting, wraith-like gray tentacles releasing their clinging hold on my parked Jeep as if reluctant to do so, and writhing back into the dark forest.

I looked at my watch and saw I'd been out for no more than ten minutes. Ten minutes! But what I'd just experienced had lasted two days! What's more it had felt like two days.

Pulling my sheepskin coat tight around me for comfort, nestling into its fleecy lining and raising the collar high over my ears, I sank back into my seat, my mind feeling too numb to even think about this latest experience.

Peering through the murk as the fog receded, the dirt track for which I'd been making emerged more and more into view, curving between the trees as it followed the course of the river. Then the road reached the top of a rise and continued over the brow, deeper into the forest and out of sight.

Seeing the dark trees again, and despite the sheepskin's thickness, I suddenly came all over shivery, my flesh felt icy cold. Then I thought: *This is stupid.* Realistic though it again was, it was only a *dream*, for goodness sake.

Out for only ten minutes. It had to be. There was no other explanation.

The same recurring dream I'd been having for weeks now. Except that this time it had continued for longer, two days longer than before – but only in my illusory imagination, that was all.

I nerved myself to relive the events of it, wondering whether, in some mysterious way, and for some unknown reason, I'd been given...been given what? A sort of revelation maybe? Of events that actually happened there, some four hundred years back in time?

Damaris's same desperate flight through the forest, chased by the Pequot war-party – but this time being rescued by Samoset, then pursued and finding the hidden valley. But most of all I thought of their passionate love for each other, and the terrible way Snake-eyes, with his implacable will for vengeance, had ended it before it had a chance to flourish.

Except there was nothing, either in history or my family's records, for any of it. As for Samoset, he quite obviously hadn't been killed there, in the hidden valley. The two parcels of tribal land he'd sold, one in that same year, 1627, and the second twenty-five years later, in 1653, were proof of that. He had lived to a ripe old age.

In which case, I said (sternly) to myself, pull yourself together, forget the "revelation" nonsense. The dreams were of my own creation. Somewhat lifelike maybe, tangible even, but nothing more. But my inner self wouldn't accept this. There *had* to be a reason for them, it argued back. Messages from my subconscious perhaps, caused by my own longings, my physical desires, kept imprisoned for too many years, but which, no longer able to contain them, were now coming to the surface? And not just my physical desires, but wanting to be loved...?

Oh, yes, I felt my heart responding, to be loved.

More than anything, to be loved...

I took a grip of myself and forced my mind back to the dream, not wanting to dwell on this thought.

What, to repeat, were they all about?

What did the uncanny likeness between Andrew and Snake-eyes mean?

If my psyche was trying to reinforce my indifference for him, it needn't bother. I cared nothing for him anymore, and certainly didn't feel the need to give him a gory death in a dream. As for Samoset again, how did he get into all this. I didn't (sadly) know anyone of his description to fall for. Nor, back once again to cloud-cuckoo-land, if they were *more* than dreams, was I wanting to start musing on all the time travelling craziness of them, or–

Screw it, I told myself, it was all getting too complicated. All the "maybes", "perhapses", the "buts", the "what ifs".

Except…

If it *was* more than a dream (and putting aside that history contradicted it) what *did* happen to my namesake after I left her cresting the rise and leaving her valley of paradise behind her, and once again entering the dark forest?

It was still the year she went missing in history, so she obviously didn't make it back to New Plimoth. One conclusion was that she was caught by the main Pequot war-party – but no, I didn't want to dwell on that, its scenario was too horrible to contemplate, and besides (not wanting to think of all the terrible images that sprang from such a thought) whatever happened to her it was four centuries ago, and there was nothing I could do to change it now.

So, Damaris Moore, just pack it in – all this pointless questioning. Instead, get up to the house, question the owner about Robert, then get home as fast as you can to Katy and that turkey that's still waiting to be cooked. And if the old man can't throw any light on Robert's disappearance, it will keep until tomorrow – it will have to anyway, the police won't be interested today, not on Thanksgiving.

As for the weird dreams, the deaths of Samoset and Snake-eyes must *surely* have ended them, especially, thank goodness, the recurring–

My mind went back to earlier this morning (in today's time I mean, just to confirm I mean now, not earlier this morning back in 1627) and the weals on my face in the mirror after waking up from last night's dream. I felt them. My skin felt smooth. I looked in my rear mirror, and could hardly believe my eyes. No trace! Nothing! Completely gone!

The memory of Samoset applying his healing leaves to Damaris's face came into my mind, but I instantly rejected it. *No way* was I going to consider having regressed. As for the weals, they would just have to remain an enigma. A form of ethereal stigmata maybe? Caused by some sort of post-hypnotic suggestion, resulting from a vivid delirium…an extremely vivid delirium…which had mysteriously appeared on my face this morning, but had now…I wrestled to provide some rational explanation but couldn't and was forced to leave it…had now just as mysteriously disappeared?

I realised this was no answer. That all I was doing was evading the issue. But with no logical reason for it, how *else* could I deal with it? And stay sane?

But then I remembered the voice coming from Samoset's grave, *Don't leave me here! Don't forget the thistledown!* And Samoset's words: 'Blow over resting place…Love not die. Live forever.'

In my mind's eye, I again saw the two fluffy white balls spiralling upwards and upwards into the heavens, until they vanished from sight.

What was that all about?

- thirty-one -

Lying stretched out on the chesterfield, The Man from San Francisco could see Snake-eyes running at him, tomahawk raised, as clearly as if he was watching a film. Except he hadn't been a viewer, he'd been one of the main cast. Though he felt no pain, he could still see the arrow piercing Samoset's stomach and blood coming from the wound.

Getting to his feet, he crossed to a wall-mounted mirror in a gilt frame. Pulling up his shirt, he saw a faint red mark on his stomach and another in his back. He stared at them, not sure what he'd expected to see. In truth, nothing, but at least they weren't real wounds, and that was a relief. Whatever it was that was happening to him recently, at least his whole being wasn't being taken over by a four hundred year old ancestral spirit from the past.

Tucking his shirt back into his jeans, he lay back on the chesterfield, hands behind his head, legs sprawled out, and brooded.

There just had to be a reason for these dreams, they were so...so damned realistic. But whatever it was, they'd so far accomplished only one thing. Maybe ruined the next few years of his life. From today on, until his memory of Damaris had faded, he'd be comparing every woman-friend to her, and he doubted he'd ever find anyone to equal her.

Not that there hadn't been other women in his life. There had been. Gorgeous women. Passionate women. Fun women. But no one really singular, no one to make him fall in love with, or to want to share his life with. No one like the Damaris of his dreams, warm, caring, beautiful, brave, resilient, and with a capacity for fun – as well as being a natural lover – all combined in the one person. All, and more, that a man could possibly wish for in a woman.

He could still see her green eyes looking all impish at him – well, okay, at Samoset, but Samoset's eyes had been his. As for when she emerged from the pool, leaving nothing to the imagination, the only word to describe her was "Wow!". And that was inadequate. Way, way short of the mark. Had he ever have thought about it, he would never have expected a woman in the 17th century to have a figure like that. No modern day young woman could have bettered it. That was for sure. And the face, and the smile to go with it.

Getting to his feet, he crossed to the bookshelves. Resting against them was a canvas. Removing the dust sheet, he stared at the scene.

Painted the week before setting off in Samoset III, it resembled nothing he'd ever done before; every brush stroke seemingly guided by Kietitan. The sylvan glade. The waterfall rippling down rocks. The rocky outcrop. The pool surrounded by trees, its leafed branches trailing over the surface of the water...

Emerging nymph-like out of it, wearing nothing more than a filmy covering, clinging to her all wet and transparent, was a nubile young woman.

There was no doubt about it.

It was Damaris.

Her face, her eyes, her body.

Everything, including her cute, dark bobbed hair.

Was it this painting that was causing his dreams, influencing what she looked like?

Or had they emanated from the same source? Kietitan?

If so, what was Kietitan's purpose?

He'd give anything to know the answer.

Except go through another dream.

Especially not after this last one when, for goodness only knew how many nightmarish hours following the departure of Samoset's soul from the body, his own 21st century spirit had seemed to be trapped inside it as Damaris, despite all his screaming, had placed more and more stones on him, until she and all else were blacked out.

Hearing her prayer to Kietitan, he'd really panicked at the thought of being left there, and his own body being found comatose across his desk, incapable of being revived.

As she finished her prayer and turned away to leave, he made one last desperate attempt, shrieking up through the stones: *Don't leave me here! Don't leave me! The thistledown! Don't forget the thistledown!*

Except his voice was silent and he'd thought he was trapped there forever.

But then his spirit was suddenly free, floating beside her, watching the gossamer stems dancing on the soft breeze, then spiralling upwards, carried by a sudden gentle wind, higher and higher into the blue sky until they were out of sight. In that same moment, as his spirit ascended to meet the swirling mists of time, he'd heard her last words.

I buried him in that valley of winding waters…

The next second he was coming-to in his chair, his head still pillowed on his folded arms on the desk, with everything that happened in the dream imprinted in his mind, and thanking Kietitan for Damaris doing as Samoset had asked her and blowing–

The thistledown!

Maybe that held the answer to it all?

He should be phoning Carlo to find out how things were progressing.

But this was far more important.

He searched the shelves, selected a leather bound book, and returned to the chesterfield.

But before starting to read, he looked across at the painting hanging up on the wall above the fireplace. Begun by an ancestor, it had been passed down his family from generation to generation.

Unlike Jennie Brownscombe's famous work – showing Damaris Hopkins with her father and stepmother – the scene had her next to Samoset, a wicked smile on her face at being so reunited with her lover. Surrounding them were most of Samoset's direct descendants, right up to the present day.

Now, three hundred and more years after the painting was first started, only one outlined face remained unfinished, waiting for Kietitan to guide the chosen painter's brush.

Until the dreams had started, he'd had no doubts that the outline was waiting for him.

But maybe the thistledown said different.

He turned to the book. On its brown leather spine, in gold letters, was the title:

American Indian Beliefs and Myths.

Searching through its pages, he found the section, *North Eastern Woodlands.*

And began to read.

- thirty-two -

I eased the Jeep from the side of the road and accelerated slowly. I knew I should be thinking of Robert. Instead, my mind's eye was still filled with the events of my last dream.

It was all a jumble. Being chased by Snake-eyes…or a "Freudian" Andrew. Rescued by Samoset. The final conflict in the glade with him sacrificing himself to save Damaris. Her covering his body with stones. The desperate voice emanating from Samoset's grave. And finally, blowing the thistledown.

I turned into the dirt road and entered the forest.

From where had I got this thistledown part of my dream? If it was a Native American custom, I'd never heard of it.

So, where had that come from?

And what – if anything – did it mean?

I could still hear Samoset's last whispered words to Damaris:

"Blow over resting place. Love not die. Live forever."

And still feel the strange breeze which had come from nowhere, to carry them upwards, ever upwards, into the blue sky, until they disappeared from sight.

Like something out of a fairy tale.

But then, so many other things about the dream had been unreal.

Samoset giving up his life for Damaris.

And Damaris running out of hiding to die with her lover instead of trying to escape.

That had been completely irrational, crazy even.

No man would ever make me act like that.

Okay, so maybe Samoset had been something special, not only handsome (with the physique of a Greek god) and a fantastic lover, he'd also been caring and gentle as well. In other words – fuelled by tales of heroes of legend and fiction: Lancelot, d'Artagnan, and all the rest of them – a man who lived only in women's dreams. And watching tear-jerking films like "Sleepless in Seattle", in which Tom Hanks wanting someone "special" in his life, was answered in the shape of Meg Ryan; and when they finally get to hold hands on top of the Empire State Building, they both instantly knew it was "magic". Written in the stars. And as if to confirm it, silvery stardust descends from the heavens.

Except that such happy endings existed only in myth and Hollywood films, or in flights of the imagination.

But in the real world…never.

The real world was full of Andrew Hartfords and Paul Chapmans.

With one thing predominating their minds.

Or Roberts, concerned with their creature comforts and their careers.

But if men like Samoset had ever existed – the Samoset of my dreams, that is – they didn't anymore. They'd died out long ago.

As I turned off the South Carver road and started up the long wooded hill – the twisting forest track still following the descending course of the river, tumbling white crested down over rocks and around boulders toward me – my thoughts changed to the First Thanksgiving painting that, for some strange reason, Robert had driven here to buy.

Maybe it was just a coincidence but, instead of having Damaris standing with her father and my great-great, etcetera-etcetera grandmother, Elizabeth – as Jennie Brownscombe had painted the historic event – the artist had shown her next to Samoset.

If Damaris and Samoset had been lovers only in my imagination, why had the unknown painter shown them together, with Damaris leaning into Samoset, a secret smile on her face lighting up her eyes, and his arm encircling her shoulders, all caring and protective.

Why?

My mind went back to my dream, remembering Damaris emerging from the water, her slip clinging wet to her body, and Samoset taking her in his arms and lowering her on to the grass.

If only!

If only he'd been around today.

And my dream not a dream, but for real.

- thirty-three -

Surrounded by lawns dotted with shrubs, small trees, and the occasional tall oak and beech, the house looked down on a valley encircled by a horseshoe of hills, with a river meandering through it.

Closing the front door behind him, he headed down the gravelled drive, making for the dirt road and the glade, still brooding over what he'd just read.

Was it a belief, or was it a myth?

Being part Abenaki, he knew from his own experience that in the spiritual world of the Red Man, such things – far beyond the credibility of the White Man – were not only accepted but actually happened.

To the Native American, dreams had an importance unimaginable to the White Man. They were revelations from the spirits – a help, or a warning meant to direct the dreamer's actions – which were sent to the supplicants in their sleep, during which he or she lost all sense of the present, not knowing whether it was night or day, or in which time span they were in.

In the words of the writer of the passage he'd just read, the White Man once understood this, but no more, because "God no longer spoke to him as He once did in the Bible, using such means as a burning bush, because if He tried, the White Man wouldn't believe it anyway, but explain it away as science fiction".

But to the so called "Indian", everything that was experienced, everything that was felt, everything that was brought before his or her consciousness – either visibly, or audibly, emotionally, or manifested some other way, especially in dreams – was sufficient indication in itself of its existence, the actuality of a supernatural power, a voltage, for want of a better word, with which the Native American believed the universe to be charged.

To the Indian, the lifeline between themselves and Kietitan and this mystical power, was the sky-bridge of space which existed between Earth and Heaven. This was why the soaring eagle was regarded as the grandest of all birds, because the eagle's world was the air which was also the breath of life; and it was only up there, high in the sky, gliding free above the earth, that communication was made with the ones above, the spirits known to the Indian as other-than-human, those who possessed magical and supernatural forces.

So it was with the thistledown Samoset had released into the air, to be carried up into the heavens, to fulfil its predestined purpose.

But only provided one believed.

With "white" blood also running in his veins, did *he* believe?

Or was he just hoping it could be true?

Maybe standing alongside Samoset's grave in silent contemplation might help to influence his mind?

- thirty-four -

Approaching the brow of a hill, my mind was still with my last dream.

Just for a moment assuming that Damaris and Samoset *had* been lovers in real life–

Cresting the hill, I slammed on my brakes.

And stared down at the valley stretched below me, recognising it.

Oh no! I felt my heart suddenly going ten to the dozen. Oh, no! Please, no!

But there was no mistaking the meandering gap between the trees and, in the distance, the glade formed by the bend in the river, the gentle waterfall, and the pool where Damaris had divested herself of all but one thin layer of clothing, hoping it would tempt Samoset to make love to her.

I tried to stop myself trembling. The last time I'd driven this road, searching for scenes to paint, was over a year ago, before my dreams had started. Not being a landscape artist, I'd taken no more notice of it – other than appreciating its beauty – than other scenic spots along the road.

Now, staring at it from the exact same spot where Damaris and Samoset had crested this ridge and looked down on their 'valley of paradise', it felt as if I was about to drive four hundred years back in time.

Still staring at it, I thought: *This has got to be the strangest, the weirdest Thanksgiving, that anyone, anywhere, has ever spent...*

In an effort to pull myself together, I dragged my gaze away from the scene and on to the gearshift.

Forward?

Or Reverse?

Reverse was my first, second and third choice.

But then: Don't be a damned fool, I told myself. For some reason, probably its splendour, I must have stored the scene in my subconscious when I drove this road before, and then not only used it in the twee painting…but had also recalled it in my last dream.

Nothing more to it than that.

Cross with myself for my irrational behaviour, I shifted the stick into "Drive" and drove over the crest of the hill.

Down into the valley of my dreams.

Behind me, I heard Harrison yawn as he began waking up.

As I neared the glade, Harrison barked, letting me know he needed a tree.

I couldn't tell him to wait, poor dog, he'd suffered enough, asleep for almost two hours, so I drove onto the verge. In the rear mirror, Harrison's shaggy head was slanted to one side, regarding me with plaintive eyes, making me feel guilty.

'Okay, Harry,' I said ruffling his thick coat and opening my door. 'Out you get.'

I ducked to one side as he came crashing over my seat and leapt out on to the dirt road, tumbling over in the process. Righting himself, he took a few prancing steps to recover his feet. Finding he still had his spring, he shot-off, tail flying, for the nearest tree, and cocked his leg up against it. Then, his dime spent, he started leaping about and darting in and out of the timbers, inviting me to play. Anxious to continue on to the house, I used my firm voice: 'Here, Harrison! Here!'

He looked at me as if to say: 'What! Back in the Jeep? You must be joking!' and bounded off, pausing to see if I was following. Seeing me still seated he came tearing back, springing high in the air as the mood took him, then dashing around the Jeep and back into the woods, happy to be alive again.

I gave up. Besides, he deserved to stretch his legs. As for questioning the old man about Robert, another ten minutes wouldn't make much difference.

Here, where the river made its wide sweeping bend, the drive veered off into the forest, making for the house on the ridge, its ancient gabled roof visible above the tops of the trees. Heading away from it, I threaded a path between the pines, a carpet of fallen cones beneath my feet.

Through the trees was a clearing, and at its edge a long, log cabin. Approaching it, I saw it had it a low doorway made of animal skins. Harrison was still charging about and so, with a half interest, I walked to it. By their weathered look, the logs appeared to be centuries old, yet wonderfully preserved. As for the hut, its design was that of a North Eastern Woodlands tribal longhouse, roughly forty feet long, twenty wide, with smoke holes spaced at intervals along its arched roofline – except they were covered, not open. The lodge had clearly been intended for ceremonial purposes, not for practical use.

Behind me, Harrison barked as he tore up. But then he saw the longhouse. Skidding to a halt, he stared at it, staying absolutely still. Then, inclining his head to one side, he fixed his eyes on it. Next and even stranger, he bounded to the doorway, tail furiously wagging, barked, then flopped down on the ground and lay there with his paws over his ears...

A trick that Robert had taught him.

Feeling somewhat unnerved by it, I commanded: 'Here, Harry. Here.'

He ignored me. Not that that was unusual, but for some reason, not helped by the silence of the forest, his actions seemed distinctly eerie.

Stifling my fear, I crossed to the lodge, moved the pelt door to one side and entered.

Without windows, it was dim inside. There was just sufficient light to see. In the middle of the dirt floor was a circle of firestones forming a hearth, with a spit for roasting meat. The absence of soot showed it had never been used and I realised, with some unease, that I was inside a spirit-house, erected purely for the souls of the departed to enjoy for eternity.

Confirming this, split-log platforms encircled the fireplace, two feet above the floor, and lined with animal skins for the spirits to sleep warm in winter, with their feet to the fire. All around the lodge was a shelf lined with silver and copper artefacts. And tomahawks, knives, axes, and bows and arrows for them to hunt with in their happy hunting-ground; platters for their food, carved drinking bowls, and tubular pipes-of-peace made of bone, fashioned with effigies of animals. And tobacco, which – I'd once read – "Indians" did not smoke for pleasure. To them, the plant was sacred, holy – nurtured and grown under ceremonial rites. When the pipe was lit, the smoke carried upwards, uniting the powers of Earth and Sky and creating an unbreakable and ever-lasting link between the physical and the spiritual worlds.

Painted around the cabin, starting from the doorway, and then along its four walls, was one continuous mural of a river. At its source, the artist had written *Madamascontee* – the Abenaki name for the river now known as *Damariscotta* – then depicted its winding course, with scenes of seasonal activities along its length: wigwam villages with men, women and children living in peace, swimming, canoeing, playing lacrosse, naked infants frolicking, women planting and harvesting corn, men in coracles fishing, winter scenes of seal-hunting. And reaching the mouth of the river where it entered the sea, the artist had written the river's name as *Damariscote...*

Cote, not cotta. That made sense. The Abenaki had been more influenced by the French than the English. And in French it meant "coast". *Cote de Damaris:* "The coast of Damaris". When Maine had fallen into British hands, some colonial Jack-in-office must not only have changed the name from French, but had either misspelt the word, or had used *cotta* instead of *terra* – the nit-wit.

But having just solved the setting of my last dream when I crested the hill, it again posed the question.

If Damaris had gone missing in the year 1627, why had the river been renamed after her?

Where, if anywhere, could I find the answer? Having been with her through all her trials – dreamwise or otherwise – for two whole days, to the point that she now felt almost a part of me, I just had to know. It might also help to solve the mystery of her disappearance. I felt I at least owed her that. Even more, maybe *this* was the purpose of my dreams? To discover the truth of it. And once I had, they would stop.

Following this thought, a mural of a river that flowed hundreds of miles away from here, on what was once Abenaki tribal land, suggested that this lodge was *also* Abenaki.

But if so, what was an Abenaki spirit-house doing on Wampanoag tribal land?

To make it more disturbing: although the lodge was centuries old, the mural was recent – a couple of years old at the most – painted by someone with considerable, if raw, talent.

Furthermore, by using the name *Damariscote* for the river (rather than the official one on the maps) it suggested – well, okay, *sort* of suggested – that whoever the artist was, he or she believed Damaris and Samoset to be more than strangers who, according to history, had met only once, when the young Morattigon chief walked into New Plimoth on that momentous day in 1621, to set up the historic peace talks between Massasoit and the First Forefathers.

It was all very puzzling.

But it was also starting to feel creepy, being inside a spirit-house, and I quickly exited, glad to be back in the open.

Harrison was lying on the same spot, his paws still over his ears.

'Harrison! Heel!' I commanded, heading back for the Jeep, and the old man I'd come here to question. Whining in

249

protest, Harry didn't even turn his head. His refusal to budge was so...so weird, especially on top of the unease I'd felt inside the lodge, I decided to let him run after me when I started the engine, thinking that he'd be left behind if he didn't end his nonsense pretty damned smart.

It was then I felt a strange, almost magnetic pull coming through the trees from the glade beyond them.

Pocketing my keys, and without even resisting it – which I seemed unable to anyway – I headed through the forest toward it.

- thirty-five -

I threaded my way through the trees and emerged into the open, and stood rooted to the spot.

The bend in the river, the peaceful glade, the trees with their leafy branches trailing on the surface of the still pool, the small waterfall tumbling into it, and the rocky outcrop, it was all so uncannily as in my last dream I was literally petrified.

I desperately tried telling myself there had to be a logical explanation for it, that maybe I'd seen a photograph of it somewhere – or perhaps a painting hanging up on the wall of the old man's study the previous time I drove here – and had unconsciously stored it in my mind.

But knowing I hadn't – hadn't done either of them, seen a photograph or a painting of it – I remained paralysed.

The only difference between dream and reality, was that there was no sign of any thicket where Samoset had built Damaris a bower. In its place were the gray headstones of what I assumed was the estate's own cemetery, showing above a white paling fence. But standing there all alone, with a dark forest behind me and the vivid memory of Snake-eyes bursting out of it, tomahawk raised for the kill, a burial ground was no pacifier.

Why I didn't turn tail and run back to the Jeep, then burn my tyres getting away from the damned valley, never again to return, I'll never know.

But slowly, drawing deep breaths to slow down my heart rate, the reasoning side of my nature again took hold of me, restoring my more familiar self and reminding me what I was here for, to question the old man about Robert. I started — well, more like forced myself — to cross the glade, even though I would have to pass the cemetery on the way up to the house on the hill, its gabled roof just visible above the treetops.

It was a beautiful November day, the sky was mostly blue, with cottony clumps of white cloud drifting slowly by, and the sun almost directly overhead. But the air was keen. I raised my sheepskin collar around my face and held it under my chin with my right hand, pushing the left deep inside my pocket.

Reaching the graveyard, and with my common sense partly restored, I gritted my teeth and chose to take the short way through it rather than go around it.

The gate creaked as I opened it. In the silence it sounded spooky. Again, I felt my spine prickle, but made myself walk on, glancing at the headstones as I did so.

All made of rough-hewn granite, their differing styles, the varying degrees of weathering in their lettering, showed the cemetery to be centuries-old. As for their inscriptions, they were simply worded, recording only the deceased's names and their years of birth and death. The oldest was for a Samuel Wolf, 1640-1702, and his wife Rebecca, 1651-1710. The next also bore the same surname. And the next. In fact, so did they all, until just under a hundred years ago when an "e" had been added, making it "Wolfe".

Wolfe? I thought. *Wolfe? I've heard that name recently.*

I reached the last and newest stone. Also made of granite, the brief inscription read:

SEAN WOLFE
Aged 33

Sean Wolfe! The around-the-world-yachtsman from the TV documentary I saw earlier this morning. I thought the white-fenced burial place looked familiar. So this was where he'd lived. And one day, when the old gentleman died, it may even have been his inheritance. He must have been crazy, giving up all this to put his life at risk circumnavigating the globe. For what? Fame?

And yet, I had to admire his restless spirit that had made him forsake twentieth century security to pit himself against the ocean's wild forces. *How sad*, I thought, to have survived his boat capsizing, then be found after months alone on a remote Pacific island, only to die of a stupid heart attack the very same day he arrived home.

A man's voice from behind made me almost leap out of my skin.

'It feels weird reading my name on a gravestone.'

I stood stock-still, the shock of a voice coming from nowhere freezing my limbs.

'Maybe I should have brought myself some flowers?' it added.

I spun around.

But the shock of someone creeping up on me, especially in a lonely graveyard, all alone out in the back of beyond, was nothing compared to seeing the man's face.

My knees buckled under me.

Had he not caught me, I would have fallen to the ground.

'Samoset!'

I repeated it, my startled exclamation now no more than a whisper.

'Samoset?'

- thirty-six -

He regarded me in silence, searching my face as if he couldn't believe I was for real.

'That would make me four hundred years old,' he finally said. 'Do I look that ancient?' His probing gaze changed to a wry smile. 'In which case, living on coconuts and fish for the last fourteen months clearly couldn't have agreed with me.'

Feeling my heart beating twenty to the dozen, and my legs trembling too much to run, I stepped back, forcing him to release his grip on my arms and tried to regain my composure. All alone with a stranger miles away from anywhere (ignoring the fact that I'd mysteriously met him, or at least his double, only a short while ago in some inexplicable dream) it could turn out to be my only saving hope.

At the same time, I was cross with myself for being so stupid as to call him Samoset.

But apart from him creeping up on me like that, when I turned and saw his face…! well, I could be forgiven my mistake. Especially as my recent dream was still with me, so graphic, so pictorial, that it and reality were still tangled up in my mind.

Subduing my fear, I returned his gaze.

Despite being prepared for it, and the evidence of my own eyes, I still couldn't believe how alike he was to Samoset. The Samoset of my dreams, that is. Other than his hair being fair, he was my imagination's twin…

To my surprise, and despite my fraught situation, I found myself assessing him.

Face, physique, tall, broad-shouldered, lean-hipped... except... there was something about him that confined it to a physical resemblance. His appeal was distinctly individual, in a blue-eyed, devil-may-care sort of way–

Another perturbing thought hit me.

How could I have imagined the Samoset of my dreams to look *exactly* like him? Other than a brief shot of him on this morning's documentary, I'd never set eyes on the man bef–

It was then I realised the significance of what he'd said.

'*Your* name?' A shiver ran up my spine. I glanced nervously at the headstone. 'Are you telling me that you're...that you're...?'

I hesitated, too spooked to finish the question.

'Sean Wolfe?' he completed it for me. 'Yes, that's me.'

My eyes flashed back to the lettering. 'But you're...'

'Dead?' he again finished it for me. 'It's rather a long story. For the moment, let's just say, quoting Mark Twain, that the reports of my demise are greatly exaggerated.'

This was definitely the moment for hysteria. All alone in a graveyard surrounded by gray headstones, with someone claiming to be the dead man buried under one of them, who was the exact double of a man that I'd – in a sort of vicarious way – just made love to and seen killed by an arrow, covered with stones and read a prayer over, then if not hysteria, my heart should certainly have missed some beats. A hell of a lot of beats. And then some.

Instead, I flared up, angry at his levity. 'Exaggerated! I'm reading a headstone that says different and you creep up on me like that! You damned near scared the pants off me.'

'In that case, I'll try again,' he grinned, raising his hands in fake defense when he saw the expression on my face. 'Sorry, I shouldn't be so flippant. It's one of my very few faults. But the prospect was too tempting to pass up on. Apology accepted?'

In that moment, for some inexplicable reason – maybe it was his infectious smile, maybe the twinkle in his blue eyes, maybe the openness of his face, or maybe the warmth he exuded – all fear dissipated from my body. I know I should have stayed spooked – after all, I could have been talking to, of all things, a ghost – nevertheless, I didn't. My legs regained their strength, the shiver in my spine went away, and I found myself smiling back at him.

'Not for the fright. I'm still shaking.' I extended my right hand to show him. 'But it was my fault for giving you the line – a slip of the tongue. I was going to say near scared me to death, but being in a graveyard I changed it, though not very cleverly.'

He was suddenly serious. 'You're right. It was a stupid thing to do, coming up behind you like that, without warning. What say we start again?'

He offered his hand in introduction. 'Sean Wolfe. And you are…?'

Although I was still bewildered, I nevertheless felt myself responding. Sean? He was probably of Irish stock. He definitely had the confidence of someone full of the Gaelic charm, who if he'd not kissed the blarney-stone, didn't need to. Even more, he was certainly dishy, what with (yes, I know I'm repeating myself) his blue eyes and crooked, almost impudent grin. He had it all and he knew it. Still, if he *was* Sean Wolfe (and there was no doubting he looked like the picture I'd seen of him on TV, except it hadn't in any way done him justice) then I wished this year's Thanksgiving would stop giving me all these damn shocks, one after another, after another.

'I'm not yet convinced,' I persisted. 'Before giving you my name, if you're who you say you are, how come you're declared dead? And not just dead, but buried. I heard all about you on Channel Fifteen this morning.'

'As I said a moment ago,' he replied (I loved his voice, deep, and yes, sexy), 'it's a long story. If you'd like to hear it, I'd be happy to tell it. Provided,' he said, again holding out his hand, 'you first humour me by answering who I'm talking to?'

I hesitated, then thought "what the hell!" and accepted his hand, then hastily withdrew mine as I felt it tingle. Talk about the Tom-Meg magic in "Sleepless in Seattle", I bet it was nothing compared to what I felt, but I didn't want to be sidetracked from what I was here for. To find out about Robert.

'Damaris.' I said. 'Damaris Moore.'

There was a pause before he replied. 'Now why aren't I surprised?' he said, looking deep into my eyes again, and then – of all the damn cheek! – glancing up my figure as well, all the way from toes back to my face. 'Damaris? I'd have bet my last cent on it. The resemblance is uncanny.'

'Resemblance?' A moment ago, when I was thinking how dishy he was, I was glad I'd chosen my tight sweater and close-fitting jeans. Like most women, I wasn't averse to being admired. But with his searching look prompting a sudden flashback of Damaris emerging as good as stark naked from the pool, and Samoset gazing at her (or us? – especially with our figures being so alike) and now his near doppelganger giving me a similar all-over, maybe I should have worn something looser, less shape-hugging?

'To Damaris Hopkins,' he replied. 'She was one of the Mayflower–'

This sudden change of conversation was instantly disconcerting. I cut him short.

'Yes, I know exactly who Damaris Hopkins is – I mean *was*,' I hastily corrected myself. 'It so happens I'm descended from her. Or rather, Stephen Hopkins, her father. But as to any resemblance, I've no idea what she looked like. What's more, I don't know how you reckon you do?'

He hesitated as if, rather than answer my question he wanted to say something more, but then changed his mind.

'From a Thanksgiving painting in my study. She's next to Samoset, who also happens to be *my* ancestor. Some coincidence, don't you think, with you calling me by his name when you first saw me. Out of curiosity, you wouldn't like to tell me why you did…?'

He paused for me to explain, but I remained silent.

'No?' he raised quizzical eyebrows. 'Okay, but the likeness between you is uncanny. Other than the colour of your hair you're alike as two proverbial peas in a pod…except you have a certain *je ne sais quoi* all of your own, that makes you–'

He cut off in mid-sentence as the coldness in my right hand made me remove it from my sheepskin collar and pocket it, replacing it with my left.

I saw him look at my wedding ring, which I still wore. Just from his expression, I could almost read his thoughts. Something like: Married! Hell! Just my luck!

As for me, I had burning questions of my own. Samoset's descendant! Today was getting weirder and weirder. And how come I'd based the loinclothed man in the strange painting I'd finished a week ago, on someone I'd never met before – and whose face I'd glimpsed for the first time only a few hours ago on TV? And who, as I now knew, was also blood related to my ancestor's lover–

His voice intruded on my thoughts. 'But passing over your resemblance for the moment,' he seemed to have recovered his composure, 'I'm still curious why you called me Samoset?'

'The similarity,' I said, feeling pushed into giving him some explanation and coming up with the first answer to enter my head. 'You're also alike as your proverbial pea in a pod.'

'Is that so? And how would you know that?'

'Like you with Damaris,' I rejoined, swiftly remembering how he'd replied to my similar question. 'To the Samoset in the same painting. I was shown it a year ago when I turned into here searching for scenes to sketch, thinking it was just a forest track, but met the owner–'

'Did you, now?'

'Yes, rather a likeable old gentleman. After explaining my mistake, he invited me to see the painting, and gave me permission to return whenever I wanted. I take it you're related?'

'Unfortunately, he's my uncle, but I have to disagree with you about him being likeable. He's an old rogue, without scruples, and nothing but trouble, all of which I have to sort out. Most times he drives me crazy, but then he does have his good moments, I suppose. Otherwise I could have him shot by now and got away with it by pleading justifiable homicide.'

He paused. 'But you must have a fantastic memory – retaining Samoset's face for over a year, even if you studied the painting for some time. Yet can't recollect Damaris, your own kin, who's not only next to him, but is also – which you must surely have noticed – the very image of you?'

Again I was made to think quickly. 'There were so many faces to look at, I didn't realise she was in it, not until you told me,' I said hurriedly, yet knowing it was a lame excuse. 'As for Samoset,' I rushed on before he could challenge me on it, 'I've also seen a photo of his statue in some books I have on Native American history–'

'There isn't one.'

'Sorry?'

'There is no statue of Samoset. Anywhere. Not as far as I know.'

Getting more and more flustered, I tried to redeem my crass mistake. 'Then it must have been Massasoit's statue, the one in Plymouth.'

'On the grounds that if you've seen one Indian, you've seen them all?'

'No!' I objected angrily. 'What I meant was…' I paused, not knowing what to say next.

He hesitated, clearly wanting to still pursue me for answers, but then, as if realising my embarrassment, returned to my explanation for my previous visit here, a year ago.

'Scenes to sketch?' he quizzed. 'As in being an artist?'

Although still flustered, I appreciated his thoughtfulness.

'Just an amateur,' I said, deciding it wasn't the time or place for personal divulgences. 'What about you? Sailing around the world isn't exactly an everyday pastime. What made you attempt it?'

'Money.' He gave a wry smile. 'Or rather the lack of it. This damned estate eats it up. I had a joint publishing-television documentary deal which was supposed to solve it—'

'Supposed to?'

'Unfortunately, my on-board camera was destroyed by the storm. And the book contract date's expired. My agent's trying to renegotiate that side of it. He's even working on it today, on Thanksgiving.'

I was okay again, in possession of myself, and seized on this opening to return to one of my earlier questions, and even further away from all the inexplicable Samoset and Damaris things that had been going on here over the last few minutes or so. 'Well,' I forced myself to smile, 'if he succeeds, I hope you include a chapter telling how it's possible for you to be both alive and buried. If I remember rightly, you were going to explain.'

Sean returned my smile, though somewhat wryly. 'As I said earlier, it's rather—'

'A long story. Yes, you've already mentioned that. But maybe you can manage it now?'

'Sure,' he said, glancing toward the dirt road. 'I don't see your car?'

'It's back there, through the trees. Past the spirit-lodge.'

'You've seen that as well? That's an interesting story in itself. But look, it's getting cold out here. What would you say to walking back to the house with me, instead of driving? It's not far and I can light a fire in my study, then tell you all you want to know over a drink of coffee. Or something stronger if you'd prefer?'

I hesitated. By now I'd accepted he was Sean Wolfe, despite the headstone. But I knew nothing about him. Well, almost nothing. I knew he could be damned infuriating. Yet, there was something reassuring about him. And I still wanted to ask the old man, Sean's uncle, about Robert.

'Thanks, a hot drink would be just the ticket.'

It was only as we were making our way between the graves, that I made the connection to a proprietary remark he'd just made.

'Your study?' I asked over my shoulder. 'You mean you own all this?' I swept my arm over the surrounding forest.

'Plus the bank mortgage and back taxes,' he replied, rather dryly. 'And to make matters worse, I was stupid enough to give Uncle William power-of-attorney while I was gone. But then, when I got back and discovered the unholy mess he's created — well, I somehow doubt you'd believe me if I told you.'

He moved alongside me and took hold of my elbow. It felt nice — more than nice, being truthful. 'A slight diversion,' he explained, holding the creaky gate open for me and making for the river instead. 'Prepare yourself, I think you're going to be surprised.'

No I won't, I thought, and stopped walking, forcing him to do the same. *It may have been only a dream, but I'm not going anywhere near that damn pool; and certainly not with you, Sean*

Wolfe. Especially with me (okay, Damaris, but it still *felt* as if it was me) *walking out of it in the all-together, and Samoset — looking just like you — seeing me, her, that way...*

'Two minutes?' Sean asked.

'It's not that,' I said. 'Your hot drink's got priority.'

'Humour me,' he insisted.

Oh, hell! No point making a fuss. It's only a pool.

I gave in and turned with him toward it.

As we crossed the glade, it was even more uncannily as in my last experience. The bend in the river, the gentle waterfall, the leafy hanging trees, the still pool. It was all...so weird, so frightening, my heart started racing again, and I was finding it difficult to breathe.

Anxious for Sean not to notice I disengaged my arm and, without thinking, made straight for the spot where the hollow was in my dream, where the Samoset of my imagination had chosen for his last resting place.

I wasn't expecting it to be there...except it was!

And not just the hollow, but the rocks filling it, exactly as Damaris had placed them.

Oh, no, it couldn't be, I felt myself panicking.

It just couldn't. It was only a dream.

Sean came alongside me. 'You've been here before?' His voice was hesitant, as if seeking confirmation rather than asking a question.

'Sorry?' I replied, my mind leagues away.

'Samoset's grave.'

I spun around. 'Oh, no! You're joking! Surely? Samoset can't possibly be buried here?'

'Sure he is. With you walking right up to it, I thought you knew.'

'But Samoset's buried in Bristol, Maine? There may not be a statue of him, but his grave's there for all to see. Please tell me he is?' I was almost begging. 'Or at least tell me I'm in the middle of some other dream.'

Sean's eyes bore into mine, as if penetrating deep down into my soul. Again, he seemed about to say something more, but again changed his mind.

'That's another Samoset,' he said. 'History got it wrong.' He held my elbow again but this time I was too numb to feel it. 'Come and see for yourself, but don't forget I warned you. And hold on tight. You're in for another surprise.'

As he led me around the grave, Sean said. 'It's so peaceful here, it reminds me of an old Algonquian saying: *I buried him in that valley of winding waters. I love that place more than anywhere else in the world...*' He paused.

Feeling as if I was losing my grip on reality, I was on the tip of adding: *'A woman who does not love her lover's grave...'* but his peculiar break made me catch myself in time.

Instead, I looked at the plaque attached to one of the stones. It read:

SAMOSET and DAMARIS
Reunited for all Eternity

I stared at it, too paralysed to move. Not only Samoset, but Damaris too! *She* was buried here? With her lover? This was becoming worse than a dream, I was back in nightmare land. What the hell was going on here...?

Yet, despite all the many emotions coursing through me, and the seeming evidence that all I'd experienced today had been something far more than just a dream, a part of my mind was still able to rationalise.

How had Damaris died? Had she met the Pequot war party on her way back through the forest? If so, who had found her body? And even more than that, who had known that she and Samoset were lovers and buried her here, honouring her last, parting words at his graveside: 'Goodbye on Earth, my love; until we meet again in the spirit-world', thereby granting her heart's wish to be buried here with him, in their "garden of paradise"?

Still in a state of shock, I glanced at the pool, and the leafy branches draping the spot where Samoset and Damaris had become one body, one flesh.

In my mind's eye, I could see Damaris standing alone by the rocky graveside built with her own hands, and above her the cloud-flecked blue sky filled with dancing snowy-white stems, ascending upwards and upwards into the heavens.

'That's why Samoset begged her to blow the thistledown,' I whispered. 'So they could be together for all eternity.'

Sean turned me to face him. Again his eyes pierced mine.

'Thistledown?' he said. 'There's only one way you could have known about that. I began wondering the moment I first saw you, and even more, a second ago, when you asked to be in some other dream.'

He unbuttoned his shirt, revealing a faint red mark on his muscled stomach. 'That's where Snake-eyes' arrow entered. There's another on my back.' His hand moved to my cheeks and gently brushed them. 'But your own cuts have healed beautifully.'

Not moving away from his touch, I gazed back at him, no longer fearful.

His eyes searched mine for confirmation.

A long moment passed between us, the silence fraught as I wondered whether to tell him it was me and not Damaris who'd heard his voice calling up for her to blow the thistledown, and wrestling with my longing to throw myself into his arms.

I wanted to…Oh, how I wanted to…

But again the damned rational side of me took over.

Despite the evidence of the wound on his body, and the memory of the weals on my face, my mind still couldn't accept even the *idea* that all that had happened to me, from my very first nightmare, could be regressions, flights back to another age, not dreams.

I just couldn't.

It was contrary to every known law relating to time and space.

But perhaps, by asking Sean more questions, I could come up with a *logical* explanation.

Pulling away from him and trying to sound in control of myself, I said: 'You're right, it is cold. I think I'd prefer the something stronger.'

- thirty-seven -

Both wrapt in our own thoughts, we had let the silence continue too long, and now there was an awkwardness between us as we walked up the track through the trees to Sean's home.

Of all my many emotions, I was mostly feeling embarrassed – embarrassed to the extent of inwardly blushing, which was unlike me.

But there was a world of difference between giving oneself willingly to a man, and discovering that the man walking alongside me – a stranger – had, in some inexplicable way, been a party to the same dream (or whatever) and therefore a witness to all that happened.

I was no longer upset about the nakedness. After all, it was Damaris's body Sean had seen, not mine. But he'd known then – and more vitally, knew at this very moment – that Damaris was an innocent Elizabethan maiden when she'd given herself to Samoset – well maybe not *quite* so innocent knowing her wicked thoughts, but certainly without experience in making love. And so, as we walked shoulder to shoulder together, what if he was thinking it could have been *my* prompting that had made her so knowing and so skilled?

Which just wasn't true. Okay, I admit I *had* learned a few things from Andrew during my student days back in New York, but Damaris was a natural, everything she'd done had come from her own instinct. I couldn't speak for Sean, but when Samoset lowered her down to the ground and I knew what was going to happen, I was wishing I was miles away (preferably back in my own time, with Katy) or at the very least able to stay detached – and for Damaris to have closed her eyes, and thus mine, too. But realising this didn't help, not one bit. I remained all discomfited, feeling that my secret self had been trespassed upon and violated.

Still wordless, we began climbing the hill. Here the branches of the trees met high above us creating a high-vaulted arch. Leaves were twirling slowly to the ground like large speckled snowflakes. And the sunlight was breaking through the intertwined roof, creating shafts of gossamer rainbows along its length, and criss-crossing the earth with dark and bright patterns.

It was Sean who breached the impasse.

'Aren't you celebrating Thanksgiving?' he asked.

'Not until this evening,' I replied, looking straight ahead through the tree-pillared tunnel and beyond, to the house skylining the ridge. 'With time on my hands, I decided to drive here and take some shots of the leaves falling, before picking up Katy on the way home.'

'Katy?'

'My daughter. She's spending the morning with a friend.'

'And how old is Katy?'

'Seven. I guess I'm a little over-protective about her, but fifteen months ago she was in a car crash in which her four grandparents were killed. Miraculously, Katy survived it without a scratch, but the trauma of it left her with the loss of her speech.'

269

'Poor Katy. How dreadful for her.' Sean's concern was clearly genuine. 'Will she recover?'

'Hard to say. She's a great kid; I don't know where I'd be without her; she's my pal. The consultant says it's psychosomatic – there's no real damage – and that one day, it will come back. I keep praying for the miracle to happen, but so far nothing.'

'That must put a tremendous strain on you and your husband.'

I hesitated. It was an opening to mention Robert, except that twelve months ago, Sean was as far away from here as one can get, marooned on some remote Pacific island. So, rather than go off on a tangent, I decided to wait for his uncle.

'Yes, it does. I'd take it from her myself if only I could.'

'I've never had children but I know I'd feel exactly the same.'

We walked a few more steps.

'And what does your husband do?' Sean asked, trying to make the question sound casual but failing.

'He's an architect; the restoration old New England houses.'

'That must be fascinating,' Sean commented, still keeping his voice cool. 'And rewarding. Making neglected properties come to life again. Rather like recreating history. I wish he could do something with mine. During winter, it's like living in an ice-box.'

Despite the offhand tone in Sean's voice, the conversation was dispelling my mood. 'But your home is beautiful,' I protested. 'With its quaint nooks and crannies and beams, and that carved mantelpiece in the hall. That's not just recreating history; it is history. The moment you enter it, it's like stepping back in time.'

Sean stopped and faced me, his eyes searching mine.

'*Like* stepping back, Damaris,' his voice was intense again, '*but not actually happening*. Since seeing Samoset's and Damaris's grave you've gone quiet. I can guess what's on your mind, but no one can travel back in time. At least, not in the flesh. To the White Man – woman in your case – regressions, out-of-body experiences, as they call them, are no more than heightened dreams, except they're infinitely more realistic.'

Realistic enough for me to have weals on my face this morning, I thought, *but for them to mysteriously disappear after Samoset applied his healing leaves to my namesake's. And realistic enough for you to have a wound mark where the arrow entered his stomach, and another on your back where it emerged.*

'But to the Native American,' he stressed, 'who believe in the existence of supernatural powers, dreams are the way by which the spirits – the other-than-humans as they call them – communicate with us here on Earth. They believe that when we're dreaming a dream that seems to be real – to be actually happening to us – then the soul, which is the very core of the self, is detached from the body. Viewed by another person, the body can be seen still in its place, but its vital spark is elsewhere – on earth, or maybe in space.' He deliberately paused, 'And sometimes, even in time.'

He gripped my arms again.

'But only the *soul*, Damaris…' he emphasised,'…*never* the body.'

Realising how hard he was holding me, he dropped his hands. Looking a little sheepish, he apologised. 'Sorry, I let myself get carried away there for a moment. But I've only just read this. Just like you, I was also puzzled by it all, and thought that...' He tailed off. 'Well, that you might like to know what the book said?'

He really had the most gorgeous blue eyes.

'No need to apologise,' I said. 'And please carry on. I'm fascinated.'

'You're sure?'

'I'm positive.'

'In that case,' he said, as we turned and continued walking up the hill, 'seeing as we live in Algonquian country, they called it *manito* – the spirits speaking to us through our souls – prophesying not just what *can* happen in our lives, but what's *waiting* to happen, provided the dreamer is able not only to *listen* to what the spirit is saying but, *more importantly*, be willing to *act* upon it. He or she mustn't sit back and just leave it to fate...'

His voice was a turn on, as well. I could listen to it all day long – *and* all night, before eventually (*very, very* eventually) falling asleep in his arms.

'...according to their belief, whatever we are being told, if we want it to happen, then we must *make* it happen, creating our own circumstances as we go.'

He paused, and gave me a quizzical look. I felt my heart beat faster. 'Are you sure you want to hear this, it's beginning to sound like a sermon.'

'Nothing like Billy Brewster used to preach.'

'Billy Brewster?'

'Just someone I once knew.' I walked on. 'Please, I'd love you to continue.'

'Okay, be it on your own head.' He re-gathered his thoughts. 'According to the book's author, what we must do is listen to the voice of our spirit speaking to us through our heart. But only provided it's with our *true* heart,' he accented, 'which is a giving heart, not a taking heart. Only then can we determine the spirit's intention for us. For the way of genuine love is giving – never *exploiting* others to further self-interest, but *embracing* them – because its desire is to share...'

Embracing. That sounded good. Right now I could do with a good hug. Especially from you, Sean Wolfe, I really could.

'...To the Native American this is level four of the soul, the superconscious, the realm of our pure essence – our *true self* – which is revealed to us only in special dreams, where time and space laws do not apply.'

True love...the desire to share, I thought, *not exploiting others.*

That sounded wonderful.

Only in a perfect world, said my other self, *and there's no such thing as a perfect world.*

It brought me back down to earth.

Ideal though it all sounded, it was pure claptrap.

I'd once given myself – heart and body – to Andrew, and look where that had got me.

Made a fool of, my body used, and my heart broken.

What's more, exploiting others didn't work very well either, not unless you thought it all through very carefully first. I'd rushed into marrying Robert on the rebound, and other than

Katy and my art, the result had been a life of monotony and boredom, one dull day following another. (And in all fairness to Robert, it couldn't have been much fun for him, either.)

No, from what I'd seen of it – in my own life, and in the lives of others – it was all a game of chance, of rolling the dice hoping they're loaded in your favour. Back home, I had a recent CD re-release of Kay Starr's old record, singing "The Wheel of Fortune". And the words, "will the arrow point my way?" were so very true.

Sometimes, though rarely, it did, and you won, but more often it didn't and you lost.

In my case, I'd lost both ways. And I didn't want to lose again.

Meantime, Kay Starr's "arrow" prompted me ask the question uppermost in my mind.

'So, how do you explain you and I experiencing the exact same dreams, and at the exact same time?' I asked. This was of more interest to me. 'Is there more to come?' I wanted him to tell me they were over for good.

'To be honest, I don't know, nor can I explain them,' Sean replied, then added. 'Not with you being…' He broke off as if waiting for me to say something like, 'As it happens, my husband doesn't understand me…' and so on, ending up with, 'I'm thinking of leaving him,' but I stayed silent.

The pause felt interminable, until he continued:

'One thing I *am* certain of is that there is always a reason for them. Except that Kietitan very rarely reveals his purposes in advance. But there again, He doesn't have to. His aim is in achieving the end-result, whatever that may be.'

'Except it plays havoc with the participants in the meantime,' I said, with sudden emotion welling up from deep inside of me.

'That may be. But the reason is *always* revealed. In Kietitan's good time. Until then the only way to cope is to regard it all as if seeing a film. One so moving that we get emotionally involved in it – laughing at the happy parts, crying at the sad, falling in love with the hero and heroine, or hating the villain, to the point that some people get to think of them as true life people. It's not too many years ago that women were fainting on hearing Valentino had died – some even committed suicide, somewhat extreme.'

'More than extreme, plain stupid.'

'I couldn't agree more. Yet it still goes on, fortunately not to the suicide stage. Think of the women who fall for the latest film or pop stars. Men as well, they're no different. Take me, I'm a Diane Lane fan, she could persuade me to join her "Under the Tuscan Sun" any time she wished. Incidentally, has anyone ever told you that you look just like her younger sister? Especially when you smile, it lights up your face. You should do it more often.'

He looked at me for a response. But with Andrew having once told me almost the same thing, he didn't get one, and so he continued.

'But with most of us it lasts no more than the length of the film, until our nous reminds us they're playing only celluloid characters, not flesh and blood.'

'Except that Damaris and Samoset were real people,' I commented.

'It's the same principle. Everything that happened between them, their love for each other, occurred nearly four centuries past, and in exactly the same way as we both watched it all happen again less than an hour ago – as though we were two cinemagoers watching a remake of, say, "Gone With The Wind" – apt when you think of the thistledown. But neither of us changed, or even influenced, what happened in any way – Samoset saving Damaris from the Pequot war party, them falling in love, Samoset getting killed, Damaris being left alone in the forest, or what happened to her after – not even infinitesimally, because it all took place four hundred years before you and I were born. In exactly the way we witnessed it. No one has the power to go back and change things. The reason for our dreams, regressions – call them what you will – has nothing to do with Samoset and Damaris. We were taken back in time not to help *them* but, for some reason as yet unknown to either of us, *to do with you and me...*'

Sean's eagerness to convince me, to remove my embarrassment which he'd obviously sensed, caused me to grasp his arm and squeeze it in thanks.

'Except I'm not sure about the me and you bit' I said. 'But to be honest, and with all I've experienced since waking up this morning, I'm not sure of anything anymore. Still, thanks all the same. What you've just said has already made me feel better. With everything that went on between Damaris and Samoset back there, it was making me feel all...'

'There's no need to say it,' he responded. 'I guessed what you were thinking.' He moved my hand to under his arm. 'The hill, it gets steeper,' he explained.

Forced to move right up alongside him, I thought: *The hill's not that steep*, but what with him holding the gate open for me as we left the cemetery, and now giving me his arm, again it was rather nice being made a fuss of. And the long wooded canopy, with the bright sunshine permeating through, was somehow creating a warm, cosy atmosphere between us.

It was a lovely feeling. All sort of…well, comfy…and good.

Yet I was still puzzled. 'I assume that with Samoset being killed, the dreams are over? I certainly hope they are,' I added, with feeling. 'I don't think I could survive another one. But if they weren't to do with Damaris and Samoset – and also putting aside your "me and you, you and me" theory – have you any other explanation as to why they happened? '

Even as I asked the question, I had a sudden and vivid recollection of Snake-eyes running at Damaris, tomahawk raised and hate in his eyes.

Except it had felt as if it was *me* he was running at.

Maybe the answer was to do with Andrew? Some kind of supernatural warning?

His threat on the car phone had certainly been intimidating: '*I'm warning you, Dris. There's no way you're getting away from me.*'

What if he was at Oak House at this very moment, waiting for me to return home?

'Who can tell with Kietitan?' Sean replied, sounding evasive. Perhaps he knew more than he was telling?

'Maybe subsequent history holds some clue?' I persisted. 'Even though Damaris was my relative, you seemed to suggest a moment ago that you know what happened to her after she left the valley?'

'There's nothing there to explain the dreams.'

'Tell me, anyway,' I asked, again feeling for her losing her lover, disturbed by the thought that she'd been taken by the Pequot war-party, and really wanting to know – even though it was four hundred years ago and there was nothing I could do to change it, 'You never know what might be hidden there, way back in time.'

Unconsciously, I moved my other hand across to also hold his arm. The action turned my body into his. Within two strides, I was thinking how good it felt to be walking so close together. And natural, as if I'd known him for years.

'Sure, why not?' Sean capitulated. 'Keep holding me like this, and I'm forever yours to command.'

Don't tempt me, Sean Wolfe. Don't tempt me. At least not until I find out about Robert.

'Damaris Hopkins,' I prompted him.

'Killjoy,' he replied. 'Okay, Damaris Hopkins it is.'

Pausing for a moment to gather his thoughts, Sean began…

- thirty-eight -

Once again I was taken back in time. But not in my spirit this time, by Sean's voice as he told me what happened to Damaris.

'The morning after leaving the valley, she reached a Wampanoag village where they gave her buckskin clothes, and a brave to escort her back to New Plimoth. But her thoughts were for Brave Wolf, Samoset's son, and she asked to be taken to Massasoit. He remembered her from the first time they met, and gave her a party of braves to accompany her overland to Pemaquid – rather a long trek for a white woman unaccustomed to long walking, but as you and I know, she was somewhat determined, your namesake.'

'*That*,' I said, 'is an understatement.'

'And some,' Sean laughed. 'Anyway, having been told how his father had died, Brave Wolfe changed his own name to Samoset to honour him–'

'So it's Brave Wolf who's buried in Bristol?'

'Yes, as I've already mentioned, history's wrong on that score. Though, with the change of name and lack of records in those days, it's hardly surprising.'

'This story has been littered with surprises.'

'With more to come, I suspect. But getting back. Brave Wolf got Damaris to take him to the valley. After seeing his father's last resting place, he was determined it shouldn't fall into White Man's hands. So, with Damaris to advise him –

her father, your Mayflower forefather, Stephen, was a shrewd operator, as you'll no doubt know, and she turned out to be a chip off the block – they persuaded Massasoit to gift the valley to Brave Wolf. But to avoid any risk of it being claimed by a grasping settler, it was registered in Damaris's name."

'That, I take it, was at her suggestion?'

'It was.'

'Smart.'

'Very.'

'I'm getting to like her more and more. What happened next?'

'After drawing up and signing the deed with Massasoit, she returned with Brave Wolf to Pemaquid, where, hoping that everything would become fairer for the "Indian" over the next few years, she made a will for Brave Wolf to inherit the valley after her death. Then, to show she had every intention of honouring it, she remained living with the Abenaki rather than return to New Plimoth. As for Brave Wolf, he now had such regard for her he adopted her as his mother–'

'How touching. So she became an Abenaki princess after all? In her own right.'

'As White Dove. Because her heart was pure, and she came in peace and in love.'

White Dove. *How beautiful*, I thought. Yet how sad that the time she'd had with Samoset had been so short. But Sean was continuing.

'That same year, realising that the White Man would take the Red Man's tribal lands from them anyway, without compensation, Damaris persuaded Brave Wolf, who was now thirteen years old, to sell a small tract in Pemaquid to some Englishman–'

'One thousand, two hundred acres.'

'Exactly right. For a thousand pounds, which she put into a trust fund to protect the valley from any greedy, Puritan claim jumpers, in the event she ever had to go to law to do so. But am I telling the story, or are you taking over, just like your–'

'Except that was no *history* lesson,' I cut across him, instantly regretting my remark. It sounded distinctly coquettish. I squeezed his arm in apology, causing me to move even closer against him for a brief second. 'Sorry, carry on.'

'If you keep doing that,' Sean commented, 'your husband will never see you again. Not even if he offers a million dollar ransom.'

'*One* million? I'm worth more than that.'

'I've no doubt you are. But shall I continue?'

'Please.'

'Then behave,' Sean smiled down at me, making my toes curl. 'Except after that, where had I got to…?

Pretending to be re-gathering his thoughts, his face cleared. 'Oh, yes. After Damaris set up the trust fund, the Abenaki became so much under the influence of the French over the next decades, that Brave Wolf decided it would be safer for her to return to New Plimoth. She refused. To honour her, Brave Wolfe renamed the river Madamascontee, Damariscote.'

That explained that mystery. But it still didn't explain how Damaris…

'You've still to explain how Damaris came to be buried with Samoset?'

'Patience,' Sean said. 'It began when Brave Wolf picked up a White Man's bug. Knowing he hadn't long to live, he sold a further thousand acres for Damaris to put into a fund for his little son, Lone Wolfe, Damaris's adopted grandson. But twenty years later, Lone Wolf's own wife and child were killed in a French attack on his village. As a result – to quote Chief Joseph's famous Montana surrender speech – Lone Wolf's "heart was sick and sad, and he didn't want to fight any more, forever".'

Still arm in arm, there was now a warm and comforting feeling between us. To be honest, I was quite enjoying it and wishing the house was miles away.

'So, he relinquished the Chieftainship and came to live in peace in this valley, to find that the original spirit-lodge – Massasoit's farewell gift to Samoset all those years back, made of saplings and bark – had fallen into decay. Lone Wolf rebuilt it of the exact same design, but more substantially out of logs, and our family has kept it in pristine condition right to this day.'

'Did you paint the mural?'

'Yes, but very badly, I'm afraid.'

'On the contrary, it's rather good. As my art-tutor used to say: "A little raw, but shows considerable promise".'

'Thanks. It was painting it that prompted my interest in art. I've got a couple of works in my study you can give me your opinion on, if you've the time?'

'For an amateur critic, I'd better warn you I'm expensive.'

'That's okay. Maybe we could barter? I can think of a number of ways we might be able to negotiate a reciprocal exchange–'

'Sean Wolfe, to use one of your sailing terms, I think both our tacks are maybe straying a little too close to the wind. I suggest we get back to where your story left off.'

'With the utmost reluctance,' he smiled again. It was slightly crooked, and rather wicked.

Feeling my heart flutter, I pulled myself together. 'Whenever you're ready.'

Hamming a defeated sigh, Sean continued.

'Three years after coming to this valley, Lone Wolf fell in love with a white woman named Rebecca Kelly and she with him. He took the name Samuel Wolf and they married, set up their home here, and had two children, a son and a daughter.'

'And Damaris?'

'She was now sixty-eight and had moved here with Lone Wolfe – to be with Samoset. It's that saying again. Remember it? The one that starts, *"I buried him in that valley of winding waters. I love that land more than all the rest of the world".*'

I nodded. I remembered it. I gave it to her.

'It was always precious to her. But despite her hope for a change of attitude by the White Man toward the Red Man, it still wasn't legal for an Indian to own land and so, when Lone Wolfe married Rebecca, Damaris transferred everything – the valley and control of the trust fund – into Rebecca's name. In return, Lone Wolfe, Samuel – however you wish to think of him – built her a log cabin near Samoset's grave. It's said she put flowers on it every day without fail, but couldn't wait to be reunited with him and lived only another year. It's also said that being constitutionally healthy, she copied the way of the Indian and allowed herself to drift away, so she could be with him all the sooner. Rather like Heathcliffe with Cathy, but with Damaris in true love, rather than an obsession.'

'How sad. Yet how beautiful,' I said, feeling a tear rising in the corner of my eye. 'She must *really* have loved him. Oh, I hope there *is* an afterlife – and that they're together now at this very moment, making up for all the years they lost on Earth.'

'They are,' Sean assured me, tightening his arm to convey his empathy with my feelings. 'If there was no after-life we wouldn't have souls. Neither would the short time we're given on this unfair planet – especially for Damaris and Samoset and the few brief hours they had together – make any kind of sense.'

The sentiment prompted the memory of Samoset's last words to Damaris into my mind.

There is no death for spirit, only a passing on. Find two thistledown. Blow over resting place. Love not die. Live forever.

I was just about to remind Sean of them, being that they were in keeping with both our thoughts, and ask him did he know what they meant, but saw we'd almost reached the end of the wooded canopy with the house in sight, and decided to keep them to myself.

Besides, I now had the answer to what happened to Damaris.

Sad though the truth was, it was moving, too.

And I was satisfied with that.

- thirty-nine -

As we emerged into the open, the dirt road changed to a gravelled drive. Flanked by lawns, it swept up to the ivy-clad house. I stopped to appreciate it. 'It's magnificent.'

'As I said, you should try living in it in winter.'

'And the view.' I gazed across the multi-hued, undulating carpet of leafed trees stretching to the distant hills.

'Not much compensation when you're snowbound for two months.'

'Oh, Sean,' I protested. 'Just look at it. The whole setting. Where's your inner being?'

'Already regressed inside the study and pouring brandy into two tumblers, then enjoying mine sitting opposite you, around a roaring log fire.'

'Ah, well,' I succumbed. 'If you can't persuade them, join them.' I took his arm again. 'Lead the way, Philistine.'

I was sitting, still wearing my sheepskin, in a wing chair by a newly lit log fire, studying Sean's bookshelves as he poured the brandies.

One could determine a lot about a person from their reading taste, and Sean Wolfe was no exception. His collection covered the whole spectrum, from Shakespeare's plays to the New York wit of Damon Runyon's colorful characters, and included works by authors as diverse as Mark Twain, Charles Dickens, Tolstoy, Steinbeck, Hemingway, the humour of James

Thurber, the short stories of de Maupassant and O'Henry, modern novels by Robert Ludlum, Ken Follett, John Grisham, Michael Ondaatje and many, many more. There were also humorous travel books by Jerome K Jerome and Bill Bryson, and the more serious by Paul Theroux. Tomes on philosophy, various religions, and one shelf devoted to Native American history up to the present day, ranging from books on their origins and evolution, beliefs and myths, and many on the varying art-forms of every main family-group.

The impression they gave of him, I decided, was of someone open-minded, willing to listen before pre-judging, and definitely with a sense of humour. Someone easy to get along with. Easy to live with—

'Ginger ale?'

'Please. But not too much to swamp it.'

'Coming right up.'

My eyes moved around the room. I loved the polished floorboards, the casual rug, the antique desk and sea-captain's chair, the grandfather-clock, and in a corner a large revolving globe on its pedestal, stained brown with age. On an alcove wall above it were photographs of *Samoset III* in full sail, with Sean at the helm, fair hair windblown, clearly loving every moment of it.

On the wall opposite the inglenook fireplace were four paintings which had been hung up since my visit, fifteen months ago. Two were mine. The other two, both expressionistic, raw but powerful in their use of colour, were presumably Sean's.

'Your brandy.' Turning away from them, I took the half-filled crystal tumbler.

'There's no need to say it,' Sean commented, looking at the paintings. 'The bottom two offend your artistic eye. They're mine, I'm afraid. The other two are by a top artist; I don't know her name, she signs with only her initials 'OH'. I saw them in a Plymouth gallery, the day before I sailed, and not only fell for them, but they also brought me down to earth, and made me realise how big the gap is between the gifted and the hopeful. I put them up as a reminder to myself not to let my expectations get too high.'

'You're being unkind to yourself,' I said. 'You show exceptional talent. Your mural told me that, your canvasses just confirm it. All you require is a little guidance. As most artists, past and present, have benefited from at some stage in their lives. But you have a natural gift for expression through colour, you just need to…well, maybe use a little restraint.'

'Thanks,' Sean smiled, 'and yes, okay, when something moves me I do get carried away, it's my nature. But when I compare hers to mine, it makes me feel despondent. Apparently she's from this neck of the woods. Once my affairs are in order, I'm determined to meet her. I've already rung the gallery and left a message, asking them to send me more about her. If she'll just give me a few tips, I'll be more than grateful. But according to the gallery owner, she's well into her seventies, and – quote – defends her privacy like a vestal virgin defends her honour.'

(*Thanks, Alex,* I thought, *wait until I next see you.*)

He paused as a thought struck him. 'You don't happen to know her by any chance?'

'I'd like to get to know her myself,' I said, still not wanting to talk about my work; not at this moment. 'If you bought them from the Bristow gallery, I happen to know the owner, Alex…' (except she's not got much longer to live, not after I get my hands on her) '…who tells me she's rather a complex character as well as being an old frump. Seemingly, she's never really known what she wants out of life, and uses her paintings to express her frustrations. I think Alex is being a little unkind, but I'll see what I can do for you.'

'Thanks. I'd really appreciate it. Especially if you can arrange for me to meet her.'

'I'll do my best,' I said, turning to the "Thanksgiving" painting. 'This one's fascinating. Your uncle told me something about it. But he didn't go into detail.'

Sean dropped on to the chesterfield and leant back, looking relaxed. Before answering he sipped some brandy, then lowered his glass.

'It was painted, or rather started by Samuel, Lone Wolf. Family legend has it that he first prayed to Kietitan to guide his brush, and as a result, was led to paint three separate groups. The one gathered around the table consists of the Mayflower settlers who survived the first winter. Then there's Massasoit and his braves who were at the first Thanksgiving. The third group, with the lodge in the background, is made up of those of our family whose eternal spirits – Samuel was supposedly told by Kietitan – have been elected to live together in this chosen corner of the Happy Hunting Grounds. When he started painting it, only Samoset and Damaris were buried here. As for the others, the ones preordained by Kietitan, Samuel was influenced to draw their faces in outline only, for them to be filled in after their deaths, when Kietitan himself would guide the brushes of the ones chosen to portray their exact features.'

Sean took another sip of brandy.

'And now there's only one face left, that of the last spirit to be admitted into this secluded garden of paradise. From the outline, it's clearly a man. When he's filled in, the painting will be complete, and the sign "House Full" will hang on the valley's ethereal gates.'

I was almost reluctant to ask. 'Any inkling who it will be?'

Sean gave a wry smile. 'We're not told in advance. We have to wait for Kietitan to tell us, and guide the artist's brush. Until then, no one knows who's been chosen. Some of my ancestors never made it. Few families are without their black sheep. Our biggest is the one who built this house—'

'Why him?' I interjected, glancing through the window at the panoramic view. 'I would have thought he'd be among the first of the elect?'

'Unfortunately for him, no. He's the one who started the family's cash flow problems when he emptied the trust fund to build this grand memorial to his name, leaving us with money problems ever since. Kietitan is said to have rewarded him by banishing his spirit from the valley, but I reckon it's never been laid to rest, and lives on in the shape of family members like Uncle William. If I could exorcise it, I'd wring its blasted neck, spirit or no spirit. But until then, I'm seriously thinking of doing it to my pesky relative instead.'

'Why? What *has* poor Uncle William done to earn such disfavour?'

'More like what hasn't he done. His list of foul-ups stretch a mile long. His latest stems back to last Thanksgiving—'

'Thanksgiving? That's the day Robert drove here.'

'Robert?'

'My husband. I should have explained earlier, but that's really why I'm here, not to take photographs. He went missing exactly twelve months ago today. It's only a few hours ago that I found out he drove here last Thanksgiving to try to buy this painting. As I've already mentioned, your Uncle William showed it to me three months before that. I asked him whether he'd sell it, but he wouldn't. I told Robert about it, and found out only today that he decided to try to buy it for me as a special Thanksgiving present—'

'You mean *he* was your husband?' Sean sat bolt upright. 'Drove a Lexus SUV? Willing to go to two hundred thousand?'

I caught my breath. 'Then he *did* reach here?'

Sean didn't reply, but stood and crossed to the window. Looking down the forest road, he glanced down at his watch as if willing it to go faster. I had an uneasy feeling.

'Sean, if you know something about Robert you have to tell me. It's been twelve months of suspense. Please, I'd rather know.'

He didn't turn his head.

'Has her father's disappearance contributed any to Katy not recovering her speech?'

'It hasn't helped.'

'Hell!'

He turned to face me, his face looking strained.

At that moment there was the exhaust-roar of an approaching car.

Through another window, I saw a long, dark green Jaguar coupè speed up the hill and on to the gravelled drive, then race past and skid to a halt outside the main door.

Immaculately dressed, Sean's uncle eased his wiry frame out of the car and stood gazing over the valley, massaging the stiffness out of his elderly joints.

Sean suspended whatever he was about to say and headed past me for the door. Rising from my chair, I blocked him. "Sean, whatever it is you're avoiding, I'd rather *you* tell me.'

He hesitated, then seeing the look in my eyes, he again took tight hold of my arms.

'Damaris, I'm afraid Robert's dead.' He paused a moment then, in a gentle voice, said, 'It's his body that's in my grave.

- forty -

William Roget downed his self-poured brandy, neat, in one gulp.

'You see, my dear,' he explained from the arm-chair opposite me, 'the estate had run out of money, and the damn bank and IRS vultures were threatening us with having to sell the valley. Sean's solution was to sail around the world and write his story. He found a Boston agent, name of Vicenze, who negotiated a book publishing, television documentary deal, and an on-board camera to film the voyage. But only a minor advance, big money not until completion. Then his yacht was found, turned turtle, and both deals fell through. To make matters worse, when Sean was presumed drowned the blasted insurance company discovered our financial predicament and refused to pay up without a body.' William Roget mimicked apostrophes with the first two fingers of both hands, '"Not until it washed up somewhere". Damned rogues,' he bristled, 'Had the gall to imply it was all a deliberate scam to defraud them. Confounded cheek.'

'Could we get to Robert,' I asked in a low voice.

'Coming to him, my dear.' Pouring himself another brandy, he cleared his throat.

'The day he arrived here, I noticed the blue in his lips even as he got out of his vehicle. He introduced himself. We chatted a moment about the weather and suchlike, then, being an ex-doctor, I advised him he should go for a check-up. He said he not only had, but that it had confirmed what I suspected – a dicky heart.'

'A bad heart!' I whispered. 'So that's what was troubling him. Oh, why didn't I see it? Why didn't he share it with me?'

'Couldn't bring himself to?' William Roget suggested, taking a gulp of his drink. 'Some men are like that. Prefer to keep things to themselves so as not to worry the little woman. And don't go blaming yourself, my dear, it would have taken someone qualified like myself to notice it for what it was. But as a result of the findings, he wanted to buy you the painting, for you to remember him by in case he popped-off without any last words of goodbye, and all that sort of thing.'

I closed my eyes to stem an upsurge of tears. At the same time, I was overwhelmed by mixed feelings of guilt and anger. Facing death, Robert had gone out of his way to get me the painting I'd wanted, so why had he been so goddamned undemonstrative in life? Okay, I'd married him for all the wrong reasons, but if only he'd been able to express *some* affection, *told* me of his love – I would have much preferred that to any gift, anyway – I may have been able to return it. I could have tried, and who knows, it might have worked? Sex wasn't the be-all and end-all. Now it was too late to know.

'I told him exactly what I'd told you,' William Roget went on, stroking his thin mustache. 'That it wasn't for sale at any price. But then he produced the money in cash. Two hundred thousand. New, crisp, shiny notes. And I wavered. It would give me breathing space. Let me make payments to the grasping IRS and our equally grasping bank, while our lawyers challenged the insurance company's position. I invited him in,

293

to give me time to think it through. The painting *was, after all,* a family heirloom, and there was one face *still* to be filled in. But as he crossed the threshold, he clutched at his chest and fell to the floor. I checked his pulse and tried to revive him, but he'd gone.'

I smothered my face in my hands, trying to blot out the picture.

'He didn't suffer?' I looked up, begging him to confirm this.

'No, my dear...' William Roget hesitated, '...he wouldn't have known a thing.'

'What is it?' I demanded. 'There's something you're not telling me.'

'Well...' he looked to Sean for help, but Sean outstared him in silence, willing him to continue.

'I have to know,' I insisted.

William Roget swallowed his scrawny Adam's apple. For some peculiar reason – in the fraught circumstances – it reminded me of a turkey, and that today was still Thanksgiving, and when I got home I would have to tell Katy that Daddy was dead.

Poor Katy, I thought. Oh, hell! *What next?*

William Roget pulled at his collar to loosen it. 'There is *one* slight thing I *should* perhaps have mentioned. When your husband fell, his head hit against an antique iron doorstop. His skull must have fractured, there was blood all over the floor. I'm sure you'll sympathise with me, my dear, when I tell you this placed me in an extremely awkward situation.' He drained his brandy glass. 'You see, I'm not too *au fait* in forensic science, so if I called an ambulance, what if it was difficult – with the blow to the head happening almost simultaneously to the heart attack – for a medical examiner to determine *which* of them caused his death.'

He stretched for the decanter to refill his glass. Sean moved it out of his reach.

Swallowing his Adam's apple again, William Roget continued. 'So there I was, with your husband lying dead on my floor, blood everywhere, including all over the doorstop – which I'd picked up, leaving prints my on it. Worse, he was carrying cash. If he'd withdrawn it from his bank and said something to the manager, or to you, about where he was going, it could leave me as the prime suspect, even if I handed it back. Also, I was the only witness to the heart attack preceding the blow. So, with it all looking highly suspicious, and the circumstantial evidence pointing to one conclusion – where would that leave *me*?'

During the old loony's rambling account, I'd become more and more dumbstruck, and had let him prattle on uninterrupted. I now found my voice, and stared up at him in utter disbelief. 'Are you saying that's why you buried him here? That you calmly decided to get rid of his–'

'No, I wasn't at all calm, my dear. Not at the beginning. Quite the contrary, in fact. That's why it all went wrong, you see. Instead of first sitting down and working it through, I regret to say I panicked, and dragged his body into his SUV, intending to dispose of both, and the money, in one of the many swamps on the estate.'

William Roget's perturbed tone at recollecting the weighty (for him) moment, suddenly lightened as he recounted his reasoned (to him) thinking in solving it.

'But then my head cleared and I thought: There I was without a body, and here was one turned up on my doorstep, so to speak. What's more, I was in a fix anyway, so what had I got to lose? In for a dime, in for a dollar, as they say.'

'You thought what?' I sprang to my feet. 'You mean…' For a brief moment words failed me, and then I exploded: 'You must be stark, staring, crazy. Talk about being in *financial* trouble. When I get home and phone the police, you'll wish you'd never been born.'

Sean decided it was time for him to intervene, to try to defuse things. 'I can understand your anger,' he said. 'When he told me, just a couple of hours ago, I blew my top, too.'

I was so livid I rounded on him as well. 'You mean *you* knew all along! When we met in the glade, *and* during our walk up to the house – yet you said nothing! You're no better than your screwball uncle! Samoset's descendant! By accident of blood, maybe, but in no other way!'

'Other than your name,' Sean reminded me, 'I knew nothing about you until a moment ago. I certainly didn't know of your connection to the man who wanted to buy the painting.'

'Nor was Sean here last Thanksgiving when it happened,' William Roget chipped in, as if he was calmly exonerating Sean, 'He was stranded on some tropical island, thousands of miles away.'

The realisation did nothing to lessen my fury. Still standing, I tossed back my brandy to try to calm myself.

'Shall I continue?' William Roget asked, as if we were having a normal conversation. The man was seriously out of touch with reality.

'You might as well,' I replied, falling back into the chair as my legs gave way. 'You can't shock me any more than you already have.'

'Oh, but he can,' Sean said. 'My only consolation is that I wasn't involved.'

His uncle disregarded the remark. 'I dressed your poor husband in Sean's clothes – he wasn't as tall, but he was fuller, and the fit was good enough – then hid him away in an outbuilding. Next, I threw his own clothes into the back of his vehicle – but on reflection excluded the cash, after all it wasn't mine to dispose of – and drove it to a nearby swamp, reputed to be bottomless, then let it roll down the bank and sink out of sight.'

Again words fail me, and so I just waited for him to continue.

'I returned to the house and cleaned everything up. My next thought was the money. I finally decided to send it anonymously through the post to his next of kin, and if the police, or anyone else, came asking questions, to deny he'd ever arrived here. But with all that had happened, for the love of me, I just couldn't remember his name. It was then I realised that everything to identify him – wallet, bank card, credit cards, driver's license, vehicle-plates – were all at the bottom of the swamp.'

William Roget stood, and crossed to the "Thanksgiving" painting.

'I put it on one side, hoping to one day discover who he was, and return it to its rightful owner.'

He pressed a hidden switch. The painting swivelled open revealing a wall safe. Twiddling the combination, he opened the door, took out an envelope and handed it to me.

'There you are, my dear,' he said, like some benevolent Santa Claus. I let it drop on to my lap. 'Two hundred thousand. You needn't count it. I can assure you it's all there. And now that Vicenze's negotiating new deals – crossed fingers and all that – for hopefully twice the original amount, we'll also be able to reimburse you with the interest you've lost on it. Let me know when your bank's worked out the figure, and I'll send you a check – with extra added,' he smiled placatingly, 'as compensation for all the needless suffering I may have caused you.'

And with this, William Roget returned to his chair and beamed across at me as if to say: That puts everything right. All's well that ends well.

Again, I was so dumbstruck, I couldn't manage a reply. Just stared at him.

'We needn't dwell on the rest,' the old crackbrain prattled on, still looking unruffled. 'It's enough to say I made up – extraordinarily coincidental as it happened – a story of Sean being rescued from a deserted island and dying only hours after arriving home. I had the death certified as his, with the cause as myocardial infarction, and had your husband buried in our family cemetery – with the utmost solemnity, I assure you, my dear, a most simple, yet dignified committal service. I even found his pipe still intact, where it had fallen, and following our custom, placed it in the spirit-lodge with the pipes of our ancestors. Faced with a death certificate, the insurance company was forced to settle. And here we are. Or rather, were, until Sean arrived, out of the blue.'

William Roget sounded regretful of the fact, as though Sean turning up alive had botched up all his plans.

'Seems he'd spent the last twelve months living on fruits, yams, berries, wild boar, and all that sort of thing – until he was rescued by some passing tramp-ship on its way to San Francisco. When he arrived, he phoned Vicenze – who almost died of shock, but then told him about his apparent death. Vicenze wired him money to buy clothes and an air-ticket, the next thing Sean arrived here, breathing flames, but determined to straighten things out. No need to tell you what transpired between us, except to say we hope to be able to repay the insurance company from the new deals that Vicenze is negotiating, leaving something left over for Sean. As for me, I've agreed to be the sacrificial lamb and "take the rap", as they say in the movies – and that about brings us up to date.'

'Up to date!'

Propelled by my pent-up rage, I sprang to my feet again, grabbing the envelope, or the nutty old devil might try to keep it this time.

'You think that's it! After all the anguish you've caused!'

I stormed to the door, and paused with my hand on the brass doorknob.

'First thing tomorrow, I'll be seeing my attorney. If you think you were near to foreclosure before, wait until you get the writ!'

I slammed the study door behind me.

William Roget – so I was told later – stared after me in astonishment.

''Pon my soul!' he remarked. 'What a temper!'

'Temper!' Sean erupted. 'Can you blame her?'

Standing and crossing to the gabled window, he watched me run down the drive into the treed arch, and disappear from his view.

Behind him, he heard his uncle flick his lighter and puff at his pipe.

From habit, Sean half opened the transom to let out the smoke.

William Roget got to his feet. 'If we're to be at the "John Carver" before we're called in to dine, we'd best be off.'

Still looking down the drive, Sean saw a ball of thistledown being carried on the breeze toward the house. Reaching the study window, it floated in through the open transom and settled in Sean's cupped hands.

'You go,' he said, looking at the soft orb of white stems. 'I've changed my mind.'

Reaching my Jeep, I flung the door open and hurled myself into my seat.

In my rear mirror, I caught sight of a ball of white thistledown drifting toward me out of the trees.

'Thistledown!' I yelled, beginning to lose it. 'I've had a frigging bellyful of thistledown. Today. Tomorrow. And for all eternity.'

I slammed my door shut, savagely turned the ignition and accelerated off, tyres squealing in protest, down the dirt road.

Back to Katy and sanity.

As far from this damn valley as I could get.

I hoped...no, prayed...that I'd never see it again.

Ever.

Glancing in the rear mirror, I saw the thistledown being caught in a flurry of dust from my spinning wheels.

Ascending higher and higher, it whirled upwards and upwards.

And out of my sight.

- forty-one -

I was heading back to Sean Wolfe's estate, with Katy sitting beside me, clutching a bunch of wild flowers, still sniffling and wiping tears.

'Where's Harry?' Katy had gestured — waving 'bye' to Jo standing in the doorway holding a kind-looking maid's hand — and getting into the Jeep, wondering why Harrison wasn't in the rear window, barking and twisting his body in his usual welcome.

Confounded dog, I swore to myself, as I swept past the top-of-the-range cars and SUVs littering the Chapmans' drive, yet knowing it was my fault for forgetting him in my temper and leaving him behind. But it meant returning all the way back instead of straight home, a thought made worse by knowing that oo-lah-lah Suzanne and black-eyed Paul (even if they weren't speaking to each other) were busy partying and showing off to their guests, inside the brightly-lit house that poor Robert had designed.

Even worse, it meant another dreadful Thanksgiving for Katy. Having to drive back to where Robert was buried, made it impossible for me not to break it to her, instead of leaving it until tomorrow, as I'd intended to.

Once on South Carver road, I'd pulled into a secluded place (not the same spot as before, when the fog writhed out of the forest and encircled me) and gently told her of my discovery that Daddy had died of a heart attack, and for some reason had been mistaken for someone else and buried under that name. Katy had wept, her grief all the more heart rending to see as she tried to express it, but couldn't say the words.

I'd held her tight, smothering her hair with kisses, as I'd also finally cried.

Then, through my tears, I promised her that as soon as it could be arranged, I would have Daddy's body reburied in Plymouth, and after that, the two of us would go away on a long holiday together somewhere in the sun, Hawaii, Italy, the South of France, or wherever else we might choose, and "blow returning to school".

Katy's grief had subsided – slowly, but still sooner than I'd expected. But then, children were said to be resilient, and it was only natural that for a seven-year old, much of her grief had already been expended over the last twelve months, from when Robert went missing. It was also quite probable that in nature's protective way – the way it helps children's thoughts to cope – her tears were as much a relief that he hadn't left us for someone else after all.

She then insisted on searching the forest's edge for flowers until she'd picked enough to satisfy her she had enough, she'd sign-languaged, "for a big bouquet for Daddy".

And then we drove on.

Up ahead, I saw the estate road approaching.

'There it is,' I said, slowing down and pointing to the track winding its way into the trees. Katy sat up and peered over the instrument panel, with the posy, so lovingly gathered, already half-crushed by being clutched so tight to her body.

Driving through the forest, I prayed: *Please, God! Make sure Sean stays inside and that I don't see him again.*

But even as I said the words in my mind, I couldn't stop my heart racing as my innermost being contradicted my plea.

Which made me feel ten times worse. With Robert dead, and taking Katy to see his grave, I shouldn't be feeling this way, I rebuked myself.

I parked on the same verge. Despite the cloudless blue skies, the late Fall was coming to an abrupt end, showering the floor with coloured leaves. There was a distinct chill in the air. I pulled both Katy's and my coat-collars up around our necks, then, holding my daughter's hand, I led her into the woods.

As we skirted the spirit-house, I showed Katy that Harrison was safe, still in the same position, his front paws over his ears.

'Shall we leave him there and pick him up on our way back?' I asked.

'All right,' Katy signalled back. 'Why is he lying like that? Like he did for Daddy?'

'Who knows?' I replied. 'If you don't, then I'm sure I don't.'

But even as I said it, I remembered William Roget saying he'd found Robert's briar pipe, and had placed it inside the lodge, with the pipes of the family's departed ancestors.

Just for a moment, it made me feel all shivery again.

But then I shrugged it off.

And clutching Katy's hand tight, continued on through the trees.

As we reached the forest's edge, I could see Sean's head and shoulders above the picket fence. Judging from where he was kneeling, he was doing something to Robert's grave.

Hell! I thought, why had I bothered praying, only to be given the opposite answer? In heaven's name, what do I do now? Turn around? Or walk over to him and brazen it out?

But again my thoughts were in opposition to the reactions of my body. Like some love struck teenager, my spine was tingling, and my stomach churning.

For goodness sake, Damaris, I thought, *pull yourself together.*

Standing in the shadow of the trees, I tried to rationalise my feelings.

I couldn't deny being attracted to him – admitting the obvious, or I wouldn't be responding this way. As for being in his company, I'd loved every moment of our walk up to the house. In that brief time I'd sensed that although he was flirtatious – and maybe a little wicked with it, except it had all been innocent and playful, with no offensive double-meaning common in men on the make – he was no two-timer. An instant judgement, I know, but there was something…what was the right word?…*unique* about him. His direct gaze. His whole body language. Something *reassuring.*

He'd also, and very clearly, been upset by the effect of his uncle's wrongdoing – both on myself and on Katy.

But…

And this was the crunch: There were barriers between us – huge barriers – that made it impossible for me to even contemplate our brief acquaintanceship going any further, no matter how much I was drawn to him.

The first was Robert.

Okay, our marriage hadn't even been a marriage, not in the true sense of the word, and in actual time, measured from when he had died (not from when I thought he'd walked out on me) I'd been a widow, admittedly without realising it, for twelve months now.

But in *real* time – measured from when I'd discovered the *truth* of his disappearance – I'd been a widow for no more than two hours, and to be thinking what I was thinking, after only two hours, was positively indecent.

The second was Katy.

She was the most important person in my life. There was no place in it for anyone else. And uppermost in this was my determination that she'd get her voice back. The holiday I was planning on, far away from familiar surroundings, could well be the very thing to rid her of her bad memories and – pray God – help to make it happen. But for Katy to see me with another man, so close to finding out about her Daddy, could have the opposite effect.

The third, and final barrier, was my threat of legal action.

I still intended going through with it. I knew it wasn't Sean who'd committed the crime. Twelve months ago he was halfway around the globe, fighting just to survive in the hope of rescue, unaware what his uncle was up to back home. But William Roget was going to have to pay for what he had put us through – especially Katy, pining for her Daddy, thinking he had walked out on us, without remorse or concern, for some other woman – and Sean would inevitably be drawn into the battle. And there was no way he could be in both camps at the same time.

So, Damaris Moore, harden your heart. But at the same time, now that you're here, you may as well let Katy place her flowers on her Daddy's grave, and then drive away for what will be the last time. And once Robert is interred in Plymouth, pack your bags and fly away from it all, just you and Katy, and the only occasion you'll need to see Sean Wolfe ever again is across a courtroom.

Holding Katy's hand, I led her across the glade.

- forty-two -

Opening the cemetery gate it creaked as before, but Sean didn't turn his head.

The granite headstone was lying face down on the grass.

Thank you at least for that, Sean Wolfe, I said to myself, Katy won't see the wrong name and get herself more upset.

Had he done it deliberately to soften me, I wondered?

Then I realised he couldn't have guessed I'd be back today, not on Thanksgiving. It was only Harrison that had brought us. I felt ashamed of my suspicions. What he was doing was obviously from a genuinely compassionate heart.

In place of the headstone, he'd planted a wooden cross into the ground, and was now securing it with rocks.

Following me through the gate, Katy saw him for the first time. Staying behind me, she jerked at my sheepskin and sign-languaged: 'Who is he?'

'He owns this valley,' I hand-signalled back.

Although he must have been aware of us, Sean stayed kneeling, not turning his head as we approached him, Katy tightly gripping my hand.

The cross had been made from mahogany, with black letters painted on its cross piece. I read out the words for Katy.

ROBERT MOORE

Do not stand at my grave and weep
I am not here. I do not sleep

Over his shoulder, Sean said, 'It's from an old Abenaki poem. Translated into English and made to rhyme, it continues:

> I am a thousand winds that blow,
> I am the diamond glints on snow,
> I am sunlight on ripened grain,
> I am the gentle autumn rain,
> When you awake in the morning's hush,
> I am the swift uplifting rush
> of quiet birds in circled flight.
> I am the soft stars that shine at night,
> So do not stand at my grave and cry,
> I am not here, I did not die.

Though I'd heard the moving poem before, I held Katy to me, fighting to choke back the welling emotion that the beautiful words had created.

'Thank you,' I whispered.

'It's the least I could do,' Sean replied. Still kneeling, he turned to us. 'I wasn't expecting you back. At least, not today.' He looked at Katy. 'And this young lady must be Katy?'

Katy looked shyly up at me.

'Katy,' I said, 'this is Mr Wolfe. Not the one who blows houses down, despite his huffing and puffing after working so hard, but, I suspect, something of a wolf in a different way.'

Rubbing his palms together to remove some earth, Sean held out his hand, treating Katy seriously, as he would an adult. 'I'm very pleased to meet you, Katy. Take no notice of what your mother said, she's just trying to be clever; I'm really a big teddy bear. She's told me a lot about you, but you're even prettier than she described.'

Katy studied him carefully to see if he meant it. Sean held her serious gaze. She finally rewarded him with a cautious smile. But although cautious, it was a very definite smile, something she rarely exchanged when meeting someone for the first time. Then, with the earnest expression of a seven-year old being treated as a grown-up, she gave him her hand.

Shaking it with equal gravity, Sean asked, 'Did you choose the flowers yourself?'

Katy nodded.

'They're beautiful. I love all the colours. Are they for Daddy?'

Again Katy nodded.

'He'll love them, too. Shall I help you arrange them?'

Another solemn nod.

'Right. I'll stay kneeling here. I'm getting too old to keep moving about, not young like you. You kneel there, opposite me, and we'll place them together.'

I realised, with gratefulness, that Sean was pretending not to notice Katy's inability to speak. Despite her tender age, Katy was normally very discerning with strangers, carefully weighing them up first before responding, but with Sean she seemed to have taken to him already – the very opposite of how she'd reacted to Andrew.

As for me, he'd hardly acknowledged my presence, but knowing it was deliberate to make Katy feel special, I looked at him kneeling across from her, letting her arrange the flowers herself, and felt an overwhelming warmth towards him. A genuine warmth from the heart and not in any way sexual (well, strictly, that's not a hundred percent true, say ninety-five).

Sitting back on his heels, he looked at Katy's carefully placed, but haphazard display.

'That's great,' he said. 'Just like a real flower arranger. And without any help from me.'

Katy beamed across at him.

'And now,' Sean asked her, 'would you like me to show you where your great-great-great aunt is buried?'

Before I could say "no" for her, "we don't have time", Katy nodded and Sean smiled up at me, with no hint of ill humour because of the way I'd stormed out of his study a short time ago. It was as if it had never happened.

'Did I miss out any "greats", Mom?'

'A few,' I returned his smile. I couldn't be cold to him, not with the way he was being so warm with Katy. And it wasn't being put on for my sake, I could tell.

Getting to his feet, he offered Katy his hand to hold. To my surprise she took it and gave me her other hand. After a momentary hesitation I grasped it, making us a companionable threesome as we strolled toward the river, with Sean telling Katy all about the various birds and animals that inhabited the woods, phrasing his words in such a way there was no reason for her to ask questions. I felt myself taking to him even more.

Reaching the rocky grave, we stood side by side together reading the plaque.

Katy looked up at Sean and hand signed to him.

I was about to translate when he replied, 'Yes, the same name as your Mommy.'

Katy asked another question.

'Samoset? He's my great-great-great grandfather.'

'In your case, less a few,' I said. 'I didn't realise you knew sign-language?'

'I don't,' Sean replied, 'but Katy's face is so expressive. We understand one another just fine. Don't we, Katy?'

Katy nodded again with due earnestness, then asked him another question.

Failing to understand it, Sean pulled one of his wry faces. He looked to me for help, and saw me smiling with amusement.

'Okay,' he said. 'So I spoke too soon.'

'Or more like pride before a fall. Katy's asking: "Were they married?". I can't wait to hear how you answer that one?'

'Simple.' He returned to Katy. 'Yes, in the eyes and blessing of Kietitan.'

'Clever,' I commented. 'But maybe too clever. That's going to leave you open to a string of new questions. You're already being asked the next one.'

Sean looked down. 'Who is Kietitan?' he translated. 'Kietitan is another name for God. The Creator.'

Another question from Katy.

'Yes, as they were married, I suppose it does make us related.'

And another.

'What do you call me? How about Uncle Sean?'

Katy gave him a positive nod and asked another question.

Sean smiled. 'Of course we can find them some flowers, too. But perhaps the next time you visit? I think today Mommy will want to get back home for Thanksgiving, or you won't be eating until well past supper time.'

Oh, no, Sean! I panicked. You've just made a big mistake introducing a new subject.

Especially Thanksgiving.

Knowing Katy, it will lead to a follow up question.

It did.

'What am I having?' said Sean. 'Beans, if there's a tin in the cupboard.'

'I assumed you'd be having dinner with your dear uncle?' I cut in.

'I was. But I changed my mind. I've had enough of him for today.'

'Amen to that,' I reiterated the thought with some feeling, then turned to Katy, who was tugging at my coat. 'No Katy, I don't think so.'

'Why?' Katy sign-languaged.

'Because with Aunt Alex and Uncle John, and Andrew, not coming – and after hearing about Daddy – I thought we'd have a quiet evening together, maybe play some games.'

Katy came back at me. I hesitated before answering, I could feel us getting too deep into this. 'Yes, Uncle Sean probably does like playing games. But I'm only cooking enough for you and me.'

She offered a suggestion.

'No, I guess you don't mind sharing.'

Katy hurried her response.

313

'Sorry, I didn't catch that?'

She repeated it, very deliberately, and very, *very* definite about it.

'Oh…' I flustered, 'Would you, now?'

'I assume both you ladies realise,' Sean intruded, 'that it's impolite to discuss secrets in front of others?'

Hearing this, Katy, of course, repeated her opinion to Sean.

'Sorry, Mom. That's another you're going to have to translate.'

Choosing my words, and not translating exactly what Katy wanted me to convey, I said, 'It seems Katy would rather you have Thanksgiving with us than one of the other three I mentioned. But being that none of them are coming any more, it's now irrelevant. Come on Katy,' I said; it was meant to be a firm voice but sounded a touch shaky. 'It's time to go, or there'll be no dinner for you and me either, just like Mr Wolfe.'

Katy stood her ground, looking up at Sean for his answer.

Help, I pleaded to him with my eyes.

He responded and extended his hand back to Katy. 'Tell you what. As it's getting dusky, why don't I walk you both safely back through the woods? Mommy and I can talk on the way and agree what's best to—'

Another question from Katy.

'Sorry, may you…?'

'Run ahead and collect Harrison,' I interpreted.

'Who's Harrison?'

'Our much-beloved, crazy, and totally insane bearded collie. For some reason best known to him, he's lying outside the spirit-lodge, refusing to budge.'

'Typical of a bearded collie,' said Sean. 'I had one myself when I was young. He was the same, a law unto himself – ungovernable. Rather like Uncle William. But they do have a way of pulling at your heartstrings.'

'I'm sorry,' I said, 'but Mr Roget does nothing for mine.' I turned to Katy. 'Okay, darling, off you go. But not too far in front. Uncle Sean…(I slipped-up, using Katy's adopted name for him, and mentally kicking myself for it) '…and I will catch you up at the lodge.'

'Uncle Sean! I like the sound of it. It's got a nice ring to it. I've not been an uncle before.'

'Don't start getting too fond of it,' I warned, forcing my voice to be neutral, especially as, with Katy already running ahead of us, we were now sort of alone together. I was wanting to hold his arm just like before, when we walked up to the house. It had felt so natural and so…well, to repeat my feelings then, so *comfy*.

Katy looked back to make sure we were following her. Seeing us still standing there, she gestured, 'Come on!'

'Sorry,' Sean apologised, but his smile contradicted it. 'Looks like you're stuck with me being an uncle for a while longer.'

'Only as far as the lodge,' I reminded him, still striving to sound all dispassionate.

'That will do for starters.'

'And the final course.'

We began walking. Katy, satisfied, ran on.

'I'm afraid there's going to be some protests when you tell her you can't make it,' I said.

'If it's any help to you, I can,' Sean replied, but under his casual tone, I detected he was hoping I might change my mind.

'I don't think that would be wise, do you,' I said, 'not in the circumstances? I still intend seeing my attorney tomorrow. Except I've decided not to include the estate, only Mr Roget personally.'

I glanced up at him. Hell! What was I giving up? He was so damned handsome. But more than that he looked kind. Nor was there any trace of hardness in those fantastically blue eyes. And he'd been so good with Katy – and that told me *so* much. You can't pretend with children, they've a sixth sense for seeing through you, especially my daughter, who'd made *no* attempt to like Andrew, and had shown her opposition to him right from the start.

'If you weren't joking about the beans, I'm sorry you've got so little in,' I said, genuinely apologetic. 'They're not much of a meal, especially for Thanksgiving when everyone else will be tucking into turkey and pumpkin pie. But, as I said, the circumstances between us *are* somewhat…

I tailed-off as I had a sudden mental picture of him, that made me smile. 'I hope you're not out of plates as well, and have to eat them out of a tin.'

'Don't worry,' Sean smiled back at me. 'When I was a kid, my favourite TV repeat was "Rawhide". After seeing the cowhands having to eat Wishbone's beans, every meal from breakfast through to supper, I reckon I'll manage. And after a year of eating wild fruit and roots, they'll seem like a feast.'

'I expect they will. But "Rawhide"? I remember it. Come to think of it, there is something of a "Rowdy Yates" about you. It explains why you're never out of denims. I did wonder.'

'They're because after a year and a half on a deserted island, I needed to replace my rags for something comfortable on the flight home from San Francisco. And in my book, comfort in a crowded 319 means jeans. I do have other clothes, suits even, but after eighteen months away I'm not looking for rheumatism. They're going to have to spend at least a week in the drying closet before I'm even tempted to wear them.'

I bet you look great in a suit, I thought, *especially with your physique. Dark blue, with a gleaming, open-neck, white and blue-striped shirt to compliment your tan—*

(Hold it right there, Damaris, you're beginning to think like a lover…or a wife, even!)

We entered the forest. The trees closed around us, forcing us to walk nearer, our arms occasionally brushing. Each time we touched, it sent a high-tension charge right through me. I had to restrain myself from letting my hand hang still, inviting his fingers to interlock with mine. The bushes thickened and I was forced to walk in front. Continuing in silence, only the crunch of our shoes on the carpet of leaves broke the hushed stillness of the forest.

From behind me, Sean said, 'As Uncle John and Aunt Alex seem to be linked, I assume the dinner guest Katy's not too keen on is the Andrew guy.'

I kept walking. 'Could be.'

'Seems I've heard that name before, just recently? But in another time.'

I stayed silent.

'Good friend?'

'Way back. From student days.'

'Yours? Or Robert's?'

'Mine. Not that it's any of your concern,' I replied, regretting the remark as soon as I said it. Even to my own ears, it sounded harsh.

'Except to tell you your daughter seems very perceptive,' Sean persisted. 'Men with the name Andrew can't be trusted, especially, so I've heard, those with narrowed eyes. I should heed her opinions, if I was—'

'Sean, may we change the subject?'

'If we must?'

'I'd prefer it.'

'In that case, let's get back to Uncle William—'

'Do we have to? Why not just enjoy the walk?'

'I'm afraid this Andrew's gone and spoilt it for me. But being a magnanimous individual, I've decided not to hold that against you, and would like to make a suggestion to save you incurring legal fees. Now that I've turned up alive, my uncle's going to have to face trial – insurance fraud's not taken lightly in Massachusetts, whatever one's age. Nor is falsifying death certificates. So, why not let the DA's office handle it all and save yourself the hassle? And the effect it could have on Katy.'

'I've been thinking the same thing,' I replied over my shoulder, glad to get away from discussing Andrew. What's more, over the last few minutes, I *had* been reasoning along the same lines as Sean. 'It's far more important for Katy to recover her speech. A lengthy civil trial with hyped-up headlines of me giving evidence, and having to travel daily to

Boston, wouldn't be the best prescription for her. No, you're right, I'll let the law deal with it.'

Just then, we entered a branched aisle of trees, at the end of which was the spirit-lodge. As if from nowhere, there came the sigh of a sudden but gentle breeze. Leaves of every hue rained down on us like coloured confetti.

'Another sign,' said Sean.

'Oh, Sean,' I laughed, despite wanting to keep the atmosphere cool between us. Or maybe a little higher, say registering nice and warm. 'A part of you will always be Morattigon. You see signs everywhere. And what was that one of?'

'Kietitan telling us we're meant for each other. It made you look like a bride. Which makes Andrew, whoever he is, definitely not right for you.'

I stopped, causing Sean to almost bump into me, and turned to face him to try lowering the temperature, which had suddenly escalated to simmering. He took hold of my hand.

'Damaris, I'm truly sorry about Robert, but can't you feel it? You and I. It's been there from the first moment we saw each other. And I'm not talking about dreams or regressions. I'm talking about now. Our own time.'

The touch of his hand was galvanic, magnetising my entire body, but again in conflict with my mind, telling me my feelings were against all that was regarded as conventional. Only God, or Kietitan, knew just how much I was longing to obey my instincts which were telling me: 'Too hell with it, life's too short.' And to look into his eyes and say: 'Sean, so help me and forgive me, but put your arms around me, and hold me. For I feel exactly the same way, too.'

Instead I said: 'Sean, it's too soon. It's only an hour or so since I found out about Robert and I have to think of Katy.' Pulling my hand away and walking on, I sought to change the subject, and again over my shoulder, asked, 'The marks on your body?' Do they hurt?'

Sean took a moment to answer. 'Smart a little. Nothing more.'

'What about Snake-eyes? Just assuming – for the sheer heck of it – that he was also from the present, would the knife cut hurt more?'

'I'd guess it would pain like crazy. Samoset gave him one hell of a blow.'

Good! I thought. *I hope he's doubled-up with it.*

'Why?' Sean asked.

'Just wondering.'

There was another pause before Sean said: 'Damaris, what makes me think you're holding back on something? Remembering the name your ancestor gave him, if there *is* something between you and this Andrew, I'd rather know?'

'No, Sean, there's nothing and that's the truth. But other than that, subject closed.'

'Provided you answer one last question.'

'Which is?'

'When you drove off, earlier, did a ball of thistledown attach itself to you?'

I hesitated, remembering the thistledown floating out of the trees, then being carried up and away by the dust from my Jeep's spinning wheels.

Once again, I visualised Damaris standing by Samoset's graveside, blowing two wispy white balls into the air, and them being carried up and ever upwards into the sky by a gentle breeze from nowhere. But whatever Sean's reason for asking the question, did I want to know his answer? I was back to living in the real world, not in dreams.

'No,' I said.

'Are you sure? Like this one?'

I stopped again and looked back. Sean was holding a small box, its lid open. Inside was a ball of white down.

'It floated in through my study window just after you left.'

Seeing it, my spine went all shivery again, just as it had when thinking of Robert's briar pipe. Sean searched my eyes. He clearly didn't believe me.

'No,' I repeated. Turning away, I continued walking.

The path widened. He moved alongside me. 'According to Abenaki belief, Kietitan never sends one without the other. That's why I assumed you'd had one, too.'

'No,' I said again, a third time. 'I'm sorry if it spoils the belief, but I didn't.'

I wasn't lying. It was the truth. I didn't have one. I'd left it behind in my dust. Whatever Sean's myth said, I didn't want to take it any further.

I didn't want any unnecessary complications.

'A pity, it's a beautiful myth,' he persisted. 'According to it, when two special lovers are parted before their love has fully blossomed, then rather than waste the love they should have shared, it's regenerated by the spirits into two wisps of down and kept alive, floating up into the sky and way beyond to the heavens, far up out of sight among the stars. They then travel through time until the exact moment, predestined by Kietitan, in another season, another age, for them to descend back to Earth. The love they hold is then implanted into the hearts of two other special lovers, who'll be brought together for that love to grow and bloom anew, into an equally rare, but new and different flower.'

Taking hold of my arm, Sean turned me to face him.

'A *new* and *different* flower, Damaris…but none the less *rare*. My name is Sean, not Samoset. I wouldn't want you to make comparisons and be disappointed.'

So moved was I by the story I almost gave in. But I pulled myself together.

'If things were different Sean,' I said, returning his gaze, 'I somehow don't think I would be. Except they're not.' I turned to again lead the way, feeling more in control of myself with my back to him, talking over my shoulder. 'Katy has still just lost her Daddy, and I still have to think of her feelings. They come first. Besides,' I forced a laugh, purposely shrugging it off as nonsense, 'it's only a myth. And Damaris blowing the thistledown was nothing more than a dream.'

That was the rational side of my nature talking again.

My other side waited…

Hoping he would say something that would finally convince me otherwise.

Behind me, Sean made none.

- forty-three -

Moments later, we rounded the corner of the spirit-lodge.

Katy was sitting on the grass stroking Harrison, who was still lying stretched out near the pelt door.

'So this is Harrison.' It was now Sean who was sounding all cool.

I nodded, glad to have something else to talk about. 'Crazy dog. Nothing but trouble. But we wouldn't be without him, would we Katy?'

Katy vehemently shook her head. Getting to her feet she ran to us. Sean lifted her up and she hugged us both, trying to pull us together.

'My,' I said, extricating myself, the last thing I wanted was us getting all bugs-in-a-rug snug. 'You two have really hit it off.'

'That's because we're easy to get on with. Isn't that so, Katy?'

Katy nodded happily.

'I've got something to show you both,' Sean said. Carrying Katy, and before I could stop him, he led the way into the lodge. Again recalling William Roget saying he'd placed Robert's pipe inside it, along with the pipes of his departed ancestors, I held back, feeling all creepy about it, not wanting to go inside. But then I switched to my rational side. It's only a log cabin, I reminded myself, full of harmless old artefacts, and followed after them.

The first thing I saw, apart from Katy still on Sean's arm, her arm around his neck, was the Thanksgiving painting from Sean's study hanging up on the far wall.

Taking hold of my arm, Sean led us to it. I just stood there staring at it, suddenly unable to move. The last face was now sketched-in. Although only in pencil, it was so finely done, there was no doubting who it was.

Katy was looking at it with a child's expression of excited surprise, but none of the awe I was feeling.

'Well?' Sean asked me, his voice subdued. 'Is it Robert?'

I could only whisper, 'Yes, it's Robert.'

Eyes riveted on the painting, I studied the face in wonderment.

Sean had never met Robert, yet the features were so exact it was almost like looking at a black and white photograph, even to the briar pipe in Robert's mouth. This was, without any doubt, the weirdest day I'd ever experienced. I only hoped next year would be more normal. And not just next year, but that all these strange happenings were destined for only this one Thanksgiving – with *no* repetition of them for rest of my entire life.

'You don't have any more tricks to show?' I joked. But feeling the way I was right now, it was my only way of coping with it all. Otherwise I'd start thinking I was dreaming again.

'None that I know of,' Sean replied. 'But you never know with Kietitan. I rather think He enjoys days like this, sitting up there in the heavens looking down at us. I also like to think that giving pleasure is one of His characteristics. And when you think about it, why shouldn't it be? He's said to possess every good virtue, multiplied to infinity. I doubt He's anywhere near as exacting and judgemental as theologians would have us believe.'

Sean returned to the painting. 'I'll colour it in later, but even here, Kietitan's had the last laugh. I always assumed it was me: The Last of the Morattigons. Instead, He'd predestined for the family to adopt Robert, the same as they did with Damaris.' He looked searchingly into my face. 'But with the painting now complete, so are the numbers chosen to occupy the valley. As for me,' the tone of his voice changed, as if asking a question, 'it looks like I'm to be the start of a new line?'

Realising it was an attempt to continue his "with *you*," theme, "it's written in the stars", yet still unable, for all my same reasons, to respond, I tried to avoid the question by looking everywhere but into his eyes...and there, up on a shelf, I saw Robert's briar pipe.

Now, I know that inanimate objects don't have any life in them, but it looked all sort of comfortable, settled, at home. So much so, my spine gave another spooky shiver. But it also helped me change the subject.

'Robert's briar pipe,' I said. Sean followed my gaze.

'Maybe it would be wrong to have his body moved, after all?' I questioned. 'We were just good friends, not lovers. We didn't even share the same bedroom.'

Now why did I volunteer that? I thought. Except, I knew exactly why – despite my inner conflict it was because I wanted him to know. Yet at the same time and with a sense of inner peace, I added (really meaning it, truly feeling it was the right decision), 'I'd like to think his spirit's happy.'

'It's not for me to say,' Sean replied, his gentle change of tone evincing he had detected my genuine sense of affection. 'It has to be your decision. But if it was mine to make…'

'You wouldn't?'

'To my mind, the painting tells me he's meant to stay here.'

I looked again at the shelf, then at Robert's filled-in face, puffing contentedly at his pipe.

'But if you're unsure,' said Sean, 'Kietitan will send you a sign.'

From outside, Harrison started barking. Then went silent.

Katy wriggled free from Sean's arms and ran through the door. We hurried after her.

Harrison was on his feet, face lifted skywards, following something circling above him.

We looked up.

A hundred or so feet above us, a white dove (slightly plumpish) was flying around the lodge. Three times it wheeled, hardly moving its wings. Then, from over the treetops, a flock of more white doves appeared, led by two distinctly male and female doves, flying so close together their wings seemed to be touching. Circling above the branches, clearly waiting for the lone dove to join them, they parted for it to enter, then, as if protecting their new member, they surrounded it, and in graceful unison flew above the colourful foliage toward the glade and from our sight.

Sean murmured: *'I am the swift uplifting rush of quiet birds in circled flight.'*

Turning to me, he said: 'I think Kietitan's just answered you that Robert's spirit belongs here in the valley with Samoset and Damaris, and all the others.'

I could only nod.

Beside me, Katy remained looking, all very serious, toward the spot where the doves had disappeared. She stayed still for a long moment, then turned to Harrison. Taking hold of his collar, she said out aloud, 'Come on, Harry, I'm hungry. Let's go home.'

Realising she'd spoken, she turned excitedly to me, 'Mommy! Mommy! My voice has come back!'

Reaching out for my beautiful, precious daughter, I dropped to my knees and pulled her to me. Rocking her with joy and with tears streaming down my cheeks, I hugged her so tight she was forced to pull herself free as, with a child's acceptance of miracles as an everyday thing, she started running for the Jeep, just visible through the trees.

'Come on, Harry!' she shouted. 'Race you.'

Harrison barked and gambolled after her. Katy shrieked with laughter as he caught her up, bounding about her as she ran.

Still kneeling I watched them. Then I wiped my eyes and looked up at Sean.

He was smiling at me, the glint of tears in his own eyes, and for once too full of emotion to say anything.

'Help me up, please, Sean.' I begged. 'I don't think I've any strength left.'

He raised me to my feet. And held me. I didn't resist.

'And get me away from here before anything else happens,' I said, giving him the keys to the Jeep. 'On second thoughts, a tin of beans isn't enough for a growing man.'

Sean looked deep into my eyes, then smiled again, making my heart flutter, and hand in hand we headed after Katy.

Reaching the Jeep, Katy and Harrison were already in the back seat, playfully fighting.

Opening the door for me, Sean said, 'I'll only be a moment,' and ran back to spirit lodge. I leant back in my seat and closed my eyes, fighting a sudden wave of emotional exhaustion. By the time he returned – opening the rear door and placing something inside the back – I'd partly rallied.

As he slid into the driver's seat, I opened my eyes: 'What was that?'

'A painting. The strangest one I've ever painted. It didn't even feel I was in control of the brush. It's unfinished but I'd like you to see it – you'll know why when you do. I've placed it on top of what seems to be one of yours. They're both sheeted so they won't get damaged.'

'I'll look at it after dinner,' I promised, re-closing my eyes, then opened them again as I heard the approaching engine of a powerful car in low gear.

It appeared around the bend – a long, low, mean-looking red Ferrari.

I knew it. Paul Chapman's. What the hell was he doing here?

It drew to a halt some fifty yards away. As Paul got out, I saw him glance at my Jeep. With a sudden feeling of yet more disaster still to happen, I sank down in my seat, hoping against faint hope he hadn't recognised it as mine.

'If I'm not mistaken, it's Carlo's attorney,' Sean said, 'though I've met him only the once. What does he want here on Thanksgiving? He's got one hell of a black eye. I wonder who gave him that?' and he opened the door before I could stop him and got out of the Jeep.

'Sean!' I called out, but I was too late.

As Sean approached him, Paul looked toward the Jeep with his familiar smirk, letting me know he *had* recognised me, and offered Sean his hand. Sean took it. Paul said something to him, led him back to his Ferrari, and they both leaned against the side and began talking. Most of it came from Paul. Sean shook his head. Paul called up a number on his cellphone, spoke to someone, and handed it to Sean.

The conversation lasted hardly a minute. Switching off the phone, Sean gave it back to Paul and seemed to be relating to him what had transpired. Paul shrugged, once again shook Sean's hand as if whatever they'd been discussing was completed, but then glanced again at the Jeep and continued talking, unable to prevent his eyes flicker toward it, and I realised I was now the subject.

I sat there, my heart racing, my mind in overdrive, knowing full well that whatever Paul was saying, it wouldn't be complimentary.

Ending his exchange, he gave the Jeep a final smirk, a definite "paid you back" smirk and slid into his seat, switched on his engine, executed an extravagant turn, and sped away.

Feeling on edge I watched Sean walk back to the Jeep, his face expressionless. Avoiding my gaze he didn't get in but spoke through my open window. 'It was Carlo. He's been trying to reach me but being I was out of the house getting no reply, so he rang Chapman and asked him to drive over as a favour – seems he owed Carlo one. He's been offered a new deal, but he's flying to LA later today and wanted to know whether I agreed to it.'

'But you said "no"?' I forced myself to ask, realising that Paul must have said something really bad about me, but desperately trying to sound conversational and restore the new and warm feeling I'd finally allowed to happen between us. 'I saw you shaking your head.'

'It's nowhere near enough. So, apart from the acres encompassing the burial ground and spirit-lodge, and a right of way to get to them, I'm putting the estate on the market – with no regrets. I won't be sorry to get it off my hands. And with Robert in the last place, I think Kietitan's telling me it's time to move on.'

Move on. The words, spoken in such a casual, yet deliberate way, confirmed my fears, and for only the second time in my life, I could feel my stupid heart start to break.

'The sale should make enough to repay the insurance company,' he continued, 'and all that's still owing to the IRS and the bank. And maybe also leave something over for myself.'

'But where will you go, and what will you do?' I asked, hardening myself, already ruing letting my guard down, and trying to sound unaffected by his change of mood. If all it had taken for him to go suddenly cold on me were some lies from Paul, then he wasn't worth–

'I'll probably head south, maybe even as far as Mexico, and find a small *cabana* to rent, somewhere quiet to concentrate on writing the book. The tropical island's an added bonus, and I'll fictionalise it a little, give it a modern day Robinson Crusoe touch.'

'Then what?' I asked, hurting, despite my resolve that I would never be hurt again.

'Either they can make me a better offer,' he said, 'or I'll sell it to another publisher.'

Stubborn, I thought, even though I was hurting. A never-give-up man. I was wrong in my outburst in his study. There was plenty of Samoset's blood coursing through his veins.

'Good for you, make them pay,' I said, making another effort to restore things between us, which the Damaris Moore of but twelve hours ago would never have done. 'Meanwhile, forget it for today. Let's get home and relax. I prepared most of it last night. It won't take long to get the rest going, then I can join you. Do you like classical music?'

'If it's all the same to you,' Sean replied. 'I'll get back to my beans.'

Beans! His response couldn't have been more hurtful. But I had to know what Paul had said. 'It was Paul, wasn't it?' I demanded. 'What did he say to you?'

'Only that you and Snake-eyes,' there was a hurt look in his eyes, 'are more than good friends — if I'm right in thinking that's who Andrew is—?'

'Once!' I cut across him, 'years ago, when I was a student in New York. *Before* I married Robert—'

'Except it's continued after that,' he accused, 'not only when Robert was alive—'

'That's not true—'

'But also when he went missing—'

'I thought he'd run off with another—' I checked myself, realising I was digging an even bigger hole for myself. One I shouldn't even be in.

'And that excuses it, does it? The grieving widow, moving her lover to Plymouth to be nearer her, when all the time poor Robert's dead–'

'I didn't know that–'

'I doubt it would have mattered to you if you had. And explains why you changed your mind and asked me to dinner. If the two of you are having some lovers' quarrel, and you're trying to use me to make a point, I'd prefer to stay out of it, thanks all the same.'

A rush of anger was now bottling my words.

'There's little of Samoset in me, you said. Well that cuts both ways. There's *nothing* of Damaris in you. I now know why Kietitan sent only *one* thistledown. There was little point in sending the other.'

He opened Katy's door. 'Goodbye, Katy, I loved meeting you,' he said, gently touching her cheek. 'And I'm thrilled you got your voice back.'

'Uncle Sean…' Katy protested.

Sean looked at me. 'Goodbye,' he said, not even saying my name.

And closing Katy's door, he walked away.

Stifling my anger, and still hurting, I opened my door to run after him and tell him about *my* thistledown, and that, 'It was *me, me,* who heard you calling up through the stones, *not* Damaris! If it wasn't for me, you'd still be there.' But then I slammed it shut again.

'Mommy,' Katy rebuked me plaintively from the rear seat. 'Please call Uncle Sean back. Please, Mommy, I like Uncle Sean. I want him to have dinner with us.'

'No, Katy.' Moving over to the driver's seat, I attacked the ignition key. The engine fired. 'I've never explained myself to any man and I'm not starting now, especially one I've known only a few hours. What the hell makes them think they have the right to—'

Words failed me. I engaged "drive" and the Jeep shot off like a bullet from a gun.

'That's selfish, Mommy,' said Katy.

I gave her a look in the mirror. She avoided it, burying her face into Harrison's neck.

Too late, I remembered that Sean's painting was in the rear of the Jeep – pressed against mine (where do such thoughts come from, even in moments like this?) by the sheer force of my acceleration.

To hell with it, I thought, *I'll send it back by courier.*

- forty-four -

I sped up the drive. Through the trees I saw Andrew sitting in his silver coupè. Seeing my Jeep in his rear mirror he got out and stood there waiting for me with, all of things, a frigging smile on his face that, I assumed, was meant to be welcoming and placating, but to me, in the foul mood I was in, looked more like a smirk. Even worse, a smirking smirk. Nauseating.

'Blast!' I exclaimed. 'This I don't need. No way.'

Twenty minutes ago, purple-eyed, lying Paul.

Now Andrew Snake-eyes sodding Hartford.

Wasn't this Thanksgiving ever going to give up on me?

Still seething and recollecting his threatening, *There's no way you're getting away from me,* 'Is that so?' I said, 'Then watch this for an emergency stop, *Andy dear.*'

Katy said nothing, knowing it was the best way to be when I was this uptight.

I slammed on my brakes as I pulled up, sliding my Jeep and spraying his coupè with grit, and deriving a perverse pleasure from seeing him wince. Unable to prevent himself, he pulled a spotless handkerchief from his pocket and gave the paintwork a quick flick-over.

Getting out of the Jeep, I ignored him, opened the door for Katy and Harry to get out, and handed my daughter the back-door keys.

'Into the house, darling. And switch off the alarm. I'll be with you in a second.'

As they scampered around the corner and through the arch, Andrew walked toward me, already pleading his case. 'Dris, you must let me explain. This morning wasn't how it looked. I just happened to be passing the gallery, saw Alex's car and thought: Hey, how about giving Dris a Thanksgiving present, a painting...'

Like hell! I thought. What's more, I detested men who crawled. And as for lying with it, this – added to Paul having just lied to Sean – this made matters worse.

But I still made no attempt to control my bad temper – in truth it wasn't against Andrew, I was still incensed with Sean. For all I cared about Andrew, he could bungee jump off the nearest high bridge and keep bouncing, with his head constantly hitting the ground. 'I'm really not interested, Andrew. All I want is to be alone. Just Katy and me. To make the best of what's left of a god-awful day. So, if you don't mind–'

I paused as Andrew grimaced and held his stomach.

'You in pain, Andrew? Oh, I'm so sorr-ree. Whatever brought that on?'

'Touch of cramp after falling asleep in the car, waiting for you to get back. I had the weirdest dream; you were in it; and for some odd reason I was–'

I brushed past him, a couple of pithy comments flashing through my mind, but I rejected them. There was no purpose in saying anything, no gain to make.

'Have a crappy celebration, Andrew.'

'Dris!'

'And don't bother to phone.'

As I walked through the arch into the courtyard, I heard his engine start, his tyres spinning too fast on the gravel, probably spraying my Jeep, paying me back, and his engine roar fade into the distance.

'Good riddance,' I said aloud to myself, opening the kitchen door and stepping back at last into the security of my home.

Katy wasn't in the kitchen. I was about to call out when I heard her playing upstairs on the landing with Harrison, safely out of earshot.

Okay, I thought, that's Andrew sorted.

Now Paul.

Picking up the wall phone, I flicked through my stored numbers and dialled.

It was almost immediately answered: 'The Chapman residence.'

'May I speak to Mrs Chapman. It's Damaris Moore.'

Drumming my fingers, I waited for Suzanne to come to the phone.

There was an extension click followed by a sugary voice: 'Damaris! This is Suzanne.'

I didn't think it was Alice-in-frigging-Wonderland, I swore to myself – though on the other hand...

'Just phoning to ask about Paul's eye, Suzanne. Hope it didn't spoil the party. I'm sorry if I hit him too hard. But my cup size really didn't need checking. Especially *inside* my bra,' I added for good measure. 'Tell him it was nothing personal, it's just that I'm particular.'

I replaced the phone to a stunned silence at the other end of the line, 'That's you also sorted, Paul C', I said aloud, taking satisfaction in what I knew was going to be happening a quarter of a mile or so from where I was standing...at just about...just about...*now!*

Ignoring the half-finished dinner preparations, I crossed to the window and looked at the beech tree standing solid on the hillside, leaves fluttering down and forming a carpet around its trunk. Remembering how salvation had come from its branches, it sobered me.

Well? I asked myself, switching by habit into my practical mode – so used was I to this way of dealing with things. *You've got rid of Andrew. Had your own back on Paul. Do you feel any better?*

I should do. I damned well should do.

But I don't!

So, starting with Robert let's analyse why. Now you know the truth of his disappearance how does that make you feel?

Like I've lost a good friend.

*What about grief? After all, he **was** your husband?*

No, strangely I don't feel grief. I have a genuine sense of loss. But being completely honest with myself, no deep heartache. Maybe it's being cushioned by the release of finally knowing what happened to him. And that he didn't suffer. And assurance of mind knowing his spirit is at peace in the valley. I do feel for Katy – losing her Daddy – and I'm especially mindful there will be more pain to come when it dawns on her he's gone for ever. But even here, I'm hoping for her sake, that after all she's had to come through over the last fifteen months, the thrill of recovering her voice will soften the blow for her.

It will. She's a gutsy little girl. She also has your love to sustain her...

Nothing could be surer.

In which case and comforted by this, replied my practical mode, persisting in pressurising me even more, *let's move on.*

I hesitated over the next question I was going to ask myself, scared of asking it, and not knowing what my answer would be.

But I had to ask it.

Okay, here's the sixty-four thousand dollar question. How do you feel about Sean?

Recollecting his open smile, blue eyes, his lean body, his casual manner, his wonderful way with Katy, I found myself struggling to answer and copped-out with trying to shrug him out of my mind: Sean Wolfe? Who needs problems?

He's broke and heading south, looking for somewhere to live in the crazy hope of turning his book into a bestseller. He's not just building castles in the air, he's clearly read too many stories about writers starving themselves in garrets, and emerging with something all major publishing houses will want to buy, fighting each other with offers of huge advances, and Hollywood producers faxing and emailing astronomical film deals. But for every Nicholas Evans, Robert Waller, or Dan Brown, there are tens of thousands of hopefuls who'll never make it, who are going to have their bubbles burst.

And you think Sean's going to be one of them?

Are you kidding? The odds against him making it are...what? Million...Billion to one.

Then why not try helping him? said my practical mode, now becoming a devil's advocate.

No way! I protested, yet knowing what my next question was going to be.

How? I asked.

Give him a roof. You have plenty of spare rooms.

But why should I? I argued back. Besides, how Katy would feel about that?

Now that's just another cop-out answer, because if you have a moral problem with that – which I know damn well you don't, Damaris Moore, not for an infinitesimal second, not as far as Sean's concerned – Robert's office and the snug can easily be converted into a separate wing. As for everyone else, who cares what any of them think? What's more, despite the seeming odds against it, who knows, he might make it. One look at him and you know he's not a man to give up easily. And there's also his indisputable talent as an artist. Still raw, but maybe with some tutoring...

But why should I support him? I hardly know him. In today's world, no one goes out on a limb for a total stranger...

Out on a limb! After what he did for you! You couldn't have chosen a more apt analogy.

In my mind's eye, I again saw Samoset dropping out of the branches of the beech tree to rescue Damaris from the Pequot war party. And in the glade, giving his life to save her from Snake-eyes.

But it was Samoset who acted so bravely. Not Sean.

Was it? Or was it Sean's spirit that prompted him? Think on it before you answer. Can you be sure of that?

Don't confuse me. Don't confuse me.

I'm not trying to. I'm trying to reach the real you. And speaking of which, don't forget Damaris either, running out into the open

339

glade, her own safety forgotten, wanting only to hold her lover in her arms, for just one more time, yet knowing it would be her last.

But it was her, not me, who threw fear aside, and ran to die at Samoset's side.

Was it? Or was it your own true self that took over? Despite not knowing whether or not you would remain there in the valley, trapped inside her body if she was killed, and never be returned back to your own time?

But it couldn't have been me, I tried to argue her out of it. And other than Katy, I've never once acted that unselfishly in my entire life.

But maybe that's what love, true love, does? Love that is giving, not taking. Love which is meant to last. Don't forget what Sean said about dreaming dreams that seem to be real; in which one's soul is detached from its body, for the spirits to tell us what can happen in our life…

Don't keep pressuring me. Just give me a moment to—

But only if you act upon it. That's the essential part.

I said give me a moment—

This is that moment. Think on it, Damaris Moore. Maybe this is what the dreams were all about, to make you follow your real self, rather than keep repressing it as you do so as not be hurt again, or feel the pain…Except, it's up to you to respond to it.

But—

Now. Before it's too late.

Still looking out through the window, I saw a ball of white thistledown drifting gently across the garden toward the house. I opened the window. It floated into the room and over to me, and settled in my upturned palm.

I looked at it, cupped it in my hand...

And called up to Katy:

'Katy, put your coat on. We're going back for Uncle Sean.'

After explaining everything to him about Andrew (well, maybe not quite *everything*) when I told him it was me who heard his voice call up through the stones, he just said...

Without even blinking an eye.

'I rather guessed it was.'

I said he could be infuriating.

But then he smiled, and his eyes were full of tenderness.

And then he kissed me, all sort of gentle, with Katy looking on giggling.

And then he picked Katy up and hugged her.

And Katy hugged him back.

And that made everything okay.

Then we got into the Jeep and drove home for Thanksgiving.

- forty-five -

'Leave everything where it is,' I said, surveying the dining table. 'I'll sort it all out in the morning. I just want to relax.'

Moving through to the living room, which was softly lit with table lamps, I collapsed into the nearest chair. Harrison was stretched out on the rug in front of the blazing log-fire, full with turkey and gravy, eyes closed with contentment.

Katy was sitting all expectantly on the edge of the sofa. 'What games shall we play?' she asked.

'Not tonight, darling,' I groaned. 'I'm bushed.'

'Uncle Sean?'

'Be there in moment, Katy,' Sean replied, studying the paintings on the far wall. 'All by OH,' he remarked over his shoulder. 'You like her work, as well?'

'Some better than others,' I said, signalling to Katy with a finger to my lips.

Katy stifled a chuckle.

'By any chance, you don't happen to have her catalogue?'

'Possibly. I'll have a look some time."

Katy was now grinning from ear to ear.

'No rush.'

I caught Katy's eye and indicated to the writing-bureau. Tip-toeing to it, she opened a drawer, took out a catalogue and gave it to me, then returned to the sofa.

'Here's one,' I said.

Sean turned. 'That was quick.' Crossing the room, he took it from my hand.

'Actually it's DH,' I said. 'Her paintings aren't too bad, but her signature's terrible.'

Sitting alongside Katy, Sean turned to the first page, showing a photograph of me.

Katy burst out laughing, no longer able to suppress herself.

Sean looked at the picture in silence.

'No wonder she lives as a recluse,' he said. 'In her seventies did your friend say? She looks at least ten years older.'

He rounded on Katy: 'As for you, young lady, if you thought that was funny, then how about this?' He tickled her neck until she was squealing and imploring: 'Mommy! Get him off me. Help me, Mommy! Help me!'

Harrison cocked an ear and opened one eye, then seeing he wasn't going to be involved, replaced his ear and closed his eye.

Sean stopped. 'More!' Katy begged.

'That's enough for tonight, Miss Katherine Moore, especially after all you ate, or you'll be ill, and I'll be in Mommy's bad books.'

'Then it's Mommy's turn. She told me to get it.'

'Snitch,' I said, from the depths of my chair.

'Don't worry,' said Sean. 'I've got something else in mind for Mommy.'

'Mmm,' I murmured. 'Can't wait.'

'What can we do now?' asked Katy.

'Something quiet,' Sean suggested. 'I'm not feeling too energetic…'

'There goes the first broken promise,' I commented.

'…not right after dinner. How about a story?'

'What kind of story,' Katy persisted.

'A once upon a time story?'

She pulled a face. 'That's for babies. Tell me a sea-story.'

'How about the *Mayflower*?'

'We did that in school. It's boring…I know! I know! Tell me about you on the desert island. Did the cannonballs try to eat you?'

Not moving my head, I lifted my eyes to Sean: 'You suggested it!'

'Asleep?' Sean asked, as I entered the sitting room.

'Not yet. I've left her reading,' I replied. 'She should drop off before long.'

I crossed to the sofa and nestled up to him, my legs curled under me.

'It's been the oddest, strangest day,' I said. Raising my face, I pecked him on the lips and resumed my cosy position. 'Apart from meeting you…and Katy getting her voice back…I hope I never have another like it for the rest of my life.'

Sean turned my face to look at the grandfather clock. Inside the glass door that protected the dial and the moon-disc, were the two thistledown.

'I've trapped them in time. Just to make sure they don't escape.'

'Don't worry. They won't,' I said. 'Not if I have to glue them in place.'

Glancing around the room, I saw the two sheeted paintings propped against a wall. 'I see you brought both in?'

'I thought if I showed you mine, you might show me yours.'

'No comment, other than it being a fair exchange. What's yours of?'

'Wait and see,' Sean replied, moving me to one side and getting to his feet. Crossing to the canvasses, he took hold of both sheets, imitated a trumpet fanfare, and yanked them off.

I gasped.

Looking puzzled at my reaction, Sean turned and stared, hardly able to believe his eyes.

Both canvases were complete, his showing not just Samoset leaning against the outcrop, but also Damaris emerging from the pool, her wet slip clinging, all revealing, to her body.

Reunited.

But as for mine...

Well, it was an exact copy – except...

With facial features subtly changed and fair hair not black, the man was indisputably Sean. And with shoulder-long tawny hair instead of dark bobbed, the woman was undeniably me.

Sean dropped on to the sofa. 'It's another–'

'Don't say another word,' I warned. 'Especially about it being a sign. Or try telling me some magical Native American myth explaining how it happened. I see it...yet I don't believe it, nor will I ever, ever understand it, so let's just leave it at that.'

I paused. 'You can hang yours of Samoset and Damaris in your study. As for mine, we'll put it up in our dressing room. Apart from you, no one's seeing me like that.'

I got up and threw another log on the fire. It immediately crackled, then flamed, adding an extra cosy warmth to the lamp-dimmed room.

Returning to the sofa, I murmured, 'Now where were we?'

'I think…like this,' Sean replied. Placing his arm around my shoulder, he tilted my face up to his, and lowered his lips to mine—

'Uncle Sean!' Katy's voice came from the landing. 'I can't sleep. Will you tell me about the cannonballs again?'

'Just when I was about to start eating you,' Sean said. 'What a time to be getting her voice back.' Standing up, laughing at the untimely interruption, he made for the door.

'The joys of parenthood,' I called after him as he left the room. 'Yesterday, you'd have had a drum.'

'Whatever,' he replied, 'I wouldn't have it any other way,' and ran up the stairs to Katy.

Rising to my feet, I crossed to the window.

Silhouetted on the hill against a cloudless, night-blue sky, the spreading beech tree looked friendly, no longer threatening. From high in the sky, a full moon shone down, illuminating the garden. And the stars seemed to be twinkling brighter than ever tonight.

Gazing up at the heavens, 'No more days like this,' I pleaded. 'Please! Once is enough. Just close the book and call it a day. Call it – Once Upon A Thanksgiving.'

I glanced at my watch. It was only nine.

Three hours left to the end of Thanksgiving.

And this was Sean, not Andrew.

And it had been a very, *very* long time.

Three hundred and eighty seven years and some months ago, to be exact.

'Change that', I said. 'Make it twice.'

And closed the curtains.

From: **Nick Cronin**

To: **Amanda Nye**

Subject: **Re: TWICE UPON A THANKSGIVING**

Mandy

I've read it. It's different. Do we know what happened after? ie. with a title like "Twice Upon A Thanksgiving", do they live happily ever after?

Nick

From: **Amanda Nye**

To: **Nick Cronin**

Subject: **Re: TWICE UPON A THANKSGIVING**

Epilogue enclosed with apologies. It somehow got detached from the ms.

- epilogue -

Well, was it a dream? Or was it a regression, an out of body experience?

Who knows, who cares? Tomorrow is Christmas Day.

We've been together a month now. It's snowing outside. Inside, the log fire is crackling and the flames are leaping up the chimney. Sean's putting up the holly and the mistletoe and the presents are all gift wrapped under the candle-lit tree. Sean's to me are in shining gold paper. I can't wait to open them.

Looks like we're going to last.

Carlo got the publishers to up the advance on the book and he's discussing a film deal, with rumours of Hugh Jackman playing the part of Sean. But after it's finished, Sean's not going to write another book. He prefers painting, he has real talent and is coming on fast.

Katy adores him. And the estate's been sold to a bunch of naturists, enough to clear off everything, the insurance company, the bank and the IRS, with some left over, so all that's off our minds.

Uncle William's skipped the country with a wealthy widow from Rhode Island who has a villa in the South of France, and retains a top lawyer who's more than capable of fighting off extradition. So that takes care of him.

Alex and John are joining us tomorrow for dinner, his first volume of poems is coming out in February, and they're tying the knot in the Spring.

And Andrew's gone back to New York without saying "goodbye".

Paul and Suzanne are moving to Boston, closer to Paul's office for him to get home early from work, otherwise it's divorce, with Suzanne threatening (according to rumour) "to take him for every cent he's got".

Stella Slater's seen the light, changed her style of dress, and joined a local, clap-happy evangelical church. They have a new pastor, Reverend Billy Brewster – a forty-two year old widower, good-looking, with no children, descended from a family that stretches way back to the *Mayflower*. He also has a highly popular Sunday morning TV service beamed throughout the whole of New England. A top-of-the-range BMW. And a lovely house with grounds. Stella's just become his secretary, replacing the matronly one he had before.

Oh, and yesterday she phoned me (since her part in bringing Sean and me together we've stayed in touch) to tell me that tonight, Christmas Eve, she's carol singing in the church choir.

As for me...

My painting is really flowing from my brushes, with such a passion of colour going into it, it's expressing exactly how I'm feeling inside. Nor am I holding it back. Not in my art, or any other form of expressionism. And why should I? I don't care if the whole world knows.

Like I told Alex, all it requires is a bit of give and take.

On both sides.
And in more ways than one.
Take it from me.
Love is grand.
And…
Oh, yes…
I just adore Thanksgiving.

From: Nick Cronin

To: Amanda Nye

Subject: Re: TWICE UPON A THANKSGIVING

Mandy

Since our chance meeting in the elevator yesterday, I've had a dream of my own.

Would you accept an invitation to my place one evening to share a bottle of wine, and help me achieve it?

Very warmest,

Nick

From: Amanda Nye

To: Nick Cronin

Subject: Re: TWICE UPON A THANKSGIVING

Nick

And maybe an in-body experience, instead of an out-of-one? I'd love to! What about tonight? It's Christmas, the time to exchange gifts.

Until then,

Mandy x

Richard Rees

Richard Rees is originally from Wrexham, North Wales, where he had an accountancy practice, but became a writer after the deaths of his young wife, Richenda, and then his only daughter, Elisabeth, from ovarian cancer. He now lives a quiet life in the seaside town of Llandudno, at the foot of the Snowdonia National Park, doesn't drink or smoke, so sounds a bit of a bore, but is gregarious, keeps fit, drives fast, and doesn't play golf.

For more information on Richard's books, including where to purchase them, or to contact Richard, go to

www.richardhrees.com

25208532R00217

Printed in Great Britain
by Amazon